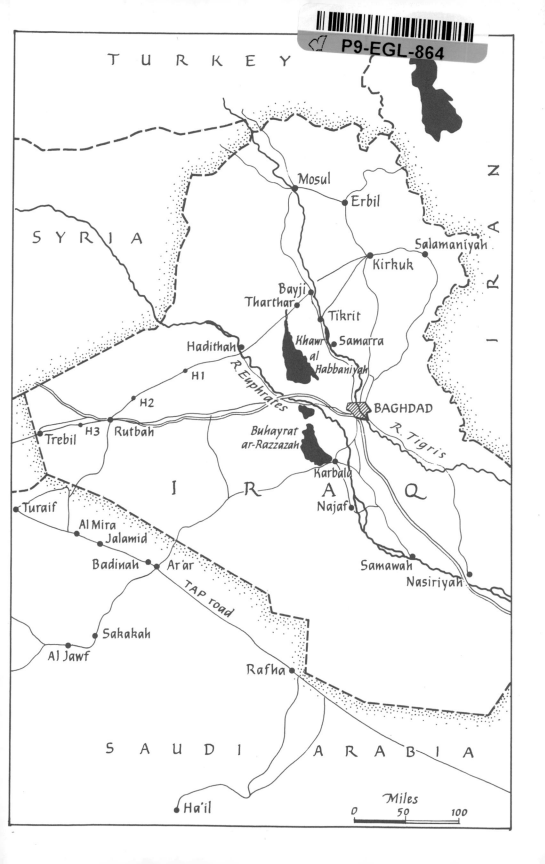

SHADOW OVER
BABYLON

DAVID MASON

SHADOW OVER BABYLON

Iustum et tenacem propositi virum
Non vultus instantis tyranni
Mente quatit solida…

The man who is just and firm of purpose
Is unshaken in his strength of mind
By the glare of a menacing tyrant…

HORACE, *Odes III (iii)*

A DUTTON BOOK

PUBLISHER'S NOTE:
This is a work of fiction. Names, characters, places, and incidents are the product of the author's imagination. To the extent that real names and places have been used, this has been done to lend an aura of authenticity to the novel. However, the use of such names and places is entirely fictitious and is not to be considered factual or truthful.

DUTTON
Published by the Penguin Group
Penguin Books USA Inc., 375 Hudson Street, New York, New York 10014, U.S.A.
Penguin Books Ltd, 27 Wrights Lane, London W8 5TZ, England
Penguin Books Australia Ltd, Ringwood, Victoria, Australia
Penguin Books Canada Ltd, 10 Alcorn Avenue, Toronto, Ontario, Canada M4V 3B2
Penguin Books (N.Z.) Ltd, 182–190 Wairau Road, Auckland 10, New Zealand

Penguin Books Ltd, Registered Offices: Harmondsworth, Middlesex, England

First published in the United States by Dutton, an imprint of Dutton Signet, a division of Penguin Books USA Inc.
Published in Great Britain by Bloomsbury Publishing Ltd.

First Printing, November, 1993
10 9 8 7 6 5 4 3 2 1

Copyright © David Mason, 1993
Endpaper maps drawn by Neil Hyslop
All rights reserved

 REGISTERED TRADEMARK—MARCA REGISTRADA

LIBRARY OF CONGRESS CATALOGING-IN-PUBLICATION DATA
Mason, David.
    Shadow over Babylon / David Mason.
        p.   cm.
    ISBN 0-525-93709-9
    1. Hussein, Saddam. 1937–   —Assassination attempts—Fiction.
    2. Assassins—Iraq—Fiction.   I. Title.
PR6063.A759S48   1993
823'.914—dc20   93-17805
                                                         CIP

Printed in the United States of America

CONTENTS

Acknowledgements

I realised soon after starting this book in March 1992 that I had badly underestimated the amount of work that would be required to complete it, and that writing it would need to become more than just a sideline activity. Since then I seem to have been able to concentrate on very little else. The encouragement of friends has been generous and unstinting throughout, and I would particularly like to thank Tim Nicholas, Jock Tillotson, George Plumptre and my brother Robert Mason for their ideas, advice and suggestions.

Desk work seems to divide people into two distinct types: those who somehow always manage to keep their papers neat and tidy, and those who for some reason appear incapable of doing so. Unfortunately I fall firmly – possibly terminally – into the latter category. But for the assistance of Tricia Joyce, and latterly Sarah Nethersole, I would many months ago have found myself buried beneath piles of unfiled documents and unanswered correspondence. I am very grateful to them and at the same time most apologetic to the many people who may have become exasperated with my failure to deal more promptly with other matters requiring my attention.

Mrs Hilary Thomas carried out research work for me in London, and James Edwards helped to monitor news and media reports and ensure that nothing of importance was overlooked. Nigel Cooper in Saudi Arabia spent many hours bringing me up to date on that country and finding out facts and figures I didn't know. Captain Rodion Cantacuzene, USN (retd), kindly advised me on the US Navy and some of its procedures. Keen students of US Naval history will observe that I have taken some licence with the service record of the USS *Missouri*: she was not, as I have suggested, involved in the Vietnam War; and she had in fact already been decommissioned by the time of the 1992 action described in this book.

Frank Sutton and Sheila Dewart most helpfully supplied statistical information, and Dr Michael Kenworthy-Browne helped to fill in some gaps in my knowledge of medical matters. Derek Cannon came up with a Latin translation which I ought to have known but didn't. Graham Markham provided much useful information about sea containers, and Stan Walker advised on general shipping matters. To the best of my knowledge there is no m.v. *Manatee*; she is loosely modelled on another ship which did in fact undertake the voyage described on the dates given. For the sake of her master and crew, I hope and trust that she did not attract quite the degree of interest from the police and Customs services in Mombasa depicted in this book.

There is a considerable amount of detail about rifle-shooting and ballistics in these pages. Although I have some personal experience of these subjects, I would not have been able to write about them convincingly without the help of John Leighton-Dyson and most particularly Malcolm Cooper, MBE. Malcolm's knowledge and experience of these matters are unequalled, and I am most grateful to him for his assistance. (Any readers concerned about the possible lack of wisdom in publishing such detailed and potentially lethal information may comfort themselves with the knowledge that I have deliberately rendered the figures inaccurate in a few minor respects.)

Dr Dave Sloggett probably knows more about satellite and space technology than anyone else alive. His energy and enthusiasm have been remarkable, and I must thank him enormously for the wealth of advice he has given me. He has been a true friend. His assistance has made it possible for me to give an accurate insight into some of the technicalities of this very specialised field; at the same time his overview has helped me to avoid disclosing any classified information – something that might otherwise have happened unintentionally. There are four further individuals who have been invaluable in settling important matters of factual accuracy on other subjects; for security reasons I cannot name them, but they know how grateful I am.

My literary agent, Vivienne Schuster, has been an unfailing source of encouragement. It is largely thanks to her that this book has been finished in the fairly short time it has taken; in fact it is very much to her credit that it has been completed at all.

I once read somewhere that writers generally have an uneasy – if not openly hostile – relationship with their publishers. For all I know this may be true in many cases, but it most certainly is *not* true in mine. I could not have received better support and encouragement than I have from everyone at Bloomsbury, particularly from Nigel Newton, David Reynolds and Penny Phillips. I am profoundly grateful to them.

My approach to this book has of necessity been a somewhat single-minded one. As a consequence I have been largely absent-minded in most other matters, but my wife Monique has been extraordinarily patient with this. I must have driven her nearly mad at times, but her support has been constant. The greatest thanks of all, and my love, go to her.

D.P.M.

The Characters

Hughie Carter	Detective Superintendent, Metropolitan Police
Paul Hallam	Detective Chief Inspector, Metropolitan Police
Jerry Willson	Detective Inspector, Metropolitan Police
The Colonel	a former Army officer
Max Goodale	Deputy Director General of MI5
Major Henry Stoner	National Rifle Association
Juliet Shelley	Johnny Bourne's flatmate
Lady Dartington	wife of Sir Peter Dartington
Dorothy Webster	Dartington's personal assistant
George and Mary Jephcott	Dartington's gardener and housekeeper
Morag Cameron	owner and licensee, Carvaig Inn
Sheila Cameron	Morag Cameron's daughter

SAUDI ARABIA

Tony Hughes	regional director, Darcon Saudi Arabia
Alvin Kennings	US Embassy, Riyadh
Jonathan Mitchell	British Embassy, Riyadh

KENYA

| Harry Cresswell | US Embassy, Nairobi |
| Robert Mwanza | Chief Inspector, Mombasa Police |

THE BAHAMAS

| Julian Smith | British Consulate, Nassau |

IRAQ

Saddam Hussein	President
Izzat Ibrahim	Vice-President
Taha Yasin Ramadan	Deputy President
Tariq Aziz	Deputy Prime Minister (ex-Foreign Minister)
Hussein Kamil Hassan	Defence Minister
Ali Hassan al-Majid	Minister of the Interior
Sa'adi Tumah Abbas	Presidential Military Adviser
Ala'a Hussein Ali	a colonel, Mukhabarat (security service)
Major Hassan Omair	a company commander, Iraqi Republican Guard
Lieutenant Saleh Masoud	a company officer, Iraqi Republican Guard
Lieutenant Aziz Ali	a company officer, Iraqi Republican Guard

PART ONE

OBSCURE MOTIVES

1

The stalker studied the ground thoughtfully through his binoculars, then stowed them away inside his jacket. "We'll have to take this next bit very, very slowly, now," he whispered to his companion. "Those three hinds on the left aren't making it easy for us. We'll be in full view of them for the next forty yards, until we reach that wee burn yonder."

The "rifle", a former Army colonel, nodded his lowered head in acknowledgement. He had absolute faith in the stalker's judgement: if Danny had said that was the only way forward, then it was the only way. It astonished him that they had got this far. For the past hour they had picked their way slowly past scattered groups of red-deer hinds and calves; it seemed to him miraculous that they had not been seen, and, with the light breeze occasionally dropping away to nothing and then picking up again in a slightly different direction, it was even more extraordinary that they had not yet been winded by the deer. Even the minutest breath of wind carrying the smell of man to the super-sensitive nose of just one of the hinds would have done it: she would have cleared off at speed, taking with her every other beast for hundreds of yards around.

Even if this stalk came to nothing, reflected the Colonel, it had been one of the most difficult and exciting he had had for a very long time. He raised his head cautiously and scanned forward across the bare patch of boggy grass they must now cross. There was no cover at all, and they would be in full view of the hinds to the left and uphill of them. They would be right out in the open – surely the hinds would see them. They were grazing, as yet unaware of any human presence, but they were scarcely a hundred and fifty yards away and would instantly notice any sudden movement. The Colonel knew that his and Danny's progress would have to be so slow and careful as to be almost imperceptible – they would have to flatten themselves to the ground and literally slither along, like snakes in slow motion. The stalker nodded at him a final time, then crept ahead, out into the open. The Colonel followed, inching his way forward.

The two men crawled slowly and with infinite care, flat on their stomachs. The Colonel concentrated on the stalker's boots, a few inches in front of his face. On several occasions the boots froze into immobility; the Colonel took his cue and remained stock-still until they moved forward once again. He knew that one of the hinds had probably raised her head from her grazing and was looking around, alert for any sign of danger. The Colonel knew better than to raise his own head to look. He would know soon enough if they had been seen: the hind would let out a short barking cough of alarm and take flight; the stalk would have failed.

The hillside was sodden from the persistent October drizzle of the previous week; both men were soaked to the skin, even though the rain had now eased off. It took them twenty more minutes to cover the fifty yards to the shallow depression of the burn, and the Colonel was breathing hard with the effort of concentration. Once at the burn, they were temporarily out of sight of the hinds; they raised themselves on to their hands and knees. The Colonel marvelled that they had made it unnoticed.

The water in the burn gurgled noisily, but the stalker still spoke in a whisper. "The stag will be about two hundred yards away now, maybe a little less. We'll go up the burn about sixty yards to that wee knoll on the right; we may be able to get a shot at him from there."

Again the Colonel nodded, and followed as the stalker led the way up the burn. He hadn't seen the stag since they had first started the stalk two hours before and nearly half a mile back along the face of the hill. He was a small, wiry man, in good physical condition at fifty-three; his eyesight was still sharp, but the stalker had had to point out to him exactly where the beast was lying.

They reached the small knoll. The stalker motioned to the Colonel to wait where he was, and crawled forward a few yards by himself, disappearing almost immediately in the grass and heather. The Colonel composed himself with deep breaths, and reflected on what he was about to do. He had been stalking for over thirty years, but the thrill and tension of it had never diminished for him. He was by nature a hunter; he loved it. After his annual week's deer-stalking, he always returned to his London office with his senses heightened, refreshed in a way no other activity would have achieved for him. In a few minutes' time now, if all went well, a stag would be dead and he would feel the usual heady mixture of elation and sadness at the ending of a life.

The stalker returned as soundlessly and invisibly as he had departed. "He's still where he was, lying down. I think we can get a reasonable shot at him from the side of this knoll."

"Where is he?" asked the Colonel. "What sort of range?"

"He's facing half towards us, about a hundred and forty yards away and slightly downhill from us," replied the stalker. "I'll try and roar him up if you like, but I'd prefer not to. We'll have to be very careful. There are some more hinds and calves only about sixty yards in front of us, between us and the stag. The nearest hind is well alert; if she takes fright, she'll be away. I think you may have to take him while he's still lying down."

"What sort of beast is he?"

"He's a very old stag, could be in his last year. He's only a seven pointer, a very poor, narrow head, but he's perfectly shootable. He'd weigh about twelve stone, maybe twelve and a half. A good beast to get off the hill. He's been with the hinds, and he's taking a rest just now. He's very black from the peat hags, and he looks pretty well tired out."

The Colonel was glad. He had never had any desire to shoot a trophy head, or a stag in his prime; he far preferred to shoot an old beast with a bad head, going back. The news that this was an old stag was just what he wanted to hear. He knew the death that awaited a stag whose last teeth had finally loosened and gone. Emaciated and weak from starvation and the cold, all last reserves of energy spent, the animal would eventually lie down to die in the bitter frosts of winter. The hoodie crows would be on to him before he died, pecking his eyes out and stabbing at him as he thrashed weakly in his final agony. Far better to end it with a bullet.

The stalker took the Rigby out of its canvas sleeve, and removed the protective plastic covers from its telescopic sight. Very quietly, he worked the bolt, easing a .275 cartridge forward from the magazine into the chamber, and then applied the safety catch. A hundred and forty yards was as close as they were going to be able to get to

5

this stag. It was a reasonable distance for a competent shot, and he had seen the Colonel's performance on the range near the lodge the day before. Perfectly adequate – in fact he was pretty good. He would be capable of a killing shot at this range or even a bit further. Nevertheless, he always got the rifle as close in as possible; and he never let even the best of them take a shot further than a hundred and eighty to two hundred yards. He motioned to the Colonel to follow him, and they crawled slowly up the last few yards on to the side of the knoll.

The landscape ahead gradually came into the Colonel's view. Straight in front of him were the hinds and calves; the nearest one seemed very close. Her head was raised, looking downhill. Beyond, he could see the old stag, lying down as the stalker had said. The stalker very gradually eased the rifle across to him, and he began to settle himself into a comfortable firing position.

Suddenly, the nearest hind flicked her head round, facing directly towards him. The Colonel froze. *God, she's looking straight at us*, he thought; *she's bound to see us now*. For what seemed an age, man and beast stared at each other.

The hind had seen a tiny flicker of movement out of the corner of her eye, and she stared intently at its source. Nothing was moving now, but something, something very small, had changed. She was uncertain, uneasy. Was it danger? She could not be sure. She shifted one of her feet, and her uneasiness communicated itself to her calf, which moved closer to her. The hind looked briefly at the calf, then back at where she thought she had seen the movement. A younger hind, ten yards away from her, looked at her curiously and followed her gaze; seeing nothing, she lost interest after a couple of minutes. The calf appeared confused, looking one way and then another. After another minute or so, its mother looked away again. She resumed feeding, but her mind was not fully on it; she remained wary.

The Colonel let out a slow sigh of relief as the hind finally lowered her head to graze. With the greatest care, he brought the telescopic sight to bear on the stag, picking out his mark. He eased the safety catch off. The stag's body was obliquely facing him; the animal was gazing downhill. The Colonel aligned the cross-hairs of the scope low down on the front of the stag's chest, near the right shoulder. The light was improving, and as he took his last breath in before the shot, a shaft of sunlight broke through, throwing the stag's body into sharper relief in the sight. *Perfect*, thought the Colonel; he started to exhale slowly, and his finger tightened on the trigger.

This time the hind was in no doubt. She had caught a flash of light from the same place; the sun had glinted on the glass optic of the telescopic sight. Now thoroughly alarmed, she barked loudly and bolted away. The other hinds followed.

The Colonel's mind registered the hind's bark, but his full concentration was now on the stag and he did not see the hinds move. Through the sight, he saw the stag turn his head sharply towards him. He squeezed the trigger. At the exact moment he fired, the stag began to struggle forward to his feet.

The roar of the rifle was deafening. In front of the Colonel, a cloud of water droplets had been atomised by the muzzle blast on the wet grass, and he and the stalker were temporarily unsighted. Just over half a second after the report from the rifle, the unmistakable *thump* of the bullet striking the stag's body carried back to them. The spray of water droplets cleared, and they took in the scene. The deer were already stampeding away.

The old stag had only just started to rise when he felt an enormous blow hit him on the right side of his body, about a foot behind his foreleg; it nearly knocked him back down. The report of the rifle reached him less than a quarter of a second later. He had heard it many times before: always it spelled danger – men. He wrenched himself up on to his feet. No human, hit by the same shot, would have been able to move, but the red deer is a phenomenally tough animal. Looking towards where the sound had come from, the stag saw the cloud of spray that had erupted from the grass. He needed no further prompting; he took off in headlong flight.

"He's hit, Colonel." The stalker was looking through his binoculars as the beasts raced away. "Yes, he's hit, right enough, but I can't tell for certain where. If it's a heart/lung shot, he'll go down in a hundred yards or less, but I think you may have hit him a little behind. You'd better give me the rifle just in case."

"The old bugger moved, Danny!" The Colonel was suddenly voluble after the tension and silence of the stalk. "He bloody moved, just as I fired! Damn it! Just half a second more, that's all I needed!"

The stag ran. He felt unusually weak and breathless, and his legs seemed a little unsteady, but adrenalin was pumping through his bloodstream. His survival instinct propelled him on.

7

The hinds had already fled, covering the rough ground at speed and without effort; the stag followed them. After a hundred yards the herd streamed over a brow down into a corrie, and was lost from view. Danny jumped to his feet. "Come on, Colonel, we mustn't lose him." He raced off, the Colonel behind him.

Danny was still well short of the edge of the corrie when he threw himself to the ground on a grassy bank and started to bring the rifle to his shoulder. He worked the bolt, ejecting the Colonel's empty case and feeding another round into the chamber. Some hinds had now come into view, way off in the distance, climbing fast up the far side of the corrie towards a saddle on the ridge of the hill. The Colonel reached his side. "Why have we stopped?" he panted. "Hadn't we better keep going?"

"You see those hinds, Colonel? They're the same ones. Either your stag will be dead in the corrie below, or he'll take much the same path out as the hinds. It will be the easiest way for him, even though he'll be climbing. If you don't mind, I think I had better take the shot."

The Colonel lay down beside Danny, and glanced sideways at him. What did he mean, he'd better take the shot? From *here*? It was a ridiculously long range. What on earth was he talking about? They would surely do better to keep after the stag and hope that he weakened and lay down.

The stalker's face was calm. After a few seconds his eyes narrowed in concentration. The Colonel followed his look. The stag had appeared as Danny had predicted, climbing directly away from them on the same track the hinds had taken.

"Oh, Christ," muttered the Colonel, "I've only wounded him. He's bloody miles away now. Jesus, what a mess!"

"I must concentrate now, Colonel." Danny locked the rifle into his shoulder, his eye to the scope.

The Colonel again glanced sideways and watched him closely. *Surely* he was not serious about attempting a shot from *here*?

The stag was about five hundred yards away, lagging well behind his hinds. He felt very weak; he was now completely numb where the blow had hit him, and a dull ache was starting deep in his gut. He had coughed and stumbled a couple of times descending into the corrie, and had nearly fallen, but now he was climbing it was easier to keep his footing. The strange feeling in his body gave him the extra edge of fear he needed. He wanted to lie down and rest, but instinct drove him on.

Danny squeezed the trigger. The bullet streaked across the void of the corrie at nearly two thousand miles an hour. Five hundred yards and just under three-quarters of a second later, it struck.

The old stag never heard the shot. Instead, he felt a second crashing blow on the back of his neck, just above his shoulders, and then — oblivion. The echo of the shot reverberated around the sides of the corrie and thundered down into the glen below.

The Colonel could hardly take it in. The stag had collapsed, stone dead. "Bloody hell," he breathed, "I've never seen anything like that in my life! Christ, the beast was bloody *miles* away! And he was still running, for God's sake! That was the most fantastic bloody shot I've ever seen!"

Danny was calmly getting to his feet. He unloaded the Rigby, replaced the scope cover and put the rifle back in its sleeve. "Och, I don't know about that, Colonel," he said easily. "Maybe it was just a bit of luck. You can never tell. Come on, sir, let's go and deal with your stag."

The Colonel followed Danny, still marvelling in disbelief. He had indeed never seen anything quite like it in his life; he would have considered it a crazy gamble to take on a moving target at that range, let alone to contemplate pulling off a clean kill with just one shot.

One thing he did know, despite all the experience that shouted at him that such a shot was a complete fluke. He had been watching the expression on the face of the stalker as he fired. The Colonel knew with absolute certainty that luck had had nothing whatever to do with it.

2

"Mr Asher, it is very kind of you to have come. I really am most grateful to you for sparing me so much of your valuable time." The Minister smiled warmly as he shook Roger Asher's hand in welcome. He hoped he was not overdoing it. He had a tendency to be perhaps a little too effusive when greeting someone he disliked. One of his friends had once told him so, and he had been irritated. He had seen the truth of it, though, and had since been more careful. Fortunately, he had sufficient personal charm to carry it off; few people had proved entirely immune. His charm had been just one of the factors that had contributed to his successful career in politics.

He surveyed Asher's face with distaste, his friendly smile giving no hint of his feelings. He realised that he should not have worried. Roger Asher was used to flattery. In fact, he was rarely subjected to anything else; he seemed almost to expect praise and servility as of right. That was what happened, supposed the Minister, if one permanently surrounded oneself with sycophants and yes-men.

"My pleasure entirely, Minister," boomed Asher. The Minister politely gestured towards a large, comfortable chair. Asher eased himself down into the leather upholstery, which wheezed under his gargantuan frame. The Minister noticed that Asher was sweating. It was beyond his comprehension that the man could have let himself get into such a state; unfit and grossly overweight, he was a physical monument to a life of overindulgence.

"A glass of lemonade? It is homemade. I find it a refreshing drink."

"That would be most kind."

The Minister poured the lemonade. He sat down in an easy chair opposite Asher and watched as the big man greedily gulped the drink down. The Minister wondered. Had bad manners somehow assisted

Asher in amassing his enormous wealth, or had the wealth, once acquired, merely rendered good manners unnecessary? An interesting question. Certainly, Asher appeared to pay only lip-service to the finer points of social behaviour. He had an ego to match his physical size, and he probably no longer cared about people's opinions of his personal habits – if he thought about other people's opinions at all. Still, there was no doubt that hobnobbing with powerful men, and being consulted by ministers, were pursuits Asher revelled in. He had accepted the invitation to the meeting with almost indecent alacrity.

"A comfortable flight, I hope?" The Minister was solicitous. Asher had flown in from New York in his private Gulfstream IV jet, which the Minister knew was opulently equipped to Asher's own questionable taste. Gaudy, yes, but hardly uncomfortable.

"Perfectly satisfactory, thank you, Minister," replied Asher, "although I can't say I really enjoy flying. I never cared for it much." He took another gulp of lemonade and set down his glass.

The pleasantries over, the Minister studied his fingernails briefly and spoke. "The Government has a rather awkward problem." He paused, as if wondering how to continue. He knew exactly what he was going to say, but he wanted to convey an impression of slight embarrassment. He knew that he was skilled at dealing with people. It was simply a question of matching the approach to the individual. He did not delude himself for one second that this man was simply a blundering oaf. Asher had been enormously successful; he was shrewd, cunning and manipulative.

Well, two can play at that game, thought the Minister. He himself had had to show great skill to maintain his position during the radical changes wrought by the politics of the 1980s. His privileged background and education had not exactly marked him out for advancement in the way that they might have done in the old days. An old family, Eton, Oxford ... that sort of upbringing and education was nowadays considered somewhat anachronistic, and that was putting it politely. The Minister had played down any reference to these things, and had survived unscathed. Now, with a new leader, a less strident and more moderate approach was being signalled. This suited the Minister, who preferred subtlety and moderation to brashness. The election due in the spring of 1992 would, he hoped, set the seal on this new approach.

11

He continued. "There is a matter that has caused the Government some difficulty. We are now anxious to see this difficulty resolved, and we considered that you might be able to offer us some advice, and perhaps some suggestions as to what measures we might take." The Minister knew that this approach would be appreciated by Asher. He glanced up at the big man's face, and could see that he had his attention. "It is a matter of some delicacy," he said finally, trying to look even more embarrassed.

"Minister, I am honoured that you think I might be of assistance," began Asher. "Naturally, I would be very willing to help. It would be an honour," he repeated.

Asher was not being honoured, thought the Minister; he was being flattered. He just could not tell the difference. He would, however, have picked up on the phrase "a matter of some delicacy". Asher was not a fool, and he would be perfectly well aware that the expression invariably meant that the matter was one of extreme *in*delicacy. So far so good, thought the Minister. As he had expected, Asher had not balked in the slightest at the suggestion that he might involve himself in potentially controversial matters. Just to be on the safe side, he would make sure that he fully understood.

"We have come to the reluctant conclusion that this matter now calls for fairly uncompromising action." Still no sign of perturbation or alarm on Asher's face, thought the Minister. He really could not have been more blunt or obvious about it, and the big man was nodding his head in understanding. This was going to be even easier than he had thought. He decided to skip the next few carefully chosen phrases. He was almost disappointed that he would not have to indulge in any skilful fencing with this man. "The problem is an individual one," he said, and paused again to let the remark sink in. He was startled by Asher's blunt reply.

"There must be many individuals who could be deemed to be a problem to the Government. How much of a problem is this particular individual?" Asher leaned heavily across to help himself to more lemonade. "Hmm, this is very good. I must get my people to make some up. I assume," he continued, "that this is not a matter of merely minor inconvenience?"

12

"I can see," observed the Minister, maintaining his composure with an effort, "that it will be unnecessary to skirt around the subject any further. I have always greatly admired your perceptiveness – I wish I could say the same for everybody I met." *Good God*, he thought, *the man is actually nodding in agreement!* "Perhaps it would be best for me to come directly to the point."

*   *   *

Fifteen minutes later, the two men concluded their discussion and rose. The Minister shook Asher's hand warmly and thanked him profusely for the assistance he had promised to give. The meeting could not have gone better. Asher had agreed to handle everything. The Government would not be seen to be involved. There would be a . . . what was that dreadful expression? Yes, a "cut-out".

As the big man left, the Minister closed the door of his office and for a moment leaned back against it, his mind almost reeling at the thought of how childishly easy it had all been.

3

Sir Peter Dartington had been intrigued by the invitation he had received. Intrigued and, he had to admit it, rather flattered and excited. Respectable businessmen like him were not supposed to get excited, of course. He reminded himself of that. Dartington set great store by his respectability; he had earned the label the hard way, and was immensely proud of his achievements.

Yes, he thought, his had been a life of back-breaking hard work. Literally so. He never tired of telling people of his humble origins, of the injury that had changed his life, and of the metamorphosis of his father's company, Dartington & Son (Builders) Ltd, into Darcon International plc. He knew the tale was an impressive one, and he had no doubt that it had inspired many people to believe that by hard work and determination anyone could succeed as he had done.

An inspiration to others – how many times had he heard himself being introduced in speeches in those terms? Dozens, if not hundreds. And he always used much the same anecdote in his answering speech. "I suppose I am what you could call a family builder made good," he would say, "in more ways than one. 'Making good' is a building term which is generally used to describe the final touches after the construction work itself is complete. Filling in small cracks, plastering over, things like that. Prettifying, if you like. Well, I can tell you that after my accident all those years ago, there were plenty of cracks to mend, and I was in plaster almost from head to foot. Whether I am any prettier as a result, however, is a matter of some doubt." It never failed to raise a laugh or two.

Dartington was a good, natural speaker; he had never for a moment considered attempting to disguise his broad provincial accent, nor had he made too many concessions to the conventions normally expected of successful businessmen. He had made a few, of course. He had found out early on that a degree of ruthlessness was required in the construction game if one was to stand any chance of success. He hadn't really liked that at first, but had discovered that the ability to make harsh decisions had come naturally to him. He had been careful, however, not to acquire a reputation for it, and had managed to disguise his ambition beneath his unaffected lack of pretentiousness and pomposity. Few people had crossed him badly; those who had done so had soon found out what he was made of and regretted it. Everyone else took him at face value. He was a well-liked figure, well liked by all. He received more invitations to attend society and business functions than he could possibly have accepted.

But this invitation had been irresistible. "Mr Roger Asher hopes that you might care to join him for the weekend on the *Princess Scheherezade*, off Cannes." Asher's personal assistant had gone on to explain that should Sir Peter find this proposal convenient – the woman sounded utterly confident that he would – Mr Asher's private jet would be placed at his disposal for the journey to Cannes and back, and a car would be waiting to take him from the airport to the marina.

Dartington had been taken completely by surprise, and for a moment was lost for words. He had heard of Asher, of course – who hadn't? – but he had never met him. He mumbled something about checking his appointments, and hurriedly buzzed his own PA. The weekend was indeed free: his wife was due to be away on one of her frequent visits to her favourite health farm – and he didn't relish the idea of being left kicking his heels at home. That had been that; he had accepted.

So now here he was on this bloody great big flashy yacht, lying on a sun-lounger, with flunkeys waiting on him hand and foot. It had come as another surprise to him that he and Asher were the only two on board – apart, that was, from the crew: eleven of them, just to look after two passengers! – but that had been nothing compared to the surprise he had felt when Asher had dismissed the steward after dinner the night before and got straight down to business. And what business! His head was still spinning. What an extraordinary proposition! *Pete, my boy*, thought Dartington to himself, *you'll have to watch yourself here.*

"Morning, Peter." Dartington turned his head to see Asher emerging from the saloon wearing a dressing-gown. The big man lumbered out on to the deck and collapsed into a large chair. "Another

15

drink? Andrew!" he bawled back in the direction of the saloon door. "Drinks for Sir Peter and myself."

"Good morning, Roger," replied Dartington. He decided not to point out that it was well past midday. How any bugger could get up that late, he thought, was beyond him. He had always been an early riser himself. And he didn't really want another drink; that poor little Andrew had already brought him three gin-and-tonics, and he'd hardly touched any of them. The young steward presumably had standing instructions to replace them the minute the ice started to melt, thought Dartington.

Andrew appeared with a large beaker of orange juice for Asher, who took it without a word and gulped it down, and a fresh gin-and-tonic for Dartington. Dartington thanked the lad. Andrew smiled at him and withdrew.

"Had any further thoughts about what we discussed last night?" Asher wiped a dribble of orange juice from his jowls.

Dartington got up from the lounger and moved to a chair under the shade of the awning, pondering his reply. "I'm sure you'll understand, Roger, that I feel a bit out of my depth in something like this. I mean . . . I've never had anything to do with this sort of thing before."

"Neither have I, my dear chap," said Asher cheerfully. "It is an unorthodox way of going about things, I know. But the main thing is that it is in the national interest. I am a patriot, and of course I know you are too. That is the main thing. We'll be doing it to help the country."

"I accept your assurance on that, Roger. In fact there can be no doubt about it. But why don't the buggers do the job themselves? I mean, why don't they get the SAS or someone to deal with it? I can't understand why they haven't done that already."

"I don't think I would be revealing any secrets if I were to tell you that they have in fact looked into that. The problem is threefold. In the first place, a very long lead time would be required to get them into a position where they could pull it off. Something in excess of a year, I believe. Secondly, not only would there be no guarantee of success, but the chance of failure and subsequent embarrassing exposure would be absolutely unacceptable to the Government. An ignominious failure – however slight the risk of such a failure might be – would be incalculably damaging." Asher paused to take another swig of orange juice. "Thirdly, and probably most significantly, there

16

is a sort of unwritten rule that governments never get personal. They can be as beastly as they like to a whole country, and frequently are, but they can never be seen to be going for individuals. I can assure you that even in this particular case, there would be an international uproar about it if it got out. It's quite ridiculous, but there it is.

"There are a few examples worth studying, where things nearly backfired when this rule was transgressed." Asher started ticking them off on his fingers. "The two most obvious cases concern actions by the United States: first, when they went after Mr Noriega in Panama, and took him prisoner; and second, when they went for that fellow Qaddafi by bombing Libya. Both were seen as highly personalised attacks; both were directed against individuals whose demise or imprisonment would have been mourned by nobody. And in both cases" – Asher shook his head sadly – "the United States was accused of unacceptable violations of national sovereignty, of bullying tactics, and of every other stupid nonsense those rock-apes at the United Nations could dream up. The problem is," he confided, "ninety per cent of the member states of the UN are ruled by tyrants and despots of one kind or another, who do not want to condone a precedent and then one day find themselves becoming the objects of similar attention. That is why they stick together, and that is why wise governments do not tempt fate by flouting the unwritten rule."

Asher appeared to have finished, but he had an afterthought. "There is of course an example of a country that has never paid any attention to this rule, and has persistently hunted down individuals, in most cases terrorists, who have committed outrages against its people. I refer, of course, to Israel. I hardly think, Peter, that I need to point out that for many years Israel has been, in the eyes of international opinion, one of the most isolated countries in the world."

Dartington had risen to his feet and was pacing the deck, a frown on his face. "So you are telling me, Roger, that when they want some dirty work done, they come to someone like you or me to put it together and do it for them?"

"I have no idea," replied Asher nonchalantly, "as I have not been approached to do anything like this before. But I must assume that that is what happens, yes."

"And why me, in particular?" *Why you?* he wanted to ask.

"That's easy. They didn't approach you. They approached me.

17

They don't yet know that I am sounding you out. I approached you, first because I know you are a patriot who has shown that his country is important to him, and second because your company is well established in the region concerned, and could therefore provide suitable assistance and a base for the operation. The third reason is a little more complicated, but I think I owe it to you to explain what it is. It will help you to understand the reason for the Government's involvement in what is, after all, a plainly illegal act in terms of international law."

Asher stopped for a moment's reflection before going on. "Believe it or not, and I think most people *do* believe it, the British Government is very careful to remain within the law. The people demand it. It makes life awkward for the Government at times, but it ensures that it remains above reproach. After all, if the Government of the oldest parliamentary democracy in the world were seen to be flouting the law, you can imagine the effect it would have on other governments with fewer scruples. At least we in Britain can — when we need to — adopt a higher moral stance in condemning the actions of others who overstep the mark in some way. It can sometimes be a drawback to have to maintain this position, but on the whole the benefits outweigh the disadvantages. I have, as you know, been an MP in my time, and I can assure you that this is the case.

"However, now and then the Government finds itself under pressure to act in a way that is contrary to this principle. Such a case has arisen here. Let me explain how." Asher paused again to drain his glass. "As you know, I am a committed European. My newspaper . . ." He waved an arm vaguely, looking off into the distance, then fixed his gaze on Dartington, who had returned to his chair and now sat rigid with concentration. "I think you will agree that my credentials in this respect are impeccable."

Dartington nodded. The big man's European credentials were indeed impeccable, although he couldn't see what he was driving at. What did the EC have to do with this?

Asher continued. "Our European partners can at times be . . . shall we say, hard negotiators. As you know, we are right now in the final stages of negotiating a treaty to be signed at Maastricht in a couple of months' time. There are some particularly difficult issues to be resolved. The majority of countries are prepared for a more federalist approach — the word has a different connotation for them, and they are less suspicious of federalism than most British people are. The British Government has in my view accurately gauged the mood of the country, and there is a point beyond which it will not be prepared to step. It is a pity, but in fact my personal opinion is that the Government is right to refuse at this stage to commit itself to more federalism. There would be no point in making a firm commitment to something that might later be rejected by the people as a whole, or cause parliamentary rebellions in the run-up to an election. The time to make such a commitment is later, when everyone can see more clearly the direction Europe is taking, and the benefits that federalism could bring. But all this can't yet be seen clearly, so however much those of us with a true vision of Europe would like things to move ahead quickly, the wiser among us are prepared to wait until we can carry the people of our country with us.

"But I'm digressing. The bald fact is, some of our other partners are more insistent on fast progress towards federalist principles. One country in particular is most insistent. You can probably guess which one."

The French, thought Dartington. *It has to be the bloody French. What have they got to do with this?*

"France's trade," continued Asher, "has taken a few knocks over the last year, owing to the international situation. You'll have heard some of the scandal stories, but I can assure you that more will emerge. Their balance of trade has been badly affected. I don't think I need to say more, given that country's fairly ruthless attitude; the simplest way to put it would be to say that in the past they have shown themselves to be prepared to sign trade agreements with any country, of any political stance, no matter what. You will no doubt recall the glee with which they sold Exocet missiles to the Argentinians during the Falklands War.

"Unfortunately for them, they now find themselves under constraint in one particular respect. One or two particularly large and lucrative contracts have been frozen. The French desperately want this situation to be reversed. There is one obstacle to this – just one. Do you see what I am driving at?"

Dartington was beginning to see. "But how does the British Government come into this?"

"It's simple," said Asher. "The French apparently do not have sufficient expertise to remove this obstacle themselves. They know it, and the British Government knows it. So the British Government has promised to do it for them. In return for this promise, they will agree to our terms for signing the Maastricht Treaty on European Unity. And the British Government is covering its position by going private with this operation, rather than using the SAS. Of course, the French don't know that part of it.

"Anyway," Asher went on, "that is the background to it all. The deal with France is the reason for the project itself; I do not think the British Government would have any particular interest in the matter otherwise — in fact there is an argument for leaving things as they are. But the imperative of an agreement at Maastricht means it is firmly in Britain's interest now to accommodate the French in this matter.

"I imagine," said Asher, holding Dartington's eyes steadily with his own, "that you can also understand why I came to you. I know you are pro-Europe, and at the same time you are a patriot. The two are not, as some would have us believe, incompatible. I hope I have given you reason enough to agree to take this on. There is an additional reason, but before I tell you what it is, I shall need your assent to the project."

"Forgive me, Roger, but it's all a bit much to take in at once." Dartington was well aware that this was a pretty hard sell he was being given. A lot of play on the old "patriotic" bit. Fair enough, he thought; he *was* a patriot. Where was the harm in that? But his natural caution told him not to be hassled into giving an answer too quickly. "Can I think about it for a while?"

"Good idea," answered Asher. "Very sensible. Let's go in and have some lunch."

They ate lunch largely in silence. Asher knocked back glass after glass of pink champagne, and rarely paused between huge mouthfuls of food for long enough to speak, while Dartington, in contrast, merely picked at his food, remaining pensive throughout. He thought hard about what he might be getting himself into. He could see the logic behind it. Asher's speech about European unity had in fact cut no ice at all with Dartington. He was a pragmatist on Europe, not an enthusiast. On a personal level, he would have preferred to keep Britain at arm's length from the increasing interference of Brussels and Strasbourg. He had nothing against the French, and indeed he admired their approach to business. He disliked the Germans, whom he regarded on the whole as stupid, arrogant and loud-mouthed, but he could get on with them if he had to.

It was on the business level that Dartington saw the necessity of remaining at the heart of Europe. There was no question about it, from his company's point of view: Europe was the only realistic way forward. All his business speeches had stressed this, and no doubt that was where Asher had picked up on his "pro-Europeanism". But he had taken that line purely from the standpoint of his company. In Dartington's view, the EC was about corruption, pure and simple. Join it, and you had a chance of competing for contracts; stay outside and you had none at all. Privately, he hated the corruption and would have described himself as a Euro-sceptic; and at times, for example whenever the odious face of Jacques Delors appeared on television, he had felt almost Eurocidal and had harboured the opinion that the late Air Marshal Sir Arthur Harris had had the most practical attitude to Europe.

What he really found hard to stomach about it was the religious fervour with which the fanatical pro-Europeans espoused their cause. They all used the same rhetoric, riddled with asinine metaphors, moronic to the point of incoherence; they talked, as Asher had done, in lofty terms of the "European dream" or the "European vision". It was neither a dream nor a vision, thought Dartington. He had looked both words up in the dictionary. There was one definition common to both and far more accurate than either – hallucination.

But he had to admit that the project Asher had put to him had appeal. What a thing to be able to tell his grandchildren! No, he thought, on reflection, he supposed he would never be able to tell anyone. But what a thing! It was exciting! There was that word again – but bloody hell, why not? He wasn't getting any younger, and every man should have something to look back on. The builder's boy, dreadfully injured in a scaffolding accident at eighteen, now about to shake the world. Before the weekend, all his energies had been bent towards steering his company through the deep recession that had hit the construction business. Maybe this was what he needed to lift him out of his gloom . . .

The two men finished lunch just before three o'clock, and wandered outside again. Andrew served coffee from a silver pot. The weather was balmy and relaxing, and Dartington realised that he felt on top of the world. What a life, he thought. Sixty years old, and something like this suddenly comes your way. *Why not!*

"OK, Roger, I'm interested. I've a good mind to do it. I think I know where to start."

"Splendid!" boomed Asher. "Splendid! A very sensible and patriotic decision, if I may say so." He paused, and his voice took on a portentous tone. "I can now confidently assure you that the Government will not be ungrateful."

"I don't understand. I thought you said that the Government doesn't know I am being approached."

"That is correct. And officially, they will continue to know nothing about your involvement – *officially*. And I stress that strongly. However, I am authorised to conclude an agreement on behalf of the Government."

"What do you mean?"

"Times are hard," said Asher, "for all of us. Forgive me, but I have done some research. And I do have a few shares in Darcon," he added, shrugging. "It is no secret that the construction business has suffered badly over the last year or so."

"What are you driving at, Roger?" Dartington's composure had slipped, and his face assumed a pugnacious expression. "We aren't for sale, if that's what you had in mind."

"No, no, good heavens, no!" protested Asher. "My dear fellow! Far from it! I am suggesting a very different solution to your problems. Please bear with me while I explain." Asher gathered his thoughts and smiled reassuringly.

Dartington remained silent and suspicious.

"Darcon is, if I am correct, currently preparing tenders for a total of eleven major construction contracts worldwide, three of them in the UK, two more in Europe, and the remainder overseas. By major," he added, "I mean tenders for contracts exceeding fifty million US dollars in value each."

Dartington's mouth was hanging open as Asher ploughed on, unstoppable now.

"Any one of these contracts, should Darcon prove to be successful in its tender, would enable your company to keep its head above water for a while. You would survive. If *two* contracts were to be awarded to you, Darcon's future would be rosy indeed. But competition is of course fierce." Asher drained his coffee-cup loudly. "I shall be blunt.

Should this project be a success, the Government will ensure that two of your tenders are accepted. It is always possible, of course, that you may win a third contract, and perhaps even a fourth, on merit alone. But you have a bottom-line guarantee from me that you will get at least two."

Dartington's jaw had now dropped to somewhere down near his lower ribs. He gaped dumbly at Asher and considered the extraordinary promise that he had just been made. It had to be a promise. The man had made it *after* he had agreed to the proposal, not before. Why would he have done that if he had not meant it and could not deliver? It must be true.

Asher stood up; he clapped Dartington reassuringly on the shoulder and went inside, leaving Dartington sitting where he was in utter astonishment.

*   *   *

Three hours later, the stewardess in the Gulfstream IV commented to the pilot that Sir Peter Dartington was behaving rather strangely. It was a bit odd, she said. Every few minutes, the man would suddenly start tittering like a schoolgirl. For no reason, she said. Did he think Dartington was all right?

The pilot told her not to worry. The boss often had a strange effect on people.

4

Ed Howard was forty-five years old. He was tall, thin and dark-eyed, and had thirteen years of active military experience behind him; from 1966 to 1979 he had been a commissioned officer in the Royal Marines and the Special Boat Service.

He had married in 1976; his wife, Claire, soon began to put pressure on him to leave the Forces and find a job offering better pay and more regular hours. When he was offered a job in the City by the father of a friend in the American Special Forces, Claire pushed him hard to take it; reluctantly, he resigned his commission and accepted the offer.

Howard had known he would miss Forces life, but he had had no idea how much of a wrench leaving would be. He felt uncomfortable in London. He didn't know anyone in the City, knew nothing of the commodities business, and had never run an office. After a week of floundering, he told his employer that he was the wrong man for the job, but old man Ziegler was not put out in the least. In fact, he was pleased – Howard had shown honesty and candour. "Ed, I didn't hire you for your knowledge of the futures market. I hired you for your judgement and your ability to get things done. You find the right people to run the thing, and you keep an eye on them. That's all I want." The old man had been honest about that, thought Howard, but only up to a point. He hadn't mentioned his other motive: he wanted to cite Howard's example and get his son Mike to follow it. Old man Ziegler had frequently told Howard that he hoped his son would "quit horsing around in the military and get on with making a life for himself in business".

Over the next three years, the old man's faith in Howard was vindicated. Howard trawled the market, found a frustrated and ambitious young trader working for a large company, and persuaded him to move. The trader brought his team with him; Howard gave him his head and a generous bonus package, which resulted in hard work, loyalty and, after three months in the doldrums, the start of an extremely successful operation. Old man Ziegler was delighted; and Howard, to his surprise, found that he was actually rather good at running a business. His trading team were content – even relieved – to leave the administration to him.

Howard was treated well, and paid even better, but he never overcame his dislike of the stifling confines of the City. He stuck it for three years and then told his employer he wanted out. The old man was sad, but accepted it. "What are you going to do, Ed?"

"Personal and corporate security – advising companies and individuals on security problems, and making sure they don't lay themselves too open to extortion from terrorists and kidnappers. It's a big market these days. It's also more the sort of thing I was trained for."

"You taking Mike too?" Mike's father guessed he would; his son had followed Howard's example, as he had hoped, but the old man had recognised after a while that Mike was not cut out for a life in commerce.

"I haven't asked him," said Howard, "and I wouldn't, without your blessing. But he may want to come in with me when he hears about it. I won't ask him; but if he comes to me, I'll take him like a shot."

The old man sighed resignedly. He wished Howard well, and they parted firm friends.

Claire was horrified when he told her he was jacking the job in, and she went completely potty when he told her what he was going to do instead. She bitched, swore and ranted at him for two weeks. Finally he got bored with it and told her she would do better to find herself a doormat, not a husband – someone who could put up with her tantrums and keep her in the pampered style to which she had, thanks to him, become accustomed. She screamed and threw a meat-cleaver at him; it missed, smashing the kitchen window and nearly decapitating a grey squirrel raiding her bird-table outside. He responded by calmly pouring a mixing bowl of cold gazpacho soup over her head to cool her off, and then went to the telephone to cancel the dinner party. He had always disliked gazpacho – it gave him indigestion.

Claire's expensive dress was taken to the cleaners the next day to remove the acid stains caused by the soup; Howard was also taken to the cleaners, shortly afterwards, in the subsequent acidic proceedings for divorce. Somehow, thanks to his distaste for legal wrangling and a rather feeble solicitor, he ended up with fifty per cent of the Fulham house but one hundred per cent of the heavy mortgage liability – in fact, with nothing. His savings went on legal fees, a hefty financial settlement for Claire and a small flat in Wandsworth; precious little was left over to put into his new business.

It was Mike Ziegler, the old man's son, who helped with the finances. They went into business together and recruited a team of ex-Forces acquaintances, mostly ex-Special Forces, to join them. XF Securities was born. Mike Ziegler and his team of four handled the American and Far Eastern market from Los Angeles, while Howard and half a dozen others looked after the larger market of Europe, Africa and the Middle East from the London office.

They had an early success when there was a kidnap attempt on a wealthy Italian client; it was the kidnappers' bad luck that one of Howard's men was actually with the client at the time. He foiled the attempt in impressive style. The three Sardinian kidnappers were vigorously disarmed and spent several weeks prior to their trial in hospital, under what was in the circumstances a ridiculously heavy police guard. Even if the four armed *carabinieri* had spent the entire time fast asleep or blind drunk, or both, which they didn't, the kidnappers were in no fit state to attempt escape. Their lawyer at the trial made much of what he said was the excessive degree of violence to which his unfortunate clients had been subjected by Howard's operative, the sinister-looking Mr Harris. He did not have to labour the point; the physical condition of the three "victims" of Mr Harris's attentions, each wheeled into court with his right leg and both arms still encased in plaster, stated their case eloquently enough.

The judge, however, proved entirely unsympathetic to their misfortune. Instead he listened with interest to the testimony of Mr Harris. Here, thought the judge, was a man who made sure of things. He nodded sagely as Harris explained in simple language that the best way to prevent a man armed with a gun from using it was to break both his wrists; he nodded again as Harris went on to explain that the most reliable method of preventing him from leaving the scene before the arrival of the police was to smash his right knee-joint.

It had been simply and quickly accomplished, said Harris. No, he hadn't remembered to look at his watch to time it, but the process had taken perhaps five or ten seconds in all. No, not for each man, he said. For all three.

Yes indeed, thought the judge. The logic of what Mr Harris had said was inescapable. In his summing-up he said so, adding that in his opinion Mr Harris had shown laudable initiative, that he had performed a valuable public service, and that anyone concerned about the risk of being kidnapped would be foolish indeed if they failed to avail themselves of the services of Mr Harris and the organisation for which he worked.

The trial received considerable publicity; a number of prominent citizens and organisations took the judge's recommendation seriously, and work flooded in. XF Securities flourished. There was a temporary setback when Howard himself, along with one of his men, spent six months in jail in Ankara, in Turkey. They had been arrested and convicted of paying off a ransom demand on a kidnap victim, but even this had redounded to their credit; the victim would otherwise have joined the ranks of disappeared industrialists, and instead he had been released unharmed. The kidnapped man's company, which had sent for Howard only after the kidnap had occurred, had been duly grateful; the Turkish authorities, however, had not been so understanding. Despite the fact that thanks to Howard the ransom money had been recovered and the kidnappers arrested and shot, in that order, by the Turkish police, Howard and his colleague had nevertheless been prosecuted for taking part in illegal negotiations with criminals. The victim's company had very much appreciated the fact that Howard had remained silent and had not implicated them in this charge, and had since retained XF Securities for all its security work.

The company concerned had been Dartington Construction Ltd, later Darcon International plc. Howard now sat facing its Chairman across the desk, in the study of the Chairman's house in Kent.

"Peter, are you serious about this?" Ed Howard already knew the answer. He could see the determined look in Peter Dartington's eye, a look he had seen before. He wondered briefly whether Dartington had gone mad. His association with Dartington had been a long and mutually beneficial one; it would be a pity, thought Howard, if he had to lose one of his best clients.

"I'm deadly serious, Ed. I would like you to examine the problem – hypothetically if you like – and let me know what you think. If you really do come to the conclusion that it's a non-starter, then we will both have to forget that this conversation ever took place; but if you think it might be possible, I want to know how it might be done and who might be prepared to do it. Could you let me have a report, say in a couple of weeks' time?"

Howard stroked his chin thoughtfully. "I won't get far in just two weeks, Peter. But I can do some background research and have a look at the possibilities. To be frank, I don't know much more about the situation than I read in the papers. But I'll have a look at it for you, yes."

"Good. Now there are various constraints you will have to build in, I'm afraid. First, this must remain between you and me alone. No one in Darcon other than myself must know about it, so please don't talk about it to any of my people. If you need to talk to any of your own people, and I would suggest that you keep the number you consult to an absolute minimum, they must not *in any circumstances* learn of my involvement." Dartington paused to light a cigarette. "Second, and equally important, you must not approach anyone who might report back to the authorities. I'm afraid that must rule out any contact at all, for any reason whatever, with friends you may have in the police or the security forces. This is entirely unofficial, and it must remain that way. Silly, in the circumstances, but there it is."

That wasn't very clever of you, Peter, thought Howard. *That last throwaway remark was illuminating.* "Peter, I have a couple of questions. First, I take it that if I can come up with a feasible plan, you will actually want me to set it up and run it. Is that correct?"

"Correct."

"Right. That was just for the record, so that I know. Now my second point. This is a very high-risk project. Certainly more high-risk than anything I have done before, and that will go for anyone else who might agree to be involved. Do you see what I'm getting at?"

"Not exactly. But go on."

"What I mean is, nothing could be the same again for anyone after something like this. For anyone to agree to take this job on, he would have to be provided with an overwhelmingly powerful incentive, given the chances of his being terminally fucked if something goes wrong. We're talking major business here, so I hope you don't mind. What is the budget?"

Dartington drew on his cigarette and fixed Howard with a level gaze before answering. "Ed, I told you I was serious. This is big, I know. If you can pull it off, I am prepared to pay you five million pounds."

"Peter, I'm afraid that just isn't going to be enough." Howard paused and studied Dartington's face. Had there been a flicker of surprise? "Look at it this way. I will need to put together a team of highly specialised people for this. Together, such a team would probably be capable of taking out the Bank of England, if anyone is. Certainly they could pull off a series of major robberies, with a potential total reward of ten million or more to split between them. And they wouldn't face the risk of being killed in the process. OK, anyone I chose would be legit, so they wouldn't go for something like that; otherwise I wouldn't hire them. But then what you are asking them to do isn't exactly legit, either."

Without lowering his eyes, Dartington tapped cigarette ash into a small silver ashtray on the desk in front of him.

"For a start," Howard went on, "I must ask fifty thousand just for preparing the report. If it turns out not to be worth that much, I'll tell you. If you accept it and commission the job, we're probably talking about a further half a mill in retainers, minimum. Then there will be expenses." He paused again; Dartington's face was impassive. "Expenses alone may amount to a million quid. On top of all that, there is the question of remuneration. As I say, it has got to be made worthwhile for those involved, considering the risks. I would have to see what they think about it. I'd say you're looking at at least a tenner, all up. I honestly don't think anyone competent would touch it for less."

Dartington looked hard and finally spoke. "I quite see your point, Ed. I can see what you mean. OK. Go ahead with the report." He reflected for a moment. "I'll see where I can get to with the finance. You'll understand" – he smiled reassuringly at Howard – "ten million pounds is a lot to come up with. But I'll see what I can do."

Dartington made as if to stand up, but Howard held up his hand. "There's just one more thing, Peter. There are all sorts of things that can go wrong with a project like this. You've already put your finger on one of them – security. I appreciate your wish not to have anyone else from your side involved. In fact, I would have insisted on it if you hadn't mentioned it yourself. As far as this project is concerned, you are going to have to start living a double life in your own company, even with your own family. No secretaries, no records, no notes, no traces, nothing at all. It will be the same for me, until I have to start recruiting. Nix. Do you follow me?"

Dartington was nodding.

"So perhaps," Howard continued, "we could start as we mean to carry on."

Dartington looked puzzled.

Howard held out his hand. "The tape, Peter." He stretched his open hand forward, palm up. "Let me have the tape, would you?"

Dartington's face suddenly showed that he realised what Howard meant. Howard could not be sure whether he was being genuine about it, but he opened the desk drawer and switched off the machine that had been running silently throughout the conversation. He ejected the cassette tape and handed it over to Howard, looking slightly apologetic.

"It's OK, Peter. It would have been a sensible routine precaution in normal circumstances. I'm sorry I had to ask. In fact I'm glad to see you have been taking my advice. But this meeting is neither normal nor routine, is it?" Howard grinned and stood up. "I'll get back to you in a fortnight's time. If I get anywhere with it, I'll include the necessary pricing details and payment arrangements. I'll bring the report with me – one copy – for you to read. Then I'll take it away and destroy it. Is there anything else?"

There wasn't. Dartington showed Howard out to his car and waved him off as he drove down the gravel drive.

Howard's thoughts were only half on his driving as the Saab cruised up the M2 motorway back to London. His mind was turning over the implications of the meeting with Dartington. He forced himself for the time being to concentrate on the things Dartington *hadn't* said, rather than those he had. Leave aside the project itself for the moment, he thought to himself; concentrate on the possible reasons for Dartington's wanting it done. Dartington had dropped his guard with the remark about it being silly not to have anything to do with the security forces "in the circumstances". He had also sounded unsure of his ground when finances were discussed. OK, ten million was a lot of cash. Wouldn't anyone be jumpy about that sort of figure? Of course they would. But he hadn't seemed agitated, just unsure. And why would Dartington want to undertake this project by himself? Howard knew the extent of Darcon's current operations and where the company's interests lay. None of them, as things stood, was being threatened to a sufficient extent to warrant the sort of action Dartington was contemplating.

Howard arrived home and let himself into his flat. He poured himself a whisky, then lit a small fire in the grate. He sat down in his armchair, slowly twirling the ice cubes in his drink as he watched the tape cassette blacken and curl up. The fire flared hotly as the acetate tape itself ignited. *Who's behind you, Peter?* he thought. *Government? Probably. But there's something funny about it.*

He went to his desk, switched on his computer, and waited as it whirred into life. When it prompted him for his password, he tapped this in, following it with the command to bring up his word-processing program. He opened a new file under the "memo" template. This was one file, he thought, that he would not save to the computer's hard disk. He would keep it only on a three-and-a-half-inch floppy while he worked on it, and it would stay in his safe or on his person at all times. The computer prompted him with the line "To:– ¶", and he typed simply "PD". Below this, it already showed "From:– EH¶". The prompt moved to "Subject:– ¶". Howard typed in the single subject line, then leaned back in his chair. Yes, he thought, this was going to be an interesting theoretical exercise, even if it came to nothing – as was most likely. He allowed his thoughts to drift and run over a few of the many issues that would have to be addressed. His eyes gazed out of the window, hardly registering the gentle movements of the leaves on the cherry tree outside. His mind wandered far away.

On his computer screen, the cursor winked patiently, waiting for further instructions, at the end of the three lines of typing.

To:–   PD¶
From:–   EH¶
Subject:–   The assassination of President Saddam Hussein of Iraq.¶

5

Over the next ten days, Howard spent his time in what a casual observer might have considered to be a state of unproductive idleness. Initially, he emerged from his flat only to make forays to bookshops, returning with piles of books on the Middle East, the 1991 Gulf War, and Saddam Hussein; he paid for all of them in cash rather than by credit card. He spent hours poring over the books, annotating passages with a green highlighter pen and bookmark stickers.

A friend in the BBC, who had covered the Gulf War from Tel Aviv, obtained for him copy videotapes from the BBC archives of all the reports of the invasion of Kuwait and the Gulf War. There were dozens of hours of footage, a good deal of it repetitive, and Howard spent much time with his finger pressed on the fast-forward button on his video recorder's remote-control unit, skimming through until he found passages of interest. He began to wish he had been able to be more specific with his reporter friend, and ask only for those passages featuring Saddam himself, but he had deliberately made the scope of his interest seem as wide as possible. The picture quality of the VHS recorder wasn't particularly good, and the action of its remote control was infuriatingly slow; he wished he still had his old Betamax machine, which had been far better and faster. The familiar face of the dictator now featured regularly on the television screen in Howard's flat; he studied every reference to Saddam with care, taking in every detail of his appearance and surroundings. Of the rare footage of Saddam making a public appearance, Howard examined almost every frame in detail.

He spent hours in the British Newspaper Library in Colindale Avenue, poring over back numbers of newspapers and periodicals, making notes and occasionally taking photocopies; and he visited

Edward Stanford Ltd in Long Acre, where he bought copies of all the maps he could find of Iraq and the Middle East.

By the end of a week, after a visit to Felixstowe docks, the beginnings of a plan were formulating in his mind, but he knew he didn't have enough. For one thing, there was not quite enough detail on the maps he had been able to get. For another, although he had read himself fairly well into the country, he was no expert on the Middle East; he would have to talk to Johnny Bourne and get his reactions. No problem there; he would be talking to him about it in due course anyway. The third problem seemed insuperable, and he doubted whether Johnny would be able to help. He would start with the maps; it was probably the simplest problem, although it would involve a potential security risk. He picked up the telephone and rang the home number of a friend in 21 SAS who had been on the staff at Northwood during the Gulf War.

"Derek? Ed Howard. Can you do me a favour?" Howard spun a plausible yarn about a client company which was getting involved in post-war reconstruction projects in Kuwait and northern Saudi Arabia. "The problem is, odd as it may seem, there seem to be no detailed maps of the region available, apart from the 1:500,000 Tactical Pilotage and 1:1,000,000 Operational Navigation Charts I've got from Stanfords. The TPCs are good, but not quite detailed enough for what I need, and they are 1981 editions. The ONCs are more recent, 1990, but not as detailed. I was wondering whether the MoD might have anything better. Any ideas?"

Derek hummed and hawed for a bit; he suggested the London Map Centre, which Howard had already tried, and then mentioned the Army Map Centre in Guildford. "The trouble is, I would have to indent for them and send a driver down there," he pointed out.

"I could go and pick them up myself, if that's any help," offered Howard. "But are they really up to date? That is the problem."

"Quite honestly, I don't know what they've got. Probably no more than you've managed to get from Stanfords – the TPCs and ONCs. If Stanfords haven't got anything better, it doesn't exist – they stock everything."

Howard knew. Stanfords had been extremely efficient. "So there's nothing new that the MoD might have? No satellite-generated ones, made for the Gulf War?"

"Well . . ." – Derek sounded a little doubtful – "there were some

33

things like that floating around, but they were pretty highly classified, and the coverage was by no means complete – they were only produced for specific targets and areas. They might not be classified any more, now that the war is over, but they would certainly still be pretty up to date, apart from various structural modifications made to the landscape, courtesy of the RAF and USAF. Bridges and buildings blown up, you know. But then that was all in Iraq, and you said you wanted Saudi and Kuwait. Kuwait's not quite what it was, of course. Covered with soot from Saddam's farewell bonfire party, new tracks made by our tanks, bullet-holes in palaces, that sort of thing."

Getting warmer, thought Howard. "They sound more like the business. Any way I can get hold of a set of them?"

"Rare as rocking-horse shit, mate. But I've still got mine, somewhere . . ."

Bingo, thought Howard. *Careful, now.* "Any chance I could borrow what you've got for a day or two, just to compare them with mine?" His voice sounded light and casual.

"Don't see why not. Come round for a drink and I'll let you have the whole set. I think they're upstairs in a box in my attic here. But I really would like to have them back."

"That would be marvellous, Derek. No problem – I'll drop them back on Wednesday. I only need to do a quick comparison. Actually, I could come straight round to collect them now, if that's not a nuisance . . . Be with you in fifteen minutes?"

"About 7.45 then. Fine." Derek rang off.

Howard reached for his jacket and let himself out, the floppy disk safely in his pocket.

An hour later, he was back with Derek's set of maps; a quick look had confirmed that they were exactly what he needed. He would get them xeroxed first thing on Wednesday and return them to Derek. One problem down, two to go.

He decided to fix himself a quick bite to eat and get the BBC nine o'clock news headlines. Then he would ring Johnny.

6

"Well, how do I look?"

"Hmm? Fine, just fine." Johnny Bourne was sitting at his desk in his shirt-sleeves, facing the window, going over a report he had to finish drafting before the morning.

"Hey, at least look at me, you rat!"

"Oh, sorry, Juliet, I was concentrating." Johnny swivelled the chair round and looked at his flatmate. "Hey, not bad!" *Bloody hell*, he thought; *what a transformation.*

He hardly recognised her. Gone were the shapeless jeans and sloppy, paint-stained pullover, the tied-back hair and the unmade-up face – quite a pretty face even then, now he thought about it – that he had grown used to since she had moved in three weeks earlier and started doing up the spare room. When she hadn't been deep in her books, she'd usually been covered in paint, wallpaper glue, some damn thing. She had always looked . . . well, a bit of a mess – although she hadn't *made* any mess, thank goodness.

She had immediately struck him as a straightforward, down-to-earth character when she had answered the ad for the room; she had no silly airs or pretences, and they had quickly come to an agreement for her to move in. She had actually proved to be a very good flatmate, thought Johnny. She always replaced things she'd finished off – coffee, sugar, stuff like that; she hadn't filled the fridge up with weird items of fad food; she'd helped keep the place tidy, and she hadn't brought a lot of female clutter with her, just a few nice little touches. Her boyfriend Mark had been no bother – he'd only called round for her a couple of times, and he'd never stayed for more than a few minutes. Best of all, there had never been cobwebby festoons of tights and other female apparel draped all around the bathroom day and night. Yes, she'd turned out to be an excellent flatmate. Easy to get on with, no trouble at all. He hoped she'd found him as easy as he had found her. She had sometimes even put together something for him to eat in the evening when she had seen he was working hard; and he had done the same for her once or twice. A good, easy, completely undemanding friendship had developed between them. But he hadn't . . . well, he'd never really *noticed* her before.

Now she looked terrific, thought Johnny. The simple, classical black shift dress, modestly showing off the curves of the slim figure which hadn't registered with him before, the dark hair tumbling down over her shoulders, framing her face, the touch of make-up accentuating her dark eyes . . . Christ, yes, she looked wonderful. Stunning. "Big night out, huh? Where's he taking you?"

"Oh, just out to dinner. He's supposed to be calling round for me in about twenty minutes, around nine." She had caught the expression of surprise on Johnny Bourne's face as he turned round. A little smile began at the corner of her mouth. She turned away before he could notice it. "Can I get you a drink, Johnny?"

"Hmm? Oh, yes – thanks, that's kind of you. Whisky, please, with a couple of ice cubes if they're there. Hey, Juliet. Sorry I was flippant. You look really nice." She glanced at him over her shoulder as she poured his drink, smiling at his compliment. He returned to his work, tapping his pencil on his chin as he read. *Sod these Germans*, he thought, his concentration gone.

Juliet brought the drink over to his desk. She set the glass down on a coaster and stood next to his chair. "What's all this stuff you're working on?" She leaned forward, peering at the papers.

"Oh, just a security report for one of our German clients. Nothing very interesting, I'm afraid." Christ, he thought, what was that scent she was wearing? A delicious breath of femininity had suddenly caught him unawares. He looked up at her, smiling. "It's rather dull, really."

"*Really* dull?" She returned the smile and rested her left hand on his shoulder as he took a shot of the neat whisky. He set the glass down, tilted the chair back and slipped his right arm comfortably round her waist, looking up at her. His arm round her waist felt natural, good. Really good. *Careful, Johnny boy*, he thought. *Remember your golden rule. Never fool around with flatmates. It always ends in disaster.*

"Yes, Juliet, you wouldn't be at *all* interested." He gazed up into her eyes, grinning mischievously. "Boring bloody Germans." His hand rested on her hip. *God, she feels nice.*

Juliet's long fingernails moved, and played delicately on the back of Johnny's neck, beneath his thick brown hair. Her fingers were ice-cold from the whisky glass. *Jesus*, he thought. The effect of her touch was sudden and electric; a tingling feeling seemed to break out down his back, and he shivered involuntarily. Another breath of her scent reached him. His smile faded a little as he looked up into her eyes. Her expression had changed somehow, almost imperceptibly. Her fingers continued playing about his neck. It felt extraordinarily erotic. *God, what is going on here?* He allowed his hand to slip down the outside of her leg, caressing her through the soft material of the dress. She swayed slightly towards him, her hip gently resting against his shoulder. His hand slipped lower.

"Mmm. Juliet, you know something? You feel really nice." Her mouth was slightly open; he could see her tongue just moving against her teeth. *Christ, is this really the same girl?*

"You're a kind man, Johnny Bourne. And *you* feel nice, too." Her hand continued moving on his neck, then down towards his chest, little light touches. Her nostrils flared slightly, her mouth opening a little more.

God in heaven, thought Johnny as her fingers played down his neck. *What is happening?* His head was swimming. Her hand was inside his shirt now, the fingernails tracing delicious patterns across his chest. *Steady, Johnny, don't forget the rule . . .* His third shirt-button had somehow come undone.

His hand reached the bottom hem of her dress, and he was touching her leg. *It's only her calf*, he forced himself to think. *How can a leg feel so impossibly sexy as this?* His heart was pounding now, and he knew his eyes were betraying him. His hand moved slowly up her leg, just inside the skirt, finding the curve of her left knee. *Sweet God, it feels wonderful.*

"You've forgotten your drink, Johnny." Her voice was low and husky. As he looked up again into her eyes he could see they had

37

turned a smoky black, and her pupils were almost completely dilated.

His hand was now just above her knee, caressing, gently exploring. Her slim, taut leg felt out of this world. *Oh, Jesus, these are silk, not nylon. And that scent* . . . "I don't seem to be able to reach my glass. There's a beautiful girl in the way . . ." He controlled his voice with an effort, but there seemed to be a roaring sound in his ears. He was losing control. She would move away now, before things went too far . . . Her thigh . . . *Oh, dear God* . . .

Juliet leaned across and held the glass to his lips. He took a small mouthful of whisky. Her hand was trembling slightly – or was it his mouth? A little of the drink escaped over the rim of the glass and ran down his face. With a quick movement, she bent down and gently licked the trickle from his chin with her lips and tongue.

The sudden feeling of her lips was shattering, and he stifled a groan. *What is happening, what is happening?* . . . His hand was now on the inside of her thigh, exploring the gentle curves of her leg; firm, but so soft through the silk . . . *Please, God, don't let her pull away now* . . . Her lips seemed to brush against his cheek as she gradually straightened up again. He caught the scent again, this time mixed with the sweet smell of her breath . . . He let out a long, deep sigh, his resistance going, his eyes closed. His hand now higher on her thigh, and . . . *Oh, Christ.* The top of her stockings. Not tights . . . Little delicate clips holding them up . . . silky soft, bare flesh now, so beautifully soft and warm . . . *Heaven* . . .

He felt her shiver as his hand caressed the top of her thigh, tracing softly round the line of the little lace knickers. *This must be just a lovely dream, it can't be true* . . . His will-power was going now, going . . . She slowly reached down, unbuttoning his shirt completely, then reached further down to the belt-buckle . . . His left hand came up at last, tangling in the dark hair behind her neck to stop the dream flying away, all control gone, pulling her face down to his . . . Their mouths devoured each other in an explosion of passion, Johnny shuddering as her right hand found him, gently coaxing him free, caressing. The roaring in his ears was deafening now, nothing else existed but this beautiful child of paradise . . .

Slowly, he stood up, shaking feverishly, and their bodies pressed urgently against each other, abandoned to the irresistible force of their desire. He picked her up lightly. She clung tightly to him, nuzzling his chest and neck, as he carried her through into the bedroom, kicking the door shut behind him.

*   *   *

"Jesus Christ, Julie!" Johnny's voice was soft, almost reverent. "What the hell happened back there?" He lay on his back, naked amid the chaos that twenty minutes before had been a tidily-made bed. The girl, naked too, lay half on top of him, her left arm and leg draped across his body, her breasts pressed softly against his chest. There was a faint sheen of perspiration on her back, down to the perfect curves of her behind. He held her to him, her scent still intoxicating. The intensity of their lovemaking had taken them both by storm. Their breathing had now eased; they lay relaxed, entwined languorously across the bed.

She looked up into his eyes and smiled. "Well, I rather think we both happened. To each other." She giggled happily, and reached up again anxiously for his face.

They kissed, slowly, grateful for each other. *God damn*, thought Johnny in wonderment. *She is so beautiful* . . . His head was still whirling with the suddenness of it all. It had been right off the business end of the Richter scale; in fact it was a bloody miracle the damn bed hadn't caught fire. Until only twenty minutes ago, he had scarcely ever even looked at her, and now . . . He didn't think he had ever known anything so powerful and compelling as the feeling that had overcome him. *How the hell have I never noticed her before – have I been blind?* This woman had just completely blown his mind away; he had been powerless to resist. *Wow!* "Julie, my darling, you are twenty-four-carat dynamite. You've just completely destroyed me. I didn't know what the hell'd hit me. I still don't. You're fantastic!" His voice softened. "You're so lovely, so beautiful . . ." He pulled her closer, and held her very tight.

Juliet bit her lip and suppressed a shiver at his display of tenderness. *Don't blow it now*, she thought. *Not too fast.* "So it was all my fault, huh? You old goat, you. So much for your rule about no sex with flatmates. What about that routine with your hand stroking my leg?

39

Have you any idea what it took for me just to stand there and try and stay in control while you were doing that?"

Johnny grinned and kissed her again. She lay on top of him and looked teasingly down into his face. His expression turned serious again; he pulled her down and held her close. Her heart pounded as he whispered into her ear. "Julie, I really mean it. You are . . . a wonderful, lovely girl. I've just *never* been hit like this before." His eyes burned into hers, then softened again. "You're so beautiful. I never imagined . . . I think I . . . I mean, you will stay, won't you?"

Oh, wow! she thought. Her eyes softened too, and she smiled down at him, her face radiant. Then, seeing his sudden expression of anxiety, she dropped her head to the hard muscle of his chest again, so that he wouldn't see her face. She felt tears coming as she spoke. "Well, I haven't got any plans to move just yet . . ." *That was the understatement of the decade*, she thought, biting her lip again. "Of course I'll stay, you big gorgeous ape. But on one condition." She blinked her eyes clear, raising herself on one elbow, and wagged her finger in his face with mock seriousness. "You only break that rule of yours with *me*, understand?"

"Deal," said Johnny happily, kissing her, tasting again the gentle sweetness of her mouth. Her delicate smell filled his senses, and he breathed in deeply. "Mmm, Julie, what is that lovely scent you are wearing? Are you sure it's legal?"

She gave a little sigh of pleasure. "Not wearing any scent, darling," she whispered dreamily in his ear. "That's just me."

He held her tight again, captivated. *She's adorable*, he thought. *I must be dreaming, I must be . . .*

The telephone rang, and Juliet stirred.

Johnny grimaced in irritation. "Let the damn thing ring. The machine will get it." He couldn't remember if he'd set the answering machine. Too bad if he hadn't. Who the hell could it be, anyway? . . . "CHRIST!" He sat up, a blur of movement, and was on his feet.

Juliet, astonished, found herself flung on her back on the bed. *God*, she thought, *he moves so fast. Like a cat . . .*

"Hey, Julie! Mark! What about Mark! Shit! The poor sap will be here any minute now!"

"Relax, lover." With a peal of laughter she pulled him back down on to the bed. It was his turn to look surprised. "I said *relax*, Johnny, will you? Mark's not coming. Certainly not with me, anyway." She

40

giggled. "It's OK. I called him at work this afternoon and put him off."

"You did what? Then what . . ." Understanding dawned on his face. "Do you mean you set up this whole . . . you little smoky-eyed minx!" He lay down again now, resting on one elbow, his eyes travelling slowly down her slim figure. His free hand closed gently over a breast, then his mouth came down on hers and he pulled her close again, kissing her eyes. Her mind collapsed into delicious turmoil again as he moved his mouth to her ear, murmuring between kisses. "How long have you been planning this, you lovely, wicked, perfect girl?"

She clasped him more tightly. *Ever since the start, you stunning man*, she wanted to say. *I think I knew from the moment I first saw you. But I had to find out what you were really like before I made yet another of my mistakes, so I wore baggy old clothes, acted uninteresting, so you wouldn't notice me just for my looks . . . And you were so nice, so considerate, so genuine, kind and good to me . . . Your smile, your eyes . . . pain behind them, somewhere, older than your age, and yet still the little boy in there too – the little boy, slightly embarrassed as you told me about your rule with flatmates . . . That was when.* But she knew she would never tell him, because if she did, he might change . . . "Would you settle for sudden mad impulse?"

"No, I wouldn't. And what would have happened . . . well, if nothing had happened?"

"Oh, I would have just sat around all evening, pretending to look miserable, gazing at your shoulders when you weren't looking, until you did the decent thing and took me out to dinner yourself." She giggled again and curled up gently against him. After a few seconds, her hand moved up round his neck, caressing him. "Johnny?"

"Still here, smoky eyes," he murmured.

"Do you have any more rules we could break?" Her hand moved again, downwards now.

"Just the one, I'm afraid." He caressed her shoulders and back, his fingers running lightly down her spine. "Shall we break it again?"

"Yes, please!"

As his hands and mouth moved over her body, her mind started to dissolve again in waves of ecstasy and she imagined she heard him murmur things to her in a strange foreign tongue; she could not understand anything he was saying, but the words sounded achingly beautiful, and somehow she knew that his soul was opening up to her: *"Mâ shûkani, mâ shûka al-'uyûn al-mudakhkhaniyîn, 'âshek alân wa dâ'im al-ayyâm, mâ shûkani, mâ shûka latîfa . . ."*

When he entered her again, she let the tears of joy come, unrestrained now, crying aloud as she became one with him, complete, an exquisite blur of sublime fulfilment. During those moments, she knew. Crying and shuddering in soaring, burning abandonment, she felt her heart swell with an intense happiness she had never experienced before. She had finally fallen. Completely out of control for the first time in her life, Juliet Shelley was head over heels in love.

7

"So why do they go along with it? Why do they put up with him, let him inflict all these disasters on them, one after another?"

"Oh hell, Ed, that's a huge question – we could discuss it for hours. The simple answer, that he rules by terror and lies, murder and misinformation, tells barely half the story. It's too simplistic, and although it's obviously true, the oversimplification also partly explains why the West has made so many blunders in the region over the years." Johnny paused to draw on his cigarette, and continued.

Howard let him talk, absorbing his knowledge. He was a fluent talker, and he obviously knew his subject, thought Howard. The tape was running so that he didn't have to take notes, but would be able to refer back to it if necessary. Howard found himself genuinely, not just professionally, interested in what Johnny was telling him.

". . . so let's just look at the question of truth for a minute. It is a key issue, because attitudes to it are so widely misunderstood. Westerners, and particularly us Brits – more recently Americans too – have lied, cheated and exploited these people for years – ever since we first came into contact with them, actually. They think of us as robbers, bullies, liars, out to subvert and destroy their culture. And they are largely right. We tend to think of Arabs as duplicitous and backward. Our image is of a shifty, squint-eyed, flea-ridden, treacherous character in a sort of dirty nightshirt, carrying a curved knife and looking for a back to stick it into. Dammit, we see it in all the movies, don't we? It must be true, mustn't it? Sure, every now and then there's a hero in clean robes, a desert sheikh type. And we like *him*, of course. Why? Because we think he has Western values, thinks like us, has learned from us. Bollocks! We couldn't be more wrong. Originally, we learned from *him* and *his* kind, not the other way round. They have a culture far older and more honourable than ours. Hell, the very notion of chivalry – of playing the game honourably, rather than winning at any price – originated in Arabia, not here in England as we so fondly imagine. They still try to live by it. All of them, from the humblest man in the poorest clothes. Do we live by such a code, any more? The hell we do!

"So when someone like Saddam rises up amongst them, a strong man, and tells them these things, they believe him. Then he tells them what he is going to do about it – how there will be glorious victories over the exploiters, that the Arab culture will triumph, and all the rest of it. They believe him. They believe him because they *want* to believe him. And that is partly the key to it: the truth, to an Arab, is more often than not what he *wants* the truth to be - there isn't the emphasis on cold factual accuracy that we pretend to stress in our own dealings with people. And if it comes to that, are *our* politicians truthful? Fucking liars, most of them.

"To an Arab, everything is subordinate to Islam and honour – even truth, because to them honour *is* the truth. And there are so many subtle sides to it in their culture . . .

". . . it's just a damned shame that it so often seems to be the rogues, the monsters with no morals, who rise to the top of the heap . . . "

That's the way of the world, lad, thought Howard. *You've still got a lot to learn, Johnny, even at twenty-eight.* But he sat and listened as Johnny ranged over the vast differences and complexities of the Arab world; Howard was getting a real sense of the affection and deep respect this rather idealistic young man obviously felt for these people.

". . . oh yes, now he's let them down so catastrophically and so often, most of them hate and fear him; in fact most of them always *have* hated him. But that doesn't mean they have come round to our way of thinking and now agree that we were right all along. They'll be happy if he goes, sure, but they'll want someone else, someone strong in his place, who they hope will achieve the things they want . . .

". . . a lot of the trouble in Iraq stems from the huge disparity in outlook between the three main ethnic, religious and cultural groupings there. They are further apart, within that one country, than for example we have ever been from the Russians – even at the height of the cold war . . . "

Later they got down to specifics: military capabilities, hierarchies, administrative details, structures. So far, Johnny had not asked him what it was all about. Ed often did exercises like this with his people in XF, pumping them for knowledge before the company ventured into new territory. Johnny was if anything a little surprised that he had never been asked any of this before - Ed had simply left that part of the world to him.

They broke off for a snack at one o'clock; Howard had bought some sandwiches at the corner shop, and they washed them down with a can of beer each. Looking at his watch, Howard was startled: they had been at it for four hours, and he had hardly said a word, other than to ask a few questions and occasionally steer the conversation on to a new course. The two men sat, relaxed, in the comfortable armchairs in Howard's flat. Johnny suddenly looked tired, he thought. Tired, but . . .

Howard looked at him closely. The younger man was wolfing his sandwiches down as though he hadn't eaten for a week. *I'll be damned*, he thought after a few seconds, a smile starting at the corner of his mouth. "Johnny?"

"Uhuh?"

"What's her name?" The smile was a grin now.

"What? How . . . ?" The younger man started, staring at him.

I'll be damned! Howard thought again. Young Johnny was actually *blushing*! "Come on, Johnny. Give. Tell all. Who is she?" Hell's bells! The boy had gone almost crimson! Howard groaned inwardly. This was all he needed.

Johnny was indeed tired; but his elation was obvious. He found he couldn't hold back, and it all spilled out in a rush, while Howard listened in astonishment. "Oh God, Ed, she's wonderful! She just totalled me, I tell you. I've never been so completely knocked out by anyone before . . ." He gushed on for a few minutes, then faltered to a stop, smiling sheepishly as he looked at the amused expression on Howard's face. "Come on now, Ed. Don't look at me like that. I'm being serious."

I can see that, thought Howard. *Oh yes, I can certainly see that.* "When did you meet her?"

"Well, last night, really . . ."

"Last NIGHT?!"

"Well, what I mean is, I never really noticed her before then. I mean . . . you've met her, actually. She's my new flatmate."

45

"Oh shit, Johnny!" Howard burst into laughter. "After all that crap you give out about your rules with flatmates, you haul off and . . . you mean, that little scruffy girl covered with paint the whole time?"

"ED!!" Johnny's voice cracked like a whip. The hard muscles on his neck and shoulders were standing out, his fists clenched tight, eyes blazing with anger. He was suddenly poised to spring, fast, deadly.

Jesus. Back off, Ed, Howard thought to himself. *That was fucking stupid. Don't be so bloody rude to the boy.* "Johnny, I'm sorry. I was way out of line. I really didn't mean it that way. Hey, come on. You must admit, there is a funny side to it – you and your golden rule. But I'm sorry. So – this is the real thing at last, eh?" He smiled, the tension gone.

Johnny subsided again, and his eyes dropped to the floor. He spoke in a soft, low voice. "Yes. It is. I can hardly believe it, but yes. This time it is. I . . . I said things to her I've never said to *anyone* before. Even now, thinking about it, I know I still mean what I said."

"What did you say to her, Johnny?" Howard asked, gently now.

"Well . . ." – Johnny grinned – "she didn't understand a single word of it. But I think she got the message."

"What do you mean, she didn't understand?"

"I was speaking Arabic. Part of an old Arabic poem, with some, er, modifications of my own. Afterwards, she made me translate it for her."

"What did you say, Johnny?" Gently again, insistent.

"I told her I loved her. Really loved her. And then I said . . ."

"Go on." Howard suddenly felt uneasy.

"Well, she went mad. I thought she was going to squeeze me to death. She started crying, and . . ."

"Johnny, what did you say?"

"I asked her to marry me . . ."

Oh, CHRIST!

". . . and she said yes."

Oh, SHIT!! Howard slumped back in his chair, with a moan of anguish. *I don't believe this. Not now, for Chrissake, when I need him for this . . . Oh, FUCK!!*

With a huge effort, Howard composed himself. "Johnny, hey, look, I'm delighted for you. Hell, congratulations, lad!" *Think, now*, he told himself. *Think positive. Don't try and put him off – you can't.* "Tell me about her. What does she do?"

"Well, it's funny you should ask." Johnny was off again, happily, his eyes alight as he talked about Juliet. "I didn't know until last night. I thought she was a student or something. Well, she is, in a way. But I never paid much attention to her, really. Never bothered to ask. She's studying for a career promotion. Her exams are coming up. She's a real high-flyer, Ed."

"What does she do, Johnny?"

"She's a Detective Sergeant. She's going to be a Detective Inspector! CID – you know. Imagine that! Me married to a policewoman! Hey, Ed . . . are you OK? Ed?"

Ed Howard had collapsed backwards into his chair with a groan. He lay there, stupefied, his eyes closed. He quite genuinely thought he was about to die.

* * *

Juliet Shelley woke from a deep sleep at 1.15 p.m. Her eyes gradually focused on her surroundings, and for a moment she wondered where she was – until suddenly everything came flooding back and she let out a long sigh of pleasure, a smile spreading across her face. She stretched luxuriantly, reaching out for Johnny, then had a moment of anxiety as she realised he was not there. She saw the note pinned to the bedside lampshade, reached across for it and opened the envelope.

My Darling –

I wish I could be there just to watch you wake up, but that call I didn't answer last night was from my boss – he left a message on the answering machine and I've had to go and see him. I'll be back this evening, probably around 6 p.m.

We'll go out to dinner this evening to celebrate, then tomorrow I want to take you shopping, to choose a piece of hardware – very hard ware – for your fourth finger. Don't wear that little black number you had on last night, or I doubt we'll ever make it out of the flat.

On second thoughts, don't you dare *not* wear it!

I love you – J.

She clutched the note to her, then turned over and squealed with

47

delight into the pillow. After a while she got out of bed, just managing to avoid colliding with the ice-bucket and its half-empty bottle of champagne. She retrieved Johnny's shirt from the pendant light-fitting above the bed, where it seemed somehow – she giggled – to have ended up the previous night. She held it to her face, inhaling the smell of him; then she put it on, doing up all but the top two buttons. The shirt came to her knees.

Going over to the window, she flung the curtains wide, and the October sun streamed in. Across the street, a builder on a scaffold tower caught the movement and glanced round, nearly dropping the trowel with which he had been repointing some brickwork at the sight of the half-dressed figure at the window not fifty feet away. Noticing his look, she flashed him a brilliant smile and disappeared from view.

Some lucky bleeder, thought the builder appreciatively, hazarding a guess at the reason for her sunny disposition. He returned to his work.

Juliet went to the kitchen where, suddenly ravenous, she prepared herself a salad with a large slab of Camembert and some biscuits; taking the plate into the sitting-room, she curled up in the large armchair next to Johnny's desk and the telephone, and dialled her best friend, Janey. She had to tell *someone*, she thought.

For the next hour and a half, anyone trying to telephone the flat would have found the line constantly engaged; and if anyone had chanced to get a crossed line, it would have been understandable if they had assumed that they were overhearing a conversation between two teenagers, rather than two sensible and level-headed career women in their mid-twenties. Juliet's obvious happiness was infectious.

*   *   *

The principal subject of Juliet and Janey's long telephone conversation was still sitting in the chair opposite Howard, his brow knotted in thought. He now understood Ed's initial reaction – inexplicable as it had seemed to him at the time – to his news.

Howard had decided to tell Johnny about the project; he could see no alternative. There was no other Arabist he knew he could trust so completely, and there was no one else who came near to Johnny in

48

organising ability, or who had Johnny's eye for detail. He had decided that he would need Johnny anyway, even if only for the set-up and approach phases of the operation and not the final penetration into Iraq itself. The only thing Johnny was likely to be at all interested in pene . . . *Stop it*, he told himself. *Don't be vulgar. You can't blame the boy.*

He knew he could trust Johnny to keep quiet about it, even with the girl, and he knew Johnny would give the project – if it got the green light – his usual two hundred per cent. He had had plenty of evidence of the younger man's unusual ability to focus his concentration on a problem to the exclusion of everything else; hell, for four hours just that morning, until they had broken for the sandwiches, he had given Howard and the subject under discussion his full attention, without once wavering or giving any sign that his mind might be elsewhere. Yet that had been on probably one of the most distractingly happy mornings of his life and, Howard guessed, after little sleep – if any at all.

Yes, he could trust Johnny to bend his full energies to the project; and he could also trust him to keep things to himself. Nevertheless, he had felt it necessary to point out the higher than normal degree of risk that Johnny's new liaison posed to the security of the operation.

"What you'll have to think about, Johnny, if you can bear with me and be analytical about it for a moment, are two separate factors here: one from your point of view, and one from hers. First, right now you are emotionally very vulnerable. You have just opened up to your girlfriend, and for the first time for a long time – maybe for the first time ever – you're going to want to share all your thoughts with her. All of them. That's entirely natural, and I wouldn't expect anything else. All I'm saying is, you'll have to keep that very much in mind, and find some way of squaring with your conscience any guilty feelings you may have about this constituting a deception on your part, especially at such an early stage in your relationship with her. Do you get what I'm driving at? I hope I'm not offending you – I'm just being logical here."

Johnny had nodded, his face thoughtful.

Good lad, thought Howard; he *was* keeping his mind analytical, and not going emotional on him. "Fine. Sorry I had to mention it, but I knew you'd understand. Now, the second thing. She has obviously gone for you like a ton of bricks. I'm very happy for you both – good for you. But most women in this state find themselves suddenly wanting to know absolutely everything about the new man in their life. You hardly know each other – she'll be dying to find out all about you. She'll drink it all in, ask a lot of questions, hang on your words, get you talking. She'll be intensely curious about every little thing about you. What you do, all that. I'm not for one moment suggesting she's going to start spying on you or anything, but she'll show an interest in literally *everything* connected with your life – even boring old farts like me who work with you. It's only natural. Do you see?"

Again Johnny nodded.

"What makes it more difficult is that she is obviously very bright. To have got where she has with CID at such a young age, she must be bloody smart. Actually," – Howard grinned – "on second thoughts, I'll take that back. Can't be that smart if she's fallen for a bum like you."

Johnny raised a mock fist at him, his eyes laughing.

"In all seriousness," Howard continued, "not only is she smart, but she is also by training and occupation extremely observant. I mean, I don't know her other than to say hello, but if she's a DS at twenty-five, about to be a DI at that, she is one smart lady. Really smart. You'll find it bloody difficult to fool her on anything, mate. And I mean *anything*. Forgive me, but I doubt whether you've seen anything of that side of her yet. And forgive me again, but you aren't that difficult to read, Johnny. At times you're like an open book. Hell, I had an example of that just now, didn't I? It was written all over your face, you big soppy git."

Johnny nodded resignedly, with a wry smile.

"In fact, I dare say that your openness and sincerity were partly what attracted her to you. Yeah, I know you're an outrageously good-looking, charming fellow, all that crap. But don't forget, this women spends most of her life dealing with people who are bad order – liars, crooks, phoneys, closet perverts, slags, the lot. She'll have seen them all and can spot the signs. Otherwise she wouldn't have got where she has. Suddenly, she meets a straight, honest, genuine nice guy like you, no side, not a cynical thought in his head, bit of a hero into the bargain – I bet she already knows about your Army record – she's bound to find that interesting. *Bloody* interesting." Howard paused to drain the last mouthful from his beer-can. "I'm not saying she's deliberately going to set out to find your Achilles' heel, but she'll be looking for constant reassurance that you really are as nice a guy as she thought, and if there's something there that doesn't fit, she's going to spot it, take it from me.

"Add all this up, and what have we got? We've got a big potential problem, that's what. It's going to be extremely difficult for you. Right at the time when you want to open up to someone for the first time, you're going to have to hold back on something – also for the first time. You're going to have to deceive her, just when it's the last thing you want to do, or thought you would have to do. It's going to be hard, mate. Fucking hard. Look, I'm sorry for spelling this out so baldly – the last thing I want to do is sound patronising, and I probably have. If so, I genuinely apologise. I wish I could have put it better. Perhaps I should have kept my mouth shut."

Johnny remained silent for a while, thinking about Howard's analysis of his situation. He could see the logic of it only too clearly. "No, Ed, you're right. All too right. I don't like it, but I can't deny it. I'm not much good at deceiving friends. It isn't something I've practised, I'm glad to say, but I can see I'm going to have to do it – for a few days, anyway, until we've looked at all this and you've finished the report. But one thing I *am* quite good at is compartmentalising my life. I can forget my work when I go home, when I want to, and I can leave personal considerations behind when I'm working. You've seen that this morning. That is something, you'll agree. As a back-up position, I think the best thing would be if I handed this Kraut job over to Peter and let him follow it up – that report's nearly finished already – and I'll start reviewing one of our client operations in Saudi Arabia. Darcon maybe; that would be a good one . . ."

Howard's face remained completely expressionless. He had not mentioned Sir Peter Dartington or Darcon at all; Johnny did not know the identity of the person who had commissioned the report.

Johnny went on talking, unaware of the significance of what he had just said. ". . . we're going to need to tap into one or two of the Saudi concerns anyway, if this thing gets off the ground. That way, I'll be working close to the truth but not on it, if you see what I mean. If she asks me what I'm doing, I'll be able to look her in the eye and say I'm working on a confidential project that has something to do with Saudi Arabia, and it will be substantially true. I don't want to have to tell her a single lie if I can help it. But I think I can live with not telling her the whole truth. I'll have to see; I'll let you know the moment I'm uncomfortable with that, or if I think I've slipped up with her. Hell, come to think of it," – Johnny smiled ruefully – "she didn't do a bad job on me, did she? You described her a while back as being scruffy, and I got angry. Well, she bloody well *was* scruffy. She was uninteresting, she let me think she was a student, hardly ever looked me in the eye . . . she certainly had me fooled. Jesus, you should have seen the difference last night! I tell you, it was incredible. She looked like a million dollars, Ed . . ." Johnny drifted off, lost for a moment in fond reflection, and Howard waited until he shook himself out of it.

The two men began to go over Howard's plan with a fine-toothed comb, covering every aspect. Johnny whistled in admiration at one or two of Howard's ideas, and occasionally interjected points of his own, animated again, concentrating with his usual intensity. They covered transport, routes, methods, equipment, documentation, administrative details, fall-back protection, security and deception plans. They agreed on a team of suitable individuals; by unspoken assent it was assumed for the time being that Johnny might not be in the team himself, but there would be a need for at least one fluent Arabic-speaker, and there was a question mark over one further specialist requirement – neither of them could think offhand of anyone with sufficient expertise in the field concerned.

By 5.30 p.m., having put a full day's brainstorming into the project, Howard decided to call a halt. They had covered almost everything, and Howard had virtually all the material he needed for his report to Dartington. They had in fact covered a great deal more ground than that, but most of the operational details would be excluded from the report anyway. There was no need for Dartington to know anything other than the basics.

He let Johnny out, then moved the chair he had been sitting on out of the way and pulled back the carpet. He opened up the little floor-safe and took out the floppy disk to continue working on the report. There would be six full C90 cassette tapes from today's session to join it in the safe, he thought. Just one essential detail was missing, and Howard thought it would do Dartington no harm to be given a bit of a surprise. Yes, he would leave it as a little sting in the tail, just to see how Dartington reacted.

The computer came on and Howard ran up his word-processing program, loading the file from the floppy disk. He started typing.

*　　*　　*

Two miles away and four hours later, Johnny Bourne and Juliet Shelley lay relaxed and contented in each other's arms in the darkness of the bedroom. Their lovemaking had been preceded by an evening of storybook romance: flowers, candlelight, dinner, caressing glances . . .

"Johnny?" A sleepy murmur from his side.

"Mmm?"

"You're under arrest."

"Huh? What for?"

"'ssaulting a police officer. Me," she added.

"I was provoked."

"No excuse. Do you accept the verdict and sentence of the court?"

"It was entrapment, honest. Anyway, you're not a court. Oh, all right, I plead guilty. What's the sentence, officer?"

"Life."

"With you?"

"Yes." She reached up and kissed him. "Johnny?"

"Still here."

"Are we really going to a jeweller's tomorrow?" She wriggled happily, nuzzling his neck.

"Yep."

"Which one?"

"You'll have to wait and see, nosy. If you must know, it's run by an old friend of mine from my Army days."

"You haven't told me much about your time in the Army. I want to hear all about it." She yawned dreamily, drifting off to sleep. "I want to know all about you. Everything. Every tiny detail. Every single tiny little thing . . ." She fell silent, breathing softly and regularly, asleep in his arms.

"I love you, smoky eyes," whispered Johnny.

8

Howard sat in silence as Dartington read through the thirty-page report. For the first twenty minutes there had been no comment from Dartington at all, other than a muttered "You've done your homework, haven't you?" after the first few pages. Howard had half expected Dartington to skip through the background sections covering the history of Iraq, its geography, climate and people, but Dartington had read steadily, seemingly engrossed in the contents.

On second thoughts, Howard supposed, it was perhaps not surprising that Dartington was reading the report carefully; it had, after all, cost him fifty thousand pounds. For half that money, he could have bought a rare first-edition copy of Lawrence's *Seven Pillars of Wisdom*, which itself would not have been without relevance. And he would have been able to keep it, too, whereas he was going to have to hand the report back to Howard as soon as he had finished it.

Dartington would probably realise, thought Howard, that the report had been written as much for Howard's benefit as for his own. During his two weeks of research, Howard had read and absorbed many hundreds of pages on the subject, including four contemporary historical works, one novel, three travel books, five general treatises on Middle Eastern politics, two biographies and three hastily-produced books covering the Gulf War and its immediate aftermath. He considered that his efforts to gain some understanding of Iraq, and of the tyrant who ruled its people, had been reasonably successful; and the discipline of distilling and setting out the salient facts in report form had been a useful exercise. Yes; he would have done something like this even if Dartington had not asked for it.

Finally, Dartington reached the closing section. His eyebrows shot up, but he said nothing. Instead he slowly folded over the last page and set the report down on the desk in front of him. "Yes," he said, giving Howard a beady look, "you've certainly done your homework. I've got a few questions, as you probably expected. I didn't much like that last paragraph, but we'll come on to that later." Since Howard said nothing, only nodded, Dartington carried on. "First of all, are you sure about all the previous attempts on his life you've mentioned? Is it as many as that?"

"No. There have almost certainly been *more* than the six I've mentioned in the report. The only difficulty is in establishing who was behind each attempt. Some were almost certainly home-grown; by that I mean that they were initiatives of individual Iraqis themselves, rather than plots inspired by foreign governments. Others were certainly initiated outside Iraq; the Israeli Mossad being the most likely protagonist. Israel has for years regarded Saddam as the biggest threat to its existence, and would love to be rid of him. The CIA is another possibility. Whatever the case with these attempts, no actual Israeli or American citizens were directly involved - they simply provided funds, encouragement, organisation, equipment, that sort of thing. The actual dirty work in each case was done – or rather, wasn't done – by Iraqi citizens who hated Saddam. But those six attempts are only the ones I've heard about – there may have been more. Also, I haven't mentioned the half-baked attempts, which never had a chance. And these are all since the end of the Gulf War. I haven't included any earlier ones, not even the ones during the build-up to it."

"Hmm." Dartington looked surprised. "I can understand the Israelis and some of the Iraqis themselves wanting to bump him off, but – the Americans? Hasn't George Bush said publicly that it's up to the Iraqi people to depose him? Has he been lying?"

"Not really. Three reasons. First, I am only guessing. There may not have been any plot backed by the CIA at all. But second, if there was, it's possible that the President did not authorise or know of such a plot himself – it could have been a CIA initiative. Third, if there *was* a CIA plot, there wouldn't, as I just mentioned, have been any actual CIA people directly involved – no US citizens with their fingers on the trigger, so to speak. The CIA would simply have contacted dissident elements in the Iraqi Army and elsewhere and put them up to it – promises of money, protection, power; you know, the normal inducements. So in a sense, Bush could reasonably claim that this was technically Iraqis themselves trying to kill Saddam, not the CIA. The provision of support to Iraqi dissident elements would certainly be entirely in line with his stated policy."

"How did you get to hear about these plots?"

"Oh," – Howard gestured vaguely – "I keep my ear to the ground. You've probably seen the signs yourself, but not picked up on them. Do you remember that report a couple of months back in the papers about a purge in the higher echelons of the Iraqi Army?"

"Yes. Was it true?"

"Pretty accurate. Large numbers of senior officers were rounded up, tortured and shot. Saddam personally supervised it, and shot a number of them himself. The ones who didn't die under torture, that is. Amongst them were the plotters of one of the assassination attempts."

"What about the ones who had nothing to do with the plot?"

"Oh, that is typical Saddam. They were killed too. He does that sort of thing the whole time, just to strike terror into everyone around him and make them feel insecure. He will do anything, kill anyone, to cling to power. I've gone into that in the report – you remember the section on how he deals with his cabinet members, and even members of his own family. In fact, it's those closest to him who are most at risk. He's got rid of a lot of his most loyal supporters, on no better grounds than that they had gained a degree of influence and public recognition that he perceived as a threat to him personally. He shot one cabinet member actually at the cabinet table, in front of all the others – you can imagine the effect on them. He knows terror is his best weapon, and he uses it without remorse. In fact the concept of remorse is completely alien to him – he doesn't understand the meaning of the word. The longest survivors in the Iraqi hierarchy are those who have proved completely servile, remained faceless and, strange as it may seem, shown a degree of incompetence – he sees initiative and competence in others as a potential threat. As well as being a vicious, ruthless psychopath, he's paranoid, as I mentioned. He sees plots and conspiracies wherever he looks. That is one of the reasons he has proved so difficult to kill."

"So how are you going to do it? You haven't gone into detail about that at all."

"That is deliberate, I'm afraid. It'll be safer that you don't know. No offence intended, but if someone gets at you, I have to be able to protect my own back." Noticing that Dartington suddenly looked slightly uncomfortable, Howard hurried on. "Immediately after this, I think we need to have another talk on security in general. I'll give you a few ideas on how to cover yourself. I hope it'll be unnecessary, but better safe than sorry."

Dartington appeared mollified, but he pursued the question. "I'm afraid nevertheless that I must ask you for some idea of how you are going to do it."

The question confirmed in Howard's mind his view that Dartington was not the prime mover behind the operation. He answered carefully. "We would be a small team. We would adopt a 'hit-and-run' approach, spending minimal time within Iraq, and using bluff and deception rather than pure stealth and concealment, although naturally everything will be geared to getting in and out without anyone realising who we are. I'm sorry, Peter, but I really mustn't tell you any more than that."

Dartington nodded resignedly. He changed tack. "What about this other stuff in here, the bit about Saddam having all these 'doubles'? Won't that make life more difficult for you?"

"Quite true; it could. To my certain knowledge, he has twelve doubles who are used from time to time to impersonate him. By now, there may be more than twelve. He sends them out and about so that he is 'seen' by his people, while he stays safe in his bunker in Baghdad where he can't be got at. Some of them bear only a passing resemblance to him, others are more convincing. There are two who are reputed to be extremely like him – so much so that very few people can tell the difference. For example, do you remember that footage of Saddam chatting to his soldiers actually inside Kuwait, just after the invasion?"

"Yes, I think I do. Do you mean . . . ?"

"Correct. That wasn't Saddam at all. It was one of his doubles – one of the two good ones. Saddam himself would never go anywhere like that, where he didn't feel completely secure. More tellingly, he never lets ordinary soldiers carry arms when he is present, in case one of them decides to take a pot-shot at him. Those soldiers were armed. And Saddam himself always carries a pistol. Always. He's never without it. The man in that film clip didn't have a weapon."

"How do you know about these doubles?"

"I have a friend in the SIS. Don't worry," he added, as alarm suddenly spread on Dartington's face, "I have followed your edict.

I haven't talked to him about this operation at all. This was a conversation we had ages ago, at the time of the Gulf War. He told me about the plastic surgeons."

"Plastic surgeons?"

"Two of them. Both highly skilled men, but both operating on the margins of respectability, shall we say. One was German, the other Swiss. Both – separately – were offered very lucrative contracts to operate on what they were told were European clients. Both travelled to France; both vanished. The Mossad got wind of information that they had been flown to Baghdad. An Iraqi informer – a doctor himself – later confirmed this to the Mossad and, interestingly, reported that the two surgeons were operating in two different clinics, both at the same time. So by inference, two people were being operated on. Some time later, both plastic surgeons disappeared. Neither has been heard of since. The whole thing tallied perfectly with a rumour going around at the time about Saddam's doubles, and these two stand-ins began to appear for him shortly afterwards. One of them is supposed to be particularly good – apparently he even has the voice right. But they're not allowed to carry their own weapons."

Dartington was shaking his head in amazement. "So how the hell are you going to get at Saddam?"

"That's the whole point of the final paragraph of the report, Peter," Howard said gently. "I won't be able to, without good intelligence. I wouldn't have a chance in hell. I can't simply go into Iraq and look for the bastard, or take an army into Baghdad and attack one of the myriad bunkers or tunnels on the off-chance that Saddam is lurking inside it. I have to know when and where I'll have a chance of getting near him. I need information. Without it, we might as well forget the whole thing, here and now."

"Is that what you mean by 'talking to my principal'?"

"Let's not beat about the bush any more, Peter. I know you're not behind this. In the first place, it isn't your style. In the second place, you're a rich man, but not so rich that you can spring for eleven million quid – which you haven't even batted an eyelid at – on a whim. And you can't lose that sort of expense in the books, either. None of Darcon's operations is threatened by any action Saddam might take – at least, nowhere near enough to justify the cost. That means someone else, or some other organisation, is paying the bills. And that someone or something else must be straight, otherwise you wouldn't have anything to do with it. The only candidate I can think of that fits the bill is the Government, but that's just my guess. I can understand why they would be reluctant to use 'official channels' to get rid of Saddam, and why they can't be seen to be helping either.

"Look," Howard continued, "I don't want to know who it is. I won't even guess any more. All I'm saying is, I have to talk to the guy in charge. I don't even have to meet him – we can talk by phone. I'll just have that one question to ask him, and I must ask him direct. It'll be better that you don't know what he tells me – in fact I'm afraid I have to insist on that too. The fact is simple: without my knowing where Saddam Hussein is going to be on any given day, there is simply no chance that I will be able to get at him and knock him off. I need a date and a place. I doubt that you have access to such information. Your principal may be able to provide it; so I need to talk to him direct. Let's not play around any more."

There was a long silence as the two men stared into each other's eyes. Finally, Dartington shrugged. "Very well; I thought you would probably guess, sooner or later. You're right, there is someone else behind this; for obvious reasons I can't tell you who they are. I will have to talk to them about this."

"OK," said Howard. "This is how we'll play it. In order to safeguard security for both of us, he will ring me on a number he can't trace back to me. That way, he won't be able to find out who I am. It will be a portable telephone. Not mine; yours – that one you use for outgoing calls only, so I won't get any calls intended for you. Ask him to ring me on that number on any Monday morning between eight and nine o'clock. I will answer, calling myself Mr Hatcher; your principal should identify himself as Mr Jethro. Please remind him that conversations on portable telephones can be overheard by someone with a VHF/UHF radio, so we will have to talk in somewhat cryptic terms."

"All right," agreed Dartington, "I'll set it up."

"Good," said Howard. "There is one other thing, which I hope you won't mind. I am going to have to burgle this house at some stage."

"What? What on earth for?" Dartington looked startled.

"Mainly to protect you. I'm going to have to use the Darcon set-up in Saudi Arabia as a cover for certain things. For that I will need information. Of course, you could simply give it to me, but I expect someone will realise in due course that Darcon has been used, so there will need to be an explanation as to how the information was obtained. The burglary will be it. I'll be in touch with you again by phone to give you a date. On that date, it would be better if you were away from here. Perhaps you could take Lady Dartington up to London for the night to the theatre or something. But you should make sure your office knows where you are. I want you to leave a set of files here, in your desk. I'll have to cause a little bit of damage – nothing serious, and it will only be in this study, so Lady Dartington won't have to be too upset; and I'll have to take one or two things, such as maybe that video recorder there, to make it look realistic. When you come back, I want you to make a very noisy complaint to the police about it. No need to leave the house unoccupied; by all means have Mrs Jephcott or someone sleep here if that's what you normally do when you're away, but it would be better if you weren't here yourself. It would be best if whoever it is is not a nervous type, likely to have a heart attack or anything. Mrs Jephcott seems pretty sensible and unflappable – I'd have thought she would be ideal. It would also be a help if that window was left unlocked, but don't tell Mrs Jephcott that. If she locks it, it won't matter." Howard indicated one of the two Georgian sash windows facing out on to the garden.

"What about the burglar alarm?"

"I know the specifications, remember? It won't be a problem. And it will go off – when I want it to."

Dartington agreed. Howard told him which files he would need to be left in the desk, and Dartington said he would await the telephone call. The two men rose; Dartington handed Howard his cell-phone and the report, and Howard left for London in the Saab.

9

Early on 28th October, Howard drove out of London and by eight o'clock was satisfactorily stuck, as he had intended, in the usual Monday-morning rush hour on the M25 motorway. Thousands of cars, nose to tail, crawled sluggishly along, with the Saab anonymous in their midst. Even in the unlikely event of someone's attempting to monitor the call he was expecting, there would have been no possibility of the signal being pinpointed to his car.

At 8.10 the cell-phone warbled its ringing tone, and Howard answered. "Mr Hatcher here. Who is speaking, please?"

"This is Mr Jethro. I understand that you wish to speak to me."

Howard was momentarily startled by the flat, disembodied, metallic sound that came over the telephone. He realised that "Mr Jethro" was using an electronic device to disguise his voice. "Thank you for calling, Mr Jethro. I believe you may be able to help me. As you know, I have been asked to do some business overseas on your behalf. Unfortunately, as things stand, I don't have sufficient information to act upon. The person I will need to contact is extremely difficult to track down, and I'll need to know where and when I will be able to meet him. I will need at least two months' notice to make all the travel arrangements necessary. Would you be able to give me details of a suitable appointment I might keep with him?"

"I will need some time to find out the information you require, Mr Hatcher. I'll have to ring you back. Perhaps next week at the same time. Failing that, the week after."

"Thank you very much. I look forward to hearing from you again."

"Goodbye, Mr Hatcher."

The phone went dead, leaving Howard in thought behind the wheel of the Saab. Despite the brevity of the call, and the disguised voice, Jethro had come across as a forceful and powerful man. Somewhat arrogant – or was that just his imagination? Howard instinctively disliked the man, and wondered who he was. Either Jethro was a very careful man, or his voice was well known. Howard shrugged. He wasn't going to find out, but in his mind he was fairly satisfied now that Jethro in some way represented the Government. He took the next slip-road off the M25 and headed into London. He had a lunch appointment at the Travellers' Club with a friend.

*   *   *

Roger Asher put down his telephone and switched off the voice-masking machine. He had not anticipated this. It would mean further telephone calls, and there were other pressing matters on his mind. A heavy cold, which he seemed to have been unable to shrug off, did not help.

He would have to telephone the Minister who, if the past was anything to go by, would be difficult to get hold of. The bore was, he would have to make the call himself; he could not risk going through his switchboard on a matter such as this. He would try that evening. In the meantime, he had many other things to attend to.

*   *   *

At 12.45 the taxi drew up outside the Travellers' Club and Howard got out. The hall porter informed him that his guest had already arrived and was waiting for him in the bar.

Howard walked through and greeted his friend. "Henry! Glad you could make it. Good to see you." The two men shook hands; Howard ordered a drink for himself and a refill for Stoner.

Major Henry Stoner was in his early fifties, and had been Howard's first company commander when Howard had joined 42 Commando, Royal Marines. Stoner was now retired and was the London Branch Secretary of the National Rifle Association. A keen rifle shot as well as a good organiser, he spent much of his time down at the ranges at Bisley, helping to organise the various national and international rifle meetings. No mean shot himself, he had once been second runner-up in the Queen's Medal competition. Now, although he kept his eye in, he was principally involved as coach to the South-Eastern regional team.

The two men chatted about old times over lunch, with Stoner fondly reminding Howard of some of the blunders the younger man had made as a newly-joined officer many years before. Retired officers could be just like parents, thought Howard, smiling; they never acknowledged that one had actually grown up. He was genuinely fond of Stoner, and had learned a great deal from him in his first two years with the Marines.

The conversation eventually turned, as Howard had known it would, to rifle-shooting and Bisley. A true enthusiast, Stoner could not stay off his favourite subject for long.

"It's getting rather more technical nowadays, Ed. I must get you down for a day, so that you can see what goes on. It's amazing what developments there have been – how much more technology has become involved recently."

"Don't you find that a bit of a shame? I mean, isn't it something of a pity, compared with the old days, when it was all down to pure skill and aptitude?"

"Not a bit of it. Nowadays it's more than ever a question of honing that skill. Even a superb technician will get nowhere unless he is also a damned good shot. It's still a question of whether you've actually got it or not. You can do a lot with coaching and practice, but to be really good you still have to be a natural at it."

"So how does a good rifle shot come to your attention? I mean, do you go round all the Army regiments looking for their best marksmen?"

"Surprisingly enough, no. The good Service shots will sooner or later turn up at Bisley anyway, sent there as part of their regimental shooting teams. Once they're there, one can spot the really promising ones quickly enough. The trouble is, standards of shooting in the Army have dropped off worryingly. I'm very concerned, and I'm not the only one." Stoner shook his head sadly.

"How so? I thought that the new SA 80 rifle had led to a much *better* standard, not the other way round."

"It did, for a time," replied Stoner. "But it was the guys who were originally trained on the SLR who showed the improvement. You see, they had been taught the basics. The ones who are coming through now have only ever worked with the SA 80. It's supposed to be an idiot-proof weapon, so it's now apparently considered unnecessary to give soldiers as much weapon training as before. The results we're seeing now are ... well, frankly, bloody dreadful. I'll give you an example: we held a Range Supervisors' course down at Bisley recently. You know – for officers and NCOs who go back to their battalions in order to instruct and run rifle ranges. Supposedly the best people in their regiments. Only one of them managed to get a better group than six inches at one hundred yards. And that was in the prone supported position. Half of the buggers didn't even know how to zero a rifle. There's no concept of coaching at all. None of them is taught the basics any more – how to breathe and so on. It's pathetic. It bodes very ill indeed for shooting standards in the Services.

"Nowadays, it's more often civilians who are the most exciting discoveries. They tend to find their way to Bisley too, of course, if they're keen – which is the most important thing. There are some fantastic shots who have never served in the Forces. With a bit of coaching and knowhow, they are soon as good as the best of the Service boys – many of them better. If you took the top one hundred shots in the country, the first fifteen would probably be half civvy and half military. The remainder would be predominantly civvy. The military is dropping right back; those who *are* any good were around when decent training standards were still the rule rather than the exception. Once the civilians start coming to practise they get talking to one another, exchanging knowledge and experience, and they become even more keen. There's a marvellous atmosphere at Bisley – people from all walks of life, with one thing in common: a love of the sport. A real working example of the Prime Minister's idea of a classless society, if you like."

"So among other things, you're a sort of talent scout, are you?"

"Well, everyone like me enjoys spotting talent and bringing it on. I try to keep my ear to the ground, of course. I suppose I've spotted my share over the years. Every now and then I hear of someone who sounds exciting, and try to persuade him to come and give it a go. It doesn't always work, of course, which is a pity."

"How do you mean?"

"Well, for example, a friend of mine recently told me about a young chap called MacDonald, a professional deer-stalker. All stalkers are pretty competent rifle shots, of course – they have to be. But this fellow sounded quite remarkable. I wrote to him, asking him to come down for a trial, but he wasn't interested. He lives in Scotland, of course. I'd love to get my hands on him and see what he could do."

"Tell me about him," said Howard.

*   *   *

The Minister put down the receiver and remained sitting for a few minutes, thinking carefully. He was uneasy that Asher had telephoned him at home, but he supposed it couldn't be helped. Asher would be bound to be pretty careful with the telephone, and on the face of it their conversation had sounded pretty innocent, even if someone had been monitoring it. But he couldn't risk it again. Asher had served his purpose in this matter; now that the Minister had a telephone number for "Mr Hatcher", he would deal direct with him. It sounded promising. He knew what kind of information Hatcher would need. Meanwhile, there was much to do . . .

*   *   *

On the afternoon of 30th October, two days after his telephone call to the Minister, Asher received a letter delivered by hand. The motorcycle courier had refused to hand it to one of his secretaries, adamant that he must deliver it in person. The secretary had tried to tell the courier that that would not be possible, but he had insisted.

"Tell Mr Asher that it concerns Mr Jethro." The courier's voice was indistinct inside the crash-helmet, which he hadn't bothered to take off.

"Very well, but I can tell you that it will not make any difference," the secretary replied, contriving to look both disdainful and alarmed at the same time. Privately, she was dreading a bawling-out from Asher, who had a quick temper at the best of times and had been in a particularly difficult mood recently.

She proved to be wrong. Asher immediately asked her to show the courier in; still wearing his crash-helmet, he handed Asher the envelope without a word and left. Asher tore it open and waved her out of the room. Ten minutes later, he buzzed her on the intercom

65

and told her to arrange for the Gulfstream to be ready to leave for Gibraltar early the following morning.

"Gibraltar, sir? Oh — of course. Would you like me to warn Joseph?"

"No. Joseph will not be coming with me."

"Very good, sir." She sat for a moment, shaking her head. It was like working in a madhouse, she thought. Things got odder practically by the day. A real eccentric, the boss.

Alone in his office, Asher burned the message from the Minister in a heavy glass ashtray.

*   *   *

Four days later, and two thousand miles to the south, Asher put down his telephone. *Another* change of plan. He wondered briefly whether he was being given the runaround by the Minister, but dismissed the idea. In any case, the way things were going, he had little option. And the potential rewards . . .

But it was annoying. He was due back in London the following night, Monday 4th November, to make a speech, and he had a meeting in New York on Tuesday. He'd wasted a day and a half kicking his heels in Madeira. Oh well, it couldn't be helped. He would ask his son to make the speech in his absence. And the hell with the meeting in New York.

More particularly, the hell with this bloody cold, which was still refusing to go away. More vitamin C was the answer. He pressed the intercom button to the galley. "Andrew! Bring me a fresh jug of orange juice." He flicked the switch off, then called the bridge. "Gus, I'm not going home yet after all." He glanced out of the window, looking towards the entrance to the harbour. The sea outside was almost flat calm; it was a gentle, hazy day. "Tenerife," ordered Asher. "Make for Tenerife."

At four that afternoon, the *Princess Scheherezade* left Funchal and sailed south away from Madeira. Asher, alone on board apart from the eleven crew members, worked on in his office below deck.

10

On Tuesday 5th November Dartington was a worried man. The lead item in the news that morning had shaken him to the core. He had rung in to his office saying that he was feeling unwell, and then sat around for most of the day wondering what to do. Should he telephone Howard? No. It would be too obvious. After much thought, he decided to do nothing for the time being.

Shortly before seven that evening, a motorcycle roared up the drive to his house. Dartington's wife answered the door; the helmeted rider handed her an envelope and roared off again.

Lady Dartington walked through to her husband's study. "This has just arrived for you, darling."

"Oh? Who's it from?" He studied the plain white envelope, which bore just his typed name and address.

"He didn't say. Just one of those motorbike couriers, you know."

"Thanks, dear."

Dartington's wife left the room and he slit open the envelope. There was no address, date or signature on the letter inside; just four lines of plain, anonymous typing.

Sir Peter: You will be understandably concerned at the events of the last twenty-four hours. This is to reassure you that the agreement made with you will be honoured, and that you have nothing to worry about. The project should proceed as agreed.

11

On the morning of Monday 4th November Howard had been in the Saab on the M25 awaiting a telephone call, but none had come. The following Monday, the 11th, the phone rang at 8.32 a.m.

He answered as before. "Mr Hatcher here. Who is speaking, please?

"Mr Hatcher, I am speaking for Mr Jethro. I am his assistant." Howard was surprised on hearing the new voice. This time there was no electronic disguise; the speaker had an English public-school accent, and sounded calm and self-assured. The voice continued. "I hope you do not mind my contacting you on Mr Jethro's behalf."

"No, that's fine," said Howard. "I assume that Mr Jethro has told you that I need some information about the overseas contract I am hoping to conclude on his behalf?"

"He has. The request for information was reasonable – this particular client is not easy to get hold of. He will, however, be attending a meeting in his home town next April, on the 28th. It will be a large meeting, but I hope you will be able to be there to make contact with him."

Howard thought fast. He had been given a date and a place – exactly what he needed; and it was to be a public meeting. He would have to examine the map of Iraq carefully, but from what he could recall the place shouldn't be too difficult to reach. Then he remembered – there was detailed coverage of the town itself on one of the maps he had got from Derek. Perfect!

"His home town, 28th April. Thank you. Is there anything else you think I ought to know?"

"There may be representatives from other firms at the meeting. They will be there as observers, not in any active capacity. You should not regard them as important. That is all I can tell you."

"Thank you; I think that should be enough to go on. I will look into this, but I think I should be able to attend the meeting. Can I suggest that you or Mr Jethro call me again, as before, in case I have any further queries? If there is no reply, you may assume that all is proceeding to plan. In the meantime, I would be grateful if neither you nor Mr Jethro would mention this meeting to anyone else."

"You need have no worries on that score, Mr Hatcher. One of us will telephone again in a fortnight's time, and fortnightly thereafter. Thank you for your assistance."

The line went dead. Howard tossed the cell-phone on to the passenger seat and turned his mind to the matter of Jethro's "assistant". That guy was no mere assistant, thought Howard. He was Government; little doubt about it. He had considered asking him why the Government could not do the job itself, armed with that sort of information. It was red-hot intelligence, whichever way one looked at it. It would surely be a simple matter to set the co-ordinates for a cruise missile to drop on top of Saddam's head – but of course that would plainly implicate the Government, and that was no doubt why he had been hired instead.

The "assistant" had implied that there might be a foreign diplomatic presence at the "meeting", and by saying that the diplomats were not to be regarded as important he had dropped a pretty heavy hint that it would not matter to him if they ended up being caught up in the affair – or even killed. Phew, thought Howard. Serious stuff.

One thing mildly puzzled him – the date. He would have to look up its significance. Army Day? No, that was 6th January. Anniversary of the Revolution? No, that was 8th February. Ba'ath Party Day? No again – that wasn't until 17th July. Something to do with Ramadan? He would have to look up the dates for Ramadan in 1992. He hoped it wasn't that; everything ground to a virtual halt during Ramadan, and that would complicate matters.

He was still wondering vaguely about the date when he reached the M40 slip-road. He abandoned his speculations for the time being and, as he headed back into London along the Western Avenue, began brooding about the underhand way the Government was going about this operation: nothing more than an exercise in keeping its own nose clean – not being seen to be involved. Deniability was the polite word for it. Hiding behind someone else's coat-tails, he called it. But never mind; he felt a fierce sense of anticipation now that he had all the information he needed. The operation was on. He had the green light to go ahead. Government, eh? He would have to watch his back very carefully indeed.

12

That Wednesday evening, Howard paid Dartington a brief visit at home in Kent. The two men went out for a walk in the garden.

Once outside, Howard told Dartington he wanted to talk about dates. The first was the following Tuesday, 19th November; Dartington agreed to be away for the night, and promised to see to it that the files Howard needed were left in his study desk. Howard then asked Dartington if he had made any holiday plans for the new year.

"Yes, as a matter of fact we have. We're going off to the Bahamas for three weeks in March. Why?"

"I'd like you to change the dates, Peter. Can you rebook for the last three weeks in April? From the 9th to the 30th? It's important."

"Dammit, Ed, we're going with some friends. I don't want to let them down. How important is it this time?"

"Very. During that time there may be some checking going on, and some questions winging back from one of your overseas operations. It would be best if you weren't there to answer them. Tell your office when you go away that you want a rest, and don't want to be bothered except in dire emergency. That way, they'll simply assume that you've made some new arrangements – they won't query them. When you get back, you'll be able to deny ever having made any such arrangements. It will keep you in the clear, and it may give me a bit more time. Can you do it?"

"Oh, very well; I'll see what I can do."

Dartington thought about it for a while after Howard had left. He was no fool; he had immediately realised that Howard must have been given the information he needed, and that the assassination must be planned to occur at some time between those dates. Yes, he thought, it would be a good idea to be out of the way while that was going on. Come to think of it, he thought with a shudder, he no longer fancied the idea of spending two weeks on a yacht in the Caribbean. He would cancel the bloody charter, even if it cost him his deposit, and rebook in a hotel instead. He had a perfectly reasonable excuse to give his wife and friends, and he doubted that they would make too much of a fuss about it. Not after what had happened to Asher.

13

On Thursday 14th November, Howard waited at Heathrow's Terminal 4 for the arrival of British Airways flight 282 from Los Angeles. The arrivals board reported a punctual landing at 12.25 p.m.; forty minutes later a tall, rangy figure appeared with a large rucksack and a briefcase.

"Ziggy! Good to see you!"

"How ya doin', Ed?" Mike Ziegler shook Howard's hand warmly, and the two men made their way towards the exit.

They collected the Saab from the car-park and headed towards central London. In the passenger seat, Ziegler stretched and yawned. Although it was past midday in the UK, his biological clock was trying to convince him that it was still before dawn.

"You've got me on *fire* with curiosity about this one, Ed." Ziegler's lazy drawl made him sound entirely uninterested, but Howard knew him well enough to recognise that the casual manner was deceptive. He had given little away over the telephone; he had simply told Ziegler that there was "an interesting new project" that might be coming off. When Ziegler had asked *how* interesting, Howard had just remained silent. He had known Ziegler would not be able to resist anything *that* interesting.

Howard cast his mind back to when he and Ziegler had first met, more than twenty years earlier. He had been sent over on a liaison posting to the US Navy's Sea, Air and Land Service – the SEALS – to study American Special Forces training. Mike had been the young SEALS officer who had been detailed to meet his flight at San Diego Airport and drive him out to the base at Coronado.

Howard had not expected his American hosts to be as militarily professional as they turned out to be. The SEALS, too, had thought that the British Special Boat Service would have little to offer them in the way of advice or experience. Both Howard and his hosts had been impressed and pleasantly surprised to have underestimated each other. Mike Ziegler – like his father, some years later – had become a firm friend, and a few months afterwards he had come over to England on an exchange posting to the SBS base at Poole, in Dorset; since then, the two of them had kept in regular contact and visited each other frequently. Yes, thought Howard; their friendship went back a long way . . .

Ziegler broke into his reminiscences. "Well, Ed, are you goin' to tell me what it is you've hauled me all the way over here for?"

"This is a big one, Mike." Howard decided to string it out a little further. The old adrenalin highs were starting again; it was all beginning to slot together. "I'll let you guess what it is."

"OK, we've been hired by the Queen to train those Dobermann dogs of hers."

"Not even close. Anyway, they're corgis."

"You talk to the US Ambassador here, he'll tell you Dobermann/alligator cross. The State Department had to buy him a new pair of pants for his best suit after he dropped in at Buckingham Palace one day for tea and cucumber sandwiches, or maybe it was for cold beer and pizza. I can prove it. It formed a major part of the 1990 US budget deficit. Item: one pair of pants, US Ambassador to the UK. Torn to pieces."

"Probably served him right. Anyway, guess again. I'll give you a clue. Who is the most unpopular man in the world?"

"Easy. Patrolman Morton Kleinberg of the LAPD. He gave me a speedin' ticket the other day. You have no idea how much I dislike that man. Why, we got to knock him off?"

"Wrong guy."

Ziegler shot Howard a sharp glance. The older man was concentrating on the road in front of him, but Ziegler noticed that his usually expressionless eyes were glittering with a fire he hadn't seen there for years. *Oh, boy* . . . "Old Saddam? We gonna pay him a visit? That it?"

"Got it in one. Choose your prize. Fluffy pink teddy bear or a packet of Liquorice Allsorts."

"Well, now, how about that. Am I invited along?"

"I'll have to think about it."

"I'll consider applyin'. I have some conditions, of course. First off,

I get to keep his baseball card collection and a key to his private apartment in Baghdad. You get to pay off the Iraqi national debt, and we split the oil revenues fifty-fifty."

"Sounds fair." Howard managed not to grin. "Any other conditions?"

"You write the letter of condolence to Mrs Saddam afterwards. I'm not doin' that."

"Come on, Mike. Fair's fair; that's your job. You're the one with the university education."

"No deal. You can turn this bucket round, right now. I'm goin' home to LA."

"OK. But first let's go and get some lunch, shall we? The rest of the boys are waiting for us."

During the remainder of the thirty-minute journey into London, Howard filled Ziegler in on the background to the project. As with Bourne, he made no mention of Dartington's name, but he told him of his suspicions about who was behind the project. Having laid all the facts before him, he found that Ziegler agreed with his conclusions. Ziegler had a similar concern about the security of the operation, and was relieved to hear that Howard's report to the man he called "the cut-out" had not contained full operational details of the assassination plan.

"What about the two guys on the phone?" Ziegler asked. "What's the tag on those two?"

"Difficult to say. Jethro is definitely somebody big. He has to be, if he has this particular cut-out in his pocket. The other guy, his assistant, I really can't place. English, very cool – and he didn't sound like anyone's assistant. Could be a senior civil servant, but then that would almost certainly mean he was SIS. It's possible, but I doubt it. No; I would guess he's even higher than Jethro. Jethro could simply be some arrogant prick who was asked to make the first call, of course. Who knows? But one way or another, this smells of Government involvement, somewhere. I'm sure the cut-out wouldn't have agreed to have anything to do with it otherwise."

"Yeah, I guess you're right. OK, what about the game-plan? How are we goin' to do it?"

"I'll go over that when we meet up with the others. We'll be there in a few minutes. In the meantime, I just want to clear a couple of things with you before we arrive."

"Shoot."

"First, I want to make Johnny Bourne second-in-command on this. Normally it would be you, but he knows that part of the world, and we're going to have to be guided by him on a lot of this. He's the only one apart from you who knows what this is all about yet."

"No problem. He's a good kid. I go along with that."

"Second, you ought to know that he's just got himself a new girl – this time it's serious, and he's very touchy about it. I must say, that boy has a terrific sense of timing. She could be a problem."

"How so?"

As Howard explained, Ziegler rolled his eyes and muttered, "Aw, shit!"

"By the way, Mike, we've got two guys with us who you haven't met before."

"Huh? Who?"

"A couple of ex-colonials," said Howard. "Andy Denard and Chris Palmer."

"What's their speciality?"

Howard explained. Ten minutes later, the Saab drew up outside his flat in Wandsworth. Howard parked the car and he and Ziegler went in to join the others.

*   *   *

"I've picked each one of you because you are the best I know at what you do." Howard glanced around the faces in the room. Seven pairs of eyes were watching him. "So far, only Johnny and Mike here know what this is about, and they're in. The rest of you have been told simply that it's big, that we're talking about retirement money – and I mean *luxury* retirement money – for all of us, and that we have only about a fifty-per-cent chance of pulling it off. I'll go further than that – we have an even worse chance of getting away with it afterwards. And we're not just talking about imprisonment here. This is action. Do any of you want out?"

"You mentioned prison, boss. How illegal is this?" Bob Usher, a hard-looking man in his late thirties, spoke up. Usher had developed a distaste for prison life several years earlier – it was he who had spent six months in jail with Howard in Ankara. The diet in the prison had been atrocious, and the deficiency of vitamins had been responsible

76

for his losing nearly all his hair; he was almost bald. Oddly, it made him look no older – if anything, the opposite. The strong muscles of his jaw gave him a pugnacious appearance. Before joining XF Securities, Usher had been a sergeant in the 22nd Special Air Service Regiment.

"I'm afraid we will have to break one or two little rules here in the UK, but nothing to get too concerned about. The main action will be overseas. Where we're going, it will be terminally illegal, if we're caught. But we'll be doing everyone a favour."

"Oh gawd," grimaced Usher, "here we go again."

"Thanks, Bob," said Howard with a grin. "I'll try to get you remission for good behaviour."

"As far as I'm concerned, if you, Mike and Johnny reckon it's OK, you can count me in, boss." The new speaker, Mel Harris, was a restless-looking man; he sat on the edge of an upright chair, leaning forward with his elbows on his knees and his hands clasped in front of him. In every respect but one he was of unremarkable appearance, but his eyes gave him away. They were piercingly blue; no one could fail to notice the intensity of his stare. Harris was aware of this and wore tinted or dark glasses when he did not want to be noticed. Like Usher, he was an ex-sergeant from 22 SAS. He had the fastest reactions of anyone Howard had ever met – faster even than Bourne's. It was he whom the three Sardinian would-be kidnappers had underestimated so badly.

"Thanks, Mel. Tony, how about you?"

"Count me in too, boss," said Tony Ackford, "I could do with a little holiday from the missus." Howard grinned. Ackford was a large-boned ex-Marine, as big as a small giant. He had served fifteen years with the Special Boat Service, the Marines' equivalent of the SAS, and had always turned down promotion. His tiny Irish wife was legendary for her fierce temper; Ackford, despite his immense physical strength and ability in combat both armed and unarmed, was no match for her. Ackford's reputation as a hard man had never quite recovered from the occasion when she had appeared late one night in a pub in Poole, where Ackford had been having a celebratory drink with a squad of Marines who had just finished their SBS training, and – at barely five feet tall compared to his six feet two – had ripped into her husband with a stream of imprecations and almost laid him out cold on the floor with a swipe of her handbag.

"Fine, Tony, but what's she going to do to you when you get back, huh?"

"I'll bring her a bunch of flowers, boss. They got flowers, where we're going?"

"I doubt it." Howard turned to the last two men. "Andy, Chris, how about you?" Andy Denard and Chris Palmer were the only two who were not on the XF Securities payroll. Howard's telephone call to Denard had been if anything even more cryptic than those he had made to the others, since Denard was a citizen of Zimbabwe; Howard had eventually contrived to get hold of him at his house in Borrowdale, in the northern Harare suburbs. It had been Denard's own suggestion to bring Palmer along. Howard would probably have agreed anyway, trusting Denard's judgement implicitly as he did, but Denard's casual remark that his mechanic friend not only had the necessary qualifications but was "a good scout" had not been lost on Howard. He instantly knew what it meant: Palmer had served with the feared Selous Scouts during the War of Independence in Zimbabwe. The "necessary qualifications" would also prove indispensable – Palmer was an aircraft mechanic.

Apart from Howard, only Bourne and Usher had met Denard before, and none knew Palmer, but Howard already sensed that the two ex-Rhodesian Special Forces men had been accepted by the others. Their dry humour, and their no-nonsense, modest style, seemed to have gone down well. Denard was small and wiry, while Palmer was built like a rugby prop forward. Both had tanned faces, weathered by their years under the African sun.

Denard spoke up. "What will the flying involve, Ed? Do I get to play with an F-16 or something nice like that? I'm pissed off flying bloody tourists around for UAC, you know."

"Sorry, Andy, nothing as fancy as that. In fact, with any luck there will be no combat flying at all."

"Shit. I might have known. Oh, well, I might as well come along anyway. Bloody taxi-driver, that's all I get to be nowadays."

"All you're good for, nowadays, you bum," growled Palmer. "Don't worry, boys, I'll keep the little fart in line."

Howard looked around the room with satisfaction. All of them had agreed in principle to join the team, as he had been almost certain they would. The money had little to do with it, he knew. He himself was probably the only one who was at all mercenary about it; he longed to break out of this flat and have something left over after the crippling maintenance payments he was making to Claire. None of the others, he thought, cared much about money, one way or the other. But then none of them had that bitch for an ex-wife either. Perhaps they could afford the luxury of treating this simply as a bit of excitement. He couldn't – for him it was strictly business. Well, it was just as well someone looked on it that way. It would have been daft to take this job on for nothing.

"OK, lads, here it is." Howard gave it to them rapidly, in a few clipped sentences. There were two or three whistles of surprise, and some approving looks on the faces around him. Mel Harris's eyes lit up in fierce delight; he slapped a fist into the palm of his other hand. Only Tony Ackford's face remained expressionless, as he chewed slowly on a piece of gum.

"This operation," Howard continued, "is not going to resemble anything we might have done in the military. We've got no back-up or support. We won't have much time for stealth; we'll have to rely on deception instead. We've virtually got to bluff our way in, and then bluff our way out again. We'll be breaking just about every military rule you can think of. This is a smash-and-grab job, not a sneak in and out. But I think it can work.

"Anyway, first things first." He produced seven fat manila envelopes and tossed one to each man. "There's twenty gorillas in each of these envelopes. I want you each to spend up to half that on getting yourselves some good wheels. Nothing too flashy. Anonymous, respectable, reliable motors. Second-hand would be easiest – nothing more than eighteen months or two years old. Pay cash, and make sure you fill out the registration details yourselves – in false names. Tell the seller you're buying the car for a girlfriend or something. The cars must not be connected with you, and you must use them only in connection with this job – not for normal work or when you're off duty. Don't insure them specifically; get your existing car insurance to cover you to drive all other vehicles. That way you'll be legal, but there won't be anything to connect the cars with you after this is all over. Leave them parked away from home when you aren't using them. We'll deal with how to dispose of them later.

"Johnny's the only exception – he needs a more up-market car for what he'll be doing. He's got twenty thou to spend on his. And the rest of the money is for incidental expenses. No flashing it about. I want receipts. Chris, I'm relying on you to keep that randy little pilot away from the night-spots and the casinos, OK?"

Palmer grinned and patted Denard on the head. "I'll keep him locked up after dark, don't worry."

Denard muttered an expletive.

"Now, here are some more envelopes." Howard handed them round; each man's envelope had his name on it. "Open them up."

Inside each one were general instructions and a task-list, and more money. The amount in each case depended on the likely expenses involved.

"Mel, you'll see that you and I have a small job to do next week; then you and Andy are going to have to make a trip to the States. You know Texas well, so I suggest you start there. Your job is to find a cowboy pilot who looks sufficiently like Andy to pass muster. I don't care if he's a crook or a smuggler or whatever, but he must be a competent flyer with a valid commercial pilot's licence and twin-engine rating. Andy can check out his flying ability, but I want you to assess him from the point of view of how easy it will be to keep him in line. We don't want a drunk or a hot-head. Put the cowboy on a retainer of ten thousand dollars, with a further ninety thousand when the job's done. Tell him as little as possible, and don't let him know your names. We won't need him over here until the end of March at the earliest. OK?"

Mel Harris nodded, his eyes still bright with anticipation.

"Good," said Howard. He turned to Ziegler. "Mike, you're headed back to the States too, but on a separate job. You'll see there are some high-tech items we need to get hold of. They'll be easier to find over there, and you'll know where to look. You'll be told by Johnny later where to have them shipped to.

"Chris, the first thing you've got to do is start growing a beard."

The stocky Zimbabwean's blond eyebrows lifted slightly; then he nodded in assent.

Howard continued. "You'll be operating on your own for a while, but your task shouldn't take too long. Johnny has a few commercial arrangements to make, then he can help you. You have to find and lease or buy a plane. Eight seats or more, good tough workhorse machine – something like an Islander or a Twin Otter, suitable for rough landing strips – and reasonable spares back-up. The other specific requirements for the plane are listed on your sheet. If it hasn't got them, get them fitted. Johnny will handle the finance for it as it'll be the most expensive item and we won't be able to use cash.

"I still have a major job to do myself. The problem is, this team is not yet complete. We need one more man, with a specialist skill that none of us has. Or at least, two or three of us do, but not to anything like the standard we are going to need. I have someone in mind who fits the bill, but I haven't approached him yet." Drawing on his cigarette, Howard watched the others trying to figure out what expertise it was that was not represented in the room. At last he said, "We need a top-class sniper. The best there is."

There were slow nods of understanding from all the seven except one. Tony Ackford had been slowly reading through his shopping-list, his brow knotting into a deeper frown with each successive item. Finally, the big man spluttered into indignant life. "Boss, what the fuck is all this crap here that Bob and I have got to get? I can just about understand how the tape recorder and Arabic tuition tapes might come in handy – I mean, I can imagine it might be useful to be able to say 'Stand completely fucking still you shagspot or I'll blow your poxy head off' in Arabic – and maybe the climbing kit and all these ropes and pulleys could be useful too if we were going to string the bleeder up instead of shoot him, but what the fuck's the use of a sixteen-foot rubber dinghy, waterproof stow-bags, wet-suits, paddles and an outboard motor in the middle of the sodding desert? And these flags and stickers? And this here – small lump of lead ... bag of plaster of Paris? Welding kit? Hydraulic jack? Two air-conditioning units? And this – ten tons of concrete breeze blocks? *Four* tons of TINNED MARGARINE? Chemical toilet and camping kit? A forty-foot-long commercial freezer container and artic trailer unit, for Chrissake? What the hell sort of a caper are we going on – a camping expedition to build a con-crete beach-hut near Baghdad, deep-fry a camel in margarine and bring the effing thing home deep-frozen, towing it behind a din-ghy?"

The others were rocking with laughter, and eventually Ackford's face broke into a grin too. Howard had guessed that this particular list would cause some bewilderment, and had been waiting for Ackford's explosion. "You forgot the thirty hundredweight of frozen peas,

Ack," he said now. "We deep-fry the camel, then we eat it with the peas. The chemical khazi is for afterwards."

Howard waited until the laughter had subsided; then he began to explain.

14

On Friday morning, a telephone call to Dartington's office was put through to Mrs Webster, his personal assistant; an oily and ingratiating voice asked when it might be possible to see "Pete" Dartington. The loyal Mrs Webster's disapproval was evident from her tone as she attempted to put the caller off, but he was persistent.

"It's an important matter, duckie," he smarmed.

Mrs Webster winced; she hated being called "duckie".

"I must see him sometime during the next few days," the caller went on. "Or I could go and see him at home, if that would be more convenient. I can't manage it this weekend, sadly. Would he be free sometime on Monday or Tuesday?"

"Sir Peter is a very busy man, Mr . . . ?" Mrs Webster waited for him to give a name, but there was silence. She continued. "I'm afraid I cannot make an appointment unless I know what you wish to see him about. In any case, he has a very full diary for Monday and Tuesday."

"Well, how about Tuesday evening then? The 19th? I could motor down to his place in the country. Tuesday evening would do me just fine."

"There would be no point, Mr . . . ?" Again she prompted the caller for a name, and this time she was rewarded.

"Harrington, duckie, Brian Harrington. Call me Brian."

"Well, Mr Harrington, I am afraid there would be absolutely no point in calling on Sir Peter at home. He does not receive business calls out of the office. In any case . . ." She broke off, biting her lip.

"Why, won't he be there on Tuesday?" The voice was wheedling.

"Mr Harrington," said Mrs Webster forcefully, changing tack, annoyed at having allowed herself to become flustered by the caller, "I suggest you write to Sir Peter, stating the nature of your business. You can be sure that you will receive a prompt reply. Mr Harrington?"

The line had gone dead.

Dorothy Webster put down the telephone with a frown of distaste. She thought for a second, then rose from her chair, knocked softly on her employer's door and went in. Dartington looked up questioningly.

"Sir Peter, I'm afraid I have just received a rather strange telephone call. A man calling himself Brian Harrington insisted that he wanted to see you on what he described as an important matter."

"Harrington? I don't know anyone called Harrington. What did he want?"

"He wouldn't say, sir. He said that he might call on you at home, and mentioned next Tuesday evening. I tried to put him off as best I could."

"Well, I'll see him off if he turns up. Thanks for warning me, Dorothy."

"I'm afraid Tuesday is the night you and Lady Dartington will be staying up in London, sir, if you remember. Would you like me to alert Mr and Mrs Jephcott to the possibility of a caller?"

"Oh. Yes. Good idea. Tell Jephcott to keep an eye open for the chap and get rid of him. And don't worry, Dorothy, I get quite a lot of silly phone calls like that at home. I often wish you could be there to filter those ones out, too."

Mrs Webster smiled and returned to her office.

Dartington watched the door close behind her. He sat tapping his pencil on his teeth. It was pretty bloody obvious who *that* had been, he thought. Howard had been about as subtle as a rhinoceros. Poor Dorothy. Still, she would remember it, and put two and two together when the time came.

15

Something was nagging at Howard as he sat poring over his maps of Scotland. He had bought a complete set of 1:50,000 Landranger Ordnance Survey maps, and was methodically working through them. He had two clues – a placename and a surname. The place had not featured in the index to his road map, but the surname had told him roughly where to start.

He found the place he was looking for on the third map he tried, sheet 41. It had taken him fifty minutes' work, but the name suddenly leapt up at him. That must be it – spelt with a "C", rather than with a "K" as Henry Stoner had told him. That was why he had had no luck with the index – he should have guessed. He studied the area in detail. Wild-looking country, he thought; steep, magnificent, desolate. The little village was marked, and there was a PH sign which made him reach for his motorist's handbook. Yes, it was listed; an inn. Rooms were available. Probably fairly basic, but it would do. He felt a brief sense of achievement at having tracked it down – without needing to ask Stoner too many questions. But a fat lot of good it would do him, unless he could find out a bit more – something that would give him a handle on this fellow.

MacDonald. Where had he seen the name before? Not an unusual name, in its various forms – as hundreds of disgusting fast-food outlets reminded him practically wherever he went nowadays. But a very common name up there – almost every other person in that part of Scotland was called MacDonald. But the name was still nagging at him. He had noticed a particular reference to it somewhere, and there might be a connection. How long ago had he seen it? Recently, he was sure. Why had it registered? He could not remember. He would have to start again from scratch.

He had kept all his enquiry notes; he gathered them together and set off again for the British Newspaper Library. The Northern Line underground took him all the way there, and by 11.30 he was deep into the stack of newspapers he had requested. At 4.35 p.m. he located the reference he had noticed before. He was just in time to put in a request for a photocopy for the next day before the fifteen-minute-warning bell sounded in the Reading Room, signalling closing time at five o'clock.

He was back again at ten o'clock sharp the next morning, Saturday, when the library opened. He put in requests for specific editions of nine more newspapers: four Scottish editions of national dailies, two national weeklies, two Scottish dailies and one Scottish weekly. There were references to the same story in three of them, but the most detailed coverage was in the Lochaber edition of the Aberdeen-based *Press & Journal*. He briefly considered asking for other local papers, but decided not to bother. He made some notes, and for good measure put in a request for a copy of the *P & J* article, asking for it to be posted to him at his flat.

Howard left the library just before eleven. It had been a stroke of luck; he had found what he had been looking for. He was fairly certain it would be enough to persuade MacDonald to co-operate.

16

Mel Harris reversed his recently-acquired Golf GTi into the farm gateway and switched off the lights. He and Howard opened the two front windows and sat for ten minutes in silence, listening, while their night vision adjusted. Eventually, Howard nodded and they got out. Howard pointed out the big house on the other side of the field; at three o'clock in the morning, only the outside-porch security light was still on. The two men each put on overalls and gloves, and unloaded a bulky black sports bag and a slim metal tube from the boot of the car.

Harris's voice was a whisper. "I feel a proper Jumblatt with these kids' trainers on, boss."

"Don't let it bother you, Mel," murmured Howard. "Think of the admiring glances you'll get down the nick after we get picked up for this little caper. Come on, let's go."

Harris and Howard walked briskly across the field and climbed the wall into the kitchen garden at the back of the house. Making no sound, they approached the house, skirting round the flower beds until they came to the windows of the study at the front. The gravel drive stretched away down to the gatehouse; Jephcott would almost certainly be there, so as to be near the gate, but Mrs Jephcott would probably be sleeping up here in the main house. Howard examined the window and gave the thumbs-up: the latch was open. Harris, ignorant of Dartington's involvement, rolled his eyes in disapproval of the laxity of house-owners who didn't bother to lock up properly. Oh, well, he thought; it would save a bit of time.

While Howard noiselessly pushed the sash window up, Harris unpacked the telescopic fishing-rod from its tube. He taped a small wire frame to the tip of the rod, and stuck pieces of putty on the arms of the wire that ran at right angles to the rod. He peeled the backing off a double-sided adhesive strip, the other side of which was already fixed to a six-inch-square piece of card, and then pushed the reverse side of the card against the putty on the frame. The frame and putty now held the card in place at the end of the rod.

Careful not to put his hand through the window, Howard silently indicated the location of the passive infra-red alarm sensor. Harris eased the rod through the window, card first.

The sensor was in the corner of the room, on the same wall as the window. Its arc was ninety degrees, so it covered the whole room; it would sense a change in position of any heat source, such as a human body, within the four walls. It could not detect the window being opened – since it was on the same wall, the sensor's gaze swept right past it. If it had had eyes, all the sensor would have seen would have been a square piece of card coming straight towards it. Because the card gave off a neutral infra-red signature, its presence did not register. The sticky fixing strip on the front of the card made contact with the sensor's plastic surface and stuck tight. Harris gently pulled the fishing-rod, which disengaged itself from the loose grip of the putty. The card was now stuck fast to the sensor, covering its small window and leaving it completely blind. As Harris withdrew the rod, Howard checked his watch; the two men waited outside the window. After six minutes Howard nodded, and they climbed soundlessly into the room.

They stood listening for a while, but there was no noise from inside the house. The two overfed dogs would be snoring in the kitchen at the far end of the hall corridor; Mrs Jephcott would be asleep too, in a spare room two floors above.

Harris unzipped the sports bag and took out four heavy, dark-coloured blankets and a packet of large map-pins. Working together in silence, he and Howard pinned a blanket over each window and over the door to the hall. When they finally drew the heavy curtains over the blankets, the room was in total darkness. Howard snapped on his small pen-torch and went to the desk. Checking the drawers, he took a small crowbar out of the bag and began quietly and slowly levering open the only two that were locked. Harris used his own torch to check that none of the putty had fallen from the card over the sensor.

Harris switched on the photocopier at the side of the desk, and the machine hummed quietly into life. Leafing through the three files he had taken from the desk to find what he wanted, Howard extracted a total of thirty-eight pages; he laid the first of these on the flat glass platen of the copier and closed the top cover. Harris covered the machine and Howard's hand, which was resting on the green "COPY" button, with the fourth blanket. As soon as it was in place, Howard pressed the button.

The noise from the photocopier was almost inaudible, and no light escaped. Harris removed the blanket, and they repeated the procedure until all thirty-eight pages had been copied. Howard gave a nod, and Harris switched off the machine. The copies of the documents, along with some Darcon headed paper and company envelopes from the desk, were placed in a document folder which in turn went into the bottom of the sports bag.

Howard deftly rifled through the other drawers of the desk; a pocket dictating machine, a camera and some loose cash were removed and joined the folder in the sports bag. Harris disconnected Dartington's fax machine and video recorder. Both went into the bag. A pair of Georgian silver candle-holders and two silver ashtrays, the only small objects of obvious value in the room, were placed by the window-sill. The two men then spent three minutes carefully ransacking the room – pulling books quietly from shelves, opening drawers and cupboards – creating the impression that someone had been searching hastily for small valuables.

When Howard was satisfied, he strewed the contents of the files about the floor. The previously tidy room now looked a convincing shambles. Switching their torches off, he and Harris removed the blankets from the door and windows, packing them and the map-pins into the now bulging bag. When the last item was zipped up inside, Howard climbed out of the window, taking the silver candle-holders and ashtrays loose in his gloved hands and lowering the bag to the ground.

Inside the room, Harris replaced the fishing-rod in its tube and handed it back out of the window to Howard. Then he walked across to the alarm sensor and removed the card, checking that all the adhesive tape came away with it. He folded the card and slipped it in his inside pocket.

The alarm sensor immediately registered the presence of an intruder. Down the hall, the alarm control box silently sent its instruction to the autodialling unit in the cupboard nearby; the unit began dialling the number of the alarm company's central monitoring station.

By the time the unit finished dialling, Harris had climbed out of the window and dropped lightly to the ground. Reaching up, he drew the window down, then used one end of the fishing-rod tube to smash a pane of glass near the latch lock. He pushed the window up again and left it open.

Taking one handle each of the bag, which was now heavy with all the booty from the study, Howard and Harris quickly retraced their steps to the kitchen garden and the wall screening it from the field beyond. At the wall, Howard dropped the candle-holders and ashtrays in the mud before climbing over.

*　　　*　　　*

Mrs Jephcott was a light sleeper. The slight sound of breaking glass woke her, and she went to the window. She saw nothing, but nevertheless telephoned the number of the gatehouse. Her husband answered on the fourth ring.

On hearing what his wife had to report, George Jephcott answered firmly and decisively. "Stay where you are, Mary; don't go down-stairs. There's a five-minute delay on the bell. We don't want to alert them. The police will be on their way. Let's catch them red-handed." He began to dress as fast as he could. Two minutes later, he left the gatehouse carrying his shotgun; he unlocked the heavy iron gate and swung it open in readiness for the arrival of the police. Then he hurried up towards the house on foot, keeping to the grass on the side of the long gravel drive.

At the same time as Mrs Jephcott was calling her husband, the police station, alerted by the alarm company, dispatched its nearest patrol car – which happened to be only three miles away – to the reported call-out. The patrol car drove at speed along the back lane to the house, without its flashing blue light or siren switched on, passing the gateway where Harris's grey Golf GTi was still hidden. Three hundred yards further on it turned right at the junction leading up to the gatehouse, then right again through the gate into the drive. Harris and Howard, making their way across the field, and by now about a hundred yards short of the GTi, watched the patrol car pass. They exchanged glances.

Neither man had said a word since leaving the GTi forty-five minutes earlier.

Exactly five minutes after Harris had pulled the piece of card away from the alarm sensor, the alarm bell on the outside of the house started to ring loudly. George Jephcott, waiting with his shotgun in the bushes near the broken window, was puzzled that no one emerged. A quarter of a mile away, beyond the field on the far side of the house, the GTi was pulling unnoticed out of the farm gateway. The police patrol car arrived at the house thirty seconds later. All the evidence, from the imprints of the training shoes in the flower beds to the nature of the stolen goods, would lead them to conclude that "youngsters" had been responsible – a view that would be reinforced by Jephcott's discovery later that morning of the items of silver amateurishly dropped near the kitchen-garden wall.

Harris headed back towards London. He drew in briefly at a lay-by to allow Howard to dump two almost brand-new pairs of training shoes, two pairs of dark-blue overalls, and a perfectly good camera, dictating machine and video recorder into a rubbish-skip.

17

The young estate agent could hardly credit his luck. It was unbelievable, he thought. One minute he had been sitting in his office
twiddling his thumbs and gloomily pondering over his future, and
the next, this round-faced fellow had walked in off the street and
said he wanted to lease some of the deadest property on the firm's
books. Unbelievable!

It wasn't that there was anything actually *wrong* with the Loundis
Road industrial units, of course. It had just been a case of bad timing
by the developer. They had been completed in 1988: ten of them, in a
row. Eminently lettable – in theory, at least. Easy access to the M4 at
junction 16; good, versatile units, all things considered. The problem
had been the recession. Only four had been let before the hard times
had begun to bite; after that, mused the estate agent, you couldn't
shift them for love nor money. The developer simply hadn't faced
up to reality; he had refused to drop the rental price, despite all the
advice he had been given. It would have been a different story if he
hadn't been in hock to his bank; by arguing a high rental value to
his bank manager, he had been able to keep him in line on the capital
value of the development. That way, he had avoided foreclosure on
the debt.

It had worked all right to start with. With the rental income on
the four let units, the developer had been able to keep up with his
interest payments, and managed to negotiate a rescheduling of capital
repayments. The trouble started when the first tenant decided to quit.
That was when the developer acted really stupid, thought the estate
agent. The tenant had nine months to go before his option to break at
three years was due, but asked to be released from this. The developer
panicked about his interest payments to the bank and got tough with

the tenant, who was held to the agreement, forced to pay the rent – and bankrupted as a result. The estate agent had pleaded with the developer to negotiate a lower rent or settle on a compensatory figure, but he would have none of it.

Anyone could have foreseen the result. The tenant was the weakest of the four; he went down owing the developer four months' rent. The other three tenants got the message loud and clear. When their break periods came up, they exercised their options and moved away. Now all ten units were empty – Loundis Road was deserted. New owner, of course. That silly sod of a developer and his equally silly bank were out of the picture. The new landlord had picked up the development at a knockdown price from the receivership, and had retained the same estate agency because the firm knew the property well. The new owner was much more reasonable, but the problem was that the development had got itself a bad name. Naturally, any prospective tenant was going to wonder why the whole place was empty. No one liked to be the first, did they? And who was renting industrial units these days, in the middle of a recession? No one. There had been no interest at all. The units had remained resolutely empty.

Until today, that was. The round-faced guy had just walked in a couple of days ago, said he liked the units, and asked if he could rent – wait for it – not one, not two, but *three* of them. Just like that. Talk about a kick-start! And he hadn't even quibbled about the rent! OK, so six quid a square foot was more reasonable than the tenner the original developer had been asking, but considering the low price the new landlord had paid for the row of units, he would easily be able to service his debt, now that three were let. And it might just stimulate interest in the others, too . . .

The round-faced Mr Bryce had been delightful to deal with. He had read through the draft tenancy agreement and agreed all the terms on the spot; he had been ready with bank references (which had checked out *very* nicely); the two of them had driven out in Bryce's car to look the units over; they had shaken hands on the deal and driven back. Nice motor, Mr Bryce had. Very nice. BMW 325i, leather sports seats, CD sound system, went like a rocket. No cashflow problems for Mr Bryce, that was obvious. Anyway, it was in the bag! The lease had been completed in a record two days, and the bank draft had been cleared. Six months' rent in advance, too, instead of the usual quarterly! Oh yes, thought the estate agent as he waved Mr Bryce off, it would be drinks all round in the office today.

*   *   *

The BMW drove away from the estate agent's office, heading out of Swindon towards junction 16 and the M4 back to London. Johnny Bourne opened his mouth and extracted the two pink rubber cheek-pads, stowing them away in a plastic bag in the glove compartment next to a small bottle of "plastic skin". The pads made him look as though he had just been for a rather painful visit to the dentist, he thought. They puffed his cheeks right out; but to anyone who didn't know what he normally looked like, they just gave him a more rounded face. The tinted contact lenses didn't itch as much as he had feared they might; he was quite used to them now. He would have to be careful not to forget to take them out, and to remember to comb his hair back to its usual style, without a parting. He rubbed his fingertips against the upholstery of the BMW; the coating of plastic skin on each finger began to peel off.

The three industrial units were perfect. No other tenants in the remaining seven, and they were at the end of a cul-de-sac. Access to the M4 was good, they were just the right size, and they would be unlikely to be disturbed.

Bourne had had a busy week. The flight to Liechtenstein, the formation of a holding company there and the transfer of a million pounds from the anonymous numbered account into a new account in the holding company's name at another bank, then back to England and the formation of three more UK-based companies: one in the food wholesale business, one in freight and transport and the third in general trading. Three separate firms of solicitors and accountants in three separate towns had handled the paperwork and VAT registration, and three printing firms had supplied a selection of company letterhead paper, invoice forms and other documentation. Then there had been further transfers of funds, this time from the holding company's Liechtenstein account into newly-opened accounts at three different British banks. There would soon begin a series of transactions between the companies which would satisfy the banks that they were trading healthily. The bank managers would not see the addresses of the other two companies with which business

94

was being conducted, and would be kept unaware that they were in fact next door to one another. The holding-company account in Liechtenstein would gradually be emptied. None of the transactions would survive a proper audit, of course; but they wouldn't have to. Messrs Bryce and Hatcher, and the other directors, would have disappeared before it came to that.

In the meantime, Bourne would have to keep remembering his hair, the tinted contact lenses, the plastic skin and those bloody cheek-pads. If Juliet saw him like that . . . the consequences didn't bear thinking about. He smiled as he thought of her, and found himself pushing his foot down on the car's accelerator. *Steady down, Johnny*, he told himself, easing it off again. *Stay below the limit. I know you can't wait to see her again, but it wouldn't do to get nicked for speeding . . .*

18

On Friday 29th November Howard arrived at Edinburgh on the midday shuttle from Heathrow. Collecting his luggage, he went to the Avis desk and completed the car-hire formalities for the Ford Escort he had booked by telephone. He drove out of the airport and headed north on the M90 motorway, skirting Perth on the new bypass and picking up the main A9 towards Inverness. An hour later, he turned off the A9 at Dalwhinnie and took the A86 towards Spean Bridge and Fort William.

It was a cold day, with squalls of northerly wind gusting across the road, at times strong enough to rock the car. Already, at 3.45 in the afternoon, the light was failing; it would be dark well before he arrived. The road was almost empty of traffic and the scenery was bleak, with snow on some of the distant hilltops beyond Loch Laggan. After a while he could no longer make them out, and by the time he arrived at Spean Bridge the sky was almost completely black. Ten miles away to the south-west, unseen in the dark and the cloud, would be the rounded summit of Ben Nevis.

Five miles past Spean Bridge he turned off on to the side-road to the small village of Carvaig. After two more miles it narrowed into a single-track road, with passing-places indicated by white diamond-shaped signs. Howard drove slowly and carefully. The eyes of black-faced sheep by the roadside were lit up by his headlamps as he passed; the animals lay in clusters on the grass verge, oblivious of the approach of his car, and a couple of times he had to stop and toot his horn to clear them off the road itself.

Finally, just after five o'clock, he saw a small scattering of lights ahead in the distance, and ten minutes later he arrived at Carvaig itself. He had no trouble locating the inn; it was prominent amongst the twenty or so cottages and bungalows in the village. He parked the car, collected his bags and rang the doorbell.

A young auburn-haired girl of about eighteen appeared, wearing jeans and a thick pullover. She had a pretty face and a soft, lilting west-coast accent. "Good evening – can I help?"

"My name is Hatcher, Edwin Hatcher. I rang and booked a room for a couple of nights. I hope that's still all right?"

"Oh, yes, of course, Mr Hatcher – I'm so sorry. Come away in! I should have known it must be you!" The girl smiled at him and offered to help with his bags.

She busied about, chattering and making him feel welcome. She showed him into the small sitting-room and went off to make him a cup of tea. A woman appeared, smiling and wiping her hands on her apron as she came up to shake his hand. She was a small, trim figure, perhaps forty years old – certainly not much more than that, Howard reckoned.

"Mr Hatcher – welcome to Carvaig! I'm Morag Cameron – Sheila's mother."

Hers had been the voice on the telephone when Howard had rung to book the room. A nice voice, soft and gentle, sounding slightly surprised at the idea of someone coming up to such a remote place in November for a weekend break. She was a very attractive woman, thought Howard as he looked at her now; his level gaze of appraisal was met with a friendly smile. The family resemblance between her and the girl was striking. Her handshake was firm and unexpectedly strong; Howard guessed that she must be used to constant hard work to earn a living. His stay at the inn would doubtless provide a welcome addition to the family finances.

Morag Cameron showed Howard upstairs to his room, which was small but comfortable – not at all the Spartan accommodation he had expected. It was simply furnished and decorated in cheerful colours, and spotlessly clean. Howard suddenly thought that this would be a good place to come for a relaxing summer holiday. It was many years since he had last been in Scotland, and as he opened the window and caught the unique, wild smell of the air mixed with the far-off tang of the sea, memories began flooding back to him. He breathed in contentedly and began to unpack.

Half an hour later, after a hot bath in wonderfully soft, peaty water, he went down to the bar. Might as well get it over with, he thought. The bar was still empty; it would begin to fill up later. He settled into a chair with a book, to all appearances a tourist relaxing after a day's motoring.

Morag's daughter came in and asked him if he would like a drink from the bar. She was visibly pleased when he chose an expensive malt whisky. He excused himself for adding a dash of water to it; he would never do such a thing down south, he said, where the water tasted so strongly of chlorine that it would murder a good whisky. She smiled.

For a while, Howard was the only customer in the bar, and he and the girl chatted amiably. He knew that curiosity would sooner or later get the better of her, and was ready, when it came, for her polite enquiry as to why he had chosen to come to Carvaig in late November.

Many years ago, he told her, he had come up here with his father; he had been a youngster of twelve at the time. His father had been invited for three days' stalking on the Glen Carvaig estate, and had taken his son along for his first experience of it. The boy had hated the idea of tramping round the hills, but in the event he had had the time of his life and had never forgotten it. He had always meant to come back to revisit the place, he said, but had only now finally got round to it. "So it's really just a little bit of nostalgia, if you like."

His story was partly true, but of course even the true parts had happened somewhere else. He had memorised enough details from the map to be able to mention some of the individual names of hills in Glen Carvaig if she asked, but knew he would be on slightly stickier ground if she asked about names of people.

"Well, it's very nice to have have old visitors back, Mr Hatcher. Oh – I'm sorry, I didn't mean to imply . . ."

He smiled. "Don't worry – you're quite right! It was all a long time ago – long before you were born. In fact, your mother would only have been a child herself. I'm forty-five, and she can't be anywhere near that. She certainly looks much younger than I do."

Sheila Cameron made as if to apologise again, but she saw that Howard genuinely hadn't minded in the least, and stopped short.

He changed the subject. "I was wondering if it would be possible to take a walk up the glen – perhaps tomorrow morning. I could take a sandwich or something with me. Is there anyone I should see to ask permission?"

"Oh, I'm sure that would be fine, Mr Hatcher. The stalking is finished for the season now, and they've not started on the hinds yet. I'm sure that as long as you stay on the road up the glen you'll be fine. And I can make you a piece for your pocket, if you tell me what you would like – we've some good beef, or there's ham or cheese."

"The beef sounds fine. That would be very kind. How would I get there? Would I drive to the lodge? I seem to remember that it's a couple of miles or so on up the road, isn't it?" It was. He had that portion of the the map clearly in his mind's eye.

"Aye, you could take your car up there. I'm sure no one would mind if you left it at the lodge for the day. From there on up the glen the track is very rough, and your car would be no good. It's a nice walk – about ten miles up the river from the lodge to the head of the glen. The gate past the lodge will be locked, but there's a stile over the deer-fence for walkers."

"That sounds excellent. But shouldn't I see someone before just setting off on my own? The stalker, perhaps?"

"Well, you may see Duncan up there at the lodge, if he's not away up the glen himself. Duncan Macrae. He's the stalker."

Howard was momentarily nonplussed. Duncan Macrae? That was the wrong name. Had he come to the right place? He thought quickly. "Glen Carvaig's a big forest for just one stalker, isn't it? I thought there were two beats."

"Aye, there are, right enough. But Duncan is the head stalker. Danny only works there part-time, during the stalking season – and of course he helps out with the hinds too."

"Danny?"

"Danny MacDonald. He's – he's a friend." The girl lowered her eyes and started to fiddle with a cloth, drying up a non-existent spill on the bar counter. She raised her eyes again to him briefly, a little embarrassed, then looked away.

But you'd like him to be more than a friend, wouldn't you, thought Howard. *Oh, Lord. As if Bourne's entanglement with the police girl wasn't enough.* He glanced at her left hand, and was relieved to see there was no ring there. Yet. "Is he a nice fellow, this Danny?"

It all came pouring out of her; she couldn't have hidden her feelings if she had tried. She was obviously in love with Danny MacDonald. The two families had known each other well and been friends for years; then had come the tragedy, when Sheila was only nine years

99

old. Her parents and Danny's were driving back late one rainy night after an evening out together in Fort William, when an oncoming van suddenly rounded a corner at speed on the single-track road. Danny's mother was driving the car. She swerved to avoid a collision and the car went off the road, careered down a steep bank and smashed into rocks forty feet below, bursting into flames. Sheila's mother, in the front passenger seat, was thrown clear; Sheila's father and both Danny's parents were killed. Morag Cameron had crawled back up to the road – with a broken leg and arm – and was found two hours later, nearly dead from exposure and shock, by a passing motorist. The van and its driver had never been traced.

Danny had been eighteen at the time of his parents' death, and Fergus, his brother, sixteen. Danny had been away at college in Edinburgh, Fergus due to start there soon. Both had worked part-time during the holidays as ghillies for their father, who had been head stalker at Glen Carvaig. John MacDonald's successor as head stalker was a disaster; fortunately he lasted only two years before he was dismissed, having been found by the estate factor one morning dead drunk and still in bed at 11.30. But by then Danny had fallen out badly with the man; he had seen through him very early on, and the bad blood that had developed between them was enough to wreck Danny's chance of getting the only job he had ever really wanted – his father's. By the time it was established that Danny had not been at fault in the quarrel, Duncan Macrae had been appointed to the post. Duncan was a good stalker, and was wise enough to recommend that Danny, a natural at it, should be given the second beat. Danny had held the position ever since.

Fergus, Danny's younger brother, had graduated from college as a qualified engineer, and had gone to Aberdeen to work in the North Sea oil business. He had travelled abroad and married; he had hardly ever come home. Then there had been the second terrible tragedy, and he would be coming home no more . . .

Howard did not ask Sheila about the tragedy that had befallen Fergus. He could see she was upset, and he quickly switched the conversation back to Danny. As the girl talked about him, a picture of the young Scot began to build up in Howard's mind. Determined, self-reliant, tough, fit and strong - all good points. Outspoken – not necessarily a bad point. A hot temper – not so good.

"So what does he do outside the season?"

"Och, he works in his uncle's sports shop in Fort William. He runs it, really. Both his uncle and aunt . . . well, they don't take much interest in anything, nowadays. Danny does everything."

Howard inwardly guessed at the reason for the uncle and aunt's lack of interest, and didn't ask for elaboration. The curse of the Highlands for so many – drink. Those long, long winter nights, with only a bottle for company . . . "Does Danny live with his uncle and aunt?"

"Oh no. He has a cottage of his own, left to him by his grandmother."

"Where is that – in the village here?" *I might as well rub it in*, thought Howard. *It would be interesting to see what happens.*

The girl looked at him strangely before replying. "No, it's away down on the Spean Bridge road," she said vaguely. "Now, Mr Hatcher," – she straightened up and assumed an air of brisk efficiency – "I'd best see to your supper before the others all come in. What would you like? We've some very nice trout, which I can recommend."

The fresh brown trout proved to be delicious; Howard ordered a bottle of white wine to go with it. Sheila's mother brought it to him and asked if everything was to his satisfaction.

"Indeed yes, Mrs Cameron," he said. "This is a most delightful and restful place. I couldn't be more comfortable." She smiled with pleasure and made to return to the kitchen; Howard gently called her back. "Mrs Cameron, would you perhaps like to join me for a drink for a short while? You've been working very hard, and I've had a long journey. Maybe we could both do with something to help us unwind a little."

Morag Cameron turned, surprise on her face. She studied his dark, almost expressionless eyes. Suddenly, she quite liked what she saw. "Well, that is kind of you, Mr Hatcher. Perhaps I will. It'll be a wee while before the bar begins to fill up. Thank you." She untied her apron and sat down; Howard poured her a glass of wine. She studied his face. *A good-looking man*, she thought. *Difficult to fathom. He's had a hard life . . . an interesting face – those dark eyes don't give much away.* She leaned her elbows on the table, resting her chin on her steepled hands. She looked coolly and with interest into his eyes. "So tell me, Mr Hatcher, what brings you up here?"

Howard began to speak in a soft voice. He answered her question with the story he had told her daughter; then he veered off on to other subjects, ranging widely, talking of his interests and asking her about her own.

They talked together for half an hour, until Morag suddenly looked at her watch and sprang to her feet. "Oh, you must excuse me, Mr Hatcher. I must attend to other things. I had no idea of the time." She held out her hand, and he stood up. She smiled at him. "Thank you for the drink. I've enjoyed our conversation."

"So have I, Mrs Cameron. Very much indeed."

"Good night to you, Mr Hatcher. I hope you find the bed comfortable."

He took her hand. "Good night, Mrs Cameron. Or may I call you Morag?"

There was still a suggestion of a smile on her face, but she said nothing, and turned to go.

Howard sat down again and drained his glass. Ten minutes later he was up in his room, trying to concentrate on his book.

Over the next hour the sounds of the public bar downstairs started to reach him through the open bedroom window; the locals had gradually drifted in to celebrate the end of another week's work. By nine o'clock, Howard calculated, the bar must have been full; the noise grew, then began to dwindle towards closing time. Howard heard the voices and footsteps of men disappearing away up the road; then, a little later, came the sound of the heavy lock on the front door being turned. Finally, at 11.30, there was silence.

Howard rose from his bed and opened the bedroom door. Stepping outside, he made his way noiselessly along the carpeted corridor to the fire-door at the far end, next to the stairs. The door was marked "PRIVATE". He pushed it open and stepped through. Beyond it there were three more doors; light filtered out from beneath one of them. After a minute or so, the light went out. He knocked softly on the door; the light inside came back on and the door opened.

Morag Cameron stood there in a nightdress, a glimmer of surprise in her expression. For a few seconds she said nothing, just looking at him. She was about to speak when his arms went round her slim body, pulling her to him. His mouth came down on hers and she was overtaken by the shocking intensity of the physical contact. The strength and passion of his embrace temporarily robbed her of thought, and for what seemed long seconds she yielded to her own sudden desire; then she abruptly pulled herself away and took a step back, her eyes bright with fury. Her slap hit his face like a whiplash.

She stared into his eyes, astonished. He hadn't even moved. Her hand stung from the force of the slap, but he gave no sign of having even felt it. Her hand came up fast to repeat the slap, and – she felt her wrist caught in his grip. She tried briefly to pull her hand free, and felt a fleeting surprise that she could not even move it. He raised the forefinger of his free hand to his lips for silence, then gently moved the finger to her own mouth. Slowly, in a caressing movement, his hand went to her cheek, then down her neck . . . she shivered and closed her eyes, and he released her captive wrist. Her face was now cupped gently in his two hands and she felt herself being pulled to him again. She raised her arms round his neck, and pressed her body against his, softening, melting, submitting to his strength . . . oh God, she had never been kissed like this before . . .

They sank slowly to the carpeted floor of her bedroom; the door clicked softly shut behind them.

As Morag Cameron lay beneath Ed Howard, the long-unfamiliar feeling slowly rose within her. She moaned softly, holding him tight, pressing her fingertips hard into his back. She moaned again, louder now, and Howard's hand clamped down across her mouth. His own mouth lowered to her ear, then to her neck, and irresistible waves of pleasure rolled up and over her, that glorious, sensual feeling she hadn't known for years . . . she writhed and screamed silently into his hand, trembling, arching her back in hunger for him . . . then gently subsiding, bathed in perspiration, relaxed as never before . . . but he was still moving, and she began to respond again, slowly and in wonderment . . . surely it wasn't possible . . . entwined, rolling over, her on top now . . . then the rising waves began to overtake her again, this time even stronger, unbearably delicious . . . she felt as though she was about to expire . . . then collapsed again . . . *Oh God, that was so wonderful, so marvellous . . . but God, he's still moving, he's never going to stop, I don't know if I can take any more . . .*

When Morag opened her eyes, she saw that he was gazing deeply into her face. She let out a long sigh of pleasure. His mouth closed on hers again, this time gently, tenderly, and he held her to him, caressing her lithe body, then whispering in her ear. Her eyes shone with contentment; she found his mouth again and kissed him deeply, lovingly. He carried her to the bed, and pulled back the covers before

103

laying her down. She lifted her arms to him; he climbed in beside her. After a little while, clasped gently in each other's arms, they began to talk, keeping their voices to no more than a whisper to avoid waking her daughter in the room next door. Gradually, Morag felt herself drifting off into sleep, curled up beside him with his arms around her; her last impression was of him murmuring softly that he had never seen a face as beautiful as hers . . .

Ed Howard rose quietly from her bed at five in the morning. The wind had dropped; outside, it was calm and peaceful. He kissed her forehead; she stirred and smiled in her sleep. He stood next to the bed for a minute, looking down at her, pale moonlight filtering through the window and illuminating her face. Gone was the careworn expression; her face was now truly beautiful, like that of a young girl. God, yes, she was beautiful . . .

Departing as silently as he had arrived, he made his way back along the corridor to his own room, his mind in unaccustomed turmoil.

19

On 29th November, Harris and Denard had been in Texas for exactly a week. They had covered nearly a thousand miles in their hired Chrysler, in a series of apparently aimless meanderings around the southern part of the state.

On arriving in Texas they had checked in at a motel on the outskirts of San Antonio, and Harris had spread out the large-scale aviator's map of southern Texas and the Mexican border on a table in his room.

Denard let out a groan when he saw the number of airfields marked. "Jeez! This whole state seems to be covered with airstrips, man. Does *everyone* here have a plane?"

"A lot of people do, Andy. The distances are big and everything is very spread out. You'd fit the whole of the UK into Texas several times over. A lot of people fly, rather than drive; so there are lots of airfields. I think our best bet will be to start looking down here in the south. To begin with, let's concentrate on places within a hundred miles of San Antonio, within striking distance of the Mexican border. You go ahead and pick out some you think might be worth a look."

An hour later, Denard had finished marking up the map; it was covered with blobs from different-coloured highlighter pens. He called Harris over. "OK. This large circle that I've drawn in red represents a distance of exactly one hundred statute miles from San Antonio International Airport. Within that circle there are two international airports – San Antonio itself and Austin. We can leave those aside. There are a further fifteen major airports with more than one runway and ample facilities for large aircraft. Five of them are US Air Force bases, so we can ignore them, and the other ten are still too big for what we're looking for so I think we can safely leave them out too. Our boy, wherever he is, will be operating out of somewhere smaller.

"Now we move on to the ones I've marked with a yellow blob. These are still technically classified as major aerodromes, but this classification is automatic for any airfield with a hard runway more than three thousand feet long. Some will be busy commercial airports serving small towns, and some will be private airstrips serving a ranch or an oilfield. All will be capable of catering for jet aircraft to a greater or lesser degree: no problem for Learjets and suchlike, and bigger aircraft could easily land there – but whether they do or not will depend on things like emergency facilities. You don't really want to put something like a 727 down in a place where the only navigation aid is a wind-sock and the only firefighting equipment is a bucket of water. Some will have good facilities for medium-size passenger aircraft, while others will be purely private strips. There are sixty-one in this category inside our one-hundred-mile circle.

"Lastly, we have possibly the most interesting category – minor airfields. There will be a big variation within this group. None will be suitable for large aircraft; either they'll have a dirt strip or, if it is tarmac, it will be less than three thousand feet long. A lot of them will be private strips, but some may be used by flying clubs, small freight carriers, crop-sprayers and suchlike. Some are marked as disused, but that doesn't necessarily mean they are. We are really spoilt for choice here – there are a hundred and forty-seven of them. That makes two hundred and twenty-five airfields in all, and all of them within just a hundred miles of here."

Harris frowned. "It'll take us for ever to check all that lot out. Isn't there any way to narrow it down a bit?"

"Yes," said Denard, "I suggest we cut out some specific areas. Look here at the map. These areas outlined in blue are military operations areas, mostly marked with the names of the USAF bases they serve, such as Randolph here in San Antonio and Randolph Auxiliary out to the east. Then there's Laughlin, way over to the west and outside our circle but with its operational areas extending inside it. It doesn't mean there's no flying allowed here, but it's controlled and subject to some restrictions, light or heavy depending on the military use. I think we might save ourselves the bother of looking at anything inside these areas. That cuts out a lot of the circle down to the east, south and west. Let's start up here, to the north."

"OK," agreed Harris, "we'll take a look at the first lot tomorrow."

He yawned. "Do you realise it's four in the morning, UK time? I'm going to get some kip."

Over the following six days, they had visited dozens of airfields. Some surprised them by their size and sophistication; others proved to be almost deserted. Harris had six flying lessons from six different instructors, Denard chartered three half-hour flights in light aircraft, and they both went up on two tourist flights. On chatting afterwards to the respective owners or pilots, however, they drew a blank each time. Three of the pilots they met seemed hungry enough for work, but the rest were apparently contented and settled in their jobs. They reluctantly decided that even the three more promising ones would not fit the bill; two were over six feet tall, and the third was about sixty years old.

"It's true, what they say about this state," groaned Denard, as they drove off having drawn yet another blank. "I haven't seen any bugger my size since we've been here."

"We've got plenty of time," Harris reassured him. "There must be somebody smaller around here somewhere who wants to earn an easy hundred thousand bucks. Of course, it would help if you weren't such a short-arse and we had more choice."

On the afternoon of Friday 29th they arrived at Los Morelos airfield, thirty miles north-west of Austin. Large hoardings at the entrance to the airfield listed the facilities on offer from a number of operators: charters, flying lessons, scenic flights over the Llano and Colorado rivers, freight services, air-taxi; the list was comprehensive.

"Looks promising," muttered Harris.

"That must be the twentieth time you've said that."

Harris drove up to the airfield control centre and parked the Chrysler. Both men got out and went inside. It was empty except for a dispatcher behind the counter and a man sprawled in an armchair, drinking coffee from a styrofoam cup.

Harris approached the counter. "We saw the notice advertising flights over the Colorado. Is that the Grand Canyon?"

The dispatcher was polite and helpful. "No sir, it's a different river. The other Colorado, the one with the Grand Canyon, is in Arizona. But this is a pretty part of the country. I can recommend it."

"All right," said Harris. "Do we have to book, or is there a plane available to take us up for a flight right now?"

"You'd want Dan Woods or his partner Gene Barcus. River Flying Services is their outfit. They're both up right now with a party each, due back in twenty minutes. Dan's got another booking for two in an hour's time, so there'd be room for the both of you on that."

Harris looked at his watch and shrugged, thinking of the extra time they would have to spend waiting. Denard caught his eye with an expression that said "Why not?", and Harris turned back to the dispatcher. They could pass the time waiting by seeing who else came in; the pilots among them would be obvious. He was about to speak when a drawling voice from behind them broke in.

"You could sure do worse than try Ray Sullivan." They turned and looked at the man in the armchair, who set down the styrofoam cup and got slowly to his feet. "He's got an office out back. I'll walk you over there. Ain't far. I got to go over there anyhow."

Harris and Denard looked at each other, then Harris said, "OK." The man led them out of the control centre, leaving the dispatcher frowning with disapproval.

"What kind of work does this guy Sullivan do?" asked Denard, as they walked across the apron. A quarter of a mile away was an old Quonsett hut with a twin-engined Cessna parked outside. The legend painted on the side of the hut in large red and white letters read "RAY SULLIVAN AIR CHARTERS, INC."

"Oh, he'll do most any darn thing you might want. One-man outfit, glad of the work. Good pilot. Does all his own maintenance, too. Old plane, but she flies just fine."

Harris and Denard exchanged another glance, following behind their guide. They reached the Quonsett hut, and the man opened a small side-door without knocking. There was a small desk in one corner, with a telephone and a mass of papers. The remainder of the interior was littered with machinery. The place was a mess; there was no one in sight.

Their guide turned to them, holding out his hand. "Well, howdy, folks! Nice of you to drop in. Ray Sullivan here, at your service." He grinned. "Sorry about the charade, but I could sure use the work."

Harris looked at Denard again, a slow smile starting on his face.

*   *   *

Ninety minutes later, they climbed down from the Cessna and had a quick conversation as Sullivan finished securing the plane for the night.

"What do you think?" asked Harris. "How do you rate his flying?"

"Perfectly OK. And I asked him about his licence. He's up to date, and fully qualified for commercial work. Plenty of experience."

"I think he'll do," said Harris, his eyes bright. "He seems pretty unflappable and steady, and he's already admitted he could use some extra dosh. Let's talk to him."

"Mel, the bugger's still a couple of inches taller than me. There's some facial resemblance, I admit. But I'm fair-haired, and he's got dark hair and a moustache."

"I'll tell you what, mate," said Harris. "Let's take him out for a beer and talk to him. We can check his licence details to make sure he isn't bluffing, and if he's OK we can offer him some work. Then, if he agrees, tomorrow we'll go shopping. I'll buy you a nice pair of cowboy boots with tall Cuban heels, a ten-gallon hat and some hair-dye. And you can start growing a 'tache. OK?"

Later that evening a delighted Ray Sullivan, now unexpectedly richer by ten thousand dollars in cash, waved the Chrysler away from the bar on the outskirts of the town of Granite Shoals. His future had just been mapped out for him by his two new friends, Mr Hoskins and Mr Dackman. He would carry on as usual at Los Morelos for a while, not attracting any attention by spending too much money; then after Christmas he would start to wind down his business and sell its only asset, the Cessna. In mid-March he would move away from the area and take a temporary rent on an apartment near Houston or Pasadena; he would telephone Mr Dackman and would be given a date in late March or early April to fly to London, England. A month after that, he would be able to retire, anywhere he liked in the world. The Far East, maybe . . .

20

Howard dressed in walking clothes and took an unhurried breakfast. Morag was nowhere to be seen. Collecting the "piece" that Sheila Cameron had made for him, he left in the car for Glen Carvaig Lodge. He found the turning off the road without trouble, and drove up the tarmac drive to the lodge itself. There was no one about. Parking his car, he changed into walking boots and set off up the glen with his map and a pair of binoculars.

The track climbed steadily, following the course of the Carvaig river. After a mile, the ancient Caledonian pine forests gave way to thinner birch woods, then petered out altogether, with the occasional lone rowan on the slopes of the hill and scattered pines and oaks down by the riverbank. The river was in spate from recent rains, and the burns running down from the hills on either side showed up white against the dull greens and browns of the grass, moss and heather, and the grey and black of exposed granite rocks. The scenery was timeless; the magnificent hills with their rounded tops, rising to two and a half thousand feet above him, were as old as any in the world.

There were several scattered groups of deer on the hillside, and Howard stopped occasionally to look at them through the binoculars. Late in the year as it was, none ventured very high up any longer; with the onset of the colder weather and the disappearance of the flies and midges that had driven them up on to the tops in the summer, they were now gradually coming down for their winter feeding on the lower slopes and riverside pastures. He could see the deer examining him curiously; their keen eyesight had picked him out from well over a mile away, long before he had seen them. None showed any particular sign of alarm at his presence, although one group moved off when he approached to within half a mile of them. Climbing away from him effortlessly and without any apparent hurry, they were soon lost to view.

Walking briskly with a long stride, it took him just under two hours to reach the empty stable at the head of the glen, where the track dwindled away. There was an enclosed paddock where the ponies would be kept during the stalking season; the stable itself was of solid stone, with a rusty corrugated-iron roof. Thick wires ran over the roof, weighted down with large rocks on each end to keep the wind from blowing the roof off in a gale. Rain was by now falling steadily and a mist was beginning to come down; Howard went inside the stable to eat his beef sandwiches. Looking out of the open stable door, he reflected that many would find the scene a dismal one: rain pouring down on a desolate landscape. Howard, pleasantly relaxed after the walk, thought it a glorious one.

*   *   *

The insistent knocking on the bedroom door gradually seeped into Morag's consciousness. Slowly she began to wake; she stretched luxuriously.

The knocking began again. "Mum? Are you all right? It's 10.30. Mum?"

Morag came fully awake with a start. She looked at her bedside clock and tried to sit up. She found she could scarcely move. *God, I feel good*, she thought, a smile of satisfaction spreading across her face. "Yes, I'm fine, love," she called in a dreamy voice. "I just slept rather well. I was tired. I'll be down in half an hour."

"OK." Sheila's voice sounded a little uncertain. It was unlike her mother, she thought. Normally she was up with the lark. She'd never been one for sleeping in. Well, she thought, it would do her no harm. She went back downstairs.

Morag heard her daughter's departing footsteps. She giggled. If she but knew, she thought. She stretched again. *Oh God, I feel so bloody marvellous. What a terrific man . . .*

After a few minutes, she forced herself to climb out of bed; initially she could hardly stand. Then her strength began to flow back, and she wandered in a daze through to the bathroom and ran a hot bath. She studied her face in the mirror. The smile startled her. *Oh God, it shows! I look . . .* For the first time in years, she appraised herself.

111

Not bad, she thought. *Not bad at all. Especially this morning* . . . She climbed gratefully into the hot water and lay there without stirring, contented and completely relaxed. Her body seemed to be glowing.

Twenty minutes later, she was dressed. Wearing a polo-neck pullover to hide the marks from his love-bites, she went downstairs to the kitchen.

Sheila gave her a strange look. "Not like you to sleep in, Mum. But I think it's done you good. You look like you've had a good rest."

Morag turned her back to hide her smile and began busying herself putting the morning's groceries away in the fridge. "I suppose I needed it, Sheila." *Oh, God, how I needed it*, she thought, suppressing a giggle. *If only the lassie knew – but no, she must not.* "Now, come on – there are customers waiting in the bar. Let's be seeing to them. By the way," she added casually, "talking of customers, where's Mr Hatcher this morning?"

"Och, he's away up the glen, like he said. He said he'd be back later on, this evening."

"Oh, fine," said Morag absently, her voice soft.

Sheila glanced at her curiously. Her mother seemed to be in an unusually relaxed mood; she was normally so brisk and businesslike. She decided to ask her; after all, what did she have to lose? "Mum?" she ventured in a small voice. "Do you think I could go out for the day tomorrow?" Behind her back, the fingers of her right hand were tightly crossed. *Please say yes, Mum*, she entreated silently. *Please!*

"All right, love," said her mother vaguely, "I don't see why not. Yes," she repeated as she walked out of the kitchen, "I'm sure that'll be fine."

Sheila watched her receding back in amazement. It had been so easy. She had said yes – just like that. She hadn't even asked where she was intending to go, and she was normally so strict and protective. She raised her eyebrows and followed her mother through into the bar.

A couple of minutes later, in between serving drinks at the bar, Morag smiled at her daughter and asked, as an afterthought, "Who are you seeing tomorrow, love?"

"Well, I had to telephone Danny this morning about something, and he asked me if I would like to go for a walk with him. I hope you don't mind. Just for a walk." *Please don't change your mind, Mum, please* . . . *For so long, I've hoped that one day he would ask me out* . . .

"Danny MacDonald?" said Morag, smiling, "He's a nice young man. Aye, he's a nice enough young man. That'll be fine, love."

"Oh, thank you, Mum!" exclaimed Sheila, flinging her arms round her mother and hugging her. "Thank you!"

*　　*　　*

Howard secured the stable door and started back down to his car. The rain continued to fall, and he was soon soaked to the skin. Normally, he hated getting wet; now he didn't seem to mind. His thoughts were a long way off as he strode along the track back down the glen. As he reached the bottom, the lodge came in sight.

The twenty-mile walk had taken him four hours, including his stop for the sandwiches. He had thoroughly enjoyed the exercise, and could fully understand the magnetic attraction that the wild and deserted splendour of the glen exerted on men such as MacDonald.

At the lodge he took a bag containing dry clothes out of the car and changed out of his wet things under the shelter of a lean-to building where firewood was cut for the lodge.

A man appeared from a barn round the back: a rather short, stocky figure in his late forties, with a broad, friendly-looking face. It was Duncan Macrae, the head stalker. Howard introduced himself as Edwin Hatcher and explained his presence, saying how much he had enjoyed his walk and that he hoped he hadn't caused any nuisance. Macrae was pleasant and civil, and asked Howard into his cottage for a cup of tea. Howard accepted gladly, and the two men talked for half an hour about Scotland in general and stalking in particular. Howard eventually excused himself and left, thanking Macrae profusely for his hospitality.

After returning to the Escort, he took the road back towards Carvaig. He drove through the village, past the inn, and down on to the main Spean Bridge–Fort William road. He arrived in Fort William just before two o'clock, parked in the station car-park, and went for a walk through the town.

The yellow-pages section of the telephone book in the inn had listed four sports shops in Fort William; that morning he had made a note of the addresses, mentally discounting one of them as it was opposite the station entrance, not in the High Street proper. He crossed over the road, past the Alexandra Hotel and into the High Street itself. The window of the first shop on his list had a display of running shoes, tracksuits, skateboards and wind-surfers. Inside he could see a young man and a girl attending to a couple of teenage customers. The young man was slim, barely twenty, and had hair cut short at the back and sides but flopping down over his forehead and eyes. Howard went on to the next address.

The second shop was two hundred yards further along the High Street, its window packed with outdoor equipment: boots, wet-weather clothing, climbing gear, fishing tackle, sticks, torches, clasp knives, rucksacks and camping equipment. A treasure-house of things for the outdoor type, thought Howard. He moved on to the third shop, which proved to be small and principally for the fisherman. The decidedly unexciting window display had a board backing, and there was a blind over the glass pane of the door preventing anyone from looking inside, so Howard opened the door and went in. A rather dour and uncommunicative man in his late fifties showed Howard a selection of trout flies in response to his enquiry. Howard bought two flies and left.

He collected his car and drove back to the second shop, parking fifty yards away facing east in the direction of Spean Bridge. He settled down to wait. At about 4.30 a large Volvo estate car drew up outside the shop; the driver got out and went inside. Five minutes later he re-emerged, followed by a fit-looking man in his late twenties carrying two 250-cartridge boxes of twelve-bore shotgun ammunition. The fit-looking man loaded the boxes into the customer's car and waved him off before going back inside. At five o'clock the fit-looking man left the shop, locking up as he went. He walked a few yards down the street to a side-road, where he got into a blue Toyota pick-up and drove away.

Howard followed the Toyota out towards Spean Bridge, keeping fairly close behind. Four miles outside Fort William, the Toyota signalled a right turn and pulled into a half-concealed gateway. Howard slowed to let the pick-up turn in; as he drove on past, the name of the cottage was briefly caught in the Toyota's lights. Howard carried on up the road for a further half-mile, then did a U-turn and headed back to Fort William. He stopped at a petrol filling station on the outskirts of the town and crossed the forecourt to the public telephone kiosk. There were a hundred and eighty-three entries in the Highlands and Islands telephone book under "MacDonald, D"; fifteen of them had Fort William telephone numbers. Howard quickly found the one with the address given as Glenside Cottage. He picked up the receiver and dialled the number.

21

Howard swung the door of the phone booth shut and drove the Escort back out of Fort William towards Spean Bridge. Ten minutes later he pulled into the gateway of MacDonald's cottage, got out of the car and walked up the short gravel path to the front door.

The fair-haired man who answered the door looked as fit as Howard would have expected a professional deer-stalker to be, despite the thick pullover and rough corduroys concealing his athletic frame. His level gaze met Howard's own, and the two men studied each other; Howard was struck by the paleness of the blue-grey eyes – you almost felt you could look right through them.

"Mr MacDonald? I'm Peter Hanbury. I rang you. It's good of you to see me."

"Danny MacDonald. My pleasure. Come in, Mr Hanbury." They shook hands, and MacDonald led the way into the small sitting-room. "Take a seat. Can I get you a cup of tea?"

"That would be very kind." Howard glanced cursorily around the room as MacDonald disappeared into the kitchen. The sitting-room was simply furnished. Along one wall, under the window, was a large workbench which was almost covered with tools, cans, bottles and assorted pieces of machinery. No woman's influence here, thought Howard. Not yet, anyway. Apart from the bench, there were two chairs, a plain table, a television and an old mains radio. A coal fire was smoking in the grate. It had clearly only just been lit; the room was cold. On the walls were some enlarged photographs of highland landscapes; Howard recognised the Glen Carvaig hills. The only personal touch was a pair of framed black and white photographs on the chimneypiece. One showed a man and woman in their thirties, with two young boys of about six and eight; the other was of the same two boys in their teens, smiling happily at the camera, high up in the hills above the glen.

MacDonald reappeared in the doorway with two mugs of tea. "Here you are, Mr Hanbury. Please take a seat."

Howard took the proffered mug and sat down. "Well, Mr MacDonald," he began, "As I told you on the telephone, I do occasional pieces for an American magazine which is widely read by hunters and gun enthusiasts in the States. I mostly supply stories and anecdotes about shooting, stalking, big-game hunting and so on. They seem to go down well over there. Anyway, I heard through the grapevine about a remarkable shot you pulled off last year, and I thought it would make the basis for a story. I'd be prepared to offer you fifty pounds for telling me about it."

MacDonald remained impassive while Howard talked; then, when he had finished, he nodded. "Well, I don't see any great harm in that. What exactly is it that you want to know?"

"I've spoken to the Colonel, and he's told me about the stalk itself." Howard was lying. He had never met the Colonel and did not know him – he had only spoken to Stoner. "So perhaps you could just tell me how you pulled off the shot. He made it all sound quite incredible, I must say – although I didn't get the feeling that he was exaggerating. He was genuinely impressed."

"The Colonel is a fine gentleman," said MacDonald, "and quite a competent shot himself. He just had a wee bit of bad luck. The stag moved just as he committed himself to the shot; the shot went behind, missing the lungs and going into the gut. The beast took off with the hinds, and we didn't have another chance at him until he was about five hundred yards away."

"But why did you take a shot at that range, when the stag was still moving?" Howard was leaning forward in his seat, looking intently at MacDonald.

"A fair enough question, Mr Hanbury," replied MacDonald, "but I was reasonably confident about the shot. It wasn't strictly necessary, as the beast would have begun to feel very sick, and would have lain down before long. But it could have been an hour or more before we came up to him again, and I don't like to see a beast suffer unnecessarily.

"The shot was a lot easier than it sounds. There were several things that helped. First of all, there was next to no wind, and what there

117

was was directly in our faces. For example, if there had been a five-knot wind from the side, I would have had to aim off a foot into the wind at that range to compensate." MacDonald paused, assessing Howard's reaction. Howard was nodding in understanding, so he continued. "In the second place, it's not difficult to estimate the speed of a beast. The stag was moving at about seven or eight miles an hour; that means he was climbing at a vertical rate of about four feet per second, allowing for the steepness of the slope. At five hundred yards the time of flight of the bullet will be a little less than three-quarters of a second, so I had to aim just about three feet in front of where I wanted the bullet to hit."

Howard was still nodding, so MacDonald went on. "Then there was the range itself. With experience, one can judge distance fairly well, but at a distance of five hundred yards even an error of plus or minus fifty yards in one's estimation can make a difference of a foot or more in the elevation of the bullet. In normal circumstances, unless one knows the exact range at that sort of distance, there can be no certainty even of hitting a beast, let alone of killing it clean."

"So?" asked Howard. "How were you so sure you could do it?"

"It's fairly simple," said MacDonald. "You see, the beast was running directly away from us and uphill, presenting the whole length of his spine almost vertically. A shot anywhere in the spine from the top of the neck to about the eighth thoracic vertebra, about a third of the way down the back, is a killing shot. D'you see what I'm getting at? The drop of the bullet due to a slight mistake in estimating the distance was not critical. The target area was a narrow one, but it was nearly three feet high. A .275 bullet such as the one I used, in a rifle zeroed for two hundred yards, will drop fifty inches below the point of aim at five hundred yards; call it four feet. Add the three-foot lead for the continued forward movement of the stag during the bullet's flight, and all I had to do was aim seven feet in front of the centre of the target area. So I aimed five feet above the head. As it happened, my estimation was correct; the bullet hit at the base of the neck, just above the shoulder. It was a good shot, yes, but not really a risky one. At least," he added, "that was the theory. In practice, it wasn't like that at all."

Howard was puzzled. "How do you mean?"

"Theory is all very well," said MacDonald, "but you can hardly sit down on a hillside with a pocket calculator and start working these things out. It helps to have the facts and figures in your head, of course, so you know what's involved. But you ask any competent shot who has to take a snap decision about how much he has to aim off for wind, or movement, or range, and he'll tell you that it's almost entirely a matter of instinct. Either you have it or you haven't. If the Colonel had asked me at the time how far I had aimed in front of that beast, I wouldn't have been able to tell him. I worked out later how much it had been."

"And yet you were quite confident of the shot?"

MacDonald nodded. "Aye, I was." He paused for a moment, studying Howard. "Anyway, I think that covers the shot itself, unless there's anything you aren't clear about on that score?"

Howard was elated. The stalker had demonstrated his competence and knowledge beyond question. "No, Mr MacDonald, you have explained it all very clearly. I followed all that perfectly."

"I rather thought you would, Mr Hanbury." MacDonald's eyes narrowed, and now he too leaned forward in his chair, watching Howard's face closely. "So perhaps you can now tell me why you're really here. You're no more a journalist than I am. You didn't give the name of your American magazine, you didn't take any notes when I was talking, and you don't appear to be interested in anything other than the technique of the shot. A good story is about more than technicalities, as any journalist will tell you. You followed me out here in your car this evening, then you went back to telephone me before returning here again. Someone fitting your description is booked into the inn at Carvaig, and has been asking questions about me and the estate. I think, Mr Hanbury – or is it Mr Hatcher, or whatever your real name may be – that you had better explain yourself."

Howard had been trying hard to remain expressionless while MacDonald spoke; now he could contain himself no longer. His face broke into a broad grin.

119

22

After giving MacDonald his real name, Howard told him that he had an interesting proposition to put to him. He apologised for the subterfuge, and MacDonald nodded. Before he explained what the proposition was, said Howard, he wanted to establish whether or not it was a feasible one.

MacDonald was intrigued and puzzled, but he had lost some of his initial wariness. "So let's get this straight, now, Mr Howard. You are asking me whether it is theoretically possible to hit a target six inches in diameter at a range of approximately twelve hundred yards. Is that it?"

"That's right."

"Fine. Well, the answer is that in theory it *is* possible. A top-quality long-range sniper's rifle, using match-grade ammunition and properly sighted in for the range concerned, is in theory capable of grouping better than a half a minute of angle. That means an error of less than half an inch diameter at a hundred yards. At twelve hundred yards the possible error will be twelve times as large, so a group of shots should fall within a circle less than six inches in diameter. But in practice it isn't as simple as that. To take the most obvious point, that assumes no error at all on the part of the man firing the rifle. No flinching, a perfect aim, and rock steadiness. And there are all sorts of other things to take into consideration too."

"Such as?"

"Well, let's assume to start with that you're using a large-calibre and very high-velocity, very streamlined bullet. That means much bigger and faster than the standard 7.62mm NATO ammo. You'd have to anyway. The standard 7.62mm NATO bullet loses velocity and goes trans-sonic at about nine hundred yards – after that, it's travelling below the speed of sound. You'll be familiar with the problems that

120

were faced by the first pilots to break the sound barrier – their planes became unstable just as they broke it. It's the same with a bullet. It becomes unstable, and its accuracy goes haywire. So for shooting at that sort of range, you'd need a very powerful cartridge – one that's still supersonic at twelve hundred yards.

"But there are other factors to take into account. The minor ones are humidity, air temperature and barometric pressure. Taking the first one first, we can pretty well ignore variations in humidity. Even a fairly wide variation in humidity will make a difference of less than an inch at twelve hundred yards. The difference is so small that you can almost disregard it.

"Air temperature is much more significant. A single degree Centigrade difference in temperature will make a difference of about one inch at twelve hundred yards. So, for example between dawn and midday, when you might have a temperature variation of perhaps ten degrees or more, the difference will be ten inches – putting the margin of error outside the six-inch target."

"As much as that? I had no idea."

"I'm afraid so. And I'm talking about very punchy ammunition. With 7.62mm, travelling more slowly and being smaller, the difference will be far more."

"Hell, I knew it made a difference, but not that much." Howard rubbed his chin thoughtfully. He began to wish he had taken Stoner up on his offer of a trip to Bisley to see how the long-range marksmen did it.

"Unfortunately," continued MacDonald, "that's only the start of it. Let's go on to barometric pressure. This is affected by both weather and altitude. The two are bound up together, if you see what I mean. The higher the altitude, the lower the pressure – that's how most altimeters work. Altitude is easy – you can get it off a map, and work out the effect using tables. Roughly speaking, a one-hundred-foot difference in altitude or a two-millibar difference in barometric pressure will make a one-inch difference in the point of impact of the bullet at a range of twelve hundred yards. Barometric variations due to changes in the weather are often as much as thirty millibars or more, and you need a good map to get the altitude accurate to a hundred feet. The higher the altitude, and therefore the lower the pressure, the thinner the air is; so there is less air resistance and the bullet doesn't slow down so quickly. Gravity will therefore have less

121

effect on the bullet because it will reach the target quicker; so it will hit the target higher than it would at a lower altitude and higher barometric pressure. D'you follow me?"

"Yes, I think so." Howard was impressed. MacDonald obviously knew his subject well, and had facts and statistics at his fingertips.

"Fine. So in theory, if the rifle had been sighted in on a cold day, say at a temperature of ten degrees Centigrade, on a firing range in the south of England three hundred feet above sea-level, you could not expect it to perform the same way up here in the hills on a warm day. At an altitude of fifteen hundred feet, and in an air temperature of twenty Centigrade, the bullet would go somewhere between two and three feet high of your six-inch target at twelve hundred yards, missing it completely. At shorter ranges, of course, these things make far less difference, and below three hundred yards one can to all intents and purposes ignore them altogether. But even so, I'm talking about a purpose-designed match-grade bullet, fired at extremely high velocity. With NATO ammo, the errors would be far greater. You can begin to see how easy it would be to miss the six-inch target, can't you?"

"Yes, I can." Howard was beginning to feel slightly worried. It was far more complicated than he had thought.

"That's not all," said MacDonald. "Have you heard of something called the Magnus effect?"

"No. Is it something to do with the rotation of the earth?"

MacDonald smiled. "No. Fortunately, you don't have to worry about that with small arms. The Magnus effect is to do with the spin of the bullet. The grooves in the rifle barrel impart a spin to the bullet, which keeps it stable in flight. The spin is usually right-handed – in other words, clockwise. A bullet with right-handed spin will tend to veer off to the right. Luckily, the effect is a predictable constant for a given range. For the sort of bullet I'm talking about, at twelve hundred yards the deviation due to the Magnus effect will be about two minutes of angle. That's twenty-four inches – quite a difference. So you have to adjust your sights two feet to the left to compensate."

"I had no idea," said Howard, frowning. "What about if the shot is a downhill one?"

"That makes far less difference than you'd think," said MacDonald. "How much are we talking about?"

"Well," said Howard, "let's say the firing point is two hundred feet above the target. That's quite a lot, isn't it?"

"It sounds a lot, I'll agree. But it's not, over that sort of distance. It's easy enough to work out. Let's see, now . . ." MacDonald thought for a moment, then gave a nod. "Right. That's an angle of about two or three degrees. The effect would be that the shot would go about six inches high at twelve hundred yards. I'd have to work it out exactly, but it doesn't make as much difference as you might think."

"That's a relief," muttered Howard.

"Hold on," said MacDonald, "because it gets worse. There are two other factors – both far more important. They make a huge difference, and they're the ones that really matter. I mentioned them when I was telling you about the shot at that stag. Range and wind. You get just one of these even *slightly* wrong, and you've had it. Let me give you an example, still using our super high-velocity ammo. Distance isn't usually a problem, of course, as most of this sort of shooting is done on a firing range where you know the exact distance to the target, to a yard. But it is a serious problem if you don't know the range exactly – and I mean *exactly*. Taking our distance of twelve hundred yards, let's assume you make an error of one hundred yards in your estimate. In open country, that is in fact a very accurate guess. Let's say you think it's thirteen hundred yards. Let's also say that you estimate the wind speed at ten knots from right to left, but that somewhere between you and the target the wind is in fact doing something quite different, which over that sort of distance is not only possible, but actually quite likely – especially on uneven ground. It's possible even on flat ground. You can see the effect at sea: on what looks at first glance like a still day, there are often localised squalls of wind making ripples on the water. But say your average error in estimating the wind speed is five miles per hour – not a big error at all, over a long distance like that. D'you realise by how far you will miss your six-inch target?"

"Tell me," said Howard, gloomily.

"The bullet will go about six feet above the target and four feet off to the side. That's how much. D'you see what I mean?"

"Oh, Lord," groaned Howard. "I had no idea it was quite that bad."

"It's not an insurmountable problem, of course," said MacDonald, "and for target shooters it's actually made quite a lot easier. As I say, they know the distance between them and the target to the nearest yard. Also, there are usually flags flying at different places all the way down the side of the range, so they can see what the wind is doing. And of course target shooters are given sighting shots, so they can check to see they've got it right. They usually get two or three practice sighting shots immediately before they actually start their competition shoot."

"Well," said Howard, "let me be more specific. Let's say we know the altitude to the nearest hundred feet, we can read the barometric pressure, take the temperature and the humidity and allow for those . . ."

"Just a second," cut in MacDonald. "It takes time to work it out from tables and mathematical formulae. You'd probably need about twenty minutes to do that."

"Five minutes maximum."

"Not a chance, unless you'd worked out a whole lot of different possibilities beforehand. That would take literally days. But anyway, you haven't mentioned range and wind."

"Maybe we could put one or two little flags out. No more. As for range, I don't know. Let's say we get it right to within fifty yards. How about that?"

"That would be an extremely accurate estimate. I don't know . . ." MacDonald was thinking hard. "But maybe we could use the mirage effect for wind if it was a warm day . . ."

Howard broke in. "Mirage effect? What do you mean?"

"You must know what a mirage is. At long distances such as this, any heat rising from the ground between the firing point and the target distorts the air slightly and causes a shimmering effect. The target will appear to float, moving up and down. The bottom of the target can disappear. If it's a very hot day, a shot can be almost impossible, of course, but if the effect is only minor, you can see the heat shimmer moving in the wind. It's a very useful aid to estimating wind speed."

"Oh." Howard looked blank for a moment. Might it be too hot when it came to it, with a mirage that would make a shot impossible?

"Anyway," said MacDonald, "we'll assume for the sake of argument that you can estimate the range accurately and make a good guess at the wind. What about sighters?"

"What do you mean?"

"How many sighting shots can the shooter take before he has to hit this six-inch target?"

124

"He can't take any."

"You mean none *at all*?"

"Correct."

"Mr Howard," said MacDonald, shaking his head and smiling dismissively, "I can tell you straight away that in those circumstances, with a bit of wind and at an imprecisely-known distance from the target, even the best shot in the world wouldn't stand a chance of hitting it with his first shot. He would be doing very well to hit a target six *feet* square with his first shot, let alone six *inches* square. I'm not exaggerating. Honestly, it just isn't on. With a really experienced spotter working alongside him with a spotting scope, he might hit it with his second, third or fourth shot, having made the necessary adjustments. But *first* shot? No chance."

"Is there no way we could get round the problem of estimating the distance?"

"Well, you could if you had an accurate range-finder. You look like a military man. Does the Army have anything like that? Laser range-finders? I seem to remember hearing something about them."

"The first ones were designed for tanks," said Howard. "They're very heavy, and I don't suppose a civilian could get hold of one anyway. There are some smaller ones now, but they're only issued to specialist miltary units." Howard considered the matter. His SBS contacts might be able to get one for him, but he dared not ask. He knew Dartington had been right to insist on no contact with the security forces. "I wouldn't be able to get one for this particular job. I think we have to rule that idea out. Isn't there another way?"

"Well, if there's an object whose exact size is known, near the target, you can get a fairly accurate idea of the range by measuring the subtended angle on a pair of binoculars with graticule markings. The usual way is to use the height of an average man. But an inch of error in his height would mean an error of twenty yards, that far away. And you'd need something much bigger than a man to do it accurately at that sort of range. I'd say you're still looking at an error of sixty yards or more. At that distance, the bullet will be dropping nearly one inch over every yard of extra range. An error of only *six* yards, never mind sixty, would be enough to make you miss."

"Is there any other way of –"

"Hold on, I've had an idea. You could use an optical range-finder. They're large, but quite accurate – a possible error of no more than

125

two or three yards over that sort of distance. They work on the split-image principle. You sight on a vertical object and turn a drum to line the bottom and top halves up so that the vertical line isn't broken. Then you read off the range on the scale. Yes, that would work. I should've thought of it before."

"Are they easy enough to get hold of?"

"My uncle has got one. It's an old naval instrument his father brought back from the war. I used to play with it when I was young. It's a big, heavy, clumsy thing, and it's ancient, but it works. Or, at least, it did. He may still have it."

"Good," said Howard, relieved. "Now, what about wind, if we can't use flags?"

"You'd definitely need something to give the wind speed. The best thing would be a proper meteorological anemometer. Several of them, preferably. You know, those things with three little cups on them which turn round in the wind. You'd need them to be put out at various places along the flight path of the bullet, with a man on each one to read off the wind speed and radio it back to you. You can get small hand-held ones. That would be much more accurate than using flags."

"Excellent!" exclaimed Howard. "A friend of mine is an electronics expert. I'm sure he'd be able get hold of a type of anemometer that he could fix up so that two or three of them could radio a signal back to a read-out, giving the wind speed. We couldn't have them manned – they'd have to be on a remote read-out."

"What d'you mean, you couldn't have them manned? Why not?"

"Mr MacDonald, before I answer that, I just want to know one thing. Given the range-finder, the anemometers and ready-calculated tables for temperature et cetera, could *you* hit such a target with your first shot?"

MacDonald thought for a moment, then gave Howard a sideways look of curiosity before answering carefully. "Yes, Mr Howard, I think I would have a good chance. I couldn't guarantee it; nobody could do that. But if the weather wasn't too bad it might be possible. Strong or gusty wind, or heavy rain obscuring the target, would make it very difficult." MacDonald now looked directly at Howard and leaned forward. "I assume there is a point to all this. Perhaps you've made a bet with someone that this can be done, and for some reason you've gone to a lot of trouble to find me and test me out. My guess is it has something to do with that fellow from Bisley who keeps writing to me and trying to get me down there to join his shooting team. Am I right?"

Howard's face remained expressionless.

"Well," MacDonald continued, "I don't mind doing something for a bet, if you'll pay my expenses; in fact I think I'd quite enjoy the challenge. I'd need to be able to specify the rifle and ammunition, of course. There's only one manufacturer in the world who produces the sort of specialist weapon that could do a job like that. But," he said firmly, "if the ultimate purpose is to get me down there on a regular basis and into a shooting team, you can forget it here and now I'm not interested. I've been patient, Mr Howard. Now you can level with me, please. What is this all about, and what is this magic six-inch target you want me to hit?"

Howard held MacDonald's eyes with his own and replied softly. "It's not quite like that, Mr MacDonald. It's not a bet. I'm being serious. Deadly serious, in fact. The target is a man."

"WHAT?" MacDonald was up on his feet in an instant, his eyes wide with incredulity. Gradually he turned a furious red, then began jabbing his finger at Howard. He controlled his voice with an effort. "Give me just one good reason, right now, you madman, why I shouldn't go straight to the police and report what you've just said!"

Howard's voice remained soft and steady. "The target is Saddam Hussein."

The blood suddenly drained from MacDonald's face, and he sat down quickly, his expression now one of open-mouthed shock. Howard watched carefully as a surge of conflicting emotions seemed to hit MacDonald all at once. His face was a study; Howard discerned more about the stalker's character in those few seconds than he had in the whole of the previous hour's conversation. Little by little, MacDonald's blue-grey eyes seemed to change colour to a fierce bright blue. The stare was as fixed and hard as any Howard could remember. The voice, when it came, was little more than a whisper. "Tell me you're not joking. *Tell me!*"

"I'm deadly serious, Mr MacDonald. This is no joke. You know it isn't. You know it, and there are three good reasons why I don't think you'll go to the police." Howard's eyes deliberately flickered to one side.

MacDonald saw the movement of his glance; his hands tightened on the arms of the chair, and the veins on his arms and forehead stood out. His voice had risen to a quiet hiss as he spoke through tightly clenched teeth. "Oh, you bastard. You complete *bastard*. You knew, didn't you? Yes. I'll do it. *I'll do it!*"

23

Morag lay in her bed that night, her heart pounding in anticipation. Would he come to her room again? Or had it been just a single night of wonderful madness? Had he meant the things he had said to her? Oh yes, he had, she decided. He must have, he *must* have . . .

She hardly heard the sound of her door opening. Then, suddenly, he was there again, standing over her, bending down to kiss her face as she rose to embrace him . . . *Oh God*, she thought, *just the feel of his body, his arms, his strength . . .*

A little later, she felt she was about to lose all control again; she grabbed his hand and held it across her mouth as before, then let the tide of pleasure wash over and over her, over and over . . .

*   *   *

Howard didn't leave her bed until 6.30. Back in his room, he slept until nine, then rose and packed, ready to leave. Downstairs, Sheila served him breakfast. He could see the girl was preoccupied; she kept looking at her watch. For a moment, he wondered if she might have overheard them, then dismissed the thought.

"Is something the matter, Sheila?" he asked gently.

The girl seemed momentarily startled. "Oh no, Mr Hatcher," she said hurriedly, "not at all. I was just wondering where my mum was. She's normally up so early, and I'm due to go out for the day . . ." She tailed off, looking embarrassed.

"Please don't hang around just on my account," he said. "If you want to get away, I shall be perfectly happy sitting here for a while, reading the paper. I'll wait to see your mother before I go."

Sheila looked at him. Her early suspicion of him had vanished. He had been polite and considerate, no trouble at all. She felt a little guilty about having telephoned Danny about him, but at least that had given her an excuse to talk to Danny, and she was now going to see him as a result . . . She smiled. "Well, if you wouldn't mind . . ."

He smiled back at her. "Off with you, then. And thank you very much," he said, standing to shake her hand, "for looking after me so well. I've really enjoyed my stay here. More than I can say. I hope I'll be able to come back one day."

She blushed and said goodbye, hurrying off. He watched out of the window as she drove off in her Fiesta, then he turned and went upstairs.

He knocked on the door of Morag's room. As he opened it, she stirred and smiled with pleasure on seeing him, then sat up in alarm. "Ed! Are you mad? Sheila will find out!"

He waved his hand in reassurance and came over to sit on the edge of the bed. "It's all right. Sheila's gone off for the day. We're alone in the inn – just the two of us." He kissed her. "I've come to say goodbye. I have to leave."

She held his face in her hands, looking deeply into his eyes. "I hope you don't think I behave like this with all my guests here."

"There'd be trouble from me if you did," he answered, grinning. "Can I come and see you again sometime?"

"There'll be trouble from me if you don't," she said tenderly. "Goodbye, stranger."

"Goodbye, Morag," he said, softly.

They embraced, holding each other tight, and then he was gone.

*   *   *

Howard drove back to Edinburgh, deep in thought. He checked in the hire-car and caught the shuttle to London. It was Sunday 1st December. Sitting on the plane, he realised he would not forget the events of that weekend in a hurry. With the successful recruitment of Danny MacDonald, the last major piece of the plan was now in place; and there had been Morag too . . . He recognised that he had taken a foolish risk with her, that he could so easily have jeopardised everything. He forced himself to acknowledge that it had been unprofessional to take such a risk. But there had been something about her . . . something irresistible . . .

On Monday morning he drove down to Swindon, where he found

Bob Usher checking off goods that had been delivered to Unit 8 on the industrial estate. Bourne was sitting at a desk in the side office, dealing with paperwork. The unit had taken on the appearance of a warehouse, with packing cases and pallets stacked in neat lines. A leased fork-lift truck was parked in the corner, plugged in for recharging.

Howard walked over to the office and went in. "Morning, Johnny. How's it going?"

"Pretty good. We're well ahead of schedule. Mel and Andy arrived back from Texas yesterday morning – looks like they've already found themselves a suitable pilot." Bourne told him about Sullivan.

"Sounds fine. Any news from Mike?"

"No. He's been in the States a week now. Those NVGs are probably tricky to get hold of. As for the other stuff, I don't know. I expect he'll ring if he has problems with any of it. How did you get on in Scotland? You look pretty cheerful."

"No problem at all. Danny MacDonald is good – really knows his stuff. He's better than I dared hope." Howard recounted the details of their meeting, relishing the part when MacDonald had challenged him for his real name. "He's pretty alert. I made it fairly obvious with my questioning of the girl at the inn – I was sure she would report back to him. And I followed pretty close up the arse of his pick-up on his way out to his cottage. Still, bearing in mind that he has no particular reason to be watching his back, he did well to put two and two together."

Bourne nodded approvingly. "I look forward to meeting the guy. By the way, when Andy and Mel rang in, I told them to join up with Chris – he's still looking for an aircraft."

Howard nodded. Chris Palmer had warned him that finding a suitable plane might take some while, but had been reasonably confident that it would only be a matter of time. "Couldn't you have gone to help him yourself?"

Bourne shook his head regretfully. "Afraid not, more's the pity. I've been completely bogged down here. Running three companies at once is not as easy as I thought it would be."

"You have my deepest sympathy, bookworm." Howard grinned. "Keep at it. Right; I'm off to talk to the others. Where's Tony? I've got a job for him."

"Next door in Unit 9. He's already got his machine tools set up.

We're using Unit 9 as the workshop, leaving this one for deliveries and storage only. He's busy on those AK silencers. Thought he might as well get on with them."

"Anything in Unit 10 yet?"

"No. The container's coming later this week; we'll put it in there. We'll have to work on it *in situ*, on its trailer. Unit 10's got a hoist, but it's only rated for ten tons."

"Fine. OK, back to your statutory company duties, lad!" Howard left him in the office and went to talk to Usher.

"All right, boss?" enquired Usher jauntily as he approached.

"Bob, I've got an extra job for you. Can you fix up something like this?" Howard handed him the notes he had made on the anemometers. "Have a think about it and let me know if it's a starter. I must go and have a word with Tony about the rifle we need."

He left Usher studying the notes and went next door to find Ackford bent over a workbench, wearing protective goggles. A five-inch cylinder of steel was spinning between the chucks of a lathe, the bit cutting into one end to form a neck.

Ackford looked up as Howard's shadow fell over the bench; he switched the machine off. "Morning, boss. Good trip north?"

"Yes thanks, Tony. Our boy has agreed. He's given me a list of requirements. How are you getting on?"

"Fine. I've done one silencer already, as a sample. I've only just started on this one. Want to see what it will end up looking like?" Ackford showed Howard the finished article. "It was easy, like I said. This end screws off like so, and inside are the sound baffles. The other end is tapped to the same thread as a standard AK muzzle brake. All we have to do is take the muzzle brake off and screw this on instead. Here, I've got a deactivated AK 47 to show you how it fits. I bought it at one of those places that sell replica guns." Ackford brought out the AK 47 assault rifle. The barrel had been plugged with steel, and the breech block had been drilled out and welded to make it impossible to fire the weapon. As such, it could be sold freely, without a Firearm Certificate, although outwardly its appearance was unchanged. Ackford depressed a small metal lug on the end of the barrel, and unscrewed a half-inch-long collar, leaving the screw-thread on the end of the barrel exposed. Then he screwed the finished silencer in place.

Howard inspected it. "It looks fine, Tony. Do all AKs have this same threading on the end of the barrel?"

"Yes. AK 47, AKM, AKMS, the lot. Even the Chinese versions do. The AK 74 doesn't, of course – it has its own special muzzle brake." The AK was the most widely produced and most copied assault rifle in the world. The original design of the Avtomat Kalashnikova 47, named after the Soviet citizen who had designed it in 1947, had remained largely unchanged since then. To save weight, later models were produced from stamped, rather than milled, steel, and a screw-on cutaway muzzle brake had replaced the simple collar – its effect was to eliminate the tendency of the muzzle to climb to the right when fired on automatic. It was a simple but effective mechanism. The AKMS was a version with a folding stock, issued to Soviet airborne forces and tank crews. Most of the Warsaw Pact countries, and a number of others, had produced their own versions of the same design. The AK 74 was a newer version; it fired the smaller 5.45mm calibre, in place of the old AK 47's 7.62mm. The AK 74 had not surfaced in large numbers outside the former Soviet Union; the AK 47 or the AKM was still standard issue in the vast majority of cases.

"How long will it take to finish all eight silencers?"

"Another few hours should do it, boss. It's a simple job with this machinery." Ackford indicated the other tools – stamps, cutters, presses, drills, and tap and die machinery. "Then I'll get on with making some modified gas ports for them – they may take a little longer. I should be through by late tomorrow."

"Good. We'll just have to remember that the bullets will still be supersonic at short range, so they'll make a crack when they're fired. There will also be quite a lot of clatter from the action working. But at least the silencers will cut out the muzzle blast. Anyway, I've got the details of the sniper rifle we need. Does this mean anything to you?" Howard passed him a piece of paper.

Ackford studied it. "Accuracy International, eh? Couldn't have chosen better. What are we going to get – the L96?" Accuracy International Ltd had designed the L96 sniper rifle to replace the British Army's ageing L42.

"Actually, no. There's now a second-generation version of the L96, which is even better. It's called the AW. But we're getting the specialist version of that – the Super Magnum." The Swedish Army had already ordered the AW. Both the L96 and the AW were produced in the NATO standard 7.62mm (.308 Winchester); this calibre was adequate for accurate sniper work up to a range of about eight hundred yards, but above that range, trajectory became a problem and the striking power of the bullet dropped significantly. Accuracy International had therefore developed the Super Magnum version in more powerful calibres. One of these was .338 Lapua Magnum, an extremely powerful round with nearly six times the striking energy of 7.62mm at a thousand yards. Some Special Forces units had already taken delivery of the Super Magnum in .338 for ultra-long-range work.

"I've heard of .338 Winchester Magnum, but not .338 Lapua Magnum," said Ackford.

"I had heard of it, but I didn't know much about it until the day before yesterday," Howard told him. "It's much more powerful. It's based on a necked-down Rigby .416 case. It's a thumping great big cartridge, firing a two-hundred-and-fifty-grain bullet at a muzzle velocity of three thousand feet per second."

"Phew. That'll give him a sore shoulder, if he fires more than a couple of them. At what range does the bullet velocity go subsonic?"

"Not until about thirteen or fourteen hundred yards out – at least four hundred yards further than 7.62mm." The muzzle velocity of three thousand feet per second was nearly three times the speed of sound; but a bullet rapidly lost velocity and power owing to air resistance, eventually dropping below Mach 1 – eleven hundred and twenty feet per second – at long range. For a high-velocity, heavy bullet with good aerodynamic characteristics, this happened at a longer range than with more conventional ammunition.

"Wouldn't it be better if we had something that went subsonic within the range we need, to avoid the noise?"

"Danny and I talked about that. He was very definite about it. In the first place, a bullet goes haywire as it changes from supersonic to subsonic, so accuracy suffers. Also, the crack of a supersonic bullet arriving will be very disorientating, and won't give any clue as to where it's come from. A bullet that had dropped to subsonic velocity would just make the normal zipping noise when it arrived, and the trajectory would be worse. It would be just as obvious that it was a bullet, but instead of being disoriented by a supersonic crack, someone might have the presence of mind to listen out for the muzzle blast. We talked about silencing the rifle, but that's right out. In any case, it has a good muzzle brake which will cut out a lot of the blast. We'll be far enough away for the time lag to be quite long, and at that distance the muzzle noise won't be too loud."

"OK. You want me to put the order in? I don't suppose it'll be easy. I know Accuracy International are extremely security-conscious. They won't sell to just anyone. I'll have to use the firm's RFD ticket to get it, and I'll probably have to dress this up as a request from a friendly foreign government." XF Securities was, among other things, a Registered Firearms Dealer. Clients occasionally requested specialist weaponry for security purposes, and the RFD licence, along with a Department of Trade and Industry Export Licence where required, officially enabled Howard's company to supply it.

"Fine. Use Colombia. Ziggy can fix that when he comes back – he's doing some work for the authorities out there, with the British Government's blessing. You know, the drugs problem. The new Colombian Government is trying to stamp out the cartels. Come to think of it, Johnny knows the details too – get him to do it. And remember that we want two of these rifles, not one. Can you see any problem with the other gear he's asked for?"

Ackford scanned down the list, verbally ticking each item off. "A hundred rounds of ammo – two-hundred-and-fifty-grain full-metal-jacket boat-tail – OK, fifty rounds of armour-piercing incendiary OK, portable ballistic chronometer OK, scope mounts OK, Bausch and Lomb ten-by-forty Tactical sniper scope OK. Yeah, no problem with that. In fact, Accuracy will fix it all up and sight it in for the ammo, if I tell them we want it batched and calibrated. I shouldn't have to do any work on it. What's this scope like? I don't know it."

"It's a very good one, with very fine adjustments. Each click is one quarter of a minute of angle, instead of the more usual half or one MOA you get on most sniper scopes. That's two and a half inches per click adjustment at a thousand yards, instead of five or ten inches. It's much more precise."

"But sniper scopes have to have large click adjustments because the variations in trajectory are huge over these long ranges."

"Not this one. It has a full adjustment of over seventy MOA – more than enough. Anyway, we know the rough distance we'll be using it at. Danny can have a few practice shots with it before we

135

go. And don't forget the two spotter scopes. Thirty-to-sixty power, variable zoom, plus small tripods."

"OK, boss, I'll get on with it."

Howard slapped him on the back and returned next door, pleased at how things seemed to be progressing.

Usher came over to him. "These anemometers shouldn't be a problem, boss. Some of the modern ones give a digital read-out. It won't be difficult to convert that into a radio signal. I'd like to get Chris to help me with this, when he's free – he might have an idea or two. He's pretty hot on electronics."

"Excellent. But remember, they must be as small and inconspicuous as possible, and there must be enough battery life for forty-eight hours if necessary. Get some modeller's enamel paint and cam them up in matt khaki and sand colours. And pick a frequency that isn't likely to get any interference. Something slightly above the normal commercial VHF band, but below the international air band – say about a hundred and ten kilohertz. You'll have to do a bit of research on that. We don't want passing aircraft or whatever wondering what this strange electronic signal is."

"OK, I'll look into it. Hey, boss?"

"Yes, Bob?"

"You haven't forgotten Turkey, have you?" Usher grinned.

Howard smiled at the grim memory of the Turkish prison cell he had shared with Usher for six months. The tough, muscular ex-SAS man had been the perfect cellmate; despite the harsh regime of the prison and the poor diet, neither had even spoken a cross word to the other. Most of the other inmates had been so desperate that they had fought like rats, instead of sticking together and supporting one another. Howard was genuinely fond of Usher; an experience like that made one either a friend or an enemy for life. The mutual respect between them was unbreakable. "Don't worry, Bob," he said, grinning evilly. "I can guarantee you one thing, whatever happens. You won't lose any more hair, like you did there."

Usher laughed and jokingly punched him on the shoulder. "That's a weight off my mind, then," he said, "or perhaps in the circumstances that's a rather unfortunate expression. In case you hadn't noticed," he added sarcastically, "the last hair on my head gave up the unequal struggle some years ago."

24

On Thursday, Palmer telephoned Bourne from Dublin to announce success in locating a suitable aircraft. The normally impassive Rhodesian sounded delighted with his find; the plane, a twin-engined Pilatus Britten-Norman Islander BN2B-20, was in excellent condition and had recently been given a major overhaul. Tip tanks were not standard on the BN2B-20, but they had already been fitted to this one, giving it a total fuel capacity of 814 litres and a payload, with full tanks, of 966 pounds – 438 kilos. That gave a maximum VFR (visual flight rules) range, at the recommended economical cruising speed of 128 knots, of 1,075 nautical miles.

The Islander had almost all the other fittings required, including an autopilot; the only modifications Palmer would need to make would be to strip out the rear seats and install a GPS satellite-navigation system. The two rear doors, staggered on either side of the fuselage, were wide enough for cargo-loading, and the low-pressure tyres were suitable for soft-field operation in harsh environments; the Islander had been specifically designed to have a short-take-off-and-landing (STOL) capability and the BN2B-20 needed only two hundred and fifteen metres to take off and land.

"She's just about perfect for what we want, Johnny," said Palmer, concluding his run-down of the Islander's specifications. "I think we ought to move fast, and snap her up."

Bourne congratulated Palmer on his find. "Excellent work, Chris," he said. "Ed will be thrilled to hear about it. I'll come straight out to meet you tonight and close the deal."

Later that evening, Bourne flew out to Dublin. The next morning, in his "Bryce" disguise, he went with Palmer to meet the Islander's owners and set in motion the formalities for the transfer of funds and re-registration of ownership.

25

The big articulated lorry pulled into Loundis Road and drove slowly up towards the end. There was a loud hiss of air-brakes; the lorry-driver climbed out of his cab and rang the bell on the side-door of Unit 10. A round-faced man wearing jeans emerged through the door and introduced himself as Mr Bryce; he and the driver had a brief conversation. "Mr Bryce" started to raise the large roller door of the unit; the driver returned to the wheel.

Ten minutes later, the trailer had been reversed into the empty industrial unit and Mr Bryce was completing the paperwork, signing for the trailer and its cargo, an empty forty-foot freezer container. The lorry-driver disconnected the hydraulic, electric and air lines of the trailer from the Scania tractor unit and jacked up the forward strut wheels; collecting the signed documents from Mr Bryce, he climbed back into the cab and drove away.

Mr Bryce lowered the roller door, obscuring the trailer from outside view. He removed the cheek-pads, and became Johnny Bourne once again, then let himself out of the small side-door and went to fetch the others.

Usher, Harris and Howard walked slowly and in silence round the large yellow-painted container sitting on the trailer. Inside the building it looked enormous. Externally, it was forty feet long, eight feet wide and eight feet high. Ackford went to the rear end; pulling up a set of steps, he reached up and undid the two heavy loading doors. As he swung them back, he muttered a curse. "Sod it. They've had the damn thing switched on. It's bloody freezing in there. We'll have to wait until it warms up before I can start working on it. I'll leave these doors open."

"They probably thought we'd be loading it up straight away,

Tony," said Howard. "These things don't spend too much time sitting around empty, if the owners can help it."

"Well, it's certainly going to be sitting around empty *here* for quite a while. Anyway, we own it now, don't we? When I've finished with it, it'll be carrying a rather unusual cargo."

"We've got all the time we need, and more. In between working on this, most of us can even go back to our normal work with XF, to keep up appearances. There's nothing much more to do for the next three months or so. It'll be Christmas soon, and everyone can take the usual time off. If you need a hand with anything over the next couple of weeks, you can call on Chris and Andy when they've finished work on the plane. Mike too, when he gets back from the States. Give me a shout if you run into any problems. Have you got everything you need?"

"Everything's here, boss. There shouldn't be any problem." Ackford climbed down from the steps and went to the other end of the container to examine the protruding refrigeration unit itself. He frowned. "There's not as much space here as I thought there would be." He pulled out a tape measure. "The freezer unit takes up nearly the whole end. There's only twenty inches or so either side of it. The largest opening I'll be able to cut will be about eighteen inches wide. Is that going to be enough? What's the biggest item to go in?"

Howard thought about it. "The domestic refrigerator, I'd say. Everything else ought to fit. You'd better see what the actual opening is when you've stripped it down and cut it. If the fridge is too big, we'll have to get a smaller one. I'd rather not risk the noise involved in breaking it up, although we could do that if we have to. Of course, there might be access to the rear doors, but we can't guarantee that."

"I'll start on it tomorrow. It should have warmed up by then. I'll leave the building's heaters on overnight. By the way, boss," Ackford added, "I'd just as soon work on over Christmas and New Year if I haven't finished it by then. The wife'll be off on her annual pilgrimage to her family in Dublin, and I can't stand the thought of going there again. I hate sitting around on my arse watching everyone get pissed and stuffing themselves sick. Also, I won't be interrupted. Can you give me a chit or something I can show her to prove I'll be working?"

"OK, Tony." Howard smiled. "I'll fix something. But get the

noisy work done before the holiday, will you? I don't want too much attention drawn to this place."

The following morning, 10th December, Ackford started work on the container. Undoing the eight large bolts that held the refrigeration unit in place, he detached it from the front of the container. He left the unit suspended from the ten-ton hoist.

Over the next two weeks, working on the inside of the container, he turned his attention to the interior lining panels at the closed end. There were two alloy panels, each one just under three feet wide and seven feet high, separated by the ducting and air vents that circulated the cold air within the container. Examining them closely, he saw that the two panels were identical in size – nothing to choose between them. He decided to work on the right-hand one, and detached it carefully. Leaving the air ducting in place, he removed the insulating material between the panel and the outside steel skin of the container.

On the outside, he marked a line where one side of the freezer unit bolted on to the end of the container. He drilled two tiny holes through on this line, then went back inside. He marked the line between the two holes, and drilled further holes through from the inside, to mark the four corners of the opening to be made. Then he went outside again and marked up the lines between the holes. When he had finished, he fetched an electric saw, fitted a thin diamond-coated cutting blade, set it in a clamp, and began to cut very carefully through the steel skin of the container, along the lines he had drawn.

Christmas came and went; Ackford worked on. He was enjoying himself; he liked the peace and solitude. With no one to interrupt him, he made faster progress than he had anticipated. By Tuesday 31st December he had completed his work on the container; he went across to Unit 8 to fetch Bourne, who had dropped in briefly to collect the mail.

Bourne walked carefully round the container, inside and out. Finally, after examining it closely for ten minutes, he spread his upturned hands in a gesture of bafflement. "OK, Tony, I give up. I saw it when you had the freezer unit off, and I saw the hole you cut. But I'm buggered if I can see anything odd about it now. How does it work?"

Ackford grinned. "Come back inside, boss."

The two men climbed back into the container through the rear loading doors, and Ackford led the way down the inside to the front end.

His voice echoed inside the empty container. "OK. The freezer unit is on the outside of this end wall; you can see the air ducts behind these grilles, exactly as normal. The unit works by drawing in air, cooling it and pumping it round the inside, through these ducts. The unit can be set for either fresh or recirculated air. Some cargoes, like flower bulbs, need fresh air, others don't. Now, you see this panel here?" He indicated the right-hand panel; like the one on the left, which looked identical, it was held in place by screws. Ackford took out a screwdriver. "All the screws are dummies except for these three . . ." He selected the three screws, turned them each through ninety degrees, and then pulled. The entire panel hinged away, folding flat against the side wall.

"Now," he continued, "you can see the doorway I've cut in the outside steel shell of the container. The door is hinged near the ducts here, and these four clamps near the corner hold it in place." He indicated the heavy hinges near the ducts and the large steel clamps near the corner of the container. "If you unfasten the clamps the door opens outwards, forming an opening eighteen inches wide and seven feet high. I'm not going to demonstrate that now, as I've just finished filling and painting the outside."

Bourne was nodding his head as Ackford explained.

"The joins where I cut the door are sealed with filler, so it will be quite stiff to open. To help open it, I've welded on two large jacking points. A couple of car jacks, braced against these steel lugs, will be able to push it open, no problem. I've done a dummy run with it with filler set hard. It works fine. So, that's the hatch. Now . . ." He swung the lining panel shut again; it closed solidly. Ackford turned the three modified screws, locking it into place. "Right, let's go back outside again."

They climbed out and went round to inspect the freezer unit itself. Ackford uncoiled a cable and connected the unit to an electric power supply. The freezer's fan hummed noisily into life.

"Can you spot anything in there?" Shouting above the noise of the fan, he indicated the unit's motor housing.

"No, it all looks the same as before. Hey, turn that thing off. I can't hear myself think."

Ackford unplugged the lead. "Well, it looks the same, but it ain't.

Right, let me explain how this works. First of all, this isn't a normal sea-going refrigerated container — what they call a 'reefer'. This is a transport unit, the sort that goes on lorries. The reason we picked a transport unit is that a proper reefer has the whole end taken up by the freezer unit itself — in other words, there wouldn't have been any space for a door to be cut. So we picked one of these instead. It's got what's called a 'nose mount' — the unit sticks out, and it doesn't take up the whole front end, see? But the principle is the same, and these units can go on ships, just like proper reefers. This unit has two power sources — a diesel motor here for when it's standing alone, and an electric one. The electric one can be hooked up to the reefer point on a ship, just the same. The power supply is four hundred and sixty volts. Can you see anything funny about this unit?"

Bourne looked closely and shook his head. "It all looks perfectly normal to me. But then I'm no expert."

"Actually, hardly anything has been changed," said Ackford. "The fan still works, as you heard, but I've made one or two small alterations. For a start, I've set it to blow fresh air, not recirculated." He unbolted the unit's grille, exposing the machinery inside. "Can you see anything now?"

Bourne was still none the wiser. "I can't see anything odd about it. Just a freezer motor, condensers, pipes and things."

"What do you suppose these two gizmos are?" Ackford indicated two smaller items nestling amidst the freezer unit's machinery, connected to separate pipes, tubes and wires.

"Oh, of course. I've got it. Now I know what I'm looking for, I've got it. That's where you've put them."

"I was thinking of putting them inside somewhere to start with, but then I had a thought. Why not put them here? Unless you were actually looking for them, you'd never spot them. And there's an added bonus — they'll drip, just like the freezer unit would if it was working properly."

"Got it. And the thermometer?"

"Here, on the outside. I'm rather pleased with this part." Ackford swung the grille and cover back over the freezer unit, bolting them into place. The thermostat dial and the read-out of the interior temperature were visible for inspection. "All I did was take the thermostat to bits and reassemble it with the wrong setting. When it's set on minus twenty Centigrade, it will actually maintain a temperature inside of *plus* twenty – normal room temperature instead of deep-freeze. I've also fixed the thermometer read-out to give the wrong reading – it will say that the interior is cold when it isn't. You can see – it says minus twenty-two at the moment."

"Ack, it's brilliant. It's a fantastic job. You'd never know, to look at it." Bourne peered closely at the outside of the steel container, below the freezer unit. "I can't see the join of the new doorway at all." He ran his finger over it to feel for any raised metal.

"Aw, watch out, boss, the paint's still wet . . ." Ackford grinned as Bourne's hand came away with a smear of paint on it. "Look what you've gone and done. Ruined me paintwork. I'll have to retouch it."

"Sorry, Tony." He wiped his hand on his jeans. "I haven't wrecked it, have I?"

"Nah. The filler's hard, that what matters. It'll only take a couple of minutes to repaint it."

"Well, Ed's going to be delighted. It's a marvellous job."

"He's coming down next week to see it. Then we can start fitting it out and loading it up. Shouldn't take long. A week, maybe two."

"And that's it? Nothing left to do after that?"

"Only the rifle, when it comes. We'll have to get our Scotsman down so that he and I can go over the details. Besides, it's about time we met the guy."

"Yes," said Bourne. "I must admit I'm curious to meet him, too. Well, Tony, I suggest you take a few days off now. You've earned it, and there's nothing else to do. I'll see you on Monday."

Ackford nodded. "Yeah, I suppose I ought to go and drop in on me mum and dad for New Year. See how they're getting on, like. The wife's still away in Ireland."

When Bourne had left, Ackford finished retouching the paintwork on the container, locked up and headed west along the M4. Pulling into the Leigh Delamere service area, in the large car-park he transferred from the Vauxhall Astra he had bought – for cash – into his own Honda Civic. He rejoined the motorway, and twenty minutes later turned off on to the M5, southbound. He arrived at his parents' house in Taunton at five that afternoon.

Seven hours later the various team members – with the exception of Mike Ziegler, who was still away in the USA – celebrated the arrival of the new year in their own ways, scattered around the country. Tony

Ackford took his parents out to their local pub for a quiet drink; Mel Harris and his wife went to a party given by friends in Worcester; Bob Usher, further north in Manchester, was in bed with his girlfriend, a pretty blonde not much more than half his age; Johnny Bourne, in his London flat, opened a bottle of champagne and toasted the future with the newly-promoted Detective Inspector Juliet Shelley; and Andy Denard dragged Chris Palmer off to Trafalgar Square where, for once, there were few serious incidents of drunkenness and injury – although Palmer had to restrain the exuberant pilot from stripping off and attempting to jump into one of the fountains.

Ed Howard spent the midnight hour alone, in his flat in Wandsworth. A glass of whisky in his hand, he sat thinking, his dark eyes expressionless and his mind far away. As the last chime of Big Ben sounded over the radio, he wondered briefly how 1992 would turn out. A thin smile crossed his mouth, and he raised his glass. *Here's to your fifty-fifth birthday*, Saddam, he thought to himself. *We'll be there to celebrate it with you, you vicious bastard. We're going to come and spoil your party.*

26

On the morning of Monday 6th January 1992, Bourne collected the mail from the box inside each of the three industrial units and went into the inner office of Unit 8. He sat down at the desk and started flipping through the letters. Much of the correspondence appeared to be a backlog from before Christmas; there were a few of the dummy letters he regularly posted himself from London to give the postman the impression that the three companies were busy; and the remainder consisted of December's bank statements, three telephone bills and the quarterly electricity bills for each unit.

The last letter in the pile caught his eye; it was postmarked Portsmouth. He opened it; it was from Accuracy International, informing "Mr Arndale" that his order for two rifles was ready for collection.

He called Ackford in. "Tony, this is where I'm afraid one of us is going to have to go legit. I'll do it myself. We won't be able to take delivery of these without the XF Securities dealer's ticket. You spoke to them before – could you ring your contact down there and let him know to expect me?"

Ackford made the telephone call, and Bourne departed for London in his BMW. At the Heathrow Airport long-term car-park he removed his contact lenses and cheek-pads and transferred as usual into his own Alfa Romeo, leaving the BMW in a vacant parking space nearby. It was an extremely expensive place to store a car – one or other of the two was there the whole time – but the thousands of other cars guaranteed anonymity. Bourne rejoined the M4, transferred briefly to the M25, then took the turning to the M3 to Southampton and the M27 to Portsmouth.

By four in the afternoon, he had transferred back to the BMW at Heathrow and returned to Swindon with two long, slim cases and a smaller, heavy box. Inside Unit 8, he and Ackford opened them up.

Ackford's eyes widened as he saw the two big rifles. "Oh, boy. Now that is what I call workmanship." He picked up one of the two heavy rifles and worked the bolt action. "Just feel that. No doubt about what this was built to do."

"Quite something," Bourne agreed. "But don't get too attached to them. Remember what you've got to do to one of them."

"It'll be an act of vandalism, boss. I'm not sure I can bring myself to do it."

"The best way is to get on with it right now. Drill out that breech block tonight, and weld up the firing pin. Plug the barrel tomorrow Then you can get on with preparing the other one for our sniper to use."

"But which one, boss?" pleaded Ackford. "These are both works of art."

"What are the serial numbers?" Bourne quickly checked the serial numbers engraved on the barrels of the two weapons. "OK; this makes your job easier. Not only are they consecutive numbers, but they end in '8' and '9' respectively. That settles it. Here's '9'. Go and start wrecking it, right now. Internal only, of course. Make it a neat job – just enough to pass inspection. It's still got to look good from the outside."

Ackford departed with the rifle, looking mournful. A few minutes later, as Bourne was locking the other rifle and the heavy box of ammunition into the safe in Unit 8, he heard the whine of a high-powered drill as Ackford set about turning a brand-new, state-of-the-art rifle into a deadly-looking but worthless piece of scrap metal.

By Wednesday morning, the job was finished. Ackford handed the now useless rifle to Bourne, who set off in the BMW to the Birmingham Proof House. Returning that afternoon, he gave the rifle back to Ackford. "OK, Tony, it passed. I've got the Deactivation Certificate for it. Now change that '9' to an '8'. I'll get on with the Export Licence papers."

Bourne sat down in the office and began filling out the three required copies of the Department of Trade and Industry Export Licence application form, entering the details of the rifle and those of the Colombian Governmental firearms dealer with whom XF

146

Securities did regular official business. On his way back to London that evening, he posted the forms with the necessary accompanying documentation.

The application would take four weeks to process; a licence would be granted for the export of the Accuracy International rifle whose serial number ended in "8". The deactivated rifle, "9", with its serial number carefully altered to "8" by Ackford's engraving, would be air-freighted to the Colombian dealer. Customs at Heathrow would give the weapon a cursory inspection to satisfy themselves that the details were correct; they would note that the serial number, make and calibre were as entered on the form. They would not examine the rifle to check that it actually worked. Why should they? Who would go to the bother of filling out a DTI Export Licence application for a rifle that didn't work and therefore needed no licence at all? The arrival of the rifle would puzzle the Colombian dealer, who would immediately notice that it was inoperable. Bourne would telephone the dealer to confirm the error and advise him to scrap it. As far as the British authorities were concerned, rifle "8" – the one that worked – had been exported and would therefore be removed from the UK records; meanwhile rifle "9" had officially ceased to exist as a firearm – there was a Deactivation Certificate to prove it. The switch would not come to light.

*   *   *

MacDonald arrived in London on Tuesday 14th January on the overnight sleeper train from Fort William. Howard collected him from King's Cross Station and drove him out to Swindon, where the rest of the team, less Ziegler, were assembled, curious to meet the stalker. Howard introduced them to him, one by one, explaining each of their specialities.

The last man he came to was Ackford. "Tony is our armourer. He's ready to fit the rifle to your measurements whenever you are."

Ackford and MacDonald disappeared next door into Unit 9, locked in conversation about weapons in general and the big Super Magnum rifle in particular.

Howard waited until they had gone, then turned to the others. "Well, Tony seems to be getting on well with him already," he said. "What do the rest of you think of him?"

147

"He seems OK," began Harris. "He looks steady and alert, and if you say he can shoot, well . . ."

"I liked him," Denard broke in. "He looks you in the eye. He seems a direct, no-nonsense type. I think he'll do pretty well."

"But he's never seen action, boss?" Usher wanted to know. "How do you reckon his nerve will stand up to it? And is he fit?"

"Oh, he should be pretty fit," Howard reassured him. "Unfit deer-stalkers don't keep their jobs for long. And he's got good nerves, from what I've seen. He's a very determined fellow. I've got a feeling he'll do just fine, even though it'll be his first taste of real action." He paused, thinking back to his own first experience of active service. He remembered the doubts he had had about how he would react to the ultimate test – staring death in the face, and inflicting it on someone else. The problem was, one could never really tell for certain how others would react. Some of the meekest and most unlikely men came through with flying colours – cool, calm and disciplined – while others, apparently confident and able soldiers, simply went to pieces. It was unpredictable, but after a while one got an instinctive feel for how each man would react – often long before the man knew himself. He looked at Usher again, and nodded. "Yes, Bob, I think he'll do OK. Now; I've got some more news. Mike is on his way back. He sounded pretty pleased with himself when I talked to him on the phone. I think he must have got everything we wanted."

"Even the night-vision goggles?" asked Bourne. "The crafty bugger. He'll have had to call in a few favours to pull that off."

"I hope not *too* many favours," replied Howard. "But Mike knows enough not to attract too much attention to himself. He said there shouldn't be any problem with the new satnav gear, so I assume he's got that too. Anyway, we'll have to wait and see. When he gets here, I'm going to send him off up to Scotland with Danny. The rifle will need sighting in and zeroing. Danny has a place in mind on the Glen Carvaig estate, way up in the hills, where they'll be able to do it without being bothered. It'll give Mike a chance to suss him out, and see whether he's as fit as he seems."

There were nods of assent and approval all round, and the team went back to work on the fitting-out of the freezer container.

*　　　*　　　*

Ziegler arrived back the next day, the 15th, and drove straight from the airport down to Swindon.

"I got it all, Ed. You can tell Johnny to expect it to arrive air-freight next week. Eight AH-64 Apache pilots' helmets and four pocket calculators. No sweat at all."

"The NVGs are fitted to the helmets? That's terrific, Mike. How did you do it?"

"Don't ask, buddy. Don't ask. Let's just leave it that an old acquaintance of mine had to make a very difficult choice about his future." Ziegler grinned.

Howard shuddered. "OK, OK, I don't want to know. What's this about pocket calculators?"

"The latest Navstar GPS equipment. It's incredibly small. I'd expected somethin' about the size of a shoe-box, but these babies are hand-held. They're only Q-code, but that saved on the size and they give you your position accurate to one hundred metres, anywhere in the world. The P-code is accurate to ten metres, but it's heavily restricted to the military. The other problem with P-code is that you need four satellites above the horizon, not just the two you need for the Q-code. Anyhow, there are four units coming."

"So it seems you have been doing some work, after all. I had visions of you swanning around in the sun somewhere. OK; I've got a reward for you – you're going on a nice little holiday to Scotland for a couple of days. I've got just the man to show you the sights. Come and meet him."

*   *   *

It was still dark when Ziegler and MacDonald set off for Scotland in Ziegler's Ford Sierra the following Sunday, 19th January. Taking great care not to attract the attention of the police, they drove steadily for ten hours before reaching their destination. The two men spoke little during the journey; Ziegler's initial attempts at light conversation had met with taciturn responses. He realised that MacDonald was very much a loner, a man whose shell would be difficult to penetrate.

They arrived at MacDonald's cottage near Fort William at five in the afternoon; MacDonald made a brief telephone call to Duncan Macrae, then began preparing a meal.

"Duncan says it'll be just fine for us to go up to the loch tomorrow," he reported to Ziegler. "We can use one of the Argocats, if we want."

"Aw, why don't we walk, Mac?" asked Ziegler, lightly. "I wouldn't mind the exercise."

MacDonald shot him a glance. "If you like," he replied. "But it's a little way up the glen, and we'll be carrying a fair amount."

"I don't mind, if you don't," said Ziegler. For a moment, watching MacDonald studying him, Ziegler thought he saw some hesitation on the stalker's face; then he realised. *I'll be damned*, he thought. *This Scotchman is actually wondering whether I'm in good enough shape for a little walk!* He grinned. "Yeah, I feel like I could do with a work-out."

MacDonald nodded, saying nothing. The ice had not yet been broken between them; the stalker was still wary.

The two men set off from the cottage at six the next morning. In the back of the car were a bulging rucksack and an H-frame carrier with the larger items strapped to it; each load weighed nearly seventy pounds. The heaviest item, in the rucksack, was a large, lead-acid battery; the most awkward and delicate, also heavy and strapped to the H-frame with the rifle case, was a three-foot-long metal cylinder with rubber eyepieces, a heavy tripod and various accessories, all painted a dull battleship grey. "It's an old range-finder," explained MacDonald. "It belongs to my uncle."

"Looks like it belongs in a museum," muttered Ziegler. "Are you sure it works?"

They left the Sierra at the lodge. It was 6.30, long before dawn, and the January air was cold, crisp and still. They hefted the two weighty loads on to their shoulders and set off along the track up the glen, MacDonald leading.

The stalker started off at a good fast walk. After half a mile, hearing no signs of distress behind him, he increased his pace. Ziegler kept up with him without apparent effort. MacDonald could hear that the American was not even breathing hard; he increased his pace again. They reached the head of the glen, after ten miles of steady but gentle climbing, in an hour and forty-five minutes. They had climbed six hundred feet, and now a the higher altitude there was a light dusting of snow on the track. Neither man had given way; both had pushed themselves hard. It was still dark.

"It gets steeper now. About five miles to go. The ground is a little rough in places – you'll need to mind your ankles."

"No problem, Mac."

Off the track now, the going was much slower; the snow covering became thicker as they climbed. The two men laboured hard up the steep hill under their heavy loads, occasionally sinking knee-deep into the snow. Both were feeling the exertion by the time they reached the top, twelve hundred feet above the pony stable where Howard had eaten his beef sandwiches three weeks earlier. The remainder of the walk was on steeply undulating ground; MacDonald picked an unerring path over the rough terrain, avoiding the worst of the peat hags beneath the snow. When they finally came to the place they had been aiming for, high in the hills, it was nearly ten o'clock. The fifteen-mile walk had taken them three and a half hours. A reasonable degree of fitness would have been required for anyone to do the walk in that time in daylight and without carrying any load; they had done it in the dark and with seventy pounds each on their backs.

With the advent of dawn Ziegler could now see the ground they had covered. In front of them was a freshwater loch, stretching out a mile long before them; mostly free of ice, and surrounded by the snow-covered peaks of the hills, it was a smooth, inky-black surface in the silent white landscape. He drank in the scenery. "Why have I never come here before? This place is just *beautiful*, Mac. Fantastic."

MacDonald glanced at him and smiled. "Aye, I love it up here in the hills myself."

The two men started to unpack some of the equipment, including the big lead-acid battery, the rifle, the ballistic chronometer and the range-finder, which MacDonald set up on its tripod on a grassy knoll by the side of the loch. Ziegler set off along the bank of the loch with a wooden target frame and a two-way radio. After a hundred paces he turned and held the target frame vertically while MacDonald took a sighting through the range-finder. MacDonald called him back four paces, took another sighting, then pronounced himself satisfied. Ziegler planted the spike of the frame firmly into the ground. The target was eighteen inches wide and five feet high, and painted bright yellow; six inches above the bottom edge was a tiny

151

half-inch black square, as an aiming mark. Before they left Swindon, Ziegler had asked why the targets had to be yellow, instead of the more usual white; the snow-covered ground now made the reason obvious. He walked back to the firing point.

MacDonald had laid the rifle out on the grassy knoll, extending its two forward bipod legs. The barrel and action were wrapped in an electric blanket which was powered by the lead-acid battery. He set up the chronometer just in front of the knoll; a bullet passing over the looped sensors would give a velocity reading. He began filling a sandbag with fine gravel from the bank of the loch.

"Perfect for zeroing – no wind at all," he observed. "We'll not be needing the anemometers." He examined the barometer and the thermometer, and consulted a notebook. Each page was covered with figures. "These are the ballistic tables I've worked out for this altitude and these conditions. I'm going to set the elevation drum for twelve hundred yards now. At only a hundred yards, the bullet should go exactly thirty-five and a half inches high of the aiming mark." Reaching for the thermometer, he checked the temperature inside the rifle barrel, then unwrapped the electric blanket and lay down with the rifle on the firing point, using the sandbag as a rest. Both men donned protective ear-muffs.

The report of the rifle echoed and rolled around the hills above the loch. MacDonald unloaded and Ziegler studied the read-out on the chronometer. "Two thousand, nine hundred and forty-six feet per second," he declared.

"That's very good," said MacDonald, sounding pleased. "I'll fire one more."

The read-out for the second shot gave a muzzle velocity of two thousand nine hundred and sixty feet per second; MacDonald was delighted. "That really is very consistent – and it's right in line with the manufacturer's figures of two-nine-five-three." He laid down the rifle, wrapping it again in the electric blanket to prevent the barrel from cooling in the chill January air.

The two men walked over to the target. Ziegler's eyebrows shot up when he saw the two closely-grouped bullet-holes. "That's some shootin', Mac," he exclaimed. "A half-inch group! That's amazin' for a heavy rifle."

MacDonald used a tape to measure the position of the group relative to his aiming mark. It was thirty-four and a half inches high, and just half an inch to the left. He was visibly pleased. "Well, Accuracy International certainly know what they're doing. This rifle has been beautifully set up. At this rate, we'll not take very long to get it zeroed."

The two men returned to the firing point. MacDonald removed the two waterproof caps from the zeroing drums of the telescopic sight. He turned the vertical adjustment four clicks up, and the horizontal drum two clicks to the right; then he replaced the caps on the drums.

"I'll take two more shots to confirm this," he said. "If it's on, we can move straight out to twelve hundred."

The next two shots hit the target so close together that Ziegler could only just tell through the spotter scope that there wasn't only one hole. The chronometer gave muzzle-velocity readings even closer than the previous ones.

When they went forward to inspect the target, MacDonald was clearly more than satisfied. "I've never had a rifle zero so well, first time. This is amazing. Look – it's exactly on the thirty-five-and-a-half inch mark. All I need to do now is adjust the scope eight clicks left for the Magnus effect at twelve hundred yards."

"Well," commented Ziegler, "it can't just be the rifle. In my book that is real fancy shootin', Mac. I never saw anythin' quite as good as that before."

They returned to the firing point again and Ziegler collected the components of a second target frame. Taking the walkie-talkie radio, he set off along the shore of the loch at an easy jog, leaving MacDonald at the firing point. Ten minutes later, he came to a small promontory which they had measured on the map to be about twelve hundred yards from the firing point. He assembled the target: a wooden frame four feet square, with tightly stretched yellow-painted canvas. In the centre of the canvas was the aiming mark, a black circle six inches in diameter. He called MacDonald on the radio and held the target frame still for the range-finder.

A minute later, MacDonald's voice came over the radio in reply. "I measure that at twelve thirty-five. Come back this way thirty-five paces and I'll take another sight."

In a matter of minutes the posts of the target frame had been hammered into the ground, exactly twelve hundred yards from the firing point. Ziegler took cover behind a boulder ten yards away and reported that he was ready. In his hand he held an electronic split-time stop-watch. Thirty seconds later, there was a whiplash crack as the bullet passed him; instantly, he pressed the start button on the stop-watch. A second and a half later there was a distant thump as the sound of the muzzle blast of the rifle caught up. He stopped the timer and picked up the two-way radio. "Mac? That was 1.46 seconds. Is that right?"

"At this altitude, yes. The bullet took 1.75 seconds, and the sound 3.21. That means the sound of the muzzle blast arrives just under a second and a half after the bullet. Where did the shot go?"

Ziegler walked over to the frame. At first he could see no mark on it; then he noticed the hole. He let out a low whistle. "Jeez, Mac. You hit the black. First time, for Chrissake! It's seven o'clock of centre, right on the edge of the black circle."

"Fine. I'll take three more shots now, to get a four-round group."

MacDonald took his time between the shots; he had used the electric blanket to prevent the rifle from becoming cold, and now he did not want the barrel to heat up too much from firing. Keeping an eye on the thermometer, he let the temperature of the steel drop back to sixty degrees Fahrenheit each time.

As the report of the last shot died away, Ziegler walked back to the target. The four shots were in a five-inch group; the centre of the group was just below the black, five inches from the centre of the six-inch circle, and three inches to the left. "Hell, Mac," he reported over the radio, "I know plenty of guys who would be happy to get a group like that at *two* hundred yards, let alone *twelve* hundred. This is unbelievable shooting, man."

"Thanks. I'm going to do some final adjustments, then take three more shots. With luck, that'll be enough. You can patch those holes now." MacDonald put down the radio and once more removed the caps on the drums of the telescopic sight. He turned the vertical adjustment two clicks up and the horizontal adjustment one click to the right; then he replaced the caps.

Ziegler covered the three bullet-holes with small paper stickers and retired behind the rock. When MacDonald had fired four more shots, the American went over to the frame. His jaw dropped as he saw the result. He spoke into the radio. "Mac, I just don't believe what I'm seein' here. You've shot a three-inch group, smack in the middle of the black. At this distance, that is just goddam incredible. I guess we're through here, right?"

"Yes, that'll do! It's gone very well indeed." MacDonald's elation was evident in his voice. "This is a hell of a fine rifle, and that ammunition is more consistent than any I've come across before. I think you could say we're in business!"

By the time Ziegler rejoined him, MacDonald had finished packing up the rucksack and the rifle was once again secure in its hard, padded case, strapped to the H-frame carrier. The American grabbed MacDonald by the hand and shook it enthusiastically, a broad grin on his face. "Mac, for a Scotchman, you are one hell of a guy. That is just . . . hell, for once, words fail me."

"You're not so bad yourself, Yank." MacDonald smiled. "But you mean *Scots*, not Scotch. Scotch is the whisky." He pulled a small pewter hip-flask out of the pocket of his tweed jacket. "Or maybe you do mean Scotch, at that. Will you take a dram?"

Ziegler took a mouthful from the flask. In the exhilaratingly cold, clean air of the hills it seemed to him the finest drink he had ever tasted. He gave a sigh of appreciation and handed the flask back to MacDonald.

They loaded the two packs on to their shoulders. Before they set off, MacDonald turned to Ziegler. "Mike, I'd just as soon not make a competition out of getting back down the hill in the fastest possible time, if it's all the same to you. I don't want to run the risk of jolting the rifle and knocking the scope off true. The scope and mounts are very sturdy, but even a small movement could put it out and I don't want to risk it. Anyway, you've shown me you're a pretty fit fellow. I'd like to have you out on the hill one day, after a stag. Then I can see how *you* shoot. You seem to know a wee bit about it."

Ziegler laughed out loud. "As a matter of fact, I used to count myself pretty goddam handy with a rifle – until today, that is. I'm just not even in your *league*, Scotchman. And I'd count it a privilege to go out deer-huntin' with you one day. Anyway, sure, let's by all means take it easy on the way down. You damn near killed me, comin' up."

The ice was broken. The two men chatted easily on the descent, elated with the success of the day's work, exulting in the splendour of the harsh winter scenery and the occasional glimpses of deer in the distance. They swapped stories and anecdotes; both men were

155

natural story-tellers. One of Ziegler's more revolting accounts of his time in Vietnam, a tale involving a deep-trench latrine, some wild pigs, a red-smoke-discharger and a number of senior officers, had MacDonald crying with laughter. They were back at the lodge well before five o'clock; they had walked thirty miles with the heavy loads, but neither man felt particularly tired. Their friendship was sealed.

The next morning Ziegler loaded up the Sierra with the rifle and other equipment for the journey back south.

MacDonald waved him off from the door of the small cottage. "Take care now, Mike. Safe driving."

"Sure thing. We'll meet again in about a month's time. It's been great to get to know you, *Scotch*man."

"You too, *Yank*," grinned MacDonald.

27

"Pour yourself a drink, Johnny." Howard gestured towards the cabinet in the corner of the room.

"Thanks." Bourne poured himself a shot of whisky and sat down. "Well, here's to the great project. So far, so good." He raised his glass.

"Yes, it's all been going well. Not much more to do before we go. When's our American pilot arriving?"

"Mel rang him yesterday. He's coming over in just under three weeks' time, on 28th March. Apparently he's raring to go."

"Must be the thought of that ninety thousand dollars. It's funny to think I might never have to meet him. How about visas?"

"All applied for. Sullivan is going on Darcon documents which we've knocked up for him; glowing testimonials for the rest of us from PAP." Pan-Arabian Petroleum was another client of XF Securities; Bourne had made use of his access to PAP's London office to lift sufficient details of previous employees' Saudi visa applications, and had prepared statements of employment by PAP for the other team members.

"You think they'll all be granted OK?"

"We've been very thorough – we've had to be. Saudi's one of the most difficult places to get a visa for. No tourists are allowed; just bona fide businessmen and pilgrims to Mecca. That's it. You have to have a cast-iron reason for going, and unimpeachable supporting documentation, including a full medical report. And that includes proof of an AIDS test. But PAP and Darcon are highly respected businesses out there and their employees have never had any trouble."

"Good. Talking of Darcon, what about the second set of documents – the ones for the project boss out there? Is everything fixed with him?"

"Tony Hughes? Yes – he's fine. He doesn't suspect a thing. The fax message he's had from me looks convincingly as if it came from Dartington – we copied his style from the ones you nicked. We had a little competition to see who could forge Dartington's signature best; Bob won. As far as Hughes is concerned, Dartington has authorised a team of surveyors to come out and look at a confidential new project, and Hughes is to offer all the facilities requested. I thought it might put his nose out of joint, but it hasn't at all. He's been very helpful. I followed up the fax with a phone call, telling Hughes what we'd need. He's letting us use that old construction camp we wanted, and he's arranging for the vehicles and other things I asked for. From his point of view it's all pretty straightforward."

"Have you met Hughes before? Will he recognise you?"

"No. We've only spoken on the phone. The only people he'll see will be me and Chris, and we'll have false ID to show him. He'll believe we're who we say we are – why shouldn't he? There won't be any reason for him to suspect that we got into the country under different names as employees of a different company."

"Fine. What about the arrangements in Mombasa?"

"All fixed. The agent out there knows what we need. He'll get all the stuff together and make sure it's ready. He doesn't have a clue what it's about. Mel will get in touch with him from Jeddah to check that everything goes OK. Anyway, if the agent gets anything wrong we've left enough time to sort it out later. And if the worst comes to the worst, there's always the 'lost passport' dodge, which ought to work in Sudan."

"I don't want to do that unless I really have to. Now, listen, Johnny," – Howard cracked his knuckle-joints – "the time's drawing near. We ought to make a final decision soon about whether you are coming with us."

Bourne's eyebrows shot up in surprise. "Hey, Ed, I thought that was all settled. I'm all ready. You can't leave me behind now."

"I know, Johnny, I know. And believe me, I don't want to. But I don't want to take you unless you're one-hundred-per-cent certain about what you're doing. You've got other responsibilities too, to your fiancée."

"Ed, I'm sure. One hundred per cent. Besides, you need me."

"That's just it, Johnny. I don't want you to think you are indispensable. You're the best for the job, but you're not indispensable."

Bourne's eyes narrowed in anger. He leaned forward in his chair. "You've talked to someone else, haven't you? Who? Come on, Ed, who?"

"Yes, I have talked to someone else. He's prepared to step in if you can't make it. He's someone I knew many years ago, before my SBS days."

"Who is he, Ed?"

"It doesn't matter, Johnny. All I'm saying is that he would do, at a pinch. His Arabic's pretty good – not as good as yours, but it would do – and he has one other advantage. He's a good rifle shot. Better than you, me or even Mike. If something untoward were to happen to our Scotsman on the way in, he might be able to do the job. But I would prefer you, any time. All I'm saying is, if you're only doing this because you don't want to let us down, you don't have to."

"Bullshit, Ed! Don't you dare leave me out, not now after all this! Who is this other guy, anyway? Are you telling me he's got no ties at all, not even a girlfriend?"

"Actually, he's married. But then so are Mel and Tony."

"Oh, come *on*, Ed! You're lecturing *me* about *my* responsibilities, and at the same time you're prepared to take on someone in my place who's *married*? Next you'll be telling me he's got children!"

"Well . . ." Howard grinned. "OK, I give up. I'm very glad to, too. But you see why I had to mention it. I had to be sure you really want to do this."

"How could you have doubted it?" Bourne smiled broadly; his anger had disappeared as suddenly as it had arisen. Howard had a healthy respect for Bourne's mercurial swings in mood, and at least there was no side to him – he was up-front with his hot temper and his emotions. With Johnny Bourne, you got what you saw. Oh well, thought Howard, one day he'd quieten down and learn to control himself better. Maybe.

28

The chill March rain lashed down; the thunderstorm was one of unusual ferocity. The suddenness of the downpour had caught the two running figures by surprise, but they were laughing, splashing through the water already pouring down the track.

Then the girl slipped and fell. She cried out, and the man stopped and turned round. He went back to her. She was sitting on a rock by the side of the track, clutching her left knee; the wet denim of her jeans was torn and there was a streak of blood mingling with the rainwater. She set her jaw and tried to stand, but winced, giving another little cry. The man caught her before she fell a second time; he picked her up in his arms. She felt very small and light. "Come on," he said, "I'll carry you. Let's get inside that stable before we both drown."

"Oh, thank you, Danny," cried Sheila Cameron, biting her lip; the pain from her knee was sharp. "That was silly of me – and we only had a little bit further to go . . ."

Danny MacDonald glanced briefly down at her as he strode along the sodden track, carrying her against his chest. Her hair was soaked, plastered to her face and neck, and she suddenly looked as young and vulnerable as ever he remembered. He reached the stable, undid the hasp and pushed the door open. Inside, out of the rain, he set her down on a stack of straw bales and shook the streaming water from his eyes. "Bloody hell!" he said. "That's some storm. Now, let's have a look at your knee."

"Mum will kill me for this," moaned Sheila as he took out his gralloching knife and carefully enlarged the hole in the knee of her jeans to examine the cut. Her teeth were chattering from the cold; she began to shiver.

Danny looked up at her face. She really *was* cold, he thought.

"Here," he said, taking off his tweed jacket. "It's wet, but it'll still be warm." She let him wrap it round her shoulders.

"What about you, Danny?" she asked. "You've only got a shirt now, and it's soaked through . . ."

"Och, I'll be fine," he said. He glanced out of the door. The rain was coming down in torrents. He shut the door, rolling a large stone against it to keep it closed. "I think we'd better stay here a while, until it eases off." It was another four miles down to the lodge. He looked at the girl again; she was shivering uncontrollably. He frowned. "I'll light a fire," he said. "That'll help to dry you out a bit."

The small stable was a long-disused cottage; it had once been inhabited, but for many years now had served only as a store and pony shelter, a staging post half-way up the glen. On one end wall was an old fire-grate; Danny pulled a thick handful of straw from one of the bales, then started breaking up the rotting remains of a discarded piece of furniture. The straw flared as he lit it; soon the old dry wood began to spit and crackle.

"This should do us fine," he smiled at the girl, "just so long as a jackdaw hasn't taken up residence in the chimney and blocked it with a nest." For a few seconds thick smoke billowed out into the stable; then the fire started to draw and the smoke began to disappear up the chimney. "Aye, she'll be fine now. Come on," he said, picking Sheila up again, "let's be moving you nearer to the heat."

He kicked a couple of straw bales over to within a few feet of the fire-grate, and set her down on one. She was still trembling with cold, her arms wrapped tightly round her body under his jacket.

"I'm sorry, Sheila," he said gently, bending down to examine her knee again, "that was a bloody stupid thing for me to do, to let you get caught out in this weather. I should have seen it coming. You're drenched, and you look frozen. Are you all right?"

She looked at him and managed a smile. "It's just as much my fault as yours, Danny," she said through chattering teeth. "It was kind of you to carry me."

He banked up the fire; it began to burn fiercely, but the stable was cold inside and Sheila continued to shake. He sat down beside her on the straw bale and put his arm affectionately round her shoulders. Heated by the fire, their wet clothes began to give off steam. The thick smell of the stable and the damp tweed filled their nostrils.

The girl snuggled up to him; he was used to feeling protective towards her. Her head leaned on his shoulder, then lifted again. "Danny, your shirt's all wet and horrible. Take it off and dry it."

He looked at her for a moment, then stood up and took off his shirt, wringing it out and hanging it on a low wooden rafter near the fire. Her eyes never left him. "Look," he said eventually, "you ought to do the same. It'll do you no good sitting there in soaking wet clothes. Don't worry – I won't look. I'll turn the other way. Take them off and hang them up, then put my jacket around you again. You'll warm up more quickly like that. Here – let me help you with your boots." He unlaced her boots, pulled them off, then peeled off her socks. His mind went back to when he had done the same thing for her many years before, when she had been a child of six and had cried when she had fallen into a burn. He had been fifteen; he had lifted her out. Now, as then, he wrung out her woollen socks and hung them up. Her feet were cold; he held them in his hands, rubbing the circulation back into them, then stood up and turned away. "I won't look," he said again.

Sheila began to undress in front of the fire. Danny heard her shudder with disgust as she pulled off her sodden shirt and dropped it on to the straw bale. There was a little exclamation of pain as she forced the wet jeans down over the injured knee, then a shiver as she wrapped his tweed jacket round her shoulders. She sat back down on the straw bale. "Ouch! This straw is prickly!" She giggled. "All right, Danny, you can turn round now."

She sounded more cheerful now, thought Danny. He turned to see her slight figure huddled in his thick tweed jacket, her bare legs stretched out towards the fire. His jacket reached almost to her knees. The fire was burning strongly now, but nearly half of the old side-table had already gone on to it. Danny looked up to the space above the bare rafters. Laid across them were some lengths of old timber; he reached up and pulled some of them down. With sharp kicks he smashed them into pieces, then stacked them up near the fire. He squeezed the water out of Sheila's shirt and jeans and hung them up on the rafters.

The stable was beginning to warm up; Sheila's trembling subsided. "When did you last have this old jacket cleaned, Danny? It smells like something died in it!"

Danny grinned, glancing down at her. "What did you expect, girl? I can't afford to have the thing dry-cleaned after every day out on the hill, can I? It's got sweat, sheepshit, stagshit, blood, peat hag . . ."

"Oh!" said Sheila, pulling a face. "Don't be so disgusting!" Then she smiled. "Come and sit down here and keep me warm!"

He sat down, leaning over again to look at her knee. "Doesn't look too bad," he pronounced. "Can you move it?"

She straightened the knee, wincing, but nodding. "It'll be OK. It's just a bruise and a cut. It may be sore for a while, but I'll be fine when I warm up." She looked directly at him. "Thank you for looking after me, Danny," she said softly.

He smiled hesitantly and stood up to put some more wood on the fire, then sat down again and gazed into the flames. "I always used to, Sheila," he said, "or at least, I hope I did."

"Would you put your arm round me again, Danny? I'm still cold."

He did so, still staring ahead into the fire. Her head dropped to his bare shoulder. Danny said nothing; he felt suddenly awkward and embarrassed. She was no longer a little child.

"Do you have many girlfriends, Danny?"

He was startled by the question. "Och, Sheila, come on, now. What would you be wanting to ask something like that for?"

"Well, we might as well talk about something. We always used to talk, when we were children. Or at least, when I was. Anyway, do you?"

"Well, I . . ." he lapsed into silence again, shrugging.

"Are any of them serious?"

"Sheila!" he protested. "You're being very inquisitive!"

"Oh, don't be so defensive, Danny! We've known each other all our lives! All mine, anyway," she murmured. "Well?"

"Well, if you must know, the answer is yes, I have had one or two girlfriends. None serious at the moment, though."

She wriggled a bit closer to him. "There's only ever been one man for me," she said in a low voice, barely audible above the crackling fire. Her cheek slipped down off his shoulder and rested softly on his bare chest. "But I don't think he's ever realised it."

The shock of realisation hit Danny MacDonald then, and he felt as though a fire had suddenly been lit inside his head. His arm tightened involuntarily around her as he became aware of how blind he had been. He did not notice that Sheila had

163

sensed his movement; she had raised her head and was looking searchingly into his eyes. His back had stiffened and his
mind now raced, trying to clarify his thoughts. He had always
thought of her simply as little Sheila; she had been like a baby
sister to him, so much younger, so small and fragile, still only
a girl, the little child he was so fond of ... Yet although
she had still not actually said anything direct, he now knew,
with the absolute certainty of instinct ... How blind he had
been ...

Slowly, he turned to look at her, comprehension on his face,
his eyes fixing at last on hers and reading confirmation in her
expression. Without a word, he cupped her face in his hands.
He had kissed her out of affection before, when she had been
a small child, but the familiar face now so close to his was
that of a young woman. *Not a little child any more, oh God
no ...* Closing her eyes, she pushed her mouth upwards towards
his, and then her arms went round his neck as their mouths
met. Danny got a sudden shock as his jacket fell away from
her shoulders and he felt her naked body pressed hard against
his chest.

Freeing his right hand, Danny reached carefully into the back
pocket of his breeches for his knife. He opened it one-handed, out
of sight behind her back, the long, sharp blade glinting red in the
firelight. It locked open with a soft click. He brought the knife down
twice, hard.

The steel blade cut deep into the straw of the bale, severing the
two strands of red baling twine binding it together. The straw sagged
beneath them, freed from the constraint of the twine. Danny tossed
the knife away; it fell near the door with a clatter. He stood up,
pulling Sheila to her feet. They kissed again, wild and euphoric
now, then he bent down to break up the bale and spread the
straw over the stone floor. He wrenched off his boots and the
rest of his wet clothes, flinging them aside. Looking up, he saw
Sheila's elfin figure silhouetted against the fire, stepping out of her
knickers, then naked, standing above him. The gentle curves of
her body were a revelation to him: she was suddenly the prettiest,
loveliest, most irresistible thing he had ever seen. No longer the
little girl, his childhood friend – all that had now changed for
ever ...

Sheila Cameron sank gently on to the rough straw next to Danny MacDonald. They stretched out together, desperate for each other, everything else forgotten. Outside, the rain still poured down, drumming heavily on the corrugated-iron roof of the stable; inside, steam rose from the damp clothing draped along the rafters. The fire roared eagerly in the grate, casting a flickering red glow on the two young lovers.

* * *

He held her tight as her sobs subsided, stroking her hair and her back as she lay on top of him. "Sheila, I'm so sorry, I'm so sorry . . ."

"What do you mean, you're sorry, Danny, my love?" she asked in a small voice. "What are you sorry for?"

"It's my fault . . . I should never have . . ."

"Danny," she said softly, "I wanted you to. And I feel like a real woman now. Now I know what all the other girls –"

"But I hurt you . . ."

"A little, at first. But after that . . ."

"But you screamed . . ."

Sheila raised her head and looked down at his face, smiling widely through the moisture in her eyes. "Yes, I think I did," she said slowly, kissing him. "But Danny, my love, that was a scream of joy, not pain!"

"But what are you crying for?" he asked anxiously, still unsure.

"I'm not really crying," she tried to reassure him. "But – but even if I am," she stammered through tears, "it's because I'm so happy!" She hugged him tightly to her. "I've never felt so happy in my life!"

He saw in her face that it was true; his relief that he hadn't hurt her was immense. He held her close, caressing her gently, kissing her. She was so tiny, he thought, so completely feminine, and now so adult too. He felt a rush of overwhelming tenderness for her, something he had not felt before with other girls. Then his eyes clouded. "Sheila, my little love," he said slowly, "there's something I must tell you. In a few days' time I'm going away."

Her head jerked up and her eyes anxiously met his.

"It should only be for a month or so," he added quickly, and saw relief instantly flood across her face.

"Where are you going?" she asked.

165

"Abroad, on a job. It's well paid," he told her.

"What will you be doing, Danny?"

"I'm not supposed to talk about it. You'll have to trust me."

She lowered her head again and lay quietly on his chest for a few minutes. "Danny?" she murmured after a while. "Do you have many girlfriends?"

He smiled. "Only one," he said, holding her tight. "There's only one woman in my life now. I just never realised it before."

29

An observer of the comings and goings in Loundis Road during the week beginning Monday 23rd March might have noticed a rather higher level of activity than had previously been apparent. Six large commercial bulk rubbish-skips were delivered to Unit 8 on Monday morning; they were deposited in a row inside the unit, which had been largely emptied of its stacks of stores. When the delivery lorries had gone, Usher, driving the leased fork-lift truck, began to load them with scrap metal and other debris. The scrap had all been prepared by Ackford and the others, working in Unit 9. Ackford had been busy with an oxyacetylene cutter, reducing his machine tools to unrecognisable pieces of metal; the other team members had systematically smashed every other item of equipment and pulverised every bit of material that had been used or left over. The whole lot went on to the skips; in twenty-four hours Units 8 and 9 were completely empty, stripped bare. In Unit 10 the large freezer container still sat on its trailer. A smaller, twenty-foot freezer container had joined it, its refrigeration unit working. In another corner was a small pile of equipment which was to be loaded on to the aircraft.

At midday on Tuesday 24th, the lorries returned to remove the skips; they drove away to the county council tip, where the skips' contents joined thousands of tons of other anonymous rubbish and detritus.

The following morning, Wednesday, the equipment for the aircraft was loaded into Howard's, Palmer's and Usher's cars, which then set off in convoy for Southampton Airport. At the airport, Palmer and Denard supervised the loading of the various packages, all entirely innocuous, into the Islander. Leaving the plane, they returned to Swindon; Howard then handed over the keys of his Rover 820 to

Denard, who had left his Toyota Corolla in London that morning and travelled up with Palmer. The Rover had suited Howard's purpose well, but he would no longer need it. Bourne gave Howard a lift home that evening in his BMW and Alfa Romeo, doing the usual switch at the Heathrow long-term car-park. MacDonald arrived later the same evening on a train from Fort William and stayed the night at Howard's flat.

On the morning of Thursday 26th, Bourne drove Howard and MacDonald back out to Swindon where, inside Unit 10, they waited for Harris. He arrived at ten o'clock, driving a large Volvo HGV tractor unit. The final items were carefully loaded into the container; last to be loaded were pallets of food, transferred by fork-lift from the smaller container, which had been keeping them frozen. The doors of the big container were closed and locked; Harris reversed the Volvo carefully into the trailer coupling and connected the power, hydraulic and air lines. The fan of the big container's refrigeration unit hummed noisily. Harris collected the paperwork from Bourne and drove the lorry away.

Bourne switched off the refrigeration unit on the smaller container, which was now empty and would no longer be required, and went into the office to arrange for its collection by the company from which it had been leased. He made two further calls, one to Lansing Linde to arrange for the fork-lift to be collected by low-loader the next morning, and the second to a firm of contract cleaners.

As Harris drove the container out on to the M4 heading east, there began a series of apparently innocent incidents which would nevertheless have made any police crime-prevention officer's eyes roll in despair at the general carelessness of some motorists. In Bristol, a Vauxhall Astra was parked in the early afternoon in a street on a housing estate not far from Temple Meads railway station; the driver, a large, raw-boned man, got out and walked away, leaving the door unlocked, the driver's window four inches open at the top and the keys in the ignition. Reaching the railway station, Ackford looked up the times of trains to London and settled down to wait for the next one. In Oxford, a small fair-haired man left a Rover 820 in a similar state in the park-and-ride facility near the city's northern bypass. Denard caught the bus into the city centre, then walked to the station; like Ackford, he caught the next train to Paddington. Meanwhile, no more than half a mile from each other in one of the

168

less salubrious areas of south-east London, a Peugeot 205 and a Ford Escort XR3 were abandoned by Palmer and Usher respectively; and nearly ten miles further north, on the other side of the river, Ziegler's Sierra was left outside a pub in Leytonstone. Some time later Denard, on arriving back in London after disposing of Howard's Rover, drove his Toyota out towards Wembley. Choosing a side-road between the football stadium and the underground station, he left the car there, caught the Bakerloo Line back to Charing Cross, then took a taxi to his hotel.

With the strange exception of the Peugeot 205, which sat undisturbed for almost two whole days, all the cars were stolen within a matter of hours of being abandoned. The burnt out shell of the Escort was found more than a hundred miles away near Stoke-on-Trent, having apparently been driven there by young joyriders; the Rover suffered a similar fate in east Oxford; and the remainder simply disappeared to be later resold to quite unsuspecting buyers, not one of whom would ever discover that his new car had a different history to that stated on the documentation. It would be another week before Harris's Golf GTi and Bourne's BMW similarly found new homes. No thefts were reported; the Metropolitan and Thames Valley police forces both thought it odd that no one came forward to complain about the Escort or the Rover – the only two cars that were brought to their attention, because of the fires – but their inquiries in each case elicited only the information that the last registered owner had sold the car to someone who could not have bothered to notify the Vehicle Licensing Centre in Swansea of the change of ownership. In both cases there was a degree of suspicion that the car in question might have been used in some criminal activity: for a time it was considered that the Escort's previous owner, a Southend publican, might have been less than honest in his protestations of innocence; however, there was no evidence and the matter was soon dropped. National data were already showing an alarming increase in car-related crime; the Escort and the Rover became just two statistics among thousands of other cases never to be solved.

Harris arrived at Felixstowe's Trinity Terminal at three in the afternoon. Reporting to the shipping agents, he completed the paperwork, made a last check of the diesel-driven generator to ensure that the refrigeration unit would continue to function independent of external electric power, and watched while the container was lifted off the trailer by crane and deposited in one of the fourteen thousand ground slots in the huge parking area, its fan still humming. Harris departed for London; stopping at a lay-by *en route*, he unhitched the empty trailer, removed its number-plate and left it there. On his arrival back in London, he returned the Volvo tractor unit to its owners. The trailer would stay in the lay-by for several weeks before the police noticed that it had been abandoned; its ownership would become another unsolved puzzle.

The shipping agents in Felixstowe submitted the usual Form C88 to HM Customs; an officer quickly scanned through the list of contents, mentally totting up the stated weights and volumes of the cargo of frozen foodstuffs to check that they tallied with the container's given gross weight of twenty-six tonnes. They did. The Trinity Terminal alone has an annual throughput capacity of one million sea containers: such an enormous number that, for practical reasons, the vast majority – particularly of those leaving the country rather than entering – are simply never inspected. On seeing that the container did not list among its contents any frozen meat or other items that might have required a routine inspection, the officer stamped the form and authorised the Customs seal; the container's movements were from then on directed by the port's computerised container-control system. It was transferred by one of the forty huge rubber-tyred gantry cranes to the mile-long quay where the Cyprus-registered m.v. *Manatee* was berthed with five other container vessels bound for different destinations. At two o'clock in the afternoon the refrigeration unit's diesel generator was shut down while the container was slowly lifted by one of the thirteen giant Panamax cranes on the quay, swung across over the ship and set down with practised precision in a slot at deck-level, just aft of the bridge superstructure, where the ship's reefer hook-up points were situated. A deck-hand secured the container to four anchoring points on the deck and connected a hook-up cable to the refrigeration unit; the fan hummed back into life, now running on the ship's electricity supply.

Within two hours, most of the remaining containers for m.v. *Manatee*'s voyage No. 56 to East Africa had been loaded on board; there were eight hundred of them, stacked in twenty rows across the ship, each row five high and eight wide. The m.v. *Manatee* was due to sail the following morning, Friday 27th March.

If the Customs officer had decided to check the weight of the container on a weighbridge or to inspect its contents, he would not at first glance have noticed anything unusual. The weight would have tallied with the weight stated in the documentation, and on opening the rear doors he would have seen four cargo pallets of frozen vegetables, stacked two pallets high and two across. The officer might have admired the precision with which the pallets had been stacked, although he might also have considered that such tight stacking was not conducive to optimum cold-air circulation: the pallets exactly fitted into the seven feet four inches' internal width of the container, and reached right to the ceiling. There was no more than an inch of spare space, either in width or in height. The pallets appeared to be standard wooden ones, but in fact they had been cut precisely to size so that they would fit tightly and make it almost impossible for anyone to see what lay behind them. Not that the Customs officer would have been likely to wonder too deeply about this; behind, he would have reasoned, would be more of the same. If he had checked with a thermometer, he might have noticed that the packs of vegetables were not quite as cold as they should have been; but although their temperature had in fact risen from minus twenty to minus thirteen Centigrade, there was no apparent difference to the naked eye. He might, if he had checked, have put this down to the tight stacking and resulting poor circulation of cold air.

Behind the four pallets of vegetables, the officer would have found other pallets, this time of tinned margarine, also frozen. There was normally no reason for margarine to be frozen, but it was nevertheless occasionally done with a mixed cargo such as this, and it would not have been thought particularly odd. What the margarine was in fact doing was helping to keep the vegetables chilled; it acted as an efficient cold pack, insulating the vegetables from what lay nearer the closed end of the container.

Behind the margarine, eight feet back from the loading doors and invisible behind the closely-stacked pallets of food, thick black-painted insulation boards formed a bulkhead barrier across the container, sealing it from floor to ceiling and preventing the frozen cargo from chilling the remaining thirty feet of the container behind it. The floor of this remaining section was covered by a one-foot-deep layer of concrete breeze blocks, the sole purpose of which was to make up weight. This concrete floor, along with the

171

walls and ceiling, was covered by thick rubberised carpeting, as an effective means of sound insulation.

The thirty-foot space was fairly cramped; along one wall were stacked bundles of equipment and stores, mostly packed in heavy-duty rubber waterproof stow-bags. The Customs officer would have found the contents of these bags and bundles very interesting indeed; they contained all the contraband items for the operation, such as the rifle, ammunition, AK silencers, satellite-navigation gear, night-vision goggles and other unusual items. Along the other wall were a domestic refrigerator, a fire-extinguisher, a vacuum cleaner and brush, a camping stove, a kettle and cooking pots standing on a drawer unit, water and fuel cans, a small wooden cubicle containing a chemical toilet, a table and two folding canvas chairs. At the far end, near the ventilation ducts, were two further items; they would have given the Customs officer a fit. Spread out on the floor were two mattresses.

As the container bumped gently down on to the deck of the ship and the fan unit came back to life, Ed Howard stirred, unzipped his sleeping-bag and climbed out. Despite the insulation, the frozen food had noticeably chilled the interior of the container, even in the short time that the fan had been switched off. Now that it was hooked up to the ship's power, the fresh air pumped in from outside would soon warm the place up again. Two small thermostatically-controlled air-conditioners were running. They were the items that Ackford had fitted into the freezer unit's housing and which Bourne had not spotted until they were pointed out to him. They would continue to circulate air at a constant twenty degrees Centigrade.

"Twenty-four more hours like this, I'm afraid," muttered Howard. "After that we'll be at sea. Tomorrow night we can start chucking the extra food and ballast overboard and make a bit more space in here." He looked across to his companion. "Danny?" *Well I'll be damned*, he thought admiringly; *he's a cool one.*

Inside his sleeping-bag on the other mattress, Danny MacDonald was fast asleep.

PART TWO

THE SHADOW

30

The noise was lost among the normal metallic creaks and groans of the ship and the sound of the refrigerator fans, as m.v. *Manatee* made her way southwards through the night in the swell of the Bay of Biscay. It was a slight clang, similar to the popping of a rivet, not very loud. Almost invisible in the dark, a thin line of paint on the outside of a forty-foot refrigerator container cracked. A section of the container wall near one corner swung slightly ajar, leaving a one-inch aperture. The hatch Ackford had cut was open.

Inside the container, Howard released the pressure of the car jack and carefully pushed the hatch open another two inches by hand, applying his eye to the gap. He hoped no one was standing immediately outside; but the chance was small. Unless a crew member had been looking directly at the hatch when the jack had pushed it ajar, the likelihood was that the slight movement would not have been noticed anyway.

There was no one to be seen to the right, the side visible through the small opening away from the hatch hinge. He could see that there was a space some seven feet wide between the container and the ship's superstructure. Other containers stacked on either side formed a solid wall, leaving a passage from one side of the ship to the other. Instead of pushing the hatch open further to stick his head out and look round the corner to the left, Howard took a small mirror from his pocket. Using the mirror, he could see that the whole passage was clear.

Satisfied, he turned to MacDonald.

"Couldn't be better," he said in a low voice. "There's plenty of room to open the hatch, and what's more we're on the lowest level, on the container deck as I hoped, not stacked right up on top of a whole lot of others. We won't need to lower everything down by rope – all we have to do is step outside. I'll just go and check out the other end, the cargo-loading doors. It'll be a bonus if we can get at them, but I'm not counting on it. I'll be back in five minutes."

Outside, he pushed the hatch door almost closed and took stock. The container was two from the end in the row; there was no space between them. Three more were stacked on top of each one, forming a solid steel wall thirty-two feet high. Seven out of the eight on the bottom row were refrigerator containers, hitched up by cable to the ship's electrical reefer points. At each end of the passageway formed by the containers and the ship's superstructure there was a small companionway down to the main deck, ten feet below; Howard descended and made his way aft, pacing out forty feet. There was no sign of life. Leaning out over the side of the ship, looking upwards, he saw that there was a gap about six feet wide separating the row of containers from the row behind it. It would be enough for them to be able to open the main doors. He returned to the hatch and let himself back in.

"OK, Danny; they've made life really easy for us. We'll be able to get at the doors. Not only that, but we won't be disturbed there. There's no direct access to that part of the container deck. No reason for it, I suppose. Now, we've got a lot to do before it gets light. I want to finish chucking all the surplus stuff overboard, so that we can seal up this hatch and repaint it. We'll only need the main doors after that. Let's go."

They stepped out of the hatch, pushing it closed. The catches on the inside clicked firmly into place; the thin lines of cracked paint around the edges of the hatch were the only evidence of its existence. Howard wiped the line of the crack clean with a cloth, then began pressing quick-setting filler into the cracks with a palette knife, while MacDonald opened a small tin of paint. When all the filler was in place, Howard carefully brushed paint over the cracks; the hatch was once more invisible.

Descending the companionway to the main deck, the two men moved noiselessly aft; Howard shinned up a heavy steel girder to the container deck at the cargo-door end of the container. MacDonald, watching him climb up, saw Howard's angular frame scale the girder with ease and disappear over the edge on to the container deck. Howard fastened a thin climbing rope to the corner anchoring point of one of the containers and lowered it to MacDonald, who climbed up after him. They pulled the rope up and untied it. The passage between the rows of containers at the cargo-door end, as Howard had reported, was about six feet wide. There was no safety rail along the side of the container deck; it was a smooth steel platform stretching all the way from port to starboard between the wall of stacked containers. On both sides of the ship, the edge of the deck hung directly over the sea.

Using a pair of pliers, Howard cut the wire of the Customs seal on the container and pocketed it. Then he swung open the container doors, folding them both flat against the containers on either side.

The packs of frozen vegetables had thawed considerably in the forty hours since they had been loaded, but they were still very cold; the two men were glad of their heavy insulated gloves as they cut the thick nylon banding and began lifting the packs off the pallets. One by one, the ten-kilogram packs of food were carried to the side of the ship and dropped overboard, falling fifty feet into the sea below. The splash in each case was inaudible, lost in the wake of the ship. Working slowly and silently, they took nearly seven hours to jettison the surplus vegetables and margarine. By five o'clock in the morning the last pack had gone, as had the pallets. The blank wall of the insulation boards faced them. The boards too were dismantled and thrown over the side of the ship. The accommodation space in the container was revealed. They would no longer need Ackford's hatch.

"OK, Danny. That'll do for tonight. We'll start shifting the breeze blocks tomorrow. Let's go in and have a brew." Pulling the heavy doors shut behind them, Howard and MacDonald went back inside.

It took them two more nights to jettison all the concrete blocks, rolling back the rubber carpeting and moving the equipment to one side at a time. Finally, they were left with just their camping equipment and the waterproof stow-bags of contraband items. The space inside the container seemed much less confined and claustrophobic with the extra foot of headroom; Howard reckoned that the boxed-in feeling, which he himself had hated, had subsided largely because of the knowledge that they now had two means of escape – one at each end of the container – rather than just one. In three days, they had seen no sign of the crew; they knew there would have been a twice-daily check of the reefer points by a crew member to ensure that the units were functioning correctly, but they had neither seen nor heard any sign of this. They had finished well ahead of the time Howard had allowed; if the main doors had been inaccessible and they had had to unload everything via the hatch, the operation might have taken several nights longer.

By the fourth night at sea, Howard and MacDonald had settled into a routine of sleeping by day and being awake by night. Howard spent the fourth and fifth nights outside the container, deep in the shadows on the main deck; his purpose was to observe the movements of the crew and study their routine. He was encouraged to see that night activity was minimal while the vessel was at sea, and that patrols by crew members were relatively infrequent and at fixed – and therefore predictable – times.

With no more manual work to do for another ten days or so, Howard brought out the Arabic language tapes and began boning up on his very limited knowledge of the language. He had a natural ear for languages and pronunciation, but he was under no illusion that he would be able to pass muster for more than a few seconds – and then only if he stuck to a handful of standard opening phrases. He concentrated on getting the pronunciation right; that, more than anything else, would be what might give him away if he had to speak the language at all. He hoped he would not need to.

His thoughts wandered from the Arabic lesson and he pondered his decision to bring MacDonald in the container rather than one of the others. Tony Ackford would have been the obvious choice, with his SBS background, but Tony had mechanical work to do and couldn't be spared. Bob Usher would have been another good choice, but ever since his experiences in prison in Ankara he had been – understandably – somewhat claustrophobic. Besides, he would be assisting Tony with the mechanical work. Mel Harris had his own job to do, looking after Sullivan, while the two ex-colonials, Andy and Chris, had the aircraft to think about – and anyway, thought Howard, those two had virtually no experience of the sea. Johnny Bourne had administrative details to attend to, and Mike Ziegler ... No, he thought. He had been right to decide on MacDonald as a companion. And he was turning out fine – he didn't seem at all bothered by being cooped up in this bloody steel box.

"How are you getting on with your tables, Danny?" Howard asked him on the seventh night. While Howard had been observing the crew's routine, MacDonald had occupied himself with his book of tables and trajectories, working with a pocket calculator and making copious notes.

He looked up at Howard. "Nearly finished, I think. I've worked out pretty well every variation we might come across, including some extremes of variation in weather. We're pretty unlikely to get anything as drastic as some of the possibilities I've allowed for. I'm just double-checking the others, the more likely ones."

"Well, I've got a little present for you from Bob. I don't know whether it'll be any good, but I'd like you to try it. See how it compares with your tables and notes."

MacDonald looked puzzled as Howard unpacked one of the stow-bags and handed him a flat, rectangular package measuring twelve inches by ten. Gunmetal grey in colour, it was less than two inches thick and weighed just six and a half pounds. Howard pressed two catches, and a lid flipped up, exposing a small screen. He pressed the power button on the right, the screen came to life and the machine emitted a tiny hum. A green light below the screen indicated a fully-charged battery.

Howard explained the rudiments of the machine to MacDonald. "It's a laptop computer, a Grid 386NX. Bob says it's a particularly good one. The MoD has bought a lot of them. They're very sturdy, despite the small size. I don't know much about this particular machine, but I know something about computers if you get stuck and need help with it. Bob's written out some instructions for you; he says the program's very easy to understand. He saw you wrestling with those tables and thought there must be a better way. Mike found the program itself – it's an American one. See what you think of it."

"A computer? Are you joking?" MacDonald gave Howard a disbelieving look. "You realise April Fool's Day was yesterday?"

"No joke, Danny. But I don't know how useful it'll be. The ballistics program may not be as accurate as it's supposed to be. Give it a try, anyway."

MacDonald's surprise turned to fascination as he followed the simple instructions Usher had provided. Starting at the standard "C:>" prompt, he typed "EXTBAL6.EXE", then pressed the return key. After a short pause, the LCD screen flashed up the logo of the computer program "EXTERIOR BALLISTICS OF SMALL ARMS". Almost immediately, the screen cleared again; the logo was replaced by a series of rows and columns of figures, giving full statistical

179

details of a specific load of ammunition, together with a complete set of weather conditions. MacDonald saw that the details had already been set for the .338 Lapua Magnum sniper ammunition, along with a series of standard readings for temperature, altitude, humidity, range, barometric pressure and windage. He studied them eagerly. Still following Usher's written instructions, he turned to the page in his notebook that gave the same standard readings. "Now just type 'SUM'", Usher's instructions told him. MacDonald did so. Immediately the screen cleared again and "PLEASE WAIT" appeared. Two seconds later, several long columns of figures appeared. In the first column was a series of ranges from zero to fifteen hundred yards in hundred-yard increments; in the second and third, bullet velocities in feet per second and bullet energy for each range; in the fourth, bullet drop below the line of departure in inches; and in the fifth, the time of flight of the bullet over the distance concerned. The sixth and seventh columns gave the trajectory above or below the aiming point for a set zero, in minutes of angle and inches, and the eighth and ninth columns gave windage settings, again in minutes of angle and inches, for a five-miles-per-hour cross-wind.

"Oh, bloody hell, will you just look at that," breathed MacDonald. Quickly, he compared the readings for elevation and windage that the computer had worked out in just two seconds with those in his notebook. They tallied almost exactly; the largest discrepancy was less than one inch at twelve hundred yards. MacDonald was inclined to think the error was in his own manually-compiled tables, rather than in those of the machine. When he realised that he could enter any reading he wanted for the variables such as temperature and barometric pressure, he ran through them all quickly, comparing the results each time with the figures he had spent dozens of hours working out manually. It took him only half an hour to finish checking them all, for every variation he had calculated himself; occasionally he looked up at Howard, an increasingly accusatory look on his face each time.

At last Howard acknowledged MacDonald's glare; he held up his hands apologetically. "Danny, I know what you're thinking. You're wondering why we didn't give you that machine before, and save you all your hard work on the tables. For the record, all the others wanted you to have it straight away – everyone except me and Mike. The two of us reckoned it would be best if you got all your tables done before using the computer, so that you'd have some solid evidence to compare its performance with. You might not have entirely trusted it otherwise. Also, I suspect the practice with the tables has familiarised you with the ammunition enough to mean you know all its characteristics, far better than the computer would have done. I'm sorry, mate, but I hope you can see the sense of it."

MacDonald pursed his lips, considering his reply. Eventually he shrugged. "You're right. I probably wouldn't have trusted it. I don't mind telling you, I'm astonished. It's amazing – so quick. I think we'll take both with us – the computer and my notebook. Then if this thing breaks down or the battery runs flat at least I'll still have my notes. And I'll have the comfort of knowing that both are accurate."

"That's just what I wanted to hear," said Howard. "Now, come on; it'll be dark again outside. I've got another little toy to show you. We're going to find out where we are, to the nearest hundred yards. With this thing," he added, holding up a small device about eight inches long.

MacDonald examined it; he couldn't decide whether it was a large pocket calculator or a television remote-control handset.

"It's a satellite-navigation unit," said Howard.

31

On the morning of 7th April, Harris and Denard waved Sullivan off from Southampton Airport. Harris was well pleased. The American pilot had behaved himself quite creditably during his stay in London; he had not gone wild with drinking and parties, and had appeared anxious to do a good job. He had checked the flight plan Harris had given him, and had even suggested a couple of sensible modifications. The flight plan had been prepared by Denard, who had later agreed that the American's alterations were reasonable; he had been careful not to let on to Sullivan that he was a pilot himself. They were still the only two team members he had met.

"I think our boy will do nicely," mused Harris, as they watched the Islander climb away and head out over the sea on the first leg of its journey to Saudi Arabia. "Nursemaiding a cowboy out in Saudi could prove to be quite a headache, but I don't think this one'll give any trouble. Hell, he doesn't even drink much – just the occasional beer. More than I can say for you, Andy, you mad little bugger."

"Call me Superman," retorted Denard. "I never drink when I fly. Come on, let's get back to London. The first beer's on me. It'll be our last for a while," he added, mournfully. "Bleddy Saudi licensing laws."

That evening, four members of the team left London for Saudi Arabia: Bourne, Denard, Palmer and Harris took a British Airways flight, BA 133, to Jeddah. Ziegler, Ackford and Usher followed the next morning, taking BA 125 to Riyadh. All seven entered Saudi Arabia under their own names and travelling on their own passports.

Entry into Saudi Arabia is very tightly controlled. There are no tourists; only two categories of visitor are permitted entry. The first, pilgrims to Mecca and Medinah, the two holy cities, are subject to travel restrictions which confine them to those two cities and Jeddah; the majority of pilgrims are granted entry only for the period of the Hajj pilgrimage. The second category, consisting of legitimate businessmen, workers and their families, are accorded a degree of freedom of movement within the Kingdom that depends on their business there; but no non-Muslims are allowed into the two holy cities.

A visa application has to be supported by convincing proof of employment by a sponsoring firm, and the reason for the stated employment is always examined carefully by the issuing body. Occasionally the Saudi authorities, such as the Saudi Embassy in London, run a double check with a company in order to satisfy themselves that the application is a bona fide one; but a well-prepared application supported by a reputable firm usually ensures that a visa is granted without much trouble. All seven men from Howard's team had stated on their visa applications that they were employees of Pan-Arabian Petroleum which, aside from its seven hundred and fifty employees who were Saudi nationals, had forty-five Britons, twelve Americans and eighty Pakistanis working in Saudi Arabia. PAP was a highly respected corporation; the fact that it was wholly owned by the Saudi royal family assured that its operations were rarely dogged by Government bureaucratic interference.

Bourne, in his capacity as security consultant to PAP, had had no trouble in concocting adequate PAP contracts of employment for the team members. Accessing PAP's computer database in its London office, he had left false records in the computer's personnel files giving details of himself and the six others, with a note in each case that any queries should be referred immediately to him. He monitored the personnel section closely over the next few weeks. When no queries came back from the Saudi Embassy and the visa applications went through smoothly (Bourne had not expected any problems) he erased the files from the database; no records were left with PAP. He made a mental note that on his return the personnel department would benefit from a bit of tightening-up on its security; no one had even noticed the extra "employees" on file.

Initially, a person taking up employment in Saudi Arabia is granted a visitor's visa, which is valid for up to one month. If he intends to stay longer, he must at some stage during this first month convert his visitor's visa into a business or "exit-re-entry" visa. To do this, a further application is required, with a second supporting letter from the sponsoring employer. An *iqaama* (work permit) is then granted. The *iqaama*, a small six-page booklet with a brown cover, must be carried at all times by the bearer, who will normally surrender his passport – stamped to show that the *iqaama* has been issued – to his employer. Without his *iqaama*, a foreigner in Saudi Arabia is a nobody. To leave the country, an *iqaama*-bearer must apply for an exit visa, a process that takes from four to six days.

In many ways, therefore, life is simpler for the visiting businessman who intends to stay for less than one month; he retains his passport, and he carries an authorising letter from his employer stating the conditions and place of employment, which determine the extent of travel permitted within the country.

On arrival in Jeddah in the early hours of 8th April, Harris and Denard took a taxi straight to the Sheraton Hotel, on the Corniche highway, where they checked into the adjoining rooms Harris had reserved in their names. At reception, they handed in their passports, each of which had been stamped at immigration with the standard visitor's authorisation. No comment had been made about Denard's new moustache or about his hair, which was darker than in his passport photograph, and there had been no awkward questions at the airport about their occupations. Harris was an "executive" – in line with what was stated on his passport – supposedly working for Pan-Arabian Petroleum, while Denard's Zimbabwean passport gave his occupation rather grandly as "company director", a relic of the days when he had run his own private air charter company, before it had been frozen out of business by United Air Charters of Zimbabwe and he had been obliged to throw in his lot with them.

Denard went straight up to his room; he would stay there for three days, not showing his face and using room service for all his meals. The room-service deliveries would be made to Harris's room, and signed for by Harris, before being taken through the connecting door. "Bored shitless," would be Denard's sole comment on re-emerging from his isolation on 11th April.

Bourne (another "company director") and Palmer (an "engineer") checked into a different hotel, the Marriott. After breakfast that morning Bourne telephoned Tony Hughes, the senior Darcon director in Saudi. Hughes had been expecting to hear from "Mr Bryce" and sent a driver round to their hotel to pick him and "Mr Potter" up. When they arrived at his office, Hughes examined the proffered

Darcon identification Bourne had prepared, giving his and "Potter's" occupations as geologist and surveyor respectively. The fax messages Hughes had been sent on Dartington's machine had had a convincing tone of confidentiality and importance, and he was now satisfied.

Hughes was a small, energetic man and Bourne could quite see why Dartington had placed a high degree of trust in him. He didn't seem to feel in the least slighted that Dartington was apparently organising new projects on his territory behind his back; Bourne soon realised from the way Hughes spoke about Dartington that the two men had been close friends for many years, and that Hughes had an unqualified admiration for his boss. It was as well, thought Bourne, that in the fax messages purporting to come from Dartington, Hughes had been instructed not on any account to refer to the matter over the telephone except when he was speaking directly to "Mr Bryce".

"Everything's ready for you, Jim," said Hughes, addressing Bourne. "You've got the run of the old construction camp up at Badanah. As I told you, it's been empty for four months now, ever since we finished that resurfacing job on the TAP road. I've had the four vehicles you wanted driven up there, and there's a couple of our mechanics going over them right now to check that they're in good order. The other staff are three security guards, two general duty men, a storeman and a cook. All Saudis except for the cook, a Pakistani. Do you need anyone else?"

"No, thanks," answered Bourne, who privately decided that the first thing he would do would be to give the Saudi staff three weeks' paid local leave, to get rid of them. He would keep the Pakistani cook, but make sure he was confined to the camp kitchen. The cook would probably be glad to see the back of his Saudi colleagues, thought Bourne; the Saudis treated non-white immigrant labour as second-class citizens. "We're pretty self-contained, Tony. We'll be out of camp most of the time, as soon as the others join us. I've asked them to fly directly up there to join us when they arrive. You've been extremely kind."

Hughes asked the two men if they would join him and his wife for dinner at home that evening, and seemed disappointed when Bourne politely declined, saying that there was much preparatory work for them to do before they headed north. He and Palmer took their leave and returned to their hotel, where they were joined later by Ziegler,

Ackford and Usher, who had arrived on a connecting flight from Riyadh.

The following day, 9th April, Bourne, Palmer, Ackford and Usher rose early and returned by taxi to Jeddah's King Abdul Aziz International Airport, where they caught the 07.45 Saudia flight SV 738 to Ar'ar, in the far north of the country. The Darcon construction camp was ten miles along the main Trans-Arabian Pipeline (TAP) road past the nearby town of Badanah, set back about three hundred yards off the highway. They arrived there at 11.30, in the heat of the day, and began settling in. As Bourne had predicted, the eight Saudi camp staff members were delighted at unexpectedly being given three weeks' leave; they disappeared with alacrity.

Ziegler, who had accompanied the others to the airport, went to the Avis car-rental desk and hired the largest vehicle available. It was a big Dodge Ram Charger covered pick-up, with a double cab and plenty of room in the rear compartment. He drove north out of the city, breathing a sigh of relief as he picked up the motorway and left behind the city traffic, which seemed to hold normal rules of the road in scant regard. He drove slowly and carefully, in no hurry. Shortly after leaving the city he came to the permanent police checkpoint, where he showed his passport and his PAP travel authorisation. The police did not seem to be bothered about making any very close inspection, and they were friendly as Ziegler greeted them courteously in the few phrases of Arabic he had learned, but he saw them giving a couple of vehicles driven by Pakistani nationals a thorough going-over. The traffic thinned out as he drove north, and after just over an hour's driving he joined the coast road, continuing north towards Yanbu. He arrived there at midday, around the time when Bourne and the others, five hundred miles away in a north-easterly direction, were sitting down to lunch in the Badanah construction camp.

About the same distance to the north-west of Yanbu, the m.v. *Manatee*'s passage through the Mediterranean was nearly over. Howard's tiny GPS satellite-navigation receiver informed him that the ship was approaching Port Said, at the northern end of the Suez Canal.

32

Harris was waiting when Sullivan touched down at King Abdul Aziz International on the morning of the 11th. The Texan, travelling on his own passport and with supporting Darcon documentation prepared by Bourne, passed through immigration control without trouble. His friendly, relaxed manner went down well with the Saudi officials. His cheerful if linguistically incorrect "Well, howdy and salaam to you, old buddy!" made the immigration officer smile. There was extra paperwork to complete for the importation formalities for the Islander, but the Saudis were used to foreign corporations importing their own aircraft, and this too was completed without a hitch. Sullivan was a man who recognised that respectful geniality went a long way; he was a likable character, and he let it work to his advantage.

Harris drove him back to the Sheraton in his hired car. Conversationally, he asked whether Sullivan had had a good flight.

"No problems at all," reported Sullivan. "In fact, I had a real nice trip. Holy shit!" he exclaimed suddenly, startled by an alarming near-miss on the car by a recklessly-driven Mazda pick-up. "Will you look at the way some of these guys drive! They tired of living, or what?"

Harris swore viciously at the other driver who raced on, oblivious. "As you can see, they're not the world's safest," he muttered to Sullivan. "In fact, it's bloody mayhem on the roads here." A little further on he changed the subject and began the well-rehearsed tale he had prepared for Sullivan's benefit. "Look, Ray, there's been a change of plan. The boss is out of town for a while. Unexpected, like. I don't know when he'll be back, but he said it could be as long as three or four weeks. You and I have got nothing to do for a while, but I've been told we're to stay on standby. We're booked into the

Sheraton. We've got to stay there and not move until we hear from him. That OK with you?"

"You're in charge," said Sullivan. "Sounds fine by me. I'll do just whatever you say."

"Fine." Harris continued the fabrication. "I've finished with most of the registration formalities, but I'll need your passport and other papers for hotel reception. All of them. You wouldn't believe the bureaucracy here. These hotels want to see literally everything, for security reasons. Driving licence, the lot. Your pilot's licence too. They'll hold it all till we check out. I'll deal with it – I speak the lingo."

"OK. Here's my folder – everything's in there." He grinned at Harris. "I guess that old folder'll look a little better at the end of this job, with an extra ninety thousand bucks in it, huh? In the meantime, I can wait. I ain't asking *no* questions at *all*."

"Thanks," said Harris. "I've got your room key here – sixth floor. It's ready for you – just go straight on up when we get there and I'll sort the rest out. Charge anything you like to the room bill – it's all paid for."

They arrived at the hotel a few minutes later. Sullivan went up to the sixth floor and settled in; the room had been vacated that morning by Denard, who was now waiting quietly next door in Harris's, his small flight-bag packed and ready. Harris gave Sullivan ten minutes to get to his room, then rang Denard from reception, telling him to come on down.

Denard walked straight past the reception desk to Harris's car. Five minutes later, Harris joined him and handed over Sullivan's folder before driving him out to the airport. Denard, using Sullivan's identity, filed a flight plan for Al Wajh, a small town on the Red Sea coast two hundred miles to the north of Yanbu; Harris did not wait around to see him take off.

33

On the night of 11th April, Howard and MacDonald stripped the container almost bare. Howard had been consulting the tiny satellite-navigation receiver with increasing frequency; a small hole Ackford had drilled in the top of the container allowed a wire antenna to be fed through so that readings could be taken from inside. Howard calculated that they would, as expected, be roughly where he wanted them to be the following night, the 12th.

The two men emerged at six o'clock on the evening of the 12th, dressed in black neoprene wet-suits. Working quickly, they began to empty the container, stacking the items they would need on the narrow section of the container deck by the rear doors. Everything else went over the side into the sea; the largest splash was made by the domestic fridge they had used to store their food for the voyage. Unknown to either man, a crew member was an hour late in making his after-dusk patrol of the main deck, just ten feet below them. The fridge fell right past his head. If it had been its original white colour he might have seen enough to make him think something was amiss, but as it was, with the fridge's exterior painted a rough matt black by Ackford, he had no more than a fleeting impression of something dropping past him in the dark. He stopped, frowned, glanced briefly over the side of the ship just in time to see a slightly unusual disturbance in the black water below, then decided that he had been imagining things. He continued with the remainder of his rounds. Twenty minutes later he was back in his cabin, having forgotten all about it.

Howard used the vacuum cleaner to sweep every last trace of their occupation from the interior, then unplugged it from the electric socket behind the aluminium panel near the refrigeration unit. He closed the panel, gave the empty container one last visual check with his torch, and left. Closing the two cargo doors he turned to MacDonald, who was bending over the camping stove outside on the deck. A small covered pot on the stove contained four ounces of lead; when it had melted, MacDonald carefully poured it into a plaster-of-Paris mould Howard had made from the original Customs seal. Howard passed the original sealing wire – now a little shorter since it had been cut – through the locking latch on the container door and into the mould so that it would pass through the solidifying lead. MacDonald poured a trickle of cold water over the mould to cool it. Satisfied that the seal was setting, the two men jettisoned the stove, the vacuum cleaner and the final surplus items over the side of the ship. Both men had relieved themselves into the chemical toilet for the last time; this too went overboard. They were glad to see the back of it. Its cloying smell, despite the fresh air circulated by the fan and the air-conditioners, had been a constant and unpleasant feature of the previous two weeks. It was the last item to go. Howard glanced at his watch; it was 19.56 local time.

Fifteen minutes later, they had lowered all their equipment by rope and pulley down to the main deck. Acutely aware now that this was the time when they stood most risk of being discovered, they worked hurriedly to move the large rubber stow-bags and other items to the stern rail of the ship. The *Manatee*'s large hydraulic stern winch, covered by its heavy green oil-stained canvas tarpaulin, provided some concealment. Behind it, they began unpacking the bulkiest and heaviest of the bags. Inside was the sixteen-foot inflatable Gemini craft. MacDonald began inflating the air compartments using a full diver's air-bottle, while Howard quietly returned to the container. The mould was now cool to the touch; he broke the plaster away and washed the new lead seal with water. He gave it a brief inspection under his torch; it would do. He flung the bits of plaster overboard, then returned to MacDonald to help finish inflating the Gemini.

Howard made fast a two-hundred-foot rope to a heavy steel stanchion on the port side of the ship, leaving just twenty feet of the rope free. He attached this short end to the port bow-ring of the Gemini. MacDonald copied the operation for the starboard side. Then they manhandled the Gemini over the rail, stern first, and let it drop.

The rubber craft hung about twelve feet below the stern rail, suspended by its bow from the two ropes, its underside facing the stern of the ship. Using a third rope fastened to a third, central stanchion, Howard lowered himself on a climbing harness down to the swaying Gemini. He attached himself by a clip on the harness to a ring on the central thwart of the craft and detached himself from the rope. Standing on the Gemini's transom board, he signalled to MacDonald, who began lowering cargo to him using the central rope. Howard reached up for each item, grabbed it and with nylon webbing bands strapped it firmly into place on the deck of the Gemini. The heaviest item, a forty-horsepower outboard motor, was the first to be lowered; then followed fuel tanks and water jerricans, then nine heavy rubber waterproof stow-bags containing food, clothing and the other equipment. Finally, MacDonald gesticulated down to Howard to take special care as he lowered the big sniper rifle in its shockproof and watertight case. Howard smiled as he caught the rifle-case carefully. It was far from being the most delicate of the items of cargo, he knew, but he understood MacDonald's concern that the telescopic sight should not be subjected to unnecessary knocks. The stalker was showing the right attitude to the tools of his new trade.

Once all the cargo was securely lashed down inside the Gemini, Howard climbed back up. Together, he and MacDonald paid out the two side ropes, using the stanchions to take the strain, until the Gemini's transom touched the sea. The water under the *Manatee*'s stern boiled and frothed from the ship's propeller; Howard had a moment's anxiety that the Gemini would capsize, but as they paid out the remainder of the rope they saw that the rubber craft had settled satisfactorily and was being towed along steadily by the two ropes, fifty yards astern of the ship.

Howard adjusted MacDonald's inflatable life-jacket and clipped a ring on the Scot's harness on to one of the two tow-ropes. MacDonald climbed over the side. Howard used the third rope to brake MacDonald's descent along the tow-rope, and watched as he slowly lowered himself down along the tow-line towards the Gemini.

Howard had warned MacDonald to watch out for buffeting when he touched the sea, but the force of the water caught MacDonald by surprise and he was momentarily sucked under and flung hard against the rubber side of the Gemini. Recovering, he hooked an arm over the side of the craft and hauled himself aboard, spluttering and spitting the taste of sea-water from his mouth. He detached his harness from the tow-rope and re-attached it to a spare ring on the craft. Grabbing the rope that had been used as the brake for his descent, he attached it

191

to the Gemini's central bow-ring; on the ship, Howard pulled it taut and made it fast to the stanchion. Then he cut the port and starboard tow-ropes free from their stanchions and let them go, throwing the surplus ends after them into the sea, so that the Gemini was being towed by the central rope alone. Finally, Howard partially inflated his own ABLJ and cut loose the last tow-rope attached to the Gemini, which floated away, now free. He quickly cut away the remaining end of rope from the stanchion and threw it overboard; then he jumped over the side himself.

He braced himself for a hard impact against the water forty feet below, but the bubbling wake beneath the stern of the *Manatee* was unexpectedly soft. As soon as he hit the water he pulled the release on the small gas-bottle in his ABLJ, inflating it fully. After a few seconds of apprehension that he might have miscalculated and would be sucked under and into the ship's propeller, he bobbed to the surface. He was spun around for half a minute or so by the turbulence, but gradually the water settled. The sea was calm. Orienting himself by the departing lights of the *Manatee*, he began swimming directly away from her; a couple of minutes later, he made out the green glow of a beta-light in the bow of the Gemini and flashed his torch so that MacDonald would see him. MacDonald paddled over and helped him aboard. The three dripping ropes were hauled into the craft, untied from the tow-rings and stowed in the bow.

Howard unpacked the outboard motor and carefully lowered it into position on the transom, connecting the fuel line. "It'll be a bloody long paddle if this bugger doesn't start," he commented to MacDonald, priming the engine and setting it at half-choke. "It's the first time I've ever done this sort of thing without a spare engine, but we just didn't have room. The Saudi coastline is about seventy-five miles over there," he added, glancing at his wrist-compass and pointing east.

The forty-horsepower engine caught on the third pull of the starter rope. "Thank God for that," muttered Howard. "I'd have murdered Tony if it hadn't started." He consulted the compass again and examined the night sky. Polaris was clearly visible, indicated by the "W" of Cassiopeia, giving him confirmation of north. As he looked at the North Star he fancied he saw it flicker, as if a momentary shadow had crossed its face. A tiny sliver of cloud in an otherwise clear sky, he thought. A satellite perhaps? He settled the Gemini on to an easterly heading and opened up the throttle. In the light swell, the Gemini would make perhaps fifteen knots, he calculated. So – say five hours, if they were lucky. It was 22.00 local time. If the calm weather held, they should make it by about three in the morning. If they were really lucky, they might even be able to avoid a day's lay-up.

MacDonald was no stranger, with his west-coast upbringing, to small dinghies. He had been out at all hours and in all weather conditions, in a variety of boats. At that moment, however, as they started out on their passage half-way across the Red Sea in the tiny sixteen-foot craft, he felt as alone and vulnerable as he had ever felt in his life. He thought briefly of home, and of young Sheila . . . so far away . . . a different world, another existence. He looked around him – there was nothing. Nothing except the lights of the m.v. *Manatee*, gradually disappearing into the night as she steamed away from them on her journey south.

*   *   *

They made better time than Howard had expected. After the first hour he calculated that the Gemini had covered fifteen miles; at 23.00 he stopped to consult the GPS receiver. It was blank. Of the fifteen Navstar satellites circling the earth, the receiver required two to be above the horizon for it to make a calculation of its position. Never mind, he thought; a long way still to go. They were hardly likely to bump into land quite yet. During the next two hours they encountered slightly rougher sea conditions, and at 01.00 Howard considered it still not calm enough to risk getting the GPS unit wet. He guessed that in spite of the weather they had covered a further twenty miles – nearly half-way. Shortly after 01.30 the wind dropped right away, and Howard opened up the outboard to full throttle. He kept up an estimated twenty knots until 03.00, by which time he reckoned they must be within ten miles or so of the Saudi coast. He stopped to get an exact fix from the GPS; the reading gave 36 deg 54 min E, 25 deg 31 min N. Holding a beta-light to the chart, he immediately saw that the southerly wind had driven them several miles further north than he had expected; they were positioned right off the southern end of Shaybara Island, only a few miles from the coast. In daylight, the island would be clearly visible.

Hurriedly, he beckoned to MacDonald to unpack the sound-muffler

193

box for the outboard engine. He decided not to fit it straight away, but began having second thoughts when a few minutes later MacDonald saw a light approaching from the south. Howard headed north, away from the light, but it continued to draw nearer until it was only perhaps two miles distant. A searchlight stabbed on and probed the dark. A patrolling Saudi coastguard or naval vessel, thought Howard grimly; time to hide.

They fitted the muffler box and slowed to a crawl, edging towards the shore. The light of the other vessel was still approaching, but Howard could not decide whether this was accidental or whether they had been picked up on a radar screen. He considered the latter unlikely; the radar profile of the Gemini was almost non-existent. A rocky promontory showed up ahead; Howard gently steered the Gemini up to it, the engine burbling almost inaudibly. MacDonald grabbed a spur of the rock and held on to it, while Howard unrolled a bulky camouflage net and draped it over themselves and the whole craft.

They were just in time. The searchlight caught the now shapeless lump of the Gemini full in its beam. They held their breath; the beam passed on. Underneath the thickly camouflaged seaweed-coloured net, everything in the Gemini was matt black. Even someone a hundred yards away with a spotlight would not have been able to discern that it was a boat at all. The vessel kept going past, west and then south, until eventually its light was lost from view. Howard stowed the net and signalled to MacDonald to let go of the rock.

A mile further on they reached the eastern end of Shaybara Island; Howard turned north through a narrow channel and began to thread his way through the little archipelago near the main coastline.

At 03.55 they made landfall. Howard did not beach the Gemini straight away; the shore was too flat and bare. If they had to lay up for the day the Gemini, or they themselves, might be noticed; and the coastguard vessel might return at any moment. A mile up the coast, travelling slowly and almost silently with the engine-muffler in place, they came to a small inlet with steep rocky sides, providing better cover. It was perfect, Howard decided – little more than a crevice in the coastline. Unless someone stood right on the edge of the small cliff-face fifteen feet above the inlet, they would not be able to see the boat. From the sea, the Gemini would be in deep shadow.

Howard jumped out, leaving MacDonald to secure the dinghy to a rock. Climbing the small rock-face, he was immediately rewarded by a rumbling sound in the distance; less than five minutes later, the lights of a truck passed by, half a mile away. Good, thought Howard; the coastal road was close by. He returned to the boat, and the two men began unloading its cargo.

Stripping off their wet-suits, they towelled themselves dry and put on black trousers, black cotton T-shirts, windcheaters and balaclavas, and desert boots. Then Howard set off for the road, carrying a small nylon bag. Keeping a look-out and listening for any sign of more traffic, he put three small marker flags by the roadside, four hundred yards apart: a yellow one at either end and an orange one in the centre. He returned to the inlet. MacDonald had laid out the Gemini's contents and was in the process of deflating the craft.

At 04.40 Howard watched anxiously as a second set of lights approached. It was getting late; it would be light in a little more than an hour. The vehicle lights passed the place where he had put out his first yellow marker. A car horn sounded three long blasts and one short. At the central orange marker it sounded again, three short and one long; then it stopped, switching off its lights.

It was Ziegler and the Dodge Ram Charger. He had been camping out for three days, and had been driving back and forth along the road twice a night, each evening after dusk and each morning before dawn. Glad as they were to see him, Howard and MacDonald were even gladder to see that he had brought with him a large thermos flask of hot coffee. Walking ahead of the Dodge, Howard guided Ziegler off the road and down to the shore. By 05.15, the three men had all the equipment loaded and were back on the road going north.

It was 06.45 when they arrived at Al Wajh. Denard was waiting for them; by 07.30 he had clearance for the flight. Ziegler drove the Dodge up to the aircraft for loading, then returned it to the airport car-park where he locked it up, pocketed the keys and left it, walking back to the plane. At 08.00 precisely, the Islander took off and headed north-east on a course for Ar'ar.

34

"No luck with weaponry yet, I'm afraid, Ed," reported Bourne as he watched Howard and MacDonald attack large plates of food. The three men were sitting at a table in the Badanah camp cookhouse; it was midday. "But everything else seems OK. Bob and I have found some spare medical equipment, and we've stripped the camp's own medical emergency Land Rover of all its kit. Tony and Chris have knocked up some other things that look convincing enough. I think our two fake ambulances will pass inspection."

"What are the vehicles themselves like?" asked Howard through a mouthful of hot curry and chapattis. He and MacDonald were ravenous after the journey; the smiling Pakistani cook had prepared a huge lunch for them.

"Couldn't be better. All identical, and they're almost brand-new. Only a couple of thousand miles on the clocks, except for one which has done ten thousand. There's nothing to choose between them. Anyway, we've cannibalised one for spares, practically stripped it down. We should have all the mechanical work finished in a couple of days, then we'll do the repainting."

"Good. I'll come and have a look in a minute. Mmm, this is good. Living in a tin box and eating tinned food for a fortnight has not been my idea of fun." He cleaned his plate with a piece of chapatti, reflecting. "I think we'd better forget the idea of getting weapons here – it could be asking for trouble, and we weren't banking on it anyway. We'll nick some when we get into Iraq. By the way, did any of you have problems with Saudi immigration?"

"No. None at all. Well, only Andy, and that was minor. And it was with Customs, not immigration. They found a copy of *Penthouse* in his hand-baggage, so they tore the rest of his kit apart to see what else he'd got. Mine too, as I was with him. Of course, we were all clean. You should have seen Mel's face – I could've sworn he knew what was going to happen. He and Chris stood to one side and pretended not to know us. They were both laughing their bloody heads off. Just as well no one had brought any duty-free liquor with them."

Howard sighed. Just like Andy Denard to be the one to be noticed, he thought. Still, no harm done. "How's Mel getting on with his companion?" he asked.

"No problems at all. I spoke to him this morning. Apparently Sullivan's really easy to get along with – relaxed, calm, no trouble. Mel's still thoroughly fed up about being left behind, you know."

"Can't be helped," shrugged Howard. "He knew it right from the start. He agreed on that basis. It was between him and Bob, and Bob doesn't speak any Arabic. Sullivan's minder may need it if something goes wrong. Mel's got an important job to do – among other things, he'll be watching our backs. Right," he concluded happily, "I'm full. Let's go and have a look at things."

They walked over to the camp workshop. Tony Ackford was working underneath a Toyota Land Cruiser on a ramp, assisted by Bob Usher. Nearby were two other identical vehicles, and the wheelless shell of a fourth, the one that had been stripped for spare parts.

"How's it going, Tony?" Howard walked over to examine his handiwork.

"Fine, boss. No probs at all. Here – let me show you an idea I'm working on. I'm doctoring the exhaust manifold on this one. I've fitted this lever into the cab; by turning it we can bypass the silencer, see? Whenever the lever is turned, it'll sound like the exhaust's blown. Clapped-out, like. We'll be able to turn it on and off whenever we want."

Howard thought about it and nodded his head. "Good idea – I like it. Are you going to do the same for both cars?"

"I thought one would do, but I can do both if you like."

"I think one will be enough. How about the electrics?"

"That won't take long at all – very simple job. Just the roof-lights to fit – you know. By the way, did you bring the infra-red filters? I might need to modify the spotlamp fittings."

"In one of the bags," said Howard. "Mike and Danny are unpacking them now. Anything I can do to help?"

"Give us a hand with this clamp, will you? I've got to get it just right. If this hole spews out too much shit in the wrong direction, it could clog the air filter."

*　　*　　*

Juliet Shelley had immersed herself in her work to take her mind off Johnny's absence. It was her second-last working day at her old job; just tomorrow left. She would have Saturday and Sunday to herself, then on Monday, the 18th, she would report to her new post at New Scotland Yard. Meanwhile, she was determined to hand over her old desk in good order.

It would be something of a wrench leaving, she thought. They were a good bunch. They had taken her out for a farewell drink the previous night. Some of them had had a few drinks too many, but on the whole it had been a good-natured do. Even the Superintendent had joined the party. That was one for the books; she had never considered him a sociable sort, but he had been affability itself. One or two of the others had been . . . well, perhaps a little far gone for their own good; they had let their hair down rather more than might seem prudent. Juliet hoped the Superintendent wouldn't hold it against them. Not even against DC Ford. Gavin Ford had really made a fool of himself. Juliet had seen the Superintendent having a quiet word with the new DS, who had sent Ford packing shortly afterwards. Serve him right, clumsy lout.

She tidied her desk and put on her coat to go. Just one more day, and then on to a new challenge, a new life. A new life . . .

As the bus ground slowly along through the heavy evening traffic, she thought about her future with Johnny. How she missed him! He had only been away for eight days, and she missed him dreadfully. What was it? Another two weeks, possibly three . . . she would never let him go away and leave her again. Never! She took out her wallet and looked at his photograph for about the hundredth time. Just looking at him made her heart beat a little faster. It was absurd.

The bus reached her stop and she got off. Instead of walking straight to the flat, she went round the corner to the shops. The cleaners were still open, thank goodness.

As she searched for the cleaning ticket, she realised to her annoyance that she had left it behind somewhere. "I'm sorry, but I seem to have lost the ticket. The name's Shelley. I brought it in this morning. It's a black skirt."

"Address, love?" Juliet gave it, and the assistant went off to look for the skirt.

When he returned and handed the package over, Juliet opened it to see if the stain had come out; it had. Thank goodness, she thought again. She would have murdered DC Ford if it hadn't. Bloody Mary, all down her skirt. She sniffed it; there was no trace of the smell of Worcester sauce and Tabasco. "Thanks very much. How much do I owe you?"

"That'll be two pounds sixty-five, love. Do you want to take this other piece as well? That would be another two-forty."

"What other piece?"

The assistant handed over a wire hanger, with a pair of blue jeans. "Same address on the ticket, love."

Juliet looked at the ticket; it had the name "Bourne" on it. Johnny's jeans. "Yes, I'll take them. They're my fiancé's." She paid and left the shop.

As she walked home, Juliet swung her bag lightly in time with her step. Silly man, she thought. Why were men always so lazy? Too lazy to use a washing machine. It was ridiculous, sending jeans to the cleaners; far too expensive. Silly man. She smiled to herself.

She let herself into the flat and took off her coat. In the bedroom, she removed the flimsy plastic covers from the skirt and jeans and opened the wardrobe door. About to hang them up inside, she noticed a stain mark on the seat of the jeans and frowned. Stupid man! Didn't he know that if you had a particular stain, you had to tell the cleaners what it was? Anyway, he could easily have got this out himself. She carried the jeans through to the kitchen and rummaged in the cupboard under the sink for the Stain Devil tubes. The orange tube was for grease and oil stains, the yellow tube for glue and chewing-gum, the white one for rust, the light-green one for felt-tip pen . . . ah, there it was. The dark-green tube. That was the one she needed.

She began to scrub at the mark. Five minutes later she held the jeans up and inspected them with satisfaction. The stain had vanished.

*   *   *

Howard and the others had time on their hands. Their arrival date in Saudi Arabia had been largely determined by the scheduling of the once-weekly container-ship sailings from Felixstowe on the East Africa route. Howard had decided to leave extra time in hand in case of problems at Suez, or an unexpected setback in Saudi itself. He had balanced this against his wish to spend as little time in Saudi as possible; an unexpected visit from Hughes, or perhaps a routine check by the local police, could be embarrassing. They were not due to leave Badanah until 25th April.

Denard took Howard and Ziegler up for a flight on the 17th. They had chosen Friday, the Muslim *jum'a*, as a day when activity would be at a minimum. Denard had filed for a local survey flight to the west, along the Trans-Arabian Pipeline road; that was precisely the route they took. Sixty miles out from Ar'ar they passed over Al Jalamid airstrip; there was little sign of life. The TAP road itself was busy; it was the main highway from Jordan through the empty desert to the Gulf states, and large lorries thundered along it day and night. All of them, Bourne had told Howard, were Saudi-registered. The Saudi Government, which frequently passed arbitrary laws and changed the rules whenever it felt like it, had decreed that all road haulage within the Kingdom would be by Saudi contractors alone.

The landscape beneath them was monotonous and almost entirely featureless: mile upon mile of rocky, boulder-strewn nothingness. Howard noticed an odd, faintly green tinge to the surface of the desert; there had been plentiful rains that winter, and long-dormant seeds of grass and flowers were springing into brief life. Far off to the south, he glimpsed the beginning of the great sand sea of the Nafud desert itself.

Fifteen miles beyond Al Jalamid, Denard indicated a dark slash in the desert a couple of miles off to the north of the road. "Al Mira strip," he said through the throat-mike to Howard.

Howard peered out of the right-hand window as Denard circled over the airstrip; it looked deserted. "Are you going to put down there now?"

200

"Nah. Just have a look, man. Your track is only a few miles away now, if your map is right. This may be the best place to land if we need to. The road would be better, but it's too busy – someone would see us."

"They probably would," agreed Howard.

Satsified that the Al Mira strip would do, Denard climbed again and flew on west. Almost immediately, he pointed out a dirt track leading off from the TAP road to the north. "I think that must be it. What do you reckon?"

"Climb some more, Andy. I want to get a good look at the area and make sure it's the right track. There are lots of them on the map, and probably a whole lot more that aren't even marked." Denard took the Islander up to eleven thousand feet. Howard spent several minutes studying the map and comparing it with the almost featureless panorama below him. He had been right. The terrain was crossed by many tracks visible from the air; only a few of them were marked on his map. "OK, Andy, I'm pretty sure that was the right track. Take her down and we'll confirm it and leave a marker. How far north do you think you can get away with?"

"At radar altitude, maybe five or ten miles before someone starts asking questions. That's as far as I'll be able to explain away as being accidental. But it depends what's watching us, and how jumpy they are about this area. I could go lower, below radar, but if there's an AWACS up it'll spot us, and our manoeuvre will definitely be regarded as out of order. Also, air-traffic-control authorities don't like people disappearing off their radar screens. The authorities here are military, and quite strict. Understandable, I suppose, after the events of last year. Of course, I could stay low enough to avoid even the AWACS. You'll see there's a wadi marked, an old riverbed. The wadi Al Mira. If I get into that, I can keep well down, below the surrounding ground-level. But if I stay that low, it's going to be no use to you. You won't be able to make out where you are on the map or see the track. And a manoeuvre like that would *really* make an AWACS sit up and think. I'd have some questions to answer afterwards."

"Fair enough. Keep us at a height no one will think is suspicious, and follow the track as far as you think won't cause any comment. We are on a survey trip, after all. If we get any questions we can explain it away with that."

After another ten minutes, Howard was satisfied. Denard had flown north along the line of the track, far enough for Howard to see that it was heading in the direction indicated on the map. Denard brought the plane round south again, heading back down the track to where it joined the TAP road. Howard turned to Ziegler in the rear of the plane, signalling to him to get ready. Ziegler took three one-litre plastic cans out of a bag and eased open the rear cargo door.

"OK, Andy," Howard said, "we're ready to mark when you are. Come at it along the road from the west. Pick a gap when there's no traffic, and get as low as you can. Give Mike a countdown – 'one' for four hundred yards short, 'two' for the junction itself, and 'three' for four hundred yards past it. OK?"

"Will do." Denard circled for a minute until he could see the road was relatively clear. Then he put the Islander into a steep dive. He levelled out at a hundred feet, then went down to ten feet, skimming along the surface of the road. Ten seconds later, he shouted, "One."

Ziegler dropped one of the cans out of the door and picked up the second. Eight seconds later, on the shout "Two", he dropped the second can, and after another eight seconds, on "Three", the third.

Denard hauled back on the control and the aircraft climbed steeply. Howard began to feel queasy at the aerobatics. When they got back up to two thousand feet, he looked down.

Spaced out along the road there were three splashes of bright white paint where the cans had burst on impact with the tarmac. They would be unmistakable, even in the dark. The middle splash was right next to the junction of the track leading north into Iraq.

"OK, Andy, that's fine. Time to go home."

*   *   *

It took a morning to prepare the two vehicles for painting. The third Land Cruiser was a sandy beige colour, and they decided to leave it as it was. It was a spare, anyway, to be used by Denard and Palmer. Bourne, Usher, Howard and MacDonald worked with adhesive tape and paper to mask off all the glass, chrome and other unpainted surfaces of the first two Land Cruisers, while Ackford set up the paint-gun and practised on the hulk of the cannibalised vehicle.

At last everything was ready. The others left, closing the workshop doors behind them to prevent dust or sand particles from blowing about. Ackford fitted his goggles and face-mask once more and began to spray. With no ventilation, the workshop soon became as hot as an oven; Ackford was drenched in sweat. Forty minutes later he emerged, closing the doors quickly behind him. Inside, the two Land Cruisers gleamed with fresh white paint.

They left the vehicles to dry for twenty-four hours, then opened up the workshop to inspect Ackford's handiwork. The white paint looked immaculate.

"Oh, *beautiful* work, Tony," said Usher with exaggerated praise. "Just gorgeous. What a clever boy you are. You've missed your vocation, mate. What did you ever go to sea for, anyway? Did they just use you as ballast, or were you permanently assigned to painting the bilges?"

"You can bog off, you little bald bleeder," retorted Ackford with a grin. "There's nothing wrong with that job at all. Look at it – perfect. Anyway, you've just voted yourself into a job. You can do the next coat, when we've finished the modifications."

"I thought you'd never ask. Let's get the paint mixed with this extra oil. Have you cleaned out the gun?"

" 'Course I have. Right; there you are. Get practising."

Ackford supervised the careful denting of several panels on the vehicles, and removed some of the trimwork and one rear bumper in its entirety. When the team had finished, Usher was left to apply the next coat of paint. The following day, when they opened the doors, the two vehicles had been transformed – they were now a matt green colour. Ackford fussed over them as the team began peeling off the pieces of masking tape and paper. "Careful with that paint. The top coat's fragile. Pull the tape off away from the paint, like this. Careful now, Danny. This isn't a herring trawler, mate."

Once all the tape and paper had been removed, they inspected the Land Cruisers carefully. Declaring himself satisfied, Howard produced a handwritten list from his pocket. "Right," he said. "Let's do the final modifications."

As they walked round the Land Cruisers consulting the list, sharp blows were administered to the glasses of two tail-lights, smashing them. A third was taken off and the bulbs removed. A front side-light received similar treatment, and one side-window was given a star-shaped crack with a hammer. Bourne opened a large packet of red stickers with Arabic lettering and red crescent shapes. He peeled them away from their paper backing and applied them to the bonnets, front passenger doors and tailgates. With the flashing roof-lamps, the Land Cruisers now looked like paramilitary ambulance vehicles that had seen a lot of service and been poorly maintained.

"OK, boys," said Ackford, handing out large paintbrushes, "That'll do. It's top-coat time. Get painting. "

Ziegler examined the large can of liquid in front of him. "What in hell's this, Tony? It looks goddam awful."

"It is, mate," said Ackford cheerfully. "It's a nice mixture of old engine oil and grease. Now, get it on there. All over the paint. Not too thick, and keep it off the glasswork – we want to be able to see out, don't we?"

Twenty minutes later the two matt-green Land Cruisers were covered with a thin smear of dirty oil. "Right," said Howard. "we might as well get some practice driving these things. Johnny, you and me first. Six laps of the camp; three with me leading and then three with you in front. Then we change over with Mike and Danny. Then Bob and Tony. And no crashing them."

"They look crashed already," muttered MacDonald.

The camp perimeter was about a mile round, a dirt track. The two vehicles raised clouds of dust and sand and were soon smothered. As Usher and Ackford finally pulled in after the last circuit, Ackford turned the lever in the cab and the throaty roar of the unsilenced engine made a racket that brought the Pakistani cook hurrying out of his quarters to see what was wrong. Bourne quickly shepherded him back inside, reassuring him that all was well.

"Bloody hell," muttered Howard, impressed. "These cars look older than God. Even *I'm* convinced they won't last ten miles. And under all that muck they're brand-new."

"I'm glad Tony Hughes isn't here to see them," said Bourne. "He'd have a fit, poor bloke."

"I'm afraid he's due for a bit of a shock, whatever happens. But not just yet, I hope."

They locked the Land Cruisers back inside the workshop for the night. It was the afternoon of Thursday 23rd April. The next night, if all went to plan, they would cross the border into Iraq.

35

It was dusk as they left Badanah. Howard privately reflected that for some reason setting out on an operation was always the part that made him most nervous. It was ridiculous, he thought. All that it involved was driving seventy-odd miles along the TAP road until they saw the paint splashes, then turning off on to the track. What could be simpler? But the risk of discovery was there. A chance police patrol – despite Johnny's assurances that these were extremely rare; a report from a truck-driver on the road that two strange and filthy-looking ambulances with unreadable number-plates had passed that way; a breakdown; perhaps some overzealous road-maintenance gang who had cleaned the paint off the road . . . It just needed one bit of bad luck, and months of work and planning would disappear down the drain. A failure later on, when at least they had tried – that would be another matter. But to fail now – it would be so . . . *ignominious*. Howard hated contemplating failure at the best of times; an intensely competitive man, he had rarely failed in anything he had attempted. *Please, not now, not this way* . . . He scowled at the thought and tried to shake himself free of it. Unnecessarily, he consulted the GPS receiver for the fourth time.

Bourne, in the driver's seat beside Howard, noticed the tension in his passenger and said nothing. He understood the burden of responsibility on the older man. For himself, he felt only a keen excitement, a sense of anticipation – something he had not felt for a long time. He thought briefly of Juliet, and his heart gave a momentary lurch, as it always did. He tried to picture her face; the vision was only a hazy one. It surprised him. It was barely a fortnight since he had said goodbye to her, with the promise that he would only be away for three weeks, four at the most. Their wedding was set for Saturday 23rd May – only a month from now. But there had been something different in those smoky eyes as she had said goodbye, something that told him she was not sure of him any more. Johnny frowned at the memory. How could she have known anything? He had been scrupulously careful. His two lives, as Bryce and Bourne, had been kept completely separate, only briefly overlapping each day in the anonymity of the Heathrow long-term car-park when he changed cars. There was no connection that she could have made; she knew nothing of Bryce, of the BMW, or of his other work. He must have been imagining things. The look on her face must just have been concern, coupled with sadness that they would not be seeing each other for a while. Yes; that was it – concern. He shook his thoughts clear and glanced at the Land Cruiser's trip milometer. "I've got sixty miles on the clock since Badanah, Ed. How are we doing?"

"Al Jalamid should be just coming up any minute. The turning's about fifteen miles past that."

In the back of the Land Cruiser, lying on the ambulance stretcher, Danny MacDonald too kept his thoughts to himself. Occasionally he turned his head to peer out ahead into the dark. To his surprise, he realised that he was having the time of his life. He liked these men. Their lives were light-years apart from his – their strange military jargon, the way each seemed to know what the other was thinking before he spoke, their professionalism – but he knew that he had a lot in common with them, too. They were tough, fit, self-reliant, unflappable – as he was. It suddenly occurred to him that he had never once seen a single sign of bad temper from any of them. The strain must have been there – he had felt it himself – but there had never been any complaining, any hint of tetchiness. They were good men to be with. A good team. And yet, oddly, they weren't really team people at all, any more than he was. They were individuals. Perhaps that was what made them such a formidable combination; they were each quite capable of looking after themselves, but they chose to be together, to pool their talents. Not one leader with a group of mindless followers, but six strong characters – nine, including Mel, Andy and Chris – any one of whom (other than himself, he thought) could have led this operation once the plan was decided on.

Danny considered each of his companions in turn. Big, level-headed Tony Ackford - confident, easygoing, mild-natured and friendly and, although the last one he would have expected to be good with his hands, amazingly skilled, precise and patient. Bob Usher, that small, tough, shiny-headed bullet of a man, usually reserved and quiet, but with flashes of bubbling humour; he seemed kind and considerate, too – hadn't he been the one who had thought of him and his endless tables and gone to the trouble of getting the little computer fixed up for him? Danny had heard about Bob's time in the Turkish prison with Ed Howard, but he had been puzzled by the others' occasional references to Bob as "TV star". Eventually he had asked what they meant, and had been startled to hear that Bob had been one of the first two men to enter through the upstairs window of the Iranian Embassy in London's Princes Gate, during the successful SAS operation to rescue the Iranian Embassy personnel in 1979. The "flash-bang-wallop" pictures of this had been replayed on TV dozens of times since, and Danny had often wondered about the men involved – who they were, what they were like. Now he could count one of them as a friend. Yes, Bob and Tony were the two Danny felt he could identify with most closely.

He hadn't really fathomed Mel Harris at all – a restless, mercurial character, never still for long, his bright little eyes always darting about. Danny suspected he had the shortest fuse of any of them, though he had seen no sign of it. Three Sardinian kidnappers had, he gathered . . .

Andy Denard and Chris Palmer were a team apart, in a way. Andy was clearly the joker, but Danny knew from what Howard had told him that he was a brave and skilled pilot, with an ice-cool brain when he wasn't hiding it behind his clowning. And then there was Chris – stolid, utterly dependable, as calm and professional as Tony.

Johnny Bourne was another, thought Danny, who was difficult to read, in the same way that Mel Harris was. There was something about Johnny that Danny couldn't put his finger on. Of all of them, Johnny was the one Ed seemed to hold in the highest regard. That surprised him; he would have expected Mike Ziegler to be the natural number two for this operation.

Howard had told Danny a little of Bourne's Army record during their sea voyage. As a young platoon commander in the Falklands War, Johnny had stumbled with his platoon into an unmarked Argentinian minefield at night, shortly before the battle for Mount Longdon. It was sheer bad luck. His platoon sergeant trod on a mine, losing a foot. Another soldier, on seeing this, panicked and ran, treading on a second mine. His foot was also blown off, and a third soldier nearby, who had correctly stood his ground, was badly injured by mine fragments. The platoon medic, a corporal, courageously trying to make his way forward to assist the wounded, trod on a third mine and lost his foot too. In the space of two minutes, Johnny suddenly found himself with four horribly injured soldiers on his hands. He calmly picked up the wounded Sergeant and led the platoon back, out of the minefield, each man following exactly in his footsteps. Just as they reached the safety of a rocky outcrop, flares went up, bathing the plain in light, and half a dozen Argentinian machine-gun nests opened up on them from the hill in front, raking the open ground. Johnny Bourne returned alone into the minefield under heavy fire, three times, to bring the other wounded men out. He summoned a stretcher party to supervise the evacuation of the wounded to a field hospital, then gave the remainder of his platoon a fighting pep-talk and led them in a devastating attack on the enemy position.

Howard had heard about the action; always on the look-out for new talent to recruit into XF Securities, he had spoken to some of Bourne's soldiers when they returned from the Falklands. The one thing they all said, quite apart from testifying to Bourne's immense bravery, was that he had terrified them with the ferocity of his attack on the Argentinian position. And yet . . . when the Argentinians had surrendered, Bourne had taken twelve prisoners, and had been kind to them, refusing to allow his angry men to carry out any reprisals, tending to the Argentinian wounded too . . .

What could you make of a man like that, pondered Danny. Complicated, a man of many moods and passions, a brave man. And yet . . . Danny had it. It suddenly struck him that at heart Johnny Bourne still had something of the little boy in him. Somehow it seemed he had never completely grown up. There was something endearing about his enthusiasms, his capacity for absorption in his work. Unpredictable? No. He couldn't be. Ed Howard would never have chosen someone he was not sure about.

Danny could clearly understand why Mike had been chosen. Mike was one of the most impressive men he had ever met – a powerhouse of energy, an athletic, cool, humorous, brilliant soldier. On the night exercises outside the Badanah camp, Mike was the one who could disappear and reappear out of thin air; he was also the one Ed had chosen to train Danny and teach him some armed and unarmed combat techniques. When Danny had watched Mike in training demonstrations, he had never seen anyone so utterly in control of his actions, so sure and certain. Yes, he was an impressive man. Impressive, and frightening. A complete fighter. And a charming, likable man.

Ed Howard himself, mused Danny, was a complete enigma. One could never tell what he was thinking. What was one to make of those dark, expressionless eyes, and the calculating, manipulative mind that must lie behind them? Howard was something of an organisational genius, and probably the best – and certainly the most experienced – soldier of all of them. None of the others had been very forthcoming about him, although Ziegler had let it slip that Howard had served with him in the latter days of the Vietnam War, and had been nominated on two separate occasions for US military decorations for bravery. He hadn't mentioned precisely what the nominations were for, but in any case the news had baffled Danny. What the hell had British soldiers been doing in Vietnam? It was the first he had heard of such a thing, and he wasn't sure whether or not to believe it. But Mike had not sounded as though he was joking.

Just what did go on inside Howard's mind? Danny rolled over again and studied the back of Howard's head. He doubted whether anyone would ever figure him out, read that mind. By nature, Howard was the most self-contained and solitary of them all. There was some sadness there, Danny thought – perhaps due to an inability to get on with people on any basis other than a professional one. He had seen Howard's small flat in London. It was utterly impersonal; there was no clue whatsoever to the man. Perhaps he had no personal life at all . . .

Danny gave up speculating. He knew that his companions were the sort of men he would choose to be with him in time of trouble. He felt flattered that *they* had chosen *him*, had accepted him. His early resentments and suspicions had been quickly dispelled. Danny MacDonald reflected once more on the job he was to do, and the hot anger rose in his throat again. Soon, now. Only a few more days . . . His eyes glittered fiercely in the dark as he lay back and tried to relax.

In the front passenger seat of the car behind, Ziegler had been thinking much the same thing as MacDonald about his friend Ed

Howard. *What is there going to be for you after this job, Ed? What can any of us do after this? We'll all have to change. I hope you find what you're looking for . . .*

Ackford, behind the wheel, broke Ziegler's train of thought. "I must get out to the States one day. Always meant to go, you know, but never got round to it. Maybe New York to start with, to keep the missus happy. She's Irish, and keeps on about how there's a lot of Irish people there. D'you think I'd like it?"

"Sure, Tony, if you like big cities," replied Ziegler easily. Privately, he thought that Ackford would hate New York, perhaps even as much as he did. He'd be happier with the simple life on a farm somewhere, maybe out in the Midwest. Preferably with a whole lot of broken-down machinery to fix. "Yeah, New York is a fine city. If you like cities, that is," he repeated, pointedly.

"Oh." Ackford had caught the inference. He turned it over in his mind for a few seconds, his jaw working on a stick of gum. "Well, maybe I could spend just a couple of days there. Then get out and about — see something of the rest of the country."

"That sounds more like it. Say, if you do come over, let me know. We'll do somethin'. Maybe take off on a canoe trip, do some fishin'. How about that?"

"You're on, mate. Hang on." Ackford came alert as the vehicle in front slowed. Shortly afterwards, a large smear of white paint appeared in the middle of the road. "I think we've arrived. Got them NVGs ready?"

"Yeah."

The two cars pulled off the road by the second paint splash. Bourne, in front, immediately killed his lights and continued a further quarter of a mile along the track, until he was well clear of the road, before stopping. Howard's spirits lifted as he passed Bourne a flying helmet; it had two protruding optical devices attached to the front, like mechanical eyes. Bourne put the helmet on, adjusted the chinstrap and switched on the optics. Howard, and in the second vehicle Ackford and Ziegler, did likewise.

The landscape showed up clearly in the dark. The night-vision goggles gathered in the tiny amount of available light and magnified it fifty thousand times; night was turned into day, in astonishing detail.

"Let's try it with the IR lamps," said Bourne to Howard. He flicked a switch on the dashboard. Ackford had fitted each Land Cruiser with an extra set of driving lamps; these were completely covered by black-coloured filters which blocked out visible light. Only the invisible infra-red wavelengths penetrated the filter. The NVGs were sensitive to infra-red as well as visible light, and the transformation was dramatic. Good as the visibility had been before, now it was as if it was a bright summer's day, except for the fact that the NVG picture was a monochrome green.

To the naked eye, the vehicles were invisible in the dark; for the occupants, however, who could see perfectly with their image-intensification goggles, it was a simple matter to pick out the track and travel at a reasonable speed. They set off northwards. Ahead, fifty miles away, was the Iraqi border.

*   *   *

"Light there — up ahead." Bourne's voice had tensed.

"Got it," said Howard. "Slow right down. Creep up closer." He took another reading from the GPS. It gave 39 deg 40 min E, 32 deg 04 min N. Depending on which line on the map you chose, they were either just short of the actual Iraqi border, or just over the *de facto* one. And the map was so vague for these parts that the lines might be inaccurate anyway . . . but the light was about three kilometres ahead. That put it inside Iraq, whichever line you chose.

For ten miles now they had been travelling more slowly and carefully, ever since the last junction. This section of the track was abominable; it clearly hadn't been used for a long time by anyone. It looked as if it hadn't been maintained since the Flood. Pretty apt phrase, thought Howard. Seasonal flash floods had carried parts of it away. They had only just spotted the track junction ten miles back; Ziegler, in the car behind, had seen it and flashed the IR lamps. They had stopped to confer for a few minutes, and Howard had decided that Ziegler was right. The left-hand fork continued north for a few miles and then began to loop round to the west, then south again, leading back to the TAP road at Turaif, near the Jordanian border. *Not* where they wanted to end up. They had turned off on to the right-hand one, towards the Iraqi border.

The two vehicles crept towards the light, their engines running almost silently. At a distance of one kilometre, Howard motioned to Bourne for another halt. They got out of the car and peered at the light, trying to discern exactly what it was.

Howard felt a tap on his shoulder. Ziegler had joined them from the second vehicle. "Movement," he whispered in Howard's ear. "A man, I'm pretty sure. "Did you see that faint light to the left? I think it was a cigarette. The main light's movin' in the breeze. My guess is a pressure lamp, hangin' outside. There's a building on the left, set back a little from the track. A guard post, maybe."

"I agree. OK, we'll move up a little closer."

Howard, Bourne and Ziegler had talked this over before setting out. They had no idea whether or not there would be a border post, or, if there was, whether it would be a Saudi or an Iraqi one, or both. They had decided that they would just have to make an assessment if they came across one, and deal with it accordingly. Ziegler had analysed the most likely possibility. "I mean, just look at this goddam place," he had said, tapping at the spot on the map where the track crossed the border. "Pretty hot postin', huh? Terrific night-life, great recreational facilities. Every military man's dream."

"What do you mean, Mike?" Johnny had asked.

"Well, if you were a hot-shot Iraqi general, who would you put in charge of a dump like that? I'll tell you who. A real asshole. You'd put someone there who you didn't want screwin' things up someplace else. So he'd be out of the way. Also, out of sight and mind. Someone you wanted to forget about, right?"

Howard had got the drift. "I think you're right. It would be a real dead-end job. Manned by incompetents or expendables. Morale would be low. Nothing happening, day after day, night after night. Discipline would be slack, alertness almost zero, equipment probably basic. I don't think we'd encounter much trouble, but that's not the point. We'd have to make damn sure we weren't seen, either."

"OK," whispered Howard now, recalling that conversation. "It's much as we expected. A chance to get some weapons, too. Three of us should do it. We'll move up four or five hundred yards closer, in the vehicles. Then Johnny, you stay there with the cars. I'll go for something to cause a diversion. Mike, you take Tony or Bob and see what ordnance you can sneak out of their armoury. How long do you reckon? One hour be enough?"

"Let's make it 22.00 exactly for the diversion," said Ziegler.

212

"That's a nice round number. I'll get clear by then. See you about five hundred yards the other side?"

"Fine. Johnny, at about 21.45, move up very slowly to as close as you dare. Come through without lights when you see the diversion. Anything else, anyone?"

"Ed?" hissed Ziegler. "Mind if I take Danny with me instead?"

Howard shot him a glance, then smiled. "An excellent idea. It'll make him feel part of the team. And in his job, he's used to sneaking up on things unobserved, isn't he?"

"Just what I was thinkin'," replied Ziegler. He went over to Howard's vehicle and whispered through the window. "Mac, the boss has picked you and me to sneak up on that border post and do a bit of thievin'."

MacDonald suddenly felt absurdly flattered to have been chosen.

*　　　*　　　*

Howard's task proved to be easy. Approaching the border post with his NVGs on, he clearly saw the main building. A large truck was parked in front. Outside, the single Tilley lamp burned brightly in the goggles' vision; underneath it a solitary sentry sat hunched on a wooden bench, wrapped in a heavy overcoat against the chill of the night air, his head buried in his chest. The man looked only half awake; he was certainly far from alert. Howard looked to the left. There was another, smaller building behind the main one, and a third – a long, low structure – next to that. The size of the buildings and the truck suggested a platoon-strength position, perhaps something slightly smaller.

A hundred yards or so further off to the left, he saw what he was looking for. There was a low, walled emplacement without a roof. Five minutes' observation confirmed it to be unguarded. Slowly, he crawled up to a gap in the wall and looked inside. *Bingo*, he thought. *A ready-made diversion.* He took a pair of pliers out of his pocket and began to work.

*　　　*　　　*

Ziegler moved like a wraith through the dark. Following him, Danny felt utterly confident. He had quickly absorbed the basic hand-signals

213

and night-movement techniques Ziegler had taught him on their night training outside the Badanah camp; and he was no stranger, as Howard had remarked, to the principle of moving quietly and without being seen. The two men approached the rear of the main building; round at the front, the lone sentry was huddled in his coat on the bench. Ziegler motioned MacDonald to the ground and covered the last few yards alone, working his way round the side. Removing his goggles, he peered through the window. Inside was a desk, with a chair behind it. A dim light came from a kerosene heater near the middle of the room. A man with the shoulder-flashes of an Iraqi lieutenant was asleep in the chair, several days' growth of stubble on his face and his beret askew, covering his eyes. *Turkey*, thought Ziegler. A wooden partition with a door separated the guard commander's office from the rear section of the building, which Ziegler guessed was a storeroom. He returned to MacDonald. They did not need to look through the window of the second building; the loud chorus of snores emanating from within told them that it was the main bunkhouse. The third building housed a communal mess-room and kitchen; inside there were six men, clustered round a second kerosene heater. The current guard detail.

"OK, Danny," whispered Ziegler in the dark. "There are three possibilities. One, the off-duty men all have their weapons with them in the bunkhouse; two, they're locked in the store in the front buildin', in the room behind the commander's office; or three, a mixture of the two. My guess is for option three, that there are spare arms in the front buildin'. Let's go take a look."

The rear door to the store was unlocked; Ziegler didn't even have to pick it. He pulled on a pair of woollen socks over his boots, so that his footsteps would make no sound on the wooden floor. Inside the store, his NVGs enabled him to see as clearly as if the room were illuminated by a weak light-bulb. Two dozen AKM and AKMS rifles hung in a long rack on the wall; nearby on the floor was a stack of green-painted metal canisters about fourteen inches long, looking exactly like oversized sardine-cans. In another rack were the long, funnel-ended tubes of six RPG-7 anti-tank rocket-launchers, with several wooden crates of projectiles underneath them, and in a third were four RPD light machine-guns, six RPKs and one Goryunov medium machine-gun, with its folded tripod beneath it on the floor. Three more wooden crates proved to contain fragmentation hand-grenades, and there was one large crate of anti-tank mines.

Working very quietly, Ziegler handed six AKMS rifles out to MacDonald, who laid them out side by side on the ground, and six of the heavy sardine-can canisters, having checked the Cyrillic script stencilled in black on the outside of each one. He ignored the machine-gun rack and instead selected one of the RPG-7s and a crate of projectiles. Checking the mines, he was relieved to note that the crate was full: the track would not be mined. Finally, he bent to pick up one of the crates of hand-grenades.

A floorboard squeaked loudly, and Ziegler froze. *Damn!* he thought, furious with himself, his mind racing. Almost immediately he realised that the sound had come from behind the thin partition, not from under his own feet. The Lieutenant had stirred and shifted in his chair. There was no further sound, and after two precautionary minutes of immobility, Ziegler padded silently outside with the crate of grenades. Infinitely slowly, he closed the door behind him.

Not long afterwards, Ziegler and MacDonald had filled one rucksack with the sardine-cans; into the other went the RPG projectiles and the hand-grenades, the long crate of projectiles sticking out of the top. Taping the AKMS rifles together so that they would not rattle against one another, Ziegler hefted one of the packs and checked his watch. Just under twenty minutes to go. One more thing to do – empty a water-bottle into the fuel tank of the truck. MacDonald, with the other pack, followed him off into the darkness.

Nineteen and a half minutes later, several things happened almost at once. First, a small mechanical alarm clock in the front office sounded. The Lieutenant yawned and woke, and the sentry outside jerked into consciousness, glancing guiltily behind him in case he had been caught sleeping at his post. At that moment, there was a dull *whooompf!* from behind the building.

The sentry got to his feet, uncertain. He gazed about him, then knocked on the door of the Lieutenant's office. As he did so, he suddenly smelled burning, and the sky began to lighten with a red glow. Jabbering in alarm, he fell through the door just as the Lieutenant emerged, so that the two men collided. The Lieutenant swore, picked himself up and ran round to the side of the building, where the sight that met his eyes momentarily froze him to the spot. He let out a bellow of fear and anger; in the second hut, soldiers

215

were jolted awake. In the darkness and confusion, they cursed and scrambled for their boots and weapons, and began piling out into the night – except it no longer seemed like night-time.

*   *   *

Howard's job had been simple. The fuel dump contained twenty-six forty-five-gallon drums of petrol and kerosene, and one of engine oil. One half-full drum of kerosene lay on its side on a trestle cradle, with a tap screwed into its main bung. The petrol drums were stacked on their ends; one drum had a rotary hand-pump fitted to it, as did the single oil drum. Using the pliers, Howard loosened the bungs on twenty of the upright drums, without removing them; at 21.50 he began pumping out the oil and petrol on to the concrete floor of the enclosure. When both the drums with pumps were empty, he opened the tap on the kerosene drum; the fuel gurgled out on to the petrol-soaked floor, running out of a four-inch-diameter drain-hole in the wall into a concrete spill-sump outside. The sump filled to overflowing; Howard stood five yards away from it, outside, and waited.

Exactly eight seconds before 22.00, he lit his cigarette-lighter and held it to a piece of rag, which he had half soaked in kerosene. Then he tossed the rag into the spill-sump and withdrew, running silently away through the darkness.

The flame flashed back from the sump through the drain-hole and ignited the fuel inside the enclosure with a loud *whooompf!*, the sound heard by the sentry. It was nothing compared with the sounds that were to follow shortly afterwards.

The flames licked fiercely round the drums. The empty petrol drum, full of petrol vapour and therefore more unstable than the full ones, was the first to blow. A colossal bang rent the night as the petrol-air mixture exploded; shards of the drum scythed through the air. Three full drums nearby were punctured by some of the flying pieces; their contents spilled on to the concrete and added to the inferno. Seconds later, the others began to blow too. The six drums with the screw-bungs still in place were the last to explode, as they were sealed tight. It took nearly five minutes before the last one finally went up, showering burning fuel high into the air in a spectacular display.

By 21.45, fifteen minutes before the diversion was due, Bourne and

Ackford had carefully inched the vehicles up to within a couple of hundred yards of the buildings. They stopped and waited. As Bourne saw the first flash of flame, he started his engine; the noise was drowned by that of the fire and subsequent explosions. Ackford, in the car behind, did the same. They waited for the guard to turn out, to see what they would do. When to make the move, Bourne knew, would be a matter requiring quite careful judgement.

After weeks or even months of stupefying boredom and inaction, something had at last occurred to grab and hold the attention of the wretched Iraqi soldiers stationed at the god-forsaken border post. Any fire is mesmerising; when first awoken to this one, the Iraqi soldiers just stood and gawped at it. Then, chattering with excitement, they began to move towards the fire to warm themselves.

The Lieutenant made a futile attempt to goad his men into action, swearing, threatening and screaming at them above the roar of the blaze. The only animate response he received was a sarcastic utterance from a large, unkempt and now wide-awake corporal, to the effect that if he, the Lieutenant, wished to go and piss on such a volcanic fire with the useless dog's *zibb* of a hand-pump which was all that served as firefighting equipment in this prestigious military establishment, then that was his, the Lieutenant's, privilege. He, the Corporal, would pray for his, the Lieutenant's, glorious future in paradise, with its legendary abundance of beautiful, fat and attentive maidens, silken cushions, clear-running water and copious supplies of delicious fruits – in that order.

The Lieutenant gave up. Biting his nails in anxiety at the prospect of the consequences to be faced when his superiors heard of this disaster, which he almost immediately decided not to report for a few days until he could get the place cleaned up, he stood glumly to one side and watched the little that remained of his hitherto undistinguished military career ascend towards the heavens in huge billows of thick, black smoke.

If he, or any of his soldiers, had turned round to look behind him at precisely 22.05, he might just have seen the dark shapes of two rather dirty ambulance vehicles pass by on the track leading north, not thirty yards away.

But none of them looked. The two vehicles slipped past, unnoticed.

Howard's team was inside Iraq.

217

36

John Kearwin glanced up at the console on the left of his desk as the "alert" light came on. A point of light near the centre of the circular screen flashed as the scan bar rotated. Positive trace from the DSP downlink, thought Kearwin, absently; not strictly speaking his territory yet. NORAD would already be dealing with it, and he would know soon enough if it needed further investigation. He tapped in a code on the console's keyboard to run a standard analysis program of the trace, and went back to work on his main screen, finishing off the BDA composites on the Iraqi Al Ateer nuclear site.

The Al Ateer exercise had an absorbing one for Kearwin, who had spent many hundreds of hours evaluating and improving other bomb-damage assessment programs, ever since the serious failures of the Gulf War. With this latest one on Al Ateer, he had detailed on-the-ground analysis to pit himself against. Kearwin's analysis of satellite reconnaissance data was being measured against actual observation; Kearwin did not know what the observers' assessment was, and he would not be told until he had produced his own analysis. This one was being done live; Kearwin had been working on it for four hours, and was just about finished.

Kearwin enjoyed a challenge, and he loved his job. He took his work seriously. All his colleagues in the National Reconnaissance Office did, he reflected; but he could never quite manage the easy, joky style the others affected while at the same time remaining dedicated to their work. They were all exceptionally talented and able people, he knew; and he knew that he too was good at what he did. It came naturally to him; he could not see anything remarkable about his affinity for the job, and did not think of his own talent as exceptional. The only yardstick he could go by was the obvious respect in which he was held by his peers, and it sometimes puzzled

218

him that they thought he was as good as they were. Sure, time and again he had come up with results that had earned him their admiration. He had put it down to a lucky break whenever this happened, but there was no higher praise for Kearwin than the occasional nicely understated compliments he was paid by his colleagues, and the camaraderie that resulted. There was nothing Kearwin liked better than to be accepted as "one of the team".

It would have amazed and baffled him to be told that the others all thought of him as something of a whizz-kid, even by their standards; he would not have understood it at all. In his eyes he was no different to them, and in fact he wished that he found it easier to join in the off-duty – and occasionally even on-duty – banter. If he had a fault, he was perhaps a slightly too serious young man, but because he was so unassuming and modest, he was genuinely liked and respected.

Kearwin had one secret anxiety, which he had confided to his boss, Walter Sorensen, in an interview he had had with him prior to joining the NRO. He was terrified that someone might nickname him "Radar". He did in fact bear a remarkable resemblance to the actor who played the part in the long-running $M*A*S*H$ series on TV: he was fairly short, with a round face and a slightly squeaky voice, and he wore small round metal-framed glasses. He had spoken candidly of his fear to Sorensen, who had seen straight away that it really bothered the nervous young man. Kearwin, thought Sorensen, was a young guy with a bit of a confidence problem. He had looked again at Kearwin's confidential reports, and the glowing tributes paid to him by the scientists who had carefully monitored his progress. Kearwin was a natural. Sorensen was a good manager, and he knew how to get the best out of his people. The day before Kearwin was due to join the NRO, Sorensen had briefed the others. He had given them a resumé of Kearwin's qualifications; the others had been impressed. Finally he had added, "And do me and him a favour, boys, huh? This is a nice young guy. Don't josh him around too much. He really hates it when people call him Radar, like the guy on TV. If I catch any of you guys doing that, I'll have your ass. I mean it."

So they hadn't. Kearwin had followed Sorensen's advice, and changed the style of his glasses, from round to square frames. That had all been seven years before; Kearwin's confidence had since grown immeasurably. He had played a significant part in the development of the NRO's methods of analysis. And he had laughed out loud the first time someone had pointed out to him that Sorensen looked a bit like a walrus. Ironically, the nickname "Walrus" had stuck to Sorensen, who had found out about it but didn't mind, but Kearwin had never once been called Radar.

The installation of the Defense Support Program satellite real-time console four years previously had been one of Kearwin's own ideas; Sorensen himself had gone along with it, which had surprised Kearwin at the time.

"Not our job, John," the Walrus had said, gravely. "Real time ain't our job. We just deal with the medium and long-tail stuff. NORAD does the real-time analysis and handles quick-reaction situations. That's what they're for. We get the more interesting job, figuring out later what they didn't have time to do." For what must have been the fiftieth time, the Walrus had gone off into one of his favourite stand-ard finger-wagging lectures to rookie analysts, patiently explaining the role of the US National Reconnaissance Office.

Good old Walrus, Kearwin had thought; after nearly three years with the NRO, he had still been treated exactly as if it was his first day. But he had rehearsed his pitch. "You're absolutely right, Walter, but it's the time lag that bothers me. Remember what happens every time there's a positive? Every time the Soviets launch a satellite or run a test firing? The brass scream for an instant analysis. OK, they scream at the NORAD boys too, for all I know, but they mainly go for us, just to see whether we've got any detail. They figure we're the guys who can give them the detail, so they holler at us for it. They do it every time. It's not *my* ass on the line when they do, of course . . ." Kearwin let the sentence hang in the air; he knew he had Walter Sorensen's attention. It was a sore point with the Walrus; very sore. He was a patient man, but he got exasperated with having to explain to every goddam cowhide who could pick up a phone that his department was not the one to ask for quick-reaction analysis – and not only that, but that he didn't even know there was a positive yet – NORAD hadn't yet got to the stage of passing it on down the line. The Walrus never liked having to sound as though he didn't know what was going on.

"Goddam cowhides," muttered Sorensen, using his stock expres-sion for officials who pestered him when they should have known better. Each time, when he put the phone down after one of those conversations, it was the same: "Goddam cowhides."

Kearwin continued. "The way I see it, Walter, is this. If we had even just one real-time console in here, say a Defense Support Program satellite one, we would know there was something as it happened. We wouldn't have to spend much time on it. DSP would be ideal. It's really just the DSP positives that get the brass going. I could set up a quick program to give us the bones of it. Hell, it wouldn't take me more than a few seconds for each positive, and we know that ninety-five per cent of them are dealt with on the spot by NORAD and never end up coming our way. We'd just spend a little time on the five per cent. We wouldn't have lost anything – in fact maybe we'd've gained an hour or two, as we'll have to work on it anyway. And you'd have an answer for the brass."

Sorensen looked thoughtful. The idea appealed to him. He tweaked his large drooping moustache, and eventually he agreed. "OK, we'll do a trial on it. One screen, and on your desk. It's your baby. You set it up. I don't wanna know it's there unless there's a squawk. And just for one satellite, OK? I don't want you fiddling about with fancy 3-D imaging stuff, using two of them to predict trajectories or any of that crap. That's definitely NORAD's job. Just one satellite. And listen here, son," he added, solemnly wagging his finger, "don't let me catch you gazing at the goddam thing all day long and neglecting your regular duties."

"No chance," said Kearwin happily. "It'll just be there to give you ready answers for the brass. Once, maybe twice a month, if the past is anything to go by."

It wasn't. Shortly after the installation of the DSP monitor on Kearwin's desk-station in the summer of 1988, the NRO was suddenly instructed to sideline a large part of its normal tasking. Kearwin and five of the other analysts were snatched off Eastern Bloc work and reallocated to the Mid-East section. They were plunged into an analysis of the Iraqi nuclear programme, and worked round the clock for a month to get an assessment out. Kearwin could not remember a time when there had been such a rush priority job; everything else seemed to go out of the window. There was some CIA input, and what seemed like a lot of other foreign scuttlebutt, some of which turned out to be quite useful. The assessment was finished by early September 1988; it concluded that the Iraqi nuclear programme was well advanced, and gave an estimate of 1994 for a practical nuclear-weapons capability. Things then quietened down a little.

Not for long. Back came the instruction, two weeks later, to update the assessment and fill in more detail. Kearwin had expected this; the assessment had been riddled with disclaimers about more time being needed, how it was only a preliminary assessment, more data coming in all the time, blah, blah, blah. Vintage Walrus, thought Kearwin, but spot on for all that. You couldn't just shift the orbits of two KH-11 satellites and expect them to come up with instant answers on new territory. OK, there had been routine Keyhole passes over Iraq before, but there was a limit to what the small team working on that sector could come up with, and a limit to the data-archiving facility set aside for their use. Besides, those guys had mostly been involved with the Iran-Iraq War monitoring job; the "surrogate gloaters", someone had called them. Not their fault; they had only been working to orders.

So, back came the instruction: six months' work, this time. Shift the KH-11 orbits again for maximum coverage of Iraq. Just one pass a day wasn't good enough. Kearwin did rough calculations of the effect this would have on the KH-11 lifetimes before the fuel gave out. It would halve them, he reckoned: down to a mean average of maybe seven hundred and fifty days per bird. *Big* birds, too – the KH-11s were among the largest of the seven thousand or so miscellaneous objects on the loose up there. Sixty-four feet long and weighing thirty thousand pounds apiece, the KH-11 series had revolutionised the NRO's ability to keep an eye on the Soviet Union. For a long while, until the Soviets had been sold a copy of the KH-11 technical manual by a former watch officer at the Ops Center, the Sovs hadn't even known what it was there for. They had known it *was* there, but it hadn't seemed active. There seemed to be no signal coming from it; in fact it generated no apparent output at all, unlike its predecessor, the KH-9 series. The KH-11 downlink was crafty: it relayed its signal up into space to a geosynchronous data-relay satellite, rather than direct to earth. The KH-11 appeared to be electronically dead, so the Soviets hadn't bothered to hide sensitive items when it passed overhead. But the principal breakthrough utilised by the KH-11 was its ability to transmit data in real time. Previous Keyhole satellites had ejected film capsules in re-entry vehicles, later picked up for processing and analysis. The KH-11s digitally encrypted their own data and relayed it electronically, so it was ready for instant analysis – no waiting around, no delays.

So two KH-11s were going to be burned up getting this data

on Iraq. It took four days to change their orbit attitude to shift the perigee further south, over the required latitude. The lowest point of the elliptical orbit was two hundred and five kilometres, permitting detailed observation. Not content with that, they wanted to "bounce" them once an orbit, too. That meant bringing the perigee right down to one hundred and fifty kilometres over a specific target, to get maximum detail, using the "slingshot" effect to take them back up again afterwards to normal altitude. The technicians boosted the apogee from three hundred kilometres to three-fifty, but Kearwin doubted that would help make them last any longer. It was the fuel problem. Because just one pass a day wasn't considered adequate, every time the satellite slipped off to the side it was to be boosted round sideways again so that it passed over the target area on every single orbit.

Schematically, the KH-11 polar orbit track was rather like a ball of string, thought Kearwin. Each time the string wound round the ball, the next pass was normally slightly to the side of where it had been before. The earth was in the centre of the ball, and the holes at top and bottom were the north and south poles. The string passed round the ball more than a dozen times a day; for all but one of these passes, until the same time the following day, it had moved round so that it was covering another part of the ball. To get the string to cover the same place more frequently, you had to keep pushing it sideways to compensate for the earth's rotation. The satellite, travelling at a speed of six kilometres per second, had an orbit time of ninety minutes; that meant sixteen orbits per day. Sixteen fuel burns, every day! That used up a lot of hydrazine fuel, and shortened the life of the satellite. But while these two satellites lasted, they would certainly pull in a lot of data. And when they died? Up would go a couple more Titan-4Cs with replacements. An expensive business. "Time is money in this game," the Walrus said, and he wasn't kidding. "You boys had better make the best use of those two babies while they last."

Kearwin and his team really managed to get their teeth into the task. Far more detail was gathered. They had several more months of data, and could be more specific in their findings. The second assessment brought in several installations that hadn't previously been analysed in much detail, and a huge amount of eyeball and shoe-leather stuff from the CIA for cross-referencing. The Walrus's preliminary verdict, delivered as ordered half-way through the assessment, was that the Iraqis could have a nuclear bomb by 1993. The final verdict (Kearwin later told himself that he should have known better than to think it was final) brought this forward to 1992.

Bang. Back it came yet again, now top priority. A hundred days, they were given. Definitive answers required, individual Grade II speculation permitted. A third KH-11 on the job now, six more analysts. KH-12 support expected soon. Archiving storage facilities trebled. Promotion and a big raise for Kearwin. And all the time, the DSP console sat on the side of his work-station, occasionally blinking up positives. Kearwin largely left it alone during this time; the Walrus got tough with the cowhides, gleefully waving his direct instruction from Defense Secretary Dick Cheney under their noses whenever they squawked at him.

Kearwin argued at length that the indicator guidelines needed reassessment, and suggested some new parameters for evaluating developments in a Third World country like Iraq, rather than those established for a crumbling superpower like the Soviet Union. He was given his head by the Walrus. The Walrus himself had long talks with the CIA old-timers, going right back to the days when the Soviet nuclear industry was in its infancy. Civilian scientists were brought in for their input on modern off-the-shelf technology, and as a result the poor old eyeball-and-shoe-leather boys out on the ground had even more leads to follow up. Some corporations in Europe were tweaked hard for what they had been up to; there would be a lot of red faces among supposedly respectable industrialists. Governments too, maybe . . .

It had all happened with bewildering speed, Kearwin remembered, and was easily the most fascinating job he had ever worked on. By October 1989, the final report was finished. Kearwin's assessments of the newer Iraqi construction projects, and more particularly of the security surrounding them, had widened the scope for investigation, and the finished document included many of Kearwin's own projections. March 1991, the report said; possibly February. By then, Iraq would have its first nuclear weapon. Not much more than a year away.

It was when the DSP orbit was shifted that Kearwin realised how seriously it was all being taken. It wasn't even covering the eastern USSR anymore, for Chrissake. He had lost Kamchatka from the screen. The Defense Support Program satellites played an entirely different ball-game. For one thing, they didn't take pictures; they simply watched out for the intense infra-red signatures emitted by missiles, and gave a fix on the launch site. After launch, DSP monitoring would track the satellite; by the use of readings from several DSPs, a 3-D image was obtained, giving a trajectory and likely target within sixty seconds. The DSPs were geostationary, not moving relative to the earth, so they always monitored the same area, giving a new reading of the whole of their patch every ten seconds. To stay in the same place, they had to be at a much higher altitude orbit. The DSP satellite that Kearwin monitored was the thirteenth that had been launched, and until now had been geostationary over Sinkiang, in north-western China. From there, thirty-eight thousand kilometres above the earth, more than a hundred times the KH-11's altitude, it had been able to see almost half of the earth's surface, including the whole of the Soviet Union, the Warsaw Pact countries, China and the Far East. But since completion of the NRO's report on Iraq, they had shifted it nearly three thousand miles west, over . . . guess where? Right, the Gulf. There were more DSP satellites dotted about up there too, somewhere, for NORAD's 3-D tracking work.

During the last year or two there had been quite a few DSP positives from Iraq; they had been analysed as SS-1 Scud-B, Al Abbas and Al Hussein test launches. Not easy to spot, but the DSP was a good system. Cloud cover was the main drawback; with something the size of an intercontinental ballistic missile, which the DSP was principally designed to pick up, you could reckon to get it through thin cloud, and certainly once it had cleared the cloud. A Scud-B, on the other hand, was much smaller. Its heat signature had less than one per cent of the intensity of an ICBM's, and of course it didn't reach the same altitude. Not so easy to spot, especially if there was cloud. But Kearwin had seen quite a few, all the same. The practice had been useful. The section of the report on delivery systems had included information on Scud test launches, although most of the hard data on these had come from NORAD; it had been the one crumb of comfort to the brass. The Scud was a crappy system – to all intents and purposes a piece of free-flight junk, a real Stone Age guidance system, inaccurate as hell. Stick a fission warhead on the front of it though, and . . .

The brass must have known what the Iraqis were going to do, concluded Kearwin in retrospect. It comforted him that the foresight had existed. Even the Walrus acknowledged that the cowhides had got it right. Kuwait, Desert Shield . . . then Desert Storm itself. What a riot *that* had been. When the Walrus had spotted juniors crowding round Kearwin's DSP console during a live Scud launch, he had come damn near to ordering Kearwin to unplug the monitor and get rid of it. There was something irresistible about real-time analysis. Kearwin had been fascinated himself.

He ran it through his mind again. It had all been all so quick, when it happened. *Whoosh*; up would go the Scud. Within ten seconds would come the first DSP blip. Every ten seconds, another blip. The Missile Warning Center at NORAD Headquarters, buried deep underground in Cheyenne Mountain, Colorado, would have it confirmed and give a probable track and target within one minute of launch – so long as there was no cloud cover. Cloud added extra time, until the missile cleared it. The DSP sent its data to a TRDSS data satellite, which relayed it direct to NORAD; when they had computed the missile track, the information was sent back up to a MILSAT relay, which in turn flashed it to CENTCOM in the Gulf. Within three and a half minutes of launch, military commanders in the field would have received the information, and in a further ninety seconds, only five minutes after launch, the Patriot batteries themselves would be ready in Israel or Saudi Arabia. The time of flight of the Scud was eight minutes or less, so the Patriot batteries had just two to three minutes – at the most – to engage an incoming missile. In a Patriot battery, you slept with your boots on and one eye open. If you slept.

The problem with the Patriot, reflected Kearwin, was that it had been designed to deal with proper targets, not junk like the Scud or its Al Abbas and Al Hussein derivatives. Those crappy Scuds would start to break up on re-entry about fifteen to twenty kilometres up, and come down in three or more pieces. The tails fell off them, fins fell off, sometimes even the missile body broke in two. Standard procedure was to fire two Patriot PAC-2s at each target, so quite often four or more ended up being fired for each Scud in the air: two following the warhead, and two following each other piece of the Scud, sometimes all the way down to the ground. One night, thirty-five PAC-2s were fired at just seven Scuds. A million bucks a throw. The debris from falling Patriots and Scuds alike, spread over a wide area, ended up causing more physical damage than the Scud warheads would have caused by themselves. In Israel, casualties actually rose by sixty per cent per Scud after the Patriots started to be used, and damage reports per Scud tripled.

The Raytheon Corporation, Patriot's manufacturer, had to some extent anticipated this problem from earlier test firings at similar targets at White Sands, in the Arizona desert; but no one could have anticipated quite how unstable and liable to break up the Iraqi Scuds would prove to be. Raytheon came up with a solution extremely quickly; within twenty-four hours they rushed extra software out to the Gulf. The Patriot operators could now take the system out of automatic mode and use a modified procedure of manual control, which enabled them to lock on to the target with the most stable trajectory – the warhead section – although enormous presence of mind was required to select just one out of several pieces of Scud maybe only forty seconds from impact on your shirt-collar.

There was just one real tragedy – the disastrous incident when a Scud flattened a canteen at Dhahran airbase, killing twenty-eight off-duty US service personnel. The Patriots didn't engage the Scud – but that wasn't anyone's fault. The problem had occurred when the "keep-out zone" had been computed. Each Patriot battery had a very precise zone, its KOZ, to defend. There was a limit to the size of this zone – if it was too large, there wouldn't be any chance of a successful intercept. So, any Scud not heading into the KOZ had to be ignored. The KOZ depended on the trajectory of the incoming missile: if it was approaching on a low trajectory, the KOZ could be larger because it meant that the Scud wasn't travelling as fast; but if it was coming in almost vertically, at very high speed, there was less time for the Patriot to lock on to it. The missile that destroyed the canteen had been coming in on an exceptional trajectory, and it hadn't been possible to cover the whole area against such an eventuality. The canteen was just *fifteen metres* outside the nearest KOZ. It was sheer bad luck, but if that Patriot battery had been just fifteen metres nearer the canteen . . .

On the whole, Raytheon had done an amazingly good job with the Patriot, thought Kearwin. Originally, he reminded himself, it hadn't been designed as an anti-missile system – the PAC-1 had been developed for use against aircraft. It was only when the brass had seen its possibilities that they had pushed for the guidance systems to be modified for ABM purposes. The PAC-2 was essentially a very good system indeed; it had shown what could be done. Never mind the problems, it was the political significance of just having the thing that had mattered. The Patriot had kept the Israeli public reassured to some extent, and had been the main reason put forward for Israel's having stayed out of the war.

Kearwin knew better. The real reason had been the development of the successor to the Patriot, the Arrow system. Arrow would have a range of one hundred kilometres and an altitude capability of forty, as against Patriot's more limited range of ten to twenty kilometres and altitude ceiling of five. The problem was, Arrow was expensive. The Israelis wouldn't be able to develop it by themselves. The Israeli Government had bargained hard with the United States, requesting funding and technological assistance. The USA had had to be extremely careful – the 1972 ABM Treaty forbade "technical transfer", so they could not be seen to be injecting technology. Funding, however, and a commitment to buy Arrow, were another matter, and the USA had guaranteed both these to Israel. *That* was what had kept them quiet, not Patriot.

Kearwin sighed. It was all back to normal now, or almost so. The priority these days was still the Mid-East, but the task was mostly supervisory, the monitoring of movements and installations. The bomb-damage assessment on the Al Ateer installation had been a welcome change, and a challenge. The information from the KH-12 passes had been good; it would be interesting to see whether his assessment came up to scratch. He was convinced it would.

He called over to one of his juniors. "OK, Peter, I think we've got a final on this. Tidy up the composites and get it all sent through now, would you?"

The junior nodded, setting to work printing up the assessment for the Walrus's approval.

Kearwin rubbed his eyes, leaned back in his chair and yawned. Outside it would be a bright spring day in Washington. He had been on duty since six in the morning; with luck he would be clear in half an hour and could get home to spend the rest of the afternoon out in the sun with Carrie and the baby. He stretched his arms up and back, rolling his head from side to side to work the stiffness out of his neck.

The flashing light on the DSP console caught his attention again. The analysis was coming through. He looked at it and frowned. *I'll be damned*, he thought, running a quick request for more information on the positive trace. He called over his shoulder to the Walrus. "Walter, we've got a positive on the DSP. Western Iraq. Looks like a Scud launch. You want to see it?"

Sorensen got up from his desk and wandered over. "Whaddya mean, a Scud? You crazy? The goddam war's over, for Chrissake." He studied the data, his forehead creasing deeply.

"Yes, but look at the location." Kearwin was tapping out instructions on the keyboard, and more information appeared on the screen under a map overlay of the region. He zoomed the screen in on the area. "Right on the border, would you believe it?"

"How does the signature fit?" Sorensen asked, peering at the screen and fingering his moustache.

"Fits with Scud parameters on the 4.3-micrometre band, maybe a little low on the 2.7 band." The short-wave infra-red sensors on the DSP routinely monitored these two wavelengths; the relative intensity of the signals on the two bands provided analysts with a great deal of information. From this it could be established what type of missile had been fired; each propellent gave off its own signature, in a pattern individual to the missile. Once the CIA knew the propellent, you pretty well had the missile.

"Where is it now?"

Kearwin tapped in the instruction on the keyboard. A few seconds later, the trace updated itself. He blinked in surprise. "Damn, it hasn't moved! Maybe an engine test."

Sorensen's face broke into a grin. "Engine test, my ass. Look at that new figure for the 2.7. Higher, right? What does that tell you? Engine test? There? On the border? You wanna know something, hot-shot? You ain't got nothing but an oil-bucket job! Never thought you'd fall for that one. Hey, boys!" The Walrus turned and boomed out to the others in the room. They looked up in surprise at him as he hammed it up for all he was worth in an exaggerated Southern accent. "John-boy here's got hisself a goddam oil-bucket job! Called me all the way over here to admire it! How *'bout* that?" He slapped his hand on Kearwin's shoulder. "Y'all keep up the good work now, John-boy, you hear?" He stomped off, chuckling, as ragged applause broke out from the other analysts.

A screwed-up ball of paper winged over and bounced off the side of Kearwin's head. He looked up sheepishly to see the good-natured grins on the faces of his colleagues. He smiled. "Hey, cut it out, fellas. OK, anyone can make a little mistake."

"Good one, John," one of the juniors called at him.

"Nice job, John," said another.

"Yeah, yeah, OK. You guys all through now? Cut it out, huh?" Not for nothing was Kearwin an analyst. He could see that the tension of the shift had been broken. It happened infrequently enough, and the good-humoured joshing would do everyone good, even if it was at his expense. He smiled again, and returned to his work.

Fifteen minutes later, Kearwin was still annoyed with himself for his mistake. Besides, something was wrong. Why the hell would the Iraqis want to try on the old oil-bucket scam in peacetime, and right on the border at that? He thought back to the war, when the tactic had been used to mislead the F-16 Falcons on Scud bombing raids. At the same time as the Patriot batteries on the receiving end were jumping into action following a Scud launch, the F-16s would already be airborne, accompanied by F-111 Wild Weasels fitted with ALQ-131 ECM radar-jamming pods. They in turn would be followed by tanker aircraft.

It was too much yak on the radio that had done it, reflected Kearwin. The Iraqis were better at radio monitoring than the Allies realised, and although their radar screens were blinded by the ECM from the F-111s, they were able to anticipate the arrival of the F-16s because of the radio chatter. They even broke the codes for the Scud targets, and knew which ones to get out of the way, well before the F-16 strikes came in. By the time the F-16s arrived, the Scud launchers were already well clear, usually hidden underneath a bridge or a viaduct; a mock-up launcher would be left in place with containers of burning oil around it to give off a heat signature for the F-16 attack sensors to lock on to. Many "successful" bombing raids just destroyed mock-ups. Oil-bucket jobs, thought Kearwin. And now he had fallen for one himself.

But was it? And why? Why right on the Saudi border, of all places? It didn't make sense. Irritated, Kearwin decided to take a closer look. He tapped out an instruction on his main keyboard, calling up the track of the most recent KH-11 or KH-12 satellite pass over the area. A diagram of the various Keyhole satellites' tracks appeared on the big screen under the area map overlay. Perfect, thought Kearwin; a KH-12 had passed over the area only five minutes earlier. The information would already have been received back via the relay satellites and the ground-link station, and the digital signal would now be in the process of being computer decoded and relayed on for archiving. It would take a few minutes for the computer to search through the archive to find the co-ordinates he wanted. That would do, Kearwin told himself. He would have a quick look at it to see what it was, and then head on home to Carrie and the boy.

He sat back in his chair, thinking, then leaned forward again. Might as well get a couple of earlier passes for comparison while he was waiting. He tapped in another instruction. The previous pass had been a KH-11 only twenty minutes before, and would do fine. He called it up. The pass before that had been forty-five minutes earlier, but the track had been well to the east and the co-ordinates he needed were just off the edge of the optimum tracking band. It wouldn't make a good comparison. The next good one before that had been nearly two hours earlier. He called this one up as a second back-up. Down in the basement, the giant mainframe computer whirred through tape banks and sifted through the co-ordinates. One minute and thirty-five seconds later, the more recent of the two previous passes appeared on Kearwin's screen. Good, he thought; no cloud cover. A perfect picture. He spent a minute or so adjusting the digital readings for maximum contrast interpretation of the infra-red picture, until he was satisfied.

A god-forsaken spot, by the look of it. Right in the middle of the desert. The only feature of any interest was a small cluster of buildings in the centre of the screen, next to a dirt track running from the top to the bottom. Near the buildings was what looked like a small storage depot. A truck was parked by the main building. A little Mickey Mouse military post. Of course – a border post. A pretty half-assed one, at that. Not surprising, he mused; it was miles from anywhere – a token presence.

The sub-console light blinked, telling him that the pass of two hours earlier was now ready. He put it on screen. There was no discernible difference to the naked eye. Kearwin ran the routine code to overlay the two and cancel out the differences. He could appreciate the enormous computing power required to carry out this apparently simple exercise; the photographic resolution of the infra-red picture was six inches, which meant that nothing smaller than a child's football would be seen. The popular rumour of a satellite's being

231

able to read car number-plates from a hundred miles up in space was complete nonsense. There would be little point in being able to pick out such detail – a six-inch resolution was sufficient to identify small objects such as vehicles with reasonable precision, especially with the computer enhancement techniques now available. For every square foot on the ground, the picture was represented by four pixels – dots in varying grey scales of one to sixteen. For every area a hundred yards by a hundred, that meant a third of a million dots. For every square mile – which was roughly what Kearwin was looking at – that was more than a hundred million dots. Each one had to be compared with the corresponding pixel in the previous picture – not a simple job. Variations in temperature between passes had to be ironed out; some bodies cooled or heated up more quickly than others. The grey scales would have to be adjusted to compensate. That was not the most difficult problem: the computer also had to take account of the different angle of view for each pass – the pictures were obliques, not verticals, and the angles varied, depending on the track of the satellite each time. Variations due to topographical obscuration had to be ironed out too.

Kearwin watched as the two pictures overlaid each other and the computer started trying to merge them. When it was happy that the area coverage was precisely the same for both, having electronically squeezed and stretched them both ways to fit each other exactly, the compensation comparisons for each picture began. The screen slowly changed as the pixels started to cancel each other out. Gradually, the dots disappeared and the screen became emptier and emptier; finally, it was almost entirely blank except for two tiny clusters of pixels near the top of the screen and another two nearer the centre. Kearwin ran a further reconciliation program to assess the anomalous readings between the two pictures; it reported back that the anomalies were sixty per cent too high to ignore. Something positive there. Kearwin overlaid the full picture back on screen, magnifying the area of the pixel-cluster anomalies at the top. There they were. A little more adjustment to the grey, and it was clear. Two vehicles. There in the earlier pass, but not in the more recent one.

He knew what he would find in the second set of clusters nearer the centre: two vehicles again, this time in the second picture but not in the first. Almost certainly the same ones. Kearwin wondered idly why they had moved only four hundred yards or so in an hour and a half. In the second picture, they were only a couple of hundred yards away from the border post.

The console indicator light flashed again; the latest picture, the KH-12 pass which should show up the heat source the DSP had spotted, was now ready for downloading. Kearwin sent a print command for the two earlier passes he had compared, along with separate blow-ups of the vehicles in each case. He also ordered a digital read-out of the actual infra-red signatures of the vehicles. Then he ran the latest pass, keeping the previous two in background. The picture came on screen.

He saw his oil-bucket fire straight away. A nice little blaze, it looked like. The border post's fuel store, obviously. The fuel had gone up. Some asshole smoking on guard near the POL point. No more to it than that, he thought, disgusted. He ran down the grey scales until the picture went almost black, leaving just the area around the fire. He kept running it down so that even the heated-up objects near the fire disappeared from the screen, giving him the exact source of the heat. Running the grey scales down into black made it look on the screen as though the fire was going out. Then, in twenty-per-cent increments, Kearwin brought it back to normal. He ran out a set of prints at each incremental value, requesting heat-analysis readings. The set of print-outs would give information on the fire and the affected area about a hundred yards around it. From what he could see, the border-post buildings themselves seemed to be in no danger. He ran the close-down sequence on the keyboard, and started tidying up his desk, preparing to leave.

Ten minutes later, after stopping by to talk to Sorensen and initial his Al Ateer report, he was ready to go. He collected the print-outs and walked back to his desk. He would have a look at them the next day, if he had time. He placed them in the current-chart drawer near his work-station.

It was then that Kearwin noticed that his screen was still active. He had run the "compare" sequence, not the close-down one. He realised he must be tired; the Al Ateer work had taken a lot of concentration. He shouldn't have bothered with the damn oil-bucket. Now his screen was showing the comparisons between all three pictures.

There was the oil-bucket fire, a big scattering of white pixels inconsistent with the two previous pictures. There were the two tiny sets of clusters near the top and the two near the middle – the two vehicles in their different positions. And . . . that struck him as interesting – there they were again, now down near the bottom of the screen. Leaving the fire. Why? He quickly checked back on his log, to see the time of the DSP satellite's first indication of the fire. That would give it an accuracy to within ten seconds. The time flashed up: exactly 15.00 USA Eastern Time. That meant 22.00 in Iraq. A precise time. Rather too conveniently precise for an accident. Deliberate?

Frowning, he compared the times of the three KH satellite passes. The first one, a KH-11, had been at 20.13 Iraqi time. The second, another KH-11, had been at 21.48, and the third – after the fire – a KH-12 at 22.12. He thought about what he had got. Two vehicles, six hundred yards from the border post at 20.13. By 21.48 they had moved up to within two hundred yards. Then at 22.12, after the fire had started, they were five hundred yards the other side of the border post. He studied the read-outs of the vehicles. Both the same: small and boxy. Not trucks. Cars – probably four-wheel drive, judging from the poor state of the dirt track. There was something odd. The spectral-analysis read-outs showed that they had their headlamps on; one could tell that from the shadows the lights cast. But there was something not quite right about those shadows. He looked at the analysis again. The shadows showed up in the infra-red band, but not in the shorter wavelengths, the visible spectrum. Infra-red lamps!

Frowning hard now, Kearwin studied the full map overlay of the area. The dirt track only just featured. The middle of nowhere, as he had guessed. He got up slowly, and walked over to Sorensen's desk. "Walter, I've got something odd here. Maybe the Ops boys at Langley can clear it up for us. Could you come and have a look?"

The Walrus was just finishing checking through Kearwin's bomb-damage assessment report. "Just a minute, son, let me finish here." He turned over the last page, nodding as he reached the final paragraphs of the report's conclusions. He finished, initialled it, and called over to the junior. "Peter, this is fine. Have it couriered on over to the Observer Section for comparison. Pronto." He turned to Kearwin. "Nice work on that BDA report. Very thorough. Be interesting to see how it stacks up against the eyeball accounts. Now, what was that you were saying about CIA operations? What have they been up to?"

The two walked back to Kearwin's station as he explained what he had got. "It's this oil-bucket fire. Something smelled wrong, so I took a closer look at it."

The Walrus broke in with a smile. "You know what I like about you, John? You're competitive. You hate being beaten. You just never give up on something, do you?"

Kearwin had to admit it. He was a mild-mannered and unassuming character, but nevertheless he had a streak of stubbornness and persistence which surprised those who first encountered it in him. He never gave up until he knew he had the answer. He would file unexplained data away in his mind for days, sometimes months, waiting for fresh information that would give him a new angle on an old puzzle. Walter Sorensen knew it; many times he had had cause to recognise how valuable Kearwin's persistence was to his section.

"It just bothered me, Walter, that's all. Look." Kearwin ran through the data, throwing up the latest of the three pictures and the map overlay on the screen. "Here's the fire, OK? Got it from a KH-12 pass less than fifteen minutes after the DSP trace. It happened at 10.00 p.m. exactly, Iraqi time, according to the DSP. Fuel depot, near that little Iraqi border post there. Twenty, maybe thirty drums of gas, some kero, maybe a bit of naphtha. Nothing odd about that, except the time – dead on 10.00 p.m. A bit too cute for it to be an accident.

"Now, here's a couple of previous passes by KH-11s." Kearwin brought in the two earlier pictures and ran the cancellation sequence. "One's at 8.13 p.m., the other at 9.48. Now, ignore the fire and look at these three pairs of pixel clusters." The three sets of clusters gradually came up on screen.

"A couple of vehicles?"

"Right. A couple of long-wheel-base four-by-fours, is my guess. But look at the times. A hundred minutes before the fire, they're up here, about five hundred yards away from the post." Kearwin pointed at the set of clusters near the top of the screen. "Twelve minutes before the fire, they've moved to within two hundred yards of the post. Then, thirteen minutes after the fire, they're through the border and down here. Now look at these." Kearwin laid out the spectral-analysis sheets showing the shadows cast by the vehicle headlamps. "Faint, not conclusive, but I got a ten-dollar bill says those are IR lamps they're using, not white light. What does that tell you?"

"If you're right, it tells me covert," said Sorensen. "*If*," he added, with emphasis. He looked at the spectral analysis; privately, he agreed. Infra-red lamps, not much doubt about it. "So, what's your theory?"

"Two vehicles approach the border by night. They drop off some guys back here. These guys sneak up on the border post, while the vehicles wait. Fifteen minutes before the prearranged time, the vehicles mosey carefully on up to near the post. At 10.00 p.m. on the button, they torch the fuel depot as a diversion. In the confusion, the vehicles drive through, no visible lights, and wait up here, the other side of the border, to pick up the saboteurs. The Iraqi border guards probably never even noticed them – look, no sign of pursuit. That truck is still stationary."

"Yeah, it fits, except there would be some light from the fire. Someone would have spotted them."

"They can't have. The guards must all have been trying to put out the fire. Or maybe that truck was sabotaged too. Listen, Walter, I'd like to get Langley to let us know if they've got anything going on there. My guess is they don't know anything about it we would have had some non-specific warning from them, maybe telling us to look the other way. This doesn't smell of Langley, anyhow. So I'd like your authorisation to pull some records from E-8A databanks. We know they've got E-8As in the air round the clock right now, monitoring movements up north. Maybe TR-1 pictures too. Let me see what they've got. They might just have something."

"Now hold on, hot-shot," the Walrus protested, "don't get carried away here. OK, some guys jumped the border. I don't blame the poor bastards. Wouldn't you wanna do the same in their place? They'll soon be picked up. Probably harmless. Head straight for the Saudi cops, like as not, and demand political asylum. Good luck to 'em."

"Sorry, Walter, I forgot to explain something. My fault. These pictures are inverted. The top of the screen is south, not north."

The Walrus shot him a puzzled glance. "You mean . . .?"

"Yes. These guys, whoever they are, are busting *into* Iraq, not out of it. Now, who the hell would want to do that? I think someone ought to find out. Let me talk to Langley."

Walter Sorensen's brow was knitted in a tight frown of concentration

236

He fingered his moustache. "Yeah," he said, "who in hell would want to do a crazy thing like that?" He remained deep in thought for a few seconds as he studied the picture; then he jabbed his forefinger towards the screen. "Let's find out!"

37

Howard had decided to put as much distance between them and the border post as possible before he made a stop. Fortunately, the track was easy to follow; there were numerous junctions, but it was obvious that none of the other tracks had recently carried a large vehicle like the truck they had seen at the border post. Occasional checks with the GPS receiver established that they were following the correct route; the track began to bend round to the north-east. The corrugations were severe in places, and there were frequent deep pot-holes and ruts, but Howard reflected that the going was rather better than he had expected.

MacDonald, being bounced around in the back of the Land Cruiser, had other opinions. He muttered and swore as he attempted with little success to stow the stolen weapons safely out of sight, and where they wouldn't rattle about. After twenty minutes he gave up, and decided that the grenades and RPG projectiles would be much safer left in their crates, rather than skidding and bouncing about loose on the floor of the vehicle. He concentrated on trying to fit the silencers Ackford had made on to the AKMS rifles. Bracing himself with his feet against the roof of the vehicle, he managed to screw the three silencers on, but didn't even attempt the more fiddly job of fitting the gas-port clamps in place. Apart from everything else, it was too dark and he could not see what he was doing. He wondered how Usher was getting on, doing a similar job in the other vehicle.

Bourne, driving, saw the pylon first. He brought the vehicle to a halt about a quarter of a mile short of it. "There's the power line."

"OK, let me check," said Howard. The GPS reading confirmed where they were; they had come nearly twenty miles. "There may be traffic. The map shows a main track crossing here, running along the line of pylons." Bourne switched off the engine; he and Howard got out.

Ziegler joined them from the second car. "You reckon they raised the alarm, or not?"

Howard thought about it. "There's been no sign of pursuit. I pulled down their antenna wires, which should buy us some time if they do try to report something, and you fixed that truck, so they couldn't chase us even if they wanted to. But that's not what worries me."

"Yeah," said Ziegler. "I've been watchin' out. No sign of any air movement." The biggest danger on this stretch, they knew, was from patrolling helicopters. The Mi-24 Hind was a fearsome machine – as Afghan Mujahideen guerrillas had discovered to their cost in their long struggle against the Soviet occupation of their country. The Hind was heavily armed and armoured, almost impossible to shoot down, and was equipped with sophisticated radar and optical target-acquisition devices. Saddam, they knew, had Hinds; almost inexplicably, he had been allowed to continue flying them after the Gulf War, mostly using them to suppress any sign of revolt in the northern hills of Kurdistan and the southern marshes of Mesopotamia. Howard hoped fervently that he had none stationed out here in western Iraq. The chance presence of a Hind in this deserted part of the country would be bound to lead to the team's detection; two vehicles travelling alone this late at night would be investigated, and that would be that. When they hit the main road further north, they would have a better chance of escaping attention.

"No sign of anything. Let's get going. I'd like to get past Rutbah before midnight if we can."

Twelve miles further on, Howard halted again; they had reached a main track junction, where they would turn north to Rutbah. They pulled the vehicles well off the track into a shallow wadi, allowing MacDonald and Usher to complete the stowage of the weapons. The RPG-7 launch tube was placed under the mattress of the stretcher in the lead vehicle; with his knife, MacDonald slit open the mattress itself and slid the projectiles inside. The glove compartments of each car were filled with grenades, and each man was given an AKMS to conceal beneath his seat, the stock folded and the silencers fitted.

"Anyone got a tin-opener?" asked Ackford. "I fancy some of these giant Russian sardines."

239

It took ten minutes' work with a hacksaw to open the heavy metal boxes; inside each box were seven hundred rounds of 7.62 x 39mm AK ammunition. The ammunition was handed out; each man charged six thirty-round magazines. The rest of the ammunition was stowed under the stretchers. Dumping the empty crates and boxes in the wadi, they checked again that there was no sign of traffic before setting off.

The track north towards Rutbah from the junction was marginally better. After a further thirty miles it improved again dramatically; they quite quickly arrived at the main junction to Rutbah South airfield. The airfield was ten miles off to the east, and the road from the field to the town of Rutbah itself was metalled in places. Howard breathed a sigh of relief. They removed their NVGs and switched their headlights on; it was time to start acting like a couple of ambulances.

It wasn't until they were eight miles short of Rutbah that they saw the first sign of life; four sets of lights were coming towards them on the road. There would be no question of avoiding them.

"Looks like military," muttered Howard.

"What do you reckon we do?" asked Bourne.

"Flash the headlights, toot the horn a couple of times, wave cheerily and bellow something patriotic in Arabic."

Bourne complied. The occupants of the four vehicles barely acknowledged them as they swept past in the other direction. As they passed, MacDonald had a brief impression of rather uninterested and sullen-looking faces, hooded and wrapped tightly against the cold.

"Land Rovers, for Chrissake," muttered Howard. "Maybe a guard detail heading for the airfield. Anyway, it's good news that there doesn't seem to be any alert out for us."

The lights of Rutbah, such as they were, appeared in the distance. The town gave the impression of being almost deserted. The power was down, and Howard guessed that the only well-lit area, a mile or so off the road to the east, was a military installation with its own generator. Behind him, as they drove through the empty-looking town, he heard a roaring sound as Ackford tried out his exhaust-bypass lever. Howard grinned to himself. No one hearing that racket would guess that this was a group of assassins attempting to pass unnoticed through Iraq.

The first main road they came to was Route 10, the old highway from Baghdad to Jordan. They turned left on to this, then a mile further on out of town turned right and picked up the road that would lead them past the cryptically-named H2 and H1 airbases towards Kirkuk. After two miles, just as they thought they were clear, they encountered their first obstacle.

The remains of the motorway bridge lay shattered in the road. Little visible attempt had been made to clear it up. Large chunks of concrete lay where they had fallen, and the two sides of the motorway above ended in thin air. The burnt-out wreckage of a large truck, whose driver had obviously been unaware that the bridge had collapsed and had driven straight over the edge, blocked the road in front of them.

"Shit," said Howard. "Can you see a way round, Johnny?"

"There must be one. This is the main sanctions-busting route from Jordan." As he spoke, they saw a set of vehicle lights approach along the elevated motorway from the west. The lights disappeared from view as it turned off and descended the far side of the embankment. They watched the vehicle pick its way past the wreckage on the other side of the burnt-out truck, and then climb back up on the east side of the motorway. Rejoining the road, it carried on east, towards Baghdad.

"OK. Let's back up and find a way round this shambles."

Five minutes later, they had climbed the embankment, crossed straight over the motorway and descended the other side. Picking up the Kirkuk road again, they drove on.

"Do you think it was a bomb that blew that bridge up?" asked MacDonald.

"Several bombs, I should think," replied Bourne. "That motorway was known as 'Scud Alley' during the Gulf War. The Scud launchers would travel along it and launch near culverts and bridges like that one. After launching, they'd leave dummy launchers out and hide the real ones under the bridges to avoid the bombing raids. It took the Allies quite a while to cotton on to that. I hope there was a Scud hiding under that one when it collapsed."

Howard was concentrating on the map. "The H2 airbase is about twenty-five miles along this road. We come to a T-junction; left would take us to the base, so we turn right, pass an oil-pumping station and skirt round the base. A right turn after the pumping station takes us back on to the main road."

241

"Why is it called H2?" asked MacDonald.

"Dunno," said Howard. "But that's the name on the map."

As they neared the airbase there was more traffic; Bourne acted as before, waving and tooting, and they were ignored as apparently being part of the usual scenery. Howard guessed that few Iraqis, even the military, really knew what anyone else was doing or who was supposed to be where, even at this time of night. Certainly, no one they had come across up till now had seemed to care. Curfew was always a possibility, but he was hoping that the travel authority of two ambulances, with their flashing roof-lights, would not be questioned. The little they had seen of the country so far gave the impression of a gloomy and dilapidated mess.

The lights of H2 glimmered up ahead. "OK, Johnny; when we turn right towards the pumping station, put the roof lights on again. I don't know what's at that pumping station; there may be a guard on it."

The precaution was unnecessary. The pumping station was little more than a deserted pile of rubble. There were craters in the road nearby; Bourne only just spotted the first one in time. It would have been enough to tear a wheel off and ruin the front suspension of the Land Cruiser. "That was a near thing," he muttered, slowing right down. "Seems like the Allies did a fairly comprehensive job around here."

"This entire country looks screwed up," commented MacDonald. "It doesn't look as though anything works any more."

"Don't speak too soon," said Howard. "We're doubling back now; it'll take us quite near that base again. We'll have to hope there isn't too much activity."

They had done a loop round the base, to avoid going straight past it. Ahead they could see the lights once more. "Runway lights are on," observed Bourne. "All military flights are supposed to be banned. What do you suppose – "

There was a roar, and the lights of a big transport plane swept low overhead as it came in to land. All three men instinctively ducked, then swore at having been taken by surprise.

"Shit! What was that?" exclaimed Bourne.

"Big transport. Couldn't make it out. Bigger than a C-130. Antonov? I don't know." Howard stared at the lights of the plane as it descended to touch down. "Anyway, let's not hang around to find out. Right turn coming up."

"Remind me when we get home to complain to the UN about them not keeping Saddam to the terms of the resolutions," said Bourne. "OK, here's the turning."

They took the right-hand fork and settled back on to the open road. "Just under sixty miles to H1," said Howard. "All being well, we should be there in another hour. Say 01.45."

The latter part of the road to H1 was almost dead straight. What little of the scenery they could make out was featureless and empty, a stone and gravel desert with occasional patches of low scrub. Traffic was sparse, and they made good time.

Ten miles short of the airbase Howard ordered a halt. They pulled well off the road and killed the lights. "Might as well refill the tanks." Howard put on his NVGs again and scanned the horizon. There was nothing in sight.

The fuel tanks took almost three full jerricans of petrol each. Glad of the extra space this would make in the rear, they slung the empties away. Howard checked the horizon again and they rejoined the road.

Soon afterwards, the lights of H1 pierced the darkness along the skyline. "With luck, we should be able to motor straight past it," said Howard. "The road's pretty straight, and . . ."

A flashing light appeared in the road about six hundred yards in front. More lights snapped on.

"Hit the screamers, Johnny! Flashers, the lot! I'll get in the back with Danny." Howard dived over the back of his seat, wrenching on a white coat. Danny was already on the stretcher, covering himself with a blanket. "OK, Danny, time for your pill. Bite hard on it when I say so. Keep your eyes closed and moan loudly."

In the vehicle behind, Ziegler was doing the same; Usher was on the stretcher. The sirens of both ambulances wailed shrilly through the night air, and Ackford added to the din by pulling the exhaust-bypass lever. The two vehicles raced up to the road-block and screeched to a halt. Running figures appeared as Bourne leapt out, gesticulating excitedly and jabbering in Arabic. An officer approached, and Bourne latched on to him, talking nineteen to the dozen, not giving the man a chance to get a word in. Bourne tugged him round to the back of the ambulance.

"*Now*, Danny," whispered Howard in MacDonald's ear, just as the rear door was opened.

Danny bit hard on the pill and began to let out a convincing moan. The pill seemed to erupt in his mouth and he found himself spraying bright-red liquid out over his chest. He tried to close his mouth, but the liquid kept bubbling out. He moaned again.

Howard had been muttering to himself as the officer came towards the ambulance with Bourne. As the door opened, he turned and snarled one of the two speeches he had painstakingly rehearsed under Bourne's tuition. The Arabic came fluently. "Shut that door, you imbecile!" he shouted furiously. "Can't you see this man is badly injured? And get your men out of the way, or his death will be on your hands!"

The sight of blood erupting from the patient's mouth, coupled with the violent rebuff from the "doctor", proved too much for the officer. He recoiled, shutting the door. Bourne was having none of it. Still gabbling away, he hauled the officer to the second ambulance. Screams were coming from inside. Bourne pulled the door open and hauled the officer round so that he could see inside. A wild-eyed Ziegler, in white coat and stethoscope, was attempting to hold a struggling and screaming Usher down on to the stretcher. Protruding from beneath the blanket was Usher's left leg. It was dripping with blood; half-way up the shin, the white bone of the tibia stuck out at a horrible angle from an extremely messy wound. A large chunk of flesh hung loose from the mutilated limb.

The officer had had enough. Unable to think above the noise of the sirens, the broken exhaust of the second ambulance being revved excitedly by its mad-looking driver, and the strident tones of the man who persisted in jabbering into his ear, he shook himself free and broke into a run. Waving furiously at his men, he yelled for the road to be cleared and the ambulances let through. Bourne returned to the front of his car and stood in the full illumination of its headlamps, screaming dementedly after the officer, and exhorting the soldiers to hurry.

"Don't overdo it, Johnny boy," muttered Howard, as he watched Bourne's theatricals, himself having difficulty thinking above all the noise.

The vehicles blocking the road were hurriedly removed; Bourne jumped back in behind the wheel and set off with a squeal of tyres. The second ambulance followed with a deafening roar of its exhaust. As Bourne passed the soldiers, he was still shouting and wailing out

244

of the window; he kept up the performance until they were three hundred yards past the block and out of sight round a bend in the road. Two miles further on, he switched off the siren and the flashing light. Behind, Ackford did the same, and silenced the roaring of the exhaust.

"Thank God for that," said Bourne. "That bloody siren was driving me mad. As for that noise from Tony's exhaust ... You OK, Danny?"

"I'm fine," said MacDonald. "Or at least," he added disgustedly, "I think I am. What the hell was in that pill? This red muck has gone everywhere."

"Effervescent tablet, mate," said Howard. "From all good joke-shops."

In the rear ambulance, Usher was peeling off the plastic "wound", complete with its protruding "bone", while Ziegler was mopping up the worst of the "blood".

"I think maybe we'll do the stomach wound next time, Bob," said Ziegler. "I'm kind of lookin' forward to emptyin' that quart jar of goat's tripe over your gut after the way you fought me back there. Shame to bring it all the way from Badanah and not use it, huh?"

"Knackers to that," said Usher. "It's Ack's turn next."

"No thanks," said Ackford, chewing contentedly on a piece of gum. "I'm quite happy driving."

38

John Kearwin had been busy. He and Walter Sorensen had quickly identified the first problem to be dealt with – tasking priorities. Strictly speaking, the National Reconnaissance Office existed to operate the satellites and interpret the photographic evidence they supplied. Its Director, the DNRO, reported direct to the Secretary for Defense, Dick Cheney, but he did not have a free hand with tasking. It was the Central Intelligence Agency that allocated tasks and decided what the satellites and other intelligence-gathering apparatus were to look at.

Sorensen had had a word with the Director, Martin Faga; because it was night-time in Iraq and there wasn't much else going on, Faga gave him seven hours to come up with something. "You've got until 06.00 Iraqi time, Walter," said Faga, whose interest had been aroused. "That's 23.00 Eastern. If you haven't come up with anything by then, I'm afraid we'll have to revert to normal daytime operations." Although he hadn't said so, Faga rather hoped that Sorensen and his team *would* find something; it would strengthen the NRO's position if they could uncover something everyone else had missed. The CIA had certainly known nothing about an incursion into Iraq; it had already been a shot in the arm for the NRO to have discovered it first. The NRO's budget was under threat: there were moves afoot to make cuts of eighteen per cent for 1993; a success with something like this would be useful ammunition in the argument against the threatened reductions.

"Thank you, Director," said Sorensen. "Can I have your authorisation to task the JSTARS as well as the KH birds?"

Faga thought about it. "All right. Yes. I don't suppose the crews will mind. But bear in mind what we are having to pay those guys." The two E-8A JSTARS aircraft had proved themselves in the Gulf

War, arriving in the nick of time. The E-8A JSTARS was to ground movement what the E-3 AWACS was to air movement; its radar apparatus could detect vehicle movement up to two hundred miles away. Unlike the AWACS, which had a huge rotating disc on top, the JSTARS aircraft had a large pod slung underneath the fuselage. It had been in the experimental stage, a prototype still on trial, when its potential usefulness had suddenly been spotted. The two prototypes, with their crews of civilian scientists, had been rushed to the Gulf and put into service. The PhDs and DScs who manned them had been highly paid; it had proved to be money well spent. Both JSTARS aircraft had remained out in the Gulf for monitoring purposes, still for the most part manned by civilians.

Kearwin's first instruction was to give the JSTARS an area to look at, with an order to locate and track the two vehicles that had left the border post. It proved to be a relatively simple task for the JSTARS; the area Kearwin had given it to look at was virtually empty and it quickly came up with a positive sighting, forty miles south of Rutbah. Now that he had an approximate speed and track of the vehicles, Kearwin lined up a KH-12 for a "bounce" pass. It was the same KH-12 that had provided the coverage of the border-post fire at 22.12 Iraqi time; the computer instruction fired its hydrazine booster, and at 23.41 it swooped down to an altitude of one hundred and fifty kilometres, its helical-scan cameras running at ultra-high speed. By the time the pass took place, the JSTARS had reported that the two vehicles were approaching the town of Rutbah, having passed four other similar vehicles heading south, in the opposite direction; Kearwin married up the two times and the location, and at 23.47 the picture appeared on his big screen.

He thanked his lucky stars that it was still a clear night, with no cloud. Because the "bounce" had brought the satellite down to nearly half the altitude, the picture of the vehicles was much better than the previous rather indistinct ones, and would be as good as he would get. He zoomed in on the image and ran a computer enhancement sequence to optimise the picture. An examination of the shadows showed that the vehicles now had normal headlights on, not the IR lamps. Fair enough, he thought. The fact that there was other traffic about probably accounted for that. Driving along a road with no visible lights on was a good way of *attracting* attention, not avoiding it. When he was satisfied, he stored the image in background memory as a template for future matching.

So far it had been pretty straightforward, thought Kearwin. They had made it easy for him. A deserted area, nothing else moving . . . but what would happen when they stopped, or encountered other vehicles? And what were they up to? More importantly, who were they, and where had they come from?

Kearwin decided that for the time being he could do nothing more to affect the tracking exercise. The JSTARS would be crucial, and if it lost the vehicles he would just have to hope for luck in picking them up again on a KH-11 or KH-12 pass. He called over to a colleague and explained the situation. "Jerry, I want you to keep a close eye on progress here." Jerry Freedman was Kearwin's senior Grade II assistant. "I've got a good template of the vehicles now – use it. We'll do routine passes each time with the KH-11s, but I want a bounce photo with every pass of the KH-12. Walter says we can bring in the other KH-12 if we need it. Let me know if the vehicles head for a big town or get into traffic, and we'll call it up."

Kearwin handed over the tracking task to Freedman; Peter Stannard, the Grade III junior, was handling the JSTARS reports and would pass on the data to Jerry. Young Peter was doing OK. A second junior was handling print-outs, and a second Grade II, Jim Morton, was compiling a detailed movement log. Jim was a precise and well-organised analyst, perfect for the job. It was all in place. It was time for a bit of backtracking.

Working alone, Kearwin began to sift through data from previous Keyhole passes. Thousands of miles of recording tape in the archive section stored routine data from satellite images of every part of the world; being able to compare new photographic evidence with old was one of the most important capabilities the NRO possessed. It was simply a matter of finding the image you wanted, Kearwin said to himself.

He studied the map overlay, zooming out so that it showed north-western Saudi Arabia. He marked the screen with the co-ordinates of the border post and the subsequent sighting; they flashed up as blips with the date and time given alongside. OK. The journey from the border to Rutbah had taken under two hours, and the vehicles had stayed on a fairly prominently-marked track. He looked at the road and track network south of the border, on the Saudi side. There were two ways they could have come, if they had used the main tracks: either from Turaif, right over in the western corner near the Jordanian border, or from Al Mira, which didn't look much of a place. Either way, their rate of travel would put them on one of those tracks for at least an hour before the first sighting near the border at 20.13. What coverage was there available for about 19.13?

Within seven minutes, he had his answer. The computer, using the template photograph he had stored, checked through the huge quantities of data from two KH-11 passes at 19.17 and 19.35, and showed the two vehicles at 19.35 ten miles north of Al Mira. The picture wasn't a good one, but there was nothing else moving on the tracks and as far as Kearwin was concerned it was conclusive. Fine. Where had they come from before that? Had they come cross-country out of the desert, or along that pipeline road? He mentally dismissed the former option for the moment, and ordered the computer to search through archive material on the TAP road. Sure enough — there they were again, at 19.04, coming along the road from Ar'ar.

Ten minutes later, Kearwin had his first big stroke of luck. A KH-11 pass had picked up the two vehicles at the moment they had turned out of a compound outside Badanah, near Ar'ar. A previous pass of the compound showed only one difference. Outside the compound, on a perimeter track, was an aircraft, a twin-engined plane that a standard template match confirmed to be a Britten-Norman Islander. He checked one more previous pass, from the day before. The aircraft was missing from the construction camp; but a few miles away, at Ar'ar airport, there it was, parked on the apron.

Kearwin leaned back in his chair and rubbed his eyes. It was 00.45 in Iraq, 17.45 Washington time. He had been on duty for nearly twelve hours; he was tired. He thought about what he had uncovered, and came to a conclusion. He stood up and went over to Sorensen's desk. "Walter, can we get Langley to do a bit of work for us here?" He explained what he had got. "Maybe they can find out about this plane for us, and this compound here. Looks like a road-construction camp. Someone should be able to track down the plane, find out where it came from."

The Walrus fingered his moustache contemplatively and shook his head. "I'll try for you, John, but I can't see that we'll get anywhere with it before the Director's deadline. We've got about five hours left. Think about it. If Langley do try to help — look at the time. It's after midnight out there. Do you think they're gonna be able to pull some Saudi air-traffic-control guy out of bed and grill him about some little bitty airplane he's probably never heard of? I don't think there's a chance. Your best shot is to keep backtracking through the archives. Check out this airport. See how many flights go in. My guess is only a few. Maybe AWACS records will come up with something."

Kearwin inwardly groaned at the prospect of having to interrogate the AWACS records system. He considered the problem. There probably wasn't any way round it. The answer had to lie with the plane. OK, how long had it been there? Easy. He could do this with the more efficient Keyhole satellite archive. One check back for each day, say at 18.00 or thereabouts. Not too difficult. He started punching in the instructions on his keyboard.

Half an hour later, he noticed that the position of the aircraft had been slightly different before 17th April. It had taken a day-trip somewhere. Call up AWACS records? No, not yet. After all, the plane was still there. He waited a couple of minutes longer while the Keyhole passes he had requested for each of the few days before came up. Finally, the pass for 12th April showed the plane missing. He checked the two previous days, but there was no sign of it. Fine; it must have arrived sometime on the 13th.

"John?" It was Jim Morton, who had taken time out from logging to look up flight patterns in and out of Ar'ar. "Very little scheduled traffic. Four flights a week to Riyadh, one to Jeddah. I've looked the place up on the database. There's almost nothing about it. I'd say we're looking at a pretty minor outpost there, just a staging point along that highway."

"Thanks, Jim," said Kearwin. It hadn't been much help, but he had enough now to check AWACS records – if there were any for that day. He decided to put someone else on to it and check on real-time progress. It was coming up to 01.45 in Iraq. Where had these guys got to? He walked over to Jerry's work-station.

"JSTARS has lost them in clutter, John!" Young Peter Stannard's voice sounded strained.

"OK. How long ago?"

"Just now, about a minute ago! They report stationary, other clutter on the road, probably other vehicles. It's confused. They can't be sure."

"Tell them to keep watching that spot until something moves again.

Maybe they ran into a road-block or something. Either they'll move on again, or this task is over."

Kearwin decided with a sigh that he would have to check the AWACS records himself; he hated the thought, as the process took much longer than getting data from the Keyhole archive; the older AWACS database demanded exact requests. You couldn't just say, "Give me all details on light-aircraft flights heading to or away from Ar'ar, with their compass headings, for 13th April." You had to give the exact heading and aircraft type. It was about time, decided Kearwin, that the procedure was updated. It would take him at least thirty minutes to feed in all the possible headings and take the info. But he couldn't take Jerry or Peter off their tasks now. With another sigh, he began to type.

He found it after only fifteen minutes. An aircraft matching the Islander's description had been tracked by a routine AWACS flight on the morning of the 13th. It had been flying a course of 035 degrees magnetic, on a heading for Ar'ar. Understandably, no one had paid any attention to it at the time, and it had already been in the air when the AWACS had come on line.

No problem; he had the Islander's course. He fed it in and the ground track flashed up on his screen on the map overlay. There were two airfields on that approximate heading: Sakakah, only seventy-odd miles from Ar'ar, and Al Wajh, way down on the Red Sea coast. He decided to try Al Wajh first. He interrogated the computer for a probable departure time, given the AWACS computation of ground speed; it calculated 08.05. The Keyhole log indicated a KH-12 pass over Al Wajh at 07.43; that would do. He pulled the picture.

Kearwin was lucky on three counts. The KH-12 had been "bounced" on that pass, and was well down, to an altitude of one hundred and sixty-five kilometres, on its way to its designated pass over Kirkuk. Also, there was no cloud cover; the picture was a good one. The third element of luck was not so much that the plane showed up clearly on the ground at Al Wajh; it was that right alongside it was a vehicle.

Kearwin thrust his fatigue to one side. The vehicle was distinctive, the picture excellent. It was a large pick-up, with what he guessed was a canvas cover over the rear cargo compartment. Where had it come from? He studied the map, and decided to follow a hunch that it had come from the south, along the coast road.

"John?" His train of thought was interrupted. It was Jerry. "I think we've got a problem."

Kearwin looked up anxiously. "What gives? JSTARS didn't pick them up again after the road-block?"

"No, it's not that. We got them again, still heading along the same road. The problem is, they're coming into a town called Hadithah. Well, actually it's a cluster of three towns, but that's the easiest one to pronounce. There's Benny- something and Hackla- something else. We settled on Hadithah." He pronounced it wrongly.

"So?"

"Well, they have three options there, the way I see it. Either they go north-west — but that goes no-place, except towards the Syrian border, so I figured they wouldn't do that — or they go south-east, to Baghdad — I thought about that, and why would they go that way? If they wanted to go to Baghdad, they'd have taken the main highway, wouldn't they?"

Kearwin considered the matter. "OK, so what's the third option?"

"They keep going in the same direction, east. That means crossing the Euphrates."

"So, what's the problem?"

"Come and have a look at the picture we have of the bridge."

*   *   *

"Al Haqlaniyah coming up, Johnny. About five miles." Howard switched off the GPS receiver and anxiously scanned the road ahead.

"Usual routine?"

"Flashing lights on, but no sirens unless we run into trouble. Head through the town and take a left to Beni Dahir, about three miles further on. There's a big bridge there over the river, leading to the road to Bayji."

"OK."

It was 02.30 when they reached Al Haqlaniyah; the town was deserted. The ambulances cruised through the silent streets, and Howard ordered the flashing lights to be switched off. They picked up the Beni Dahir road, and three miles on came into another small town. They had descended from the plateau, down into the river valley, and it was noticeably warmer, though still cool. There were trees, orchards and fields surrounding the town. The road ran along the west bank of the Euphrates. It felt humid after the dryness of the desert; a pungent smell of animals and humans wafted in through the windows. Howard wrinkled his nose, but he noticed Bourne inhaling with apparent pleasure.

"The bridge should be coming up on the right." Howard consulted the GPS. They were at 34 deg 06 min N, 42-deg 23 min E. "Yes – there it . . . Oh, shit!"

Bourne braked the Land Cruiser to a halt. They sat in silence, staring at the sight alongside them. The huge bridge was a wreck. The central span was completely gone, one end of it protruding from the water; the main pier on the far side had collapsed sideways. The yawning gap was two hundred yards wide.

"Any other bridges, Ed?"

"There were. But the other three are shown here as definitely down. Maybe this was one of the last to be hit."

"So, what do we do?"

"The next bridge downstream is twenty miles away, and it's right by an Army base. I don't want to risk it unless we really have to. And maybe that one was hit, too."

"Upstream?"

"There's a big hydroelectric dam about five miles north of here. Beyond that, nothing for another forty miles, mainly because of the dam and its lake."

"Could we cross the dam?"

"Bound to be heavily guarded. Besides, do you notice any lights around here? Not a thing. I bet that's damaged too. No, there must be a temporary ferry or something here. Keep going along slowly, and I'll look out for it. If there's nothing, we'll go for the dam."

Howard saw the pontoon ferry just a mile further on. They stopped and switched off the lights. Ziegler joined them, and they examined the pontoon through binoculars. It looked deserted. "There'll be someone there on duty," growled Ziegler, hefting his AK. "I guess I'll just have to go wake him up."

Ten minutes later, on Ziegler's light-signal, the two Land Cruisers slipped gently down the muddy incline to the jetty. Ziegler waved them straight on to the large floating pontoon tethered alongside it.

He himself was kneeling down, one knee on the chest of a now wide-awake Iraqi corporal, the silencer of his AKMS jammed between the man's teeth. Howard and the others got out of the cars.

"This here's Corporal Abdul," said Ziegler conversationally. "He's kindly goin' to act as our tour guide of the Euphrates tonight. Isn't that right, Abdul?" Ziegler grinned down at the Iraqi soldier, who had not understood a word he had said. A mixture of fear and hatred suffused his face; fear was clearly winning the battle. "Right, Abdul. I'll guess I'll hand you over to my friend Johnny. You and he will get along just fine. You be a good boy and do what he says, you hear?" He turned to Bourne. "You better watch out for that Abdul. He's quite a character. He had a big sharp bayonet which he wanted to show me. I put it in the river for safe keepin'."

Bourne grabbed the Corporal and hauled him roughly to his feet, talking in a low, fluent voice full of menace. He kept close to the Iraqi as he moved to the rear of the pontoon and prepared to start the diesel engine.

The engine fired with a clatter; Bourne signalled to the others to cast off. The pontoon began to swing out into the lazy current of the big river, heading for the opposite bank through the black, oily water. Howard and Usher scanned the west bank behind them for any sign that the pontoon's departure had been noticed; they saw nothing.

At the far bank, they slipped alongside the jetty and made fast. Bourne turned to Howard, within earshot of the others. "Ed, take the cars on up the bank a little way. I'm just going to have a word with the Corporal."

The two vehicles moved forward off the jetty and drove up the incline. At the top, Howard stopped and waited; a minute or two later, Bourne rejoined him. "Everything OK?" asked Howard, as they set off eastwards.

"Fine. His name wasn't Abdul, actually." He paused, and then added, "It was Hamood. Hamood Nasir. Nasty piece of work, he was."

In the back of the vehicle, MacDonald noticed Bourne's use of the past tense. He shuddered and glanced out of the rear window. He could see nothing; the pontoon had already disappeared from view.

Intuition, however, told him that the body of Corporal Hamood Nasir had joined the other flotsam in the water of the Euphrates, floating slowly southwards as the huge river wound its way towards Baghdad.

*   *   *

Kearwin's eyes were red with fatigue, but curiosity had now overridden all thoughts of rest. He had traced the pick-up truck back south along the coast road. A pair of successive KH-11 passes, at 04.47 and 05.05 on 13th April, had shown the pick-up to have been stationary for a period of at least eighteen minutes in the early hours of the morning at a remote-looking spot about seventy miles south of Al Wajh.

But there had been nothing there except the pick-up. Or had there? The vehicle must have stopped for some reason. To rendezvous with some other vehicle, along the road? No. There had been no other vehicle present. Besides, the pick-up had driven off the road, a few hundred yards down towards . . .

Of course! The sea!

But there was no sign of a boat. Nothing, except a tiny two-pixel-sized blob, bright with heat, right by the shore in the earlier of the two passes. Not far from the pick-up. Something very small, almost too small to see. The computer had even ignored it as an aberration. Kearwin thought about it. It was ridiculous. Something just one foot across? One *foot*? Forget it. It was the equivalent of looking at something smaller than a single pellet of bird-shot with the naked eye at a distance of nearly a mile. Forget it!

But the heat source was there, definitely. A man? No, it couldn't be. No satellite picture had *ever* given sufficient resolution to spot one single human. Besides, this object, whatever it was, was too hot – much too hot for it to be a human. At the same time, it was not nearly hot enough to be a fire . . .

An engine! It had to be an engine!

Hammering out instructions on his keyboard now, Kearwin called up a KH-12 pass from thirty minutes before the two KH-11s. He sat chewing his nails as he waited for it to come through. It began to appear; he fixed his eyes on the screen. There was the sea, a uniform grey, warmer than the land. He studied it

255

keenly. No, there was nothing there. Damn! He adjusted the grey scales.

Then he saw it. The tiny bright spot. And it was seven hundred yards out to sea! That meant . . .

Of course, a boat or dinghy might not show up – the temperature difference would be too slight, especially if spray was cooling the boat. But an outboard engine . . .

Yes it must be the same object. It *was* an engine! *Now* he had something to work with!

Half an hour later, Kearwin threw his head back and let out a piercing whoop of triumph. The work of the NRO ground to a temporary halt as analysts looked up in astonishment.

Walter Sorensen, despite his own tiredness, jumped to his feet and hurried over to Kearwin's desk. Heads turned; no one present had ever seen the Walrus break out of a slow, measured walk. Now he was running. Even if it was only a few yards, the Walrus was definitely *running*.

"I've got them, Walter! I've got them!" Feverishly Kearwin began to explain, his high-pitched voice cracking with excitement and rising above the sudden hubbub among his colleagues. As his words came pouring out, other analysts drifted away from their stations and gathered around to hear what all the fuss was about. Kearwin told them all about the oil-bucket fire and his suspicions, the vehicles, the backtracking from the border, the aircraft sighting at the construction compound and its subsequent sighting at the Ar'ar airfield; he explained about the AWACS reports, and the computation that traced it back to Al Wajh. Then there was the pick-up truck, and how it had itself been picked up from the KH-11 scans down the coast road. Then the tiny two-pixel-sized hot-spot, alone out on the sea . . .

Walter Sorensen listened with pride as Kearwin talked. This was one of *his* boys. The excited murmuring of the other analysts washed over him as he thought about what Kearwin had achieved. He, Walter Sorensen, had trained young John Kearwin. Now the youngster – OK, maybe not a youngster any more – was explaining it all to the others, giving them a lesson that one day might wind up in a textbook. Kearwin's squeaky voice rose still higher above the chatter as he started to expound on the technicalities and bring up the images on his screen to illustrate what he was saying.

The Walrus reflected, his mind only half concentrating. There was no getting away from it. John Kearwin had just done something extraordinary, something that made him maybe the best of them all. The boy had done all that tracking – intuitive work, most of it – from inside Iraq, all the way back through Saudi to the Red Sea. Covering a period of two weeks and a vast expanse of territory, he had tracked targets that would normally have been reckoned too small to rate any attention. And he had done it with archive material – not even special tasking.

OK, thought Sorensen, he himself might have managed some of that stuff, when he was a kid. But maybe not the last part of it. He thought about that. *Wow*, was the Director going to like this!

Kearwin had backtracked a tiny target, just one foot across, over a seventy-five-mile stretch of ocean.

At last, after all these years, Sorensen had something that would make Langley sit up and notice. Oh *boy*, would they sit up! He could give them the route, the schedule, the timings, a rough idea of the vehicles, the camp they had come from, the aircraft – he could give them the lot.

Best of all, he could give them that goddam great big container ship.

39

Twenty miles clear of the Hadithah crossing, Howard was the first to spot the warehouse. He wouldn't have seen it if the turning hadn't been there. Glancing idly down the side-road, he saw the wire compound and security hut. He made a decision. "Pull up, Johnny."

They pulled off the road and studied the compound. "Nothin' movin' at all," observed Ziegler. "Hardly surprisin', at four in the mornin'."

"Things could start moving soon," said Howard. "There are only about two hours of dark left. I think we'll take a look at this place, see who's here. We won't find a more deserted spot than this, and I don't want to get too close to Bayji."

They drove the Land Cruisers quietly up to the gatehouse; nothing moved. Bourne got out and rattled the gate, shouting in Arabic. There was a sound of movement from within, and an old man appeared, dishevelled and only half awake. Bourne chatted amicably to him for a minute or so, and then suddenly produced his AK. The old man paled. He jabbered in terror, hurrying to open the gate.

They drove the vehicles through; Bourne made the old man lock the gate and hand him the key. He pulled him over to the back of the second ambulance and pushed him inside. "Look after him, Bob. We'll take a look at that warehouse. He's guarding an empty building, would you believe."

The warehouse was a large steel and concrete building; as the civilian guard had said, it was empty. He was the only man on duty. Bourne judged that he was about sixty, but he looked much older. In his fear, he was a pathetic figure. He sat silent and trembling in the rear of the Land Cruiser as MacDonald and Howard opened the two big sliding doors of the warehouse.

Once the vehicles were inside and out of sight, Bourne explained. "It's just about perfect. It's lain empty for over a year, according to our friend here – ever since the war. He and his two sons have the job of guarding it. The sons will be along at dawn to relieve him, then he's due to take over again at dusk. He spends all his nights here. No one ever comes near the place. It belongs to one of the state agricultural companies – they used to use it as a food store. The guy's not even armed. He'll cause no trouble."

"Right," said Howard. "Time for a bit of vehicle maintenance, something to eat, and some rest. We've done well. But first things first." He pulled out his packet of cigarettes. "Anyone got a light?"

40

Harry Cresswell was in a foul mood. For one thing, he didn't like being woken up at three in the morning. Especially, he muttered to himself, after a late night. What was more, he didn't like the sound of this at all. A major panic, it sounded like. What the hell was going on? An invasion, maybe? Or a nuke being smuggled in? Or what? God only knew. The whole thing sounded screwy. But it had to be important. Cresswell swore to himself. He was due his annual leave, starting tomorrow; he could kiss that goodbye, he thought gloomily.

There was no way round it. The Deputy Director (Intelligence) had been quite explicit and emphatic. He had also sounded pretty mad about something. "Get your ass down there pronto, and check it out!" the DD(I) had yelled at him down the line. It was OK for the DD(I), Cresswell thought, crossly; it was only nine in the evening at Langley . . .

Hell, that proved it. It must be important. The DD(I), calling him after hours.

Right. Well, he would start by fouling up a few other people's Sunday morning, starting with the Ambassador and working down. Yes; he would start with the Ambassador, right now. He would need his authorisation for the flight, and he would need him to get the police and Customs people into line at the other end. Cresswell picked up the telephone and buzzed the switchboard. "Get me the Ambassador."

"You could use his direct line, Mr Cresswell. But are you sure —"

"Just do it. Now! And when I'm through with him, get me the operations manager of American Airlines at Jomo Kenyatta International. On second thoughts, find out his home number and get him there." That jerk on the switchboard. Someone should put a squib under his ass.

Cresswell ran a hand through his hair as he sat waiting for the call to the Ambassador. He yawned. There was something vaguely wrong with the world this morning, and he couldn't quite put his finger on it. Hangover? No, not exactly.

Coffee! That was it. He needed a cup of coffee.

Ten minutes later, waiting for the call to the American Airlines chief, Cresswell felt a bit more human. All it had taken was a cup of coffee. He wished he was better at mornings. He never had been much good at them, ever since childhood. How he envied those guys who could leap out of bed with smiles on their faces, ready to go. He thought back over his conversation with the Ambassador, wondering if he hadn't been a bit short with him. It didn't go down well, being short with ambassadors, even if you were the CIA Head of Station. Had he been rude? He decided he hadn't. Forceful, perhaps. He would apologise later, using the urgency of the situation as an explanation. The Ambassador was OK, a decent guy.

The phone rang; it was the airline chief on the line. Cresswell introduced himself and told the astonished man what it was he wanted, giving him the authorisation. A quarter of an hour later, he was on his way to the airport; there was no traffic, and the eight-mile drive took him twelve minutes.

At 4.05 a.m. the American Airlines 747 rose from the runway and climbed gently into the pre-dawn sky above Nairobi. It banked slowly round and settled on a south-easterly course for Mombasa.

In the first-class section of the plane, Harry Cresswell settled down to a hot breakfast, oblivious of the puzzled glances of the steward. He hoped he would get there before that goddam ship docked and started discharging any passengers or cargo.

The steward had firmly decided that the world had gone mad. A whole 747, he thought; just for one passenger. Who the hell *was* this guy?

*   *   *

"They've definitely stopped, John. The JSTARS has seen no movement for twenty minutes now."

Peter Stannard sounded worried, decided Kearwin. Or was it just tiredness? Everyone was tired. It was 9.25 p.m., and they had been on duty for over fifteen hours. Maybe the guys in those vehicles felt the same. Yes, that could be it, he thought. It would be 4.25 a.m. in Iraq; maybe they were taking a break. He hoped so. "Get an exact fix on the location from the JSTARS, Peter. Jerry, see what the next Keyhole pass makes of it, and run a comparison from the archive. They could be resting up for the day."

"I've got an archive picture here now," said Freedman. "Take a look. Empty desert, except for this big building set back off the main road. Maybe they pulled in there."

There was no way of telling, Kearwin knew. But the location of the building tied in exactly with the last movement reported by the JSTARS. He looked closely at the picture on Freedman's screen. It was an oblique, showing the northern elevation. There was a small hut on the south side, near the road, and what looked like a fence surrounding the area. Nothing else. "What's the height measurement on that building?" he asked.

"About seven metres."

"OK. When is the next KH pass?"

"Ten minutes away. It's the second '12, set up for a bounce."

"Good," said Kearwin. "Get a vertical shot, and an oblique of the southern elevation, the side nearest the road."

The two pictures came through fifteen minutes later. The vertical shot indicated that the vehicles were not parked next to the building, hidden behind it, and the oblique showed the big doors at the front – easily large enough for the vehicles to get through. The doors were closed.

Kearwin consulted Sorensen. "I reckon they're holed up in there, taking a break for the day. They've been on the move for nearly twelve hours. All the same, I'd like to keep the JSTARS on station for another couple of hours, just in case it's only a temporary stop. Can we ask them that, or will it cause problems?"

The Walrus gave Kearwin an amused smile. "John, right now you are in a position to ask for just about anything you like. You'd probably get Air Force One, if you said you wanted it." Kearwin looked puzzled; the Walrus smiled again and went on. "About an hour ago, I phoned the Director to tell him what you'd found. I can tell you, the Director is one happy man. He called me back just now. He's been kicking ass all over Washington, and there's green smoke coming out of CIA Headquarters in Langley. The DCI is madder than hell. He wants to know why the CIA didn't damn well find out about

262

this first. He's put a bomb under his DD(I), and the DD(I) has been yelling his head off at his people out in Riyadh and Nairobi. A couple of dozen other places, too. They're chasing around right now, trying to find out about the plane and the container ship. The Director has heard a rumour from the Defense Department that a CIA man has commandeered a Boeing 747 all to himself, just to get his ass over to Mombasa. The National Security Council is convening for an emergency meeting in . . ." – Sorensen consulted his watch – ". . . in half an hour's time, and the President's National Security Advisor has already spoken with the President. Yes, I reckon you could say you've caused something of a stir in this here town."

Kearwin looked completely bemused. "But why? What's all this about?"

The Walrus studied him for a moment before replying. "I guess you've been too busy doing your tracking work even to think about it." He fingered his moustache and his eyes gleamed at Kearwin. "The Director, on the other hand, has given it a great deal of thought. He's made some assumptions, but they're good ones and I agree with him. These guys are clearly illegals. They sneak into Saudi from the sea, then they sneak into Iraq over the border. They must be good, and they must be very determined. They're risking their lives. The way the Director sees it, they have to be doing something big. *Real* big." The Walrus stopped for a moment and pursed his lips gravely. "What – or maybe I should say *who* – do you think they could be going for?"

There was a long pause as Kearwin realised what Sorensen was getting at. "Oh," he said lamely. "I never thought of that. Wow!"

"Exactly," said the Walrus. "Wow."

41

Harry Cresswell had no idea who the Ambassador had spoken to, but it must have been someone with clout. The Kenyan Foreign Minister, probably. Whoever it was, President Moi would have been told, thought Cresswell; nothing much happened in this country without his getting to hear about it. Anyway, it had had the required effect. A Chief Inspector of the Kenyan police was waiting for Cresswell when he arrived in Mombasa, and he was whisked straight down to the docks. He arrived there at 5.30 a.m., as the first signs of daylight were appearing. The port had been sealed off; there were Kenyan Army people everywhere, unsmiling, mean-looking men with loaded rifles. They looked as if they wouldn't hesitate to use them. Out in the harbour, the lights of three patrol boats circled as the m.v. *Manatee* was slowly towed in to her berth.

In the Port Director's air-conditioned office three hours later, Cresswell put down the telephone and sat for a moment, thinking. The DD(I) had sounded in a slightly better humour than when they had last spoken. Cresswell's initial report following the questioning of the *Manatee*'s captain must have mollified him somewhat. Not that there had been much to report. The only details of any note concerned the ship's schedule. The DD(I) had known that the ship had docked and discharged cargo in Port Sudan and Djibouti before carrying on to Mombasa, but that was all he had known. The news that her port of origin was Felixstowe, England, and that she had not stopped anywhere else *en route*, apart from Suez, seemed to have given him something to chew on.

"No sign of stowaways having been aboard?"

"We're still searching, sir. There's about a hundred Kenyan cops tearing the ship apart, and several squads of Customs guys have taken it on themselves to start opening up all the containers. I haven't told

264

them our birds have already flown – they might lose interest. The ship's captain is screaming blue murder that the cops have trashed his cabin, and from what I can see from here, they don't intend to miss much."

"Well, call me as soon as you find anything."

"I will, sir."

Cresswell looked out of the window again and raised his eyebrows at the sight of the pandemonium on the dockside. There was no earthly point in intervening, or trying to bring a more methodical approach to the search. Besides, it may have looked like mayhem down there, but those gangs certainly were moving those containers. The ship was nearly half empty already. Cresswell could see Chief Inspector Robert Mwanza in the middle of a throng of African bodies, giving orders, directing the operation. In his way, the Chief Inspector was quite efficient.

Privately, Cresswell didn't think anything would be found. The guys they were after had gone, hadn't they? It wasn't much good searching for them now. But you never knew . . .

There was a knock on the door, and a young policeman entered. "Excuse me, sah. The Chief Inspector says to come."

"I'll be right there." Cresswell left the office and ambled down the stairs. As he opened the door and stepped out into the bright morning sun, the clamour of the activity on the quay hit his ears like a volley of gunfire. He walked across towards where Chief Inspector Mwanza was leaning over a table working his way through a pile of documents. "How's it going, Chief Inspector?"

Mwanza gestured over his shoulder at a big yellow-painted freezer container. "That one is empty."

"Is that unusual?"

"The Customs say yes, but not unheard of. Occasionally they go empty if the owners cannot find a cargo for both ways."

"What does it say on the bill of lading?"

"That is what I am trying to find, Mr Cresswell." Mwanza continued sifting through the stack of papers.

Cresswell walked over to the container. Four Customs men were standing by the open doors, examining the British Customs seal. A police constable was guarding the entrance, trying to look important. He looked faintly ridiculous, guarding an empty box. Cresswell approached the Customs officials. "Is the seal OK?"

One of the men looked up and nodded. "Yes, sah."

Cresswell poked his head inside the container. Clean as a whistle. He wandered round it slowly, examining the outside. The fan unit at the other end was running noisily; it obviously had an integral power supply.

Wait a minute. What was the goddam thing running for? It was empty, right? Some idiot had switched it on by mistake. He strode back to Mwanza. "Someone put the cooler fan on by mistake."

Mwanza raised his head briefly but made no reply; he resumed his search for the bill of lading.

Cresswell walked back over to the container and went round to the rear. "Anyone know how to turn this thing off?" Blank looks greeted his question. Cresswell shrugged. Fine. Let it run. Why should he care that fuel was being wasted, keeping the thing froz . . .

Just a goddam minute! *It hadn't been cold.* Cresswell put his hand inside and felt the interior wall. It wasn't cold at all. He ran round to the other end again. The fan was still running; it was even dripping with condensation. And the temperature gauge said . . . *minus twenty*!

Cresswell hurried back over to the table. "Inspector! I think we got something here!"

"Indeed, Mr Cresswell. I think so too." Mwanza flourished a piece of paper. "There would appear to have been a fraud. The bill of lading says that this container left Felixstowe with a cargo of frozen food."

For the next thirty minutes, Cresswell was forced to wait, pacing back and forth with frustration, as the police examined the container for fingerprints. There was one set; they turned out to be Cresswell's, from where he had touched the inside. Mwanza gave him a cool glance but said nothing.

At last they had finished. Now policemen swarmed inside the container with screwdrivers and began taking the panelling apart. Five minutes later, the dummy panel had been removed and the hatch discovered. There was a series of loud clangs from inside as it was attacked by an enthusiastic policeman with a sledgehammer. Cresswell, waiting outside, saw the previously smooth surface of the paint crack, and, at 9.02 a.m. precisely, the hatch suddenly swung open on its hinges.

It would be another hour before an engineer reported the existence of two air-conditioning units mounted inside the refrigeration-unit housing, and explained how the thermostat had been deliberately tampered with.

Cresswell didn't wait for the engineer. As soon as the hatch swung open, he raced away back to the port headquarters block. Taking the steps three at a time, he ran into the Port Director's office, picked up the telephone and started dialling.

At 03.09 USA Eastern Time, the phone began to ring in the DD(I)'s office in Langley, Virginia. The DD(I) flicked on a light, rose sleepily from his couch and picked up the receiver.

When he heard what Cresswell had to report, he instantly forgot his tiredness. "Thank God for that," he muttered as he rang off. "London can take the shit from now on."

What he had no way of knowing was that just six hours later, the whole lot would bounce straight back in his face.

42

The emergency meeting of the British Joint Intelligence Committee broke up and its members began to disperse. As he headed for the door, the Commissioner of the Metropolitan Police was approached by a trim, grey-haired figure wearing a regimental tie.

"Commissioner, may I make a suggestion?"

The Commissioner looked at the speaker with interest. "Yes, Mr Goodale? I would welcome your ideas."

Max Goodale smiled. "May I first of all say how much I regret the way this business with the IRA brief has been handled. I don't believe the argument should have become such a public and acrimonious one, nor, I think, do the majority of my colleagues in Five."

The Commissioner nodded. The recent stripping of the police of responsibility for domestic anti-terrorist operations, and the handing over of that responsibility to MI5, had been a sore point with the police; pride had been dented and many in the force had felt insultingly snubbed. "It is kind of you to put it that way, Mr Goodale. I myself felt that it could have been handled better."

"I feel it is important that there should be no rancour between our organisations. I say that because it is possible that we may be able to help with one or two aspects of this new matter." The Deputy Director of MI5 studied the Commissioner carefully for signs of resentment; as he had expected, he saw none. The Commissioner had a formidable intellect and Goodale knew he would, like himself, be above petty interdepartmental rivalries. He continued. "Naturally, anything we can do will be on the basis that the investigation will be entirely under your control. It is simply that we have various resources at our disposal that could be of assistance. I would like to offer them. After all, none of us yet knows what we are dealing with here."

"Mr Goodale," said the Commissioner, "that is a generous offer, and I very much appreciate the way you have expressed it." He smiled back at the MI5 man. "I think it is an excellent idea, and I would like to take you up on it. May I ask whether you have cleared this with your Director-General?"

"Not yet," replied Goodale, "but I am confident that she will entirely approve. Perhaps, if I may suggest it, the first step would be for me to have a meeting with the officer you plan to put in charge of this investigation. He and I could take it from there."

"Good idea," said the Commissioner. "Perhaps I could give you a lift back to the Yard? We can fill him in on this together, over breakfast."

"That would be very kind," said Goodale.

They walked out towards the Commissioner's car; a smartly uni-formed police sergeant saluted and opened the rear doors. Goodale gestured to his own driver to follow on behind. The two men settled back comfortably as the police Jaguar set off at speed through the almost deserted streets. They discussed the unusual nature of the task the police had just been assigned.

"I'm going to throw this job at SO11," said the Commissioner. "Initially, at any rate, it looks like a job for the Criminal Intelligence Branch, with help of course from other departments – including, as you have kindly offered, your own. You know," he smiled, "if you hadn't suggested it, I would probably have approached you about it anyway, once I got round to thinking about it."

Goodale laughed. "Well, it's nice to know we are both thinking along the same lines. Let's hope that together we can come up with something. Can I ask who will be the officer in charge?"

"The Commander of SO11. One of the best, if not *the* best. Jones. Patrick Jones."

"I have met him," said the Deputy Director of MI5. "For obvious reasons, our paths have crossed before. We get on well together."

"If there's anything to be found, Jones will find it," said the Commissioner.

43

"All right then gentlemen. This is what we're going to do." Commander Patrick Jones leaned over the table and looked around the faces in the room. His glance settled on a small, stocky man with thinning red hair and close-set eyes. "Hughie, I want you to get down to this Swindon address. Liaise with the local Thames Valley people when you get there. Don't step on their toes, but I want it quite clear that the instruction has come from the top that this inquiry is centralised here in London. If you get any grief on that score, tell them to talk to their Headquarters in Kidlington. The Chief Constable is being put in the picture as I speak, and he'll straighten out any grumbles. There'll most likely be no one at the address; break the door down. Give the place a thorough going-over – I want every speck of dust analysed. Find out who has been there, who owns it. Ask around and find out if anyone has seen the people who used the place. If it's rented, get hold of the agent and get all the details. Names, descriptions, the works. Who has made deliveries or collections? Post, refuse collection, milk? Grab anyone who has seen any of the occupants. OK?"

Detective Superintendent Hughie Carter had been making notes; he looked up and nodded. This was going to be a major job, he was beginning to realise, judging by the number of people who had been pulled in to help. As if there wasn't enough to do on his own patch, he thought, sourly. The first thing he would do would be to call his newly-appointed assistant and hand over all his other work. That would leave him to concentrate on this. Yes, he decided, that was a good idea. A baptism of fire for his fast-track assistant. It would give him a chance to see how the kid handled things in his absence. A competent enough kid – or so she seemed so far. She had to be competent, he supposed, to have been promoted that quickly. Well, he would soon find out what she was made of.

The Commander was now addressing a tall, blond, scholarly-looking man wearing heavy-framed glasses. "Paul, I want your team to do the banks. Start with the head offices of the main clearers, and find out where this outfit had an account. When you find it, get copies of all the bank statements since the account was opened, get copies of all cheques from the branch, details of all transactions and who the payments were to or from. Get copies of letters to the bank – there'll be something on file. Go and talk to the people they did business with. Visit the registered office and grab anyone there. Find out who audits their accounts and pull them in too. Again, I want names and descriptions of these characters. Clear on that?"

Detective Chief Inspector Paul Hallam of the Fraud Squad nodded. This one sounded interesting. He liked grabbing respectable citizens out of bed on a Sunday morning.

Jones moved on to address a dark-haired man who looked like what he in fact was – an ex-middleweight boxer. "Jerry, I want you and your boys to find out about this aircraft. All we have is the British registration mark. Get some of your team to work on the mark and find out where they bought it. Has it been re-registered? If so, who to? Get the others backtracking it from Saudi Arabia. It arrived there on ..." – Jones consulted his notes – "... on 11th April. Give it a couple of days, maybe three or four, for the journey, and find out where it left from. Start with airfields in the south of England. Don't bother with those that have no Customs facilities. Pull in someone from the CAA to help you. Find out who saw it and, most importantly, who the pilot was. Get a name and description."

"Right." Detective Inspector Jerry Willson privately doubted whether he would get much joy out of civil airfields on a Sunday, but his jaw was set in determination. Like Hallam, he had every intention of making someone else suffer for yet another ruined weekend. The Civil Aviation Authority would be the first on his list of telephone calls.

"Now; I would like to introduce Mr Goodale here. Mr Goodale is from the Security Service – MI5." There were a few startled glances. Jerry Willson opened his mouth to protest, then thought better of it. Jones was continuing. "I suggest each of you thinks carefully about what Mr Goodale can offer, in terms of either personnel or resources. You've all worked with Five before, off and on. Mr Goodale will be staying in London; there will be an open line from this office to his.

271

He and I will be joint co-ordinators on this." Jones let the remark sink in. The men in the room studied Goodale with new interest, realising that he must be a high-ranking member of MI5. Jones nodded as he saw the interest. He wasn't going to elaborate on exactly how senior Goodale was. He carried on. "As I said, joint co-ordinators. The Commissioner has personally issued instructions to me that this is to be a joint operation. You will have a man from security attached to each of your teams. You are to make full use of what he has to offer. I want the highest degree of co-operation. I hope that is understood. I also," he concluded, "want results. And I want them fast."

*   *   *

Over the next few hours, the results began to come in. The preliminary work had been easy. The information on the bill of lading for the container had led to the Loundis Road address in Swindon, and the container-leasing company confirmed that the container in question had been delivered to Unit 10. Soon, a team of a dozen analysts was at work, searching the building for the minutiae of evidence. At the same time, a startled young estate agent, whose firm had been conveniently identified by the "TO LET" hoarding at the entrance to Loundis Road, was hauled unceremoniously from a late Sunday-morning lie-in with his girlfriend and subjected to a session of intensive questioning by two unsmiling and determined-looking CID officers. He rapidly decided that this was not even a bad joke, let alone a good one, and told them what he knew. The search team widened its area of operation to Units 8 and 9, and the descriptions of "Mr Bryce" and his blue H-registration BMW 325i were circulated.

The estate agent was very specific about the car. It was a blue four-door saloon, he said; it had a manual gearbox and silver-grey leather seats, and the body was the new version which had been introduced in 1991, not the previous version. The only detail the estate agent could not remember was the full registration number, so one of Hughie Carter's team was detailed to get a complete list of all cars with corresponding specifications from the main BMW distributors in Bracknell. The distributors quickly produced a print-out list of all such cars, with their chassis and engine numbers. Out of a total production of two thousand six hundred and nine H-registration 1991-model BMWs, one hundred and seven were blue manual four-door saloons with grey seats. The Driver and Vehicle Licensing Centre in Swansea matched the chassis numbers of these with registration numbers; none of the cars proved to be registered to a Mr Bryce. Police forces all over the country were given the list and asked to check up on them as a matter of urgency. In a massive operation all the owners were visited at home. Of the seventy-nine who were in when the police called, five looked sufficiently like "Mr Bryce" to be escorted down to their local stations for further enquiries. Another twelve drivers were stopped on the road; eleven, on being released after unusually lengthy questioning, furiously vowed to write to the Police Complaints Authority with allegations of harassment. The twelfth joined the five to be detained pending conclusive identification. Six sets of photographs were faxed down to Swindon; each time, the young estate agent shook his head.

Of the remaining sixteen BMW-owners, fourteen were away on holiday or business trips; neighbours, on being asked for descriptions, were in each case quite sure that the one given of Bryce applied neither to the owner concerned nor, in the case of cars owned by women, to any boyfriend or husband.

The last two cars proved to be the most interesting. One had been reported stolen in mid-January, and the other had been sold but never re-registered in the new owner's name.

"Look at the date, Trev," said Detective Superintendent Hughie Carter. "It was stolen in January. The agent says chubby-face was driving it last November. It can't be that one. Did the other guy give a description of the buyer of his?"

"Yes, sir, but it isn't conclusive," said Detective Sergeant Trevor Smith. "He's one of these uselessly vague buggers who can't remember anything much. Just says the guy was in his late twenties, maybe early thirties. 'Just looked ordinary,' was all he said."

"Did you try him with the chubby-face description?"

"Yes. He couldn't be sure. Useless sod."

Carter made a decision. "Never mind. It must be the one. OK; we'll release the registration number to the media. See what that throws up."

It would turn out to be a dead end. Bourne's BMW, having been stolen and given a completely new identity, was by now in Italy. It was no longer blue, and its new owner would remain blissfully innocent of its chequered history for ever.

Detective Chief Inspector Hallam, too, had initial success. Barclays Bank co-operated by quickly producing all the records of the freight and transport company Bourne had set up. These revealed the existence of the two other dummy companies. Hallam immediately set a team of detectives to work on each one, and was soon in his element, gleefully ordering unfortunate and entirely innocent solicitors and accountants to be brought in for questioning, and impounding documents for fingerprinting. When the main payments from the Liechtenstein bank were uncovered, he reported back to Commander Jones.

Patrick Jones pursed his lips and drummed his fingers on the desk. "That one will probably have to wait until tomorrow, Paul. We can't go after an overseas organisation just on my say-so. But I'll see what I can arrange." He put down the telephone and frowned. Liechtenstein, indeed. That rang a bell somewhere. But it probably wouldn't help. So far, chubby-face had covered his tracks pretty well. The investigations into the car would lead nowhere, Jones was sure of that. The three industrial units were as clean as a whistle, as far as Hughie Carter had been able to tell. No useful evidence of anything: the place smelled of disinfectant; it had obviously been scrubbed clean. The only evidence they had found was a small spot of yellow paint on the floor of one of the units; it would probably match up with the paint on the container. Hughie Carter had got excited when a set of dabs on a door-handle had tallied with those of someone with form for auto theft, and they had raided the suspect's flat. It had turned out that he worked for a contract cleaning company; his boss had confirmed that they had cleaned all three industrial units but had never even seen any of the occupants.

The banks and the estate agency had been as helpful as they could have been, but the documents they had surrendered bore the fingerprints only of the bank staff and the estate agent. Each had sworn that chubby-face had not been wearing gloves when he signed the leases and other agreements. Some sort of invisible coating on his fingers? Probably.

Bugger it, thought Jones. The fellow must have slipped up *some-where*. Hughie Carter would find something. *Someone* must have seen something going on at Loundis Road. One of the many people making deliveries there, most likely. Hughie had already talked to the driver who had delivered the container, but all he had seen was . . .

chubby-face. The guy couldn't have been alone; there must have been others. The driver had said he had seen other cars parked outside the unit – though he couldn't remember what any of them were.

They must have been hiding inside. Chubby-face was the front man. That meant he didn't mind being seen. Why? Obvious – disguise. The face? Contact lenses, dyed hair, maybe . . . Cheek-pads. Yes, cheek-pads. Voice? Neutral, neither one thing nor another. Classless. Could have been public school, could have been anything. Could even have been a foreigner who spoke good English. A normal-looking man, medium height, sometimes in a suit, sometimes in working clothes . . . It was pretty hopeless, unless Hughie came up with another witness, or Paul uncovered something from the bank records. The problem was, not many transactions had gone through the books. Only inter-company ones, between the three dummies and the Liechtenstein account, apart from normal things like electricity and phone bills. But what about all the gear that would have been needed to work on that container and convert it? And the stuff that must have gone into it? That must have been bought from somewhere. Cash, thought Jones, gloomily. Oh yes, chubby-face had covered his tracks well.

The telephone rang; it was DI Willson. "We've traced the plane, Chief. Southampton Airport. It left there on 7th April. And we've traced it back to Ireland, where they got it from."

"Any descriptions or names?" Jones leaned forward in his chair.

"I was rather hoping you would be able to pull a few strings with the Garda in Dublin, Chief. You know, ask them to talk to the plane's previous owners. Questions would be better coming from them."

"Consider it done," said Jones, warmly. "What about the pilot?"

"I was saving the best until last. We pulled the records from the airport log. His name's Sullivan. US citizen, commercial pilot's licence. We've got his address, passport number, everything. He flew out alone in the Islander. I've checked with immigration records and the airlines, and they've given me details of when he entered the UK. I'm faxing details to you now."

"Good work, Jerry."

"Thanks, Chief."

"And don't call me 'Chief'."

"Right, Chief."

Jones rolled his eyes and replaced the receiver with a grin. Now *that* was more like it, he thought. Some hard information to work on. More importantly, he had something he could report. He looked at his watch; it was 2.10 p.m. Not bad going, for just over half a day's work. He sat back in his chair and waited for the fax to come through.

*   *   *

Commander Jones's progress report was rapidly passed up the line; Sullivan's details were immediately relayed to CIA Headquarters in Langley, where at 9.25 a.m. Eastern Time they landed on the desk of the Deputy Director (Intelligence). The DD(I) was not best pleased to learn of the involvement of a US citizen in an affair that he thought he had safely passed to London for action; those who came into contact with him over the next hour were left in little doubt as to his displeasure.

After drafting a terse request for assistance from the Federal Bureau of Investigation in the matter of obtaining full details on Sullivan, the DD(I) turned his irritation on James Ansell, the head of the Mid-East desk. "What does that idiot in Riyadh think he's up to? Why haven't we heard any more from him about this airplane?"

"You mean Kennings?"

"Yes – Kennings. What the hell is he doing, sitting on his ass? Get him moving on this, will you? I want that plane found, and fast."

Ansell raised his eyebrows at the DD(I)'s display of irascibility. He didn't much care to be shouted at. If it went on, he would go over his head and make a complaint to the DCI. He fixed the DD(I) with a level gaze and replied, "Alvin Kennings is a good man. He did well to get the registration mark of the plane in the first place. I can tell you from my own experience that it's not easy to communicate any sense of urgency at all to the Saudis, especially when they can see no obvious reason for an enquiry. And you said yourself that there was no question at this stage of telling them what all this is about." Yes, reflected Ansell, Kennings had done pretty well, so far. He had used his brains, correctly guessing where the Islander had entered Saudi Arabia and then concentrating his enquiries on Jeddah. He must have pulled in a few favours to get the information in the short time it had taken.

The DD(I) thought about it. "Well, keep him at it, would you?

Scowcroft's on my back on this one, and that means the President is on his."

Ansell said nothing. It would be quite unnecessary to reinforce his previous message to Riyadh, he thought privately. Kennings would not let him down.

44

Unfortunately for Alvin Kennings, the Islander had disappeared nearly twenty hours earlier. Denard had left Badanah shortly after dark, having filed a flight plan with Ar'ar air-traffic control that afternoon. He had given his destination as Tabuk, three hundred miles to the south-west across the Nafud desert.

Taking off at 19.00, an hour after Howard and the ambulances had left Badanah, he climbed to ten thousand feet and settled on to the course of 204 degrees magnetic he had filed with Ar'ar control tower. After half an hour of steady flying, correctly reasoning that by then Ar'ar's interest in his progress would have diminished, he switched off all his lights, dropped altitude and skimmed northwards at low level, going almost back on his tracks.

The desert was flat and featureless, but flying at an altitude of at times little more than one hundred feet above the ground in the dark, and without using any instruments other than his compass, was a test of nerve and skill. After another half an hour he was streaming with sweat, but he did not dare climb any higher in case his disappearance from the radar screens had been noticed and a search was in progress.

In fact, he needn't have bothered. As soon as the controller at Ar'ar had satisfied himself that the Islander was following its course correctly, he stood down for the night. No other traffic was expected, and he knew he would be alerted if any emergency arose. Ar'ar was not by any standards a busy airfield.

Denard flashed over the TAP road at ninety knots, heading north towards the Iraqi border. The driver of a large lorry heading for the United Arab Emirates had the vague impression of something roaring overhead in the dark, but he had been half asleep and came to the conclusion that he must have been dreaming. Denard switched on his GPS unit, banked round and came in to land on the TAP road behind the departing lorry. There was no other traffic about. He checked his position on the map: only two miles off course. He took off again, continuing at low level for eighteen minutes; then, switching on a low-power hand-held VHF radio, he spoke just two words: "Light up."

Ten seconds later, he saw the mini-flare. It was one mile away, slightly to starboard. The tiny flare rose no more than one hundred and fifty feet and was lost in the vastness of the desert, but its brief five-second burst of life was enough for Denard. He hauled the aircraft round to starboard and headed directly for where the flare had been. Forty seconds later, he passed over two parallel lines of lights on the ground. Easing back on the throttle and lowering the flaps, he circled once at low speed and then brought the aircraft in to land between the two lines of lights. It bumped down softly on its big balloon tyres, and Denard taxied up to the end of the improvised runway.

Palmer was waiting for him in the third Land Cruiser. They had made a reconnaissance and decided on the landing strip two days earlier, fixing its exact position using the GPS. It was in the middle of nowhere, approximately thirty miles north-east of Al Jalamid in the Wadi al Ubayyid, twenty-five miles short of the Iraqi border.

Denard was exhausted from the concentration of low-level flying. Palmer had a thermos of sweet tea ready, and Denard drank two cups, sitting in the front seat of the vehicle while the engineer finished shutting down the aircraft, fitting the engine nacelle covers and anchoring it down against possible winds.

"Rather my job than yours, Chris," commented Denard when Palmer joined him in the vehicle. "I don't envy you that drive. Bleddy dull, this country."

"No problem, man," answered Palmer. "You behave yourself here, hey?"

"Oh, sure," said Denard, sarcastically. "What the hell could I get up to here, anyway?"

"I wouldn't like to guess, knowing you," grinned Palmer. "Got the papers for me?"

Denard handed over Sullivan's folder with all the documents inside. "Be off with you now. Drive carefully, and don't go bumping into any camels."

279

"And don't you go shagging any stray goats. I'll see you in a couple of days."

Denard climbed out of the vehicle and walked over to the tent Palmer had put up; he was looking forward to a long sleep. Tomorrow, he thought, yawning, he would shave off his moustache and wash out the hair-dye. There was no need for him to look like Sullivan any more.

Palmer started the car and set off southwards towards the TAP road; he wore his night-vision goggles for the cross-country drive in the dark. He hit the TAP road at 22.11, just after Bourne had led the two ambulances past the Iraqi border post and the Iraqi guards were warming themselves by Howard's diversionary fuel-depot fire. High overhead, the KH-12 satellite flew past unseen on the track that would take it past the border-post fire less than a minute later. It automatically registered the presence of Palmer's Land Cruiser as it turned on to the main road; the image would be recorded into the giant archive databank but never retrieved.

Palmer settled down for the long drive to Jeddah. It would take him eighteen hours.

45

"Come in." The double knock on the door was soft and polite, as the DD(I) liked it. He continued working on his papers, without looking up, as the visitor entered his office.

"FBI report on Sullivan, sir."

The DD(I) now glanced up at his visitor with interest. The young agent standing in front of him proffered a thin sheaf of papers.

"Well? Give me the meat of it."

Agent Jim Halsey stammered a little nervously as he began to recite. "S-subject's n-name Ray Edwin Sullivan, b-born 15th December 1945, age 46, US citizen, social-security numb—"

"Yes, yes, yes; just stick to the important details, would you?"

"S-sorry, sir." Halsey cleared his throat and continued. "Subject unmarried, only relatives a sister in Iowa and an aunt and uncle in Vermont. Subject resided in Granite Shoals, Texas, until recently, and ran a one-man air charter operation out of Los Morelos airfield, nearby. Subject closed down this business in January and sold his airplane, a twin-engined Cessna. On 14th March subject moved out of his rented accommodation, leaving no forwarding address. On 27th March subject took the 15.10 Delta Airlines flight 1632 from Houston, Texas, to Atlanta, Georgia, where he connected with the 19.20 Delta flight 10 to London, Gatwick, arriving 08.10 on the 28th. That's London, England, sir."

"I know. Any criminal record?"

"One minor conviction for possession of narcotics, sir, a long time ago, in 1967. Ten grams of marijuana."

"That's all? No record of military service?"

"No, sir. We're still looking into that."

"Have they talked to the, ah, aunt or uncle?"

"They haven't been able to trace them yet, sir. But they have talked to the sister. She says he's an easygoing type, irresponsible, lazy, gets by on his charm. Apparently he suffered very badly from asthma in his early twenties, which could explain his lack of military service. She also . . ." Halsey hesitated; the DD(I) signalled for him to continue. "The sister also says, and I quote, everyone likes him, but he's just a small-time, no-good bum."

"What? Don't the two of them get on?"

"Apparently not, sir. Seven years ago he borrowed three and a half thousand dollars from her to help finance the airplane, and never paid it back. They don't speak to each other any more. When asked whether she thought he might be involved with a major criminal organisation, she just laughed."

"Hmm. Anything else on his financial status?"

"Copies of bank statements for the last five years, sir. No known assets other than the Cessna. He just about managed to pay his bills – usually late."

"Nothing else?"

"No, sir. Shall I leave the file here with you, sir?"

"Thank you. That will be all, Agent, ah . . ."

"Halsey, sir."

"Thank you, Halsey."

The young man withdrew, leaving the DD(I) moodily pondering the case of Ray Sullivan. It was not at all what he had expected. A small-time bum, indeed. Causing all this trouble. Well, he'd make goddam sure Sullivan lived to regret it. If he ever showed his ass back here in the States, or anywhere else the CIA could get its hands on him, he'd regret it. Oh boy, would he regret it.

There was just one consolation, and thinking about it made the DD(I)'s spirits rise a little. A no-good, small-time bum wouldn't have the knowhow or the initiative to organise a major international stunt like this. Sullivan must be a nobody in this operation, strictly a bit-part player. Perhaps even a stooge. He hadn't covered his tracks like the others, according to the latest reports just in from London. And there probably weren't any other US personnel involved. It still looked like an British operation. Fine, thought the DD(I). Let the Brits carry the can.

46

Mel Harris put down the telephone and frowned. The call had gone through easily enough, more easily than he had expected. But that wasn't the problem. Why hadn't Patel answered himself? He had been forewarned to expect the call, had promised he would be in all afternoon. There wouldn't be anyone else there on a Sunday. Something was wrong. Patel never employed African staff in his office, only Indians, and mostly his own family. So why had an African voice answered the telephone?

The conversation had been brief, and Harris had given nothing away, but he hadn't liked the smooth way the African voice had simply said that Mr Patel was away and could he ask who was calling, please? Harris had promptly hung up.

If Patel had been arrested, what did he know? Nothing, thought Harris. All he had was a list of things to prepare, to re-equip the container for the return journey. Patel was a successful trader, and nothing on the list would have presented any problem. He had eagerly agreed to do the job and ask no questions when promised the thirty-thousand-dollar bonus. As far as Patel was concerned, the container was just a container; the stores and equipment he had been asked to procure were all innocuous items, even if they were rather a strange mixture. No, thought Harris; there was nothing that Patel could reveal. But if he *had* been arrested . . . Harris decided that he couldn't be sure. He would try ringing again, maybe tomorrow. Palmer would be here soon with the papers; then they could let Sullivan go. That would at least be one less thing to worry about, and he would at last be able to get out of this sodding hotel. Harris paced his room restlessly, pulling fiercely on his cigarette. The telephone conversation had made him uneasy. It was just as well, he reflected, that he had decided to check.

*   *   *

Sixteen hundred miles to the south, in Patel's Mombasa office, Chief Inspector Robert Mwanza replaced the telephone receiver. Like Harris, he frowned. So the Indian, Patel, had been telling the truth about "Mr Harmon", even though the caller hadn't given his name. The fact that he had hung up on him was enough. An English voice, as Patel had said. Not American. Why then the interest shown by the Americans? An overseas call, but too brief to trace. His mind ran over the list of items Patel had shown him. Quite obviously, most of them were for fitting out the container as living space for two men. But why the other things – the rubber boat, the wet-suits, the ropes and the rest of it? The more Mwanza thought about it, the more convinced he became that he had been misled by the American, Cresswell. This was no simple case of smuggling. He decided to file a complaint with his report. If nothing else, he thought, he had managed to put an end to whatever it was that someone had been planning.

47

"Alvin?"

"Yes; who is this?"

"Jonathan Mitchell. This is unofficial, but it might be a good idea if we pooled our resources."

Kennings was instantly wary. He knew Mitchell well, and liked him, but he had not yet received the go-ahead from Langley to work with him on this. He feigned surprise. "I don't think I quite understand you, Jonathan."

"Oh, come on, Alvin." The English voice on the other end of the line was serious, not mocking. "Don't be like that. The plane."

Kennings wasn't giving in, not just yet. "What do you mean?"

"All right," Mitchell sighed, "if you want to play hard to get, I'll tell you. I know where it is. The Islander, I mean. Or at least," he added, "I know where it should be."

"What!" Kennings's response reverberated noisily down the telephone line. "How did you find out? Where is it?"

From the other end came an equally resounding silence.

Kennings gave in, wearily. "OK, what's the deal?"

"Simple. You've got transport. HMG doesn't quite run to private jets. You share your wings, and I share my info."

Kennings wondered how on earth Mitchell had found out about the Learjet he had commandeered. Never mind. The deal was a fair one. He capitulated. "OK. It's a deal. I'll meet you at King Khaled International in twenty minutes. American Airlines ticket counter."

"Fine. See you there."

Forty minutes later, the two senior representatives of the British SIS and the American CIA in Saudi Arabia were seated in the tiny Lear as it taxied for take-off from Riyadh. Kennings turned to the Englishman. "OK, Jonathan, tell me how you found out."

"Simple, really. My Embassy people have been ringing round every airfield and airport in the country. We got lucky at a place called Tabuk."

"What! I spoke to them less than an hour ago. They didn't say anything. And why are we going to Ar'ar, if it's at Tabuk?"

"It's not at either. You'll probably find this hard to believe, but it's been overdue at Tabuk for more than fifteen hours now, and they hadn't reported it missing. They only noticed its absence when I asked if it was due in."

"Useless assholes," said Kennings warmly. "So why Ar'ar?"

"Two reasons. First, that's where it took off from at 19.00 yesterday. Second, that's where it's been based for the last couple of weeks or so. Or in that area, anyway."

"WHAT!" For the second time in less than an hour, the normally calm Kennings exploded with incredulity. Langley must have known. And they hadn't bothered to tell him. Just wait until he . . .

Mitchell had been watching Kennings's face, and imagined he knew what he was thinking. He guessed that the existence of the plane must have come to light through the CIA. "Probably just a case of a mistaken application of the 'need to know' principle, old man. If it's any comfort, no one told me, either. I had to wring it out of Ar'ar, after I spoke to Tabuk. They're closed for the rest of the day. Had to drag an off-duty official to the phone. Quite a helpful chap, actually, once I'd chatted him up a bit."

Kennings was only half listening. He was seething with anger that he had been sent on a wild-goose chase when Langley had known all along exactly where to send him. He shook his mind clear and changed the subject. "Tell me about this company Darcon, Jonathan. Are they on the level?"

"Why do you want to know?"

"Because the Islander's documentation on entry into Jeddah made out it was their airplane. I phoned a guy called Hughes – he's the senior Darcon man here – but he said he knew nothing about it. Said there had to be some mistake. They already have a plane – a little single-engined one."

Mitchell suddenly looked thoughtful. "That puts a new slant on things," he said, frowning.

"How come?"

"Because a couple of days ago the Islander apparently received clearance from Ar'ar to base itself temporarily at a construction camp just down the road. Place called Badanah. My contact in Ar'ar told me the pilot and his friends were living there. And the camp happens to be owned by Darcon."

"Well," said Kennings, "I think the first thing we'd better do is go and have a look at this camp, don't you? And after that, we'd better go back and have another chat with that nice-sounding Mr Hughes about his employees. I think he's got a bit of explaining to do."

"I've got a better idea," said Mitchell. "Let's ring him now. Save a bit of time. This thing has a phone, hasn't it?"

Using the radio telephone in the Lear, Mitchell called Hughes at his office, catching him just before he left for home. Hughes sounded genuinely perplexed and indignant, but insisted that the visitors were all bona fide, with all the correct documentation from London, signed by Sir Peter Dartington himself.

"Mr Hughes," said Mitchell, "I'm going to send round one of my people from the Embassy to see you right away. He will be accompanied" – Mitchell glanced at Kennings, who nodded – "by someone from the Embassy of the United States. I would be grateful if you would co-operate with them in full."

Hughes promised to do so.

"One more thing, Mr Hughes. You say they asked for the use of four vehicles – you're sure that's correct?"

Hughes said that it was.

"Good. What I'd like you to do is to make a report straight away to the Saudi police. Tell them that these vehicles have been stolen and give descriptions of the men you saw. I'll be at Badanah within the hour, and I'll telephone you with confirmation that the vehicles are missing." Mitchell ended the conversation and turned to Kennings. "Let the police do the legwork, eh!"

The CIA man smiled. "Nice touch, Jonathan," he said. "I like that. I like it a lot."

48

A baffled and angry Tony Hughes wasted little time in putting together details of the Land Cruisers he had sent to Badanah and the faxes he had received from England. He made three copies of each document: one for the police and the other two for the British and American Embassy men who had phoned to say they were on their way. While awaiting the arrival of the police, he placed an overseas call to the London office of his friend and colleague Sir Peter Dartington – only to be told by a secretary that he was out of the country and not contactable. Hughes was about to ask to be put through to Dorothy Webster, Dartington's PA, intending to demand point-blank to be told where he was, when there was a knock on his door and a smartly-uniformed Saudi police sergeant was shown in. Hughes put down the telephone, stood up from his desk and greeted the officer politely.

There is relatively little common crime in Saudi Arabia, essentially because police detection rates are high and penalties, even for minor offences, can be extremely severe. Incidents of theft and burglary are rare; faced with the likelihood of having his right hand cut off at the wrist in a public ceremony if he is caught, the potential criminal will generally conclude that even fairly lucrative proceeds of the crime he is considering are not worth the risk. Quite apart from the agonising nature of such a punishment – enough of a deterrent in itself – the loss of the *right* hand, rather than the left, confers a double social disgrace. The right hand is used for eating, while the left is reserved for attending to that part of the body considered most undesirable to be brought even indirectly into contact with food. Anyone who makes the mistake of passing or receiving food with the left hand is guilty of an outrage that will never be forgiven or forgotten. It is immediately and very visibly apparent to everyone what the person without a right

288

hand has done; and even in the unlikely event of his being thought to have had sufficient punishment for his crime, he would nevertheless be deemed quite unacceptable company at mealtimes.

Having been instructed by his superiors to conduct a preliminary investigation into the theft of no fewer than four vehicles, the police sergeant was in a serious mood. In the course of a twenty-minute interview, Hughes told him everything he knew and handed over the file he had prepared on "Mr Bryce" and "Mr Potter". When the sergeant heard that Bryce and Potter might have entered the country under false pretences by posing as Darcon employees, his expression became even more serious. When he was satisfied that he had all the relevant details, he thanked Hughes gravely and departed. It was exactly 17.00.

The Saudi police wasted little time. Descriptions of the two men and the four stolen Land Cruisers were circulated and flashed to police stations and mobile units all over the Kingdom. Hughes had given good descriptions of the two men, but he had seen Bourne and Palmer only in disguise. Bourne had worn his "Bryce" cheek-pads and tinted contact lenses, and Palmer the thick beard he had been growing for that purpose since November and had subsequently shaved off – as soon as he arrived in Badanah. They had entered Saudi Arabia on their own passports and under their true identities, undisguised, and the passport photos they had supplied for their visas bore little resemblance to the two men Hughes had seen. The visa photos would therefore prove to be of little value and Hughes would later be unable to identify them.

Hughes had in fact made one crucial but quite understandable error in the particulars he had given the sergeant. Although Palmer had spoken only a few words at their meeting two weeks before, Hughes had heard enough to convince him that the bearded man had a South African accent. He had stressed this point strongly to the police sergeant and it was a detail that would – not surprisingly – remain unquestioned by the Saudis; more remarkably, the British and American authorities would also fail to raise any doubts about it. The Irish Garda, on interviewing the Islander's original owners, had been informed of Palmer's "South African accent", and the new evidence from Hughes merely reinforced the notion. There is in fact a subtle difference between the accent of a South African of English (rather than Afrikaner) descent and that of a white Zimbabwean. If

Hughes had known this and been able to recognise the difference, Palmer's true identity would have been revealed very quickly from Saudi immigration records, for the simple reason that he was one of only three white Zimbabwean citizens in Saudi Arabia at that time – the other two being Denard and a children's nanny employed by the wife of an American oil-company executive.

Palmer was doubly fortunate that day. At precisely the same time as the police sergeant was being ushered into Hughes's office, Palmer was being waved through the routine police traffic checkpoint on the approach to Jeddah, near the end of his long drive south from where he had left Denard and the Islander. The bored and uninterested police officers on duty at the checkpoint paid little attention to the friendly greeting offered by the heavy-set driver of the Land Cruiser, opting instead to concentrate on a pick-up truck directly behind it containing five Indian migrant workers. One of the Indians turned out to have left his *iqaama* behind, and the pick-up and its passengers were still being detained forty minutes later when the details of the stolen Land Cruisers came through. By then the policemen at the checkpoint had forgotten all about the Land Cruiser, and Palmer, exhausted after his marathon nine-hundred-mile journey, had arrived at the Jeddah Sheraton and was relaxing in the lobby with a long cool drink.

The traffic police in Saudi Arabia are a separate entity from the regular "anti-crime" police, but in this case both branches had been put on the alert, with instructions to look for the two men whose descriptions had been given. Alvin Kennings and Jonathan Mitchell had arrived at Badanah, where they discovered the construction camp empty but for the Pakistani camp cook, who was alone in his quarters. They rapidly realised that the cook was an innocent dupe, but nevertheless grilled the unfortunate man for information about the camp's recent occupants. The highly nervous Pakistani, immediately sensing that something was badly amiss, was pathetically anxious to help. He bombarded the two men from the SIS and CIA with details; in his eagerness to please, however, he failed to appreciate that inaccurate information is worse than none at all. On being asked questions to which he did not know or could not recall the answers, he adopted the procedure of telling his interviewers what he thought they wanted to hear. The result, as Kennings soon realised, was an almost worthless stream of particulars, many of them fabricated and misleading. It did not help that the cook had a poor eye for detail; his descriptions of the eight men he had seen were to prove virtually useless.

Kennings drew Mitchell to one side. "We're getting nowhere with this guy. He's bullshitting us, trying too hard to be helpful. About the only useful information he's given is that there were eight of them, all white, and that they all left here last night in the three vehicles and the plane. I think we can rely on what he said about two of the vehicles being painted up to look like ambulances, and that stuff about one of the engines making 'a very terrible noise', as he put it. Those will be the two inside Iraq. The third vehicle has definitely left too, and we have to assume that it's still in Saudi. The fourth must be that hulk in the workshop; I guess they stripped it clean for spares. I suggest we limit what we report to the fact that we're now looking for eight white men, three vehicles and one airplane. If we assume that Sullivan is still with the plane, that leaves seven men in three vehicles, two of which we know are inside Iraq. I think if we give people any more than that it will just add to the confusion."

"You're right," said Mitchell. "I'll go and phone Hughes and get him to report that to the police. Let's hope they pick up that third car."

Mitchell telephoned Hughes, who quickly relayed the information to the Saudi police. The scope of the search was accordingly widened, and orders were issued for all white Darcon employees to be investigated. Kennings and Mitchell, had they been in direct contact with the police themselves, would have suggested that the investigation should not be confined to Darcon employees, but they knew that any blatant intervention by them would lead to diplomatic complications and cloud the issue still further. Far better for it to remain a civil matter, a straight case of Darcon reporting a serious case of theft. It was an entirely understandable assumption on Hughes's and the police's part that the criminals were posing as Darcon employees.

The trouble was, the assumption was wrong.

291

49

Tiredness had finally overcome John Kearwin. Having completed the tracking of the dinghy to the container ship, and having satisfied himself that the two vehicles in Iraq were indeed resting up for the daylight hours, he handed the job over to his relief and made his way to the rest room. Exhausted, he collapsed on to a couch and slept soundly for ten hours.

Wakened by the smell of coffee and a gentle buzz of conversation as NRO staff members drifted in and out for short breaks, he went to the men's room to freshen up. Collecting a cup of coffee on the way back, he returned to the control centre.

His relief looked up in surprise. "Oh, hello, John. I wasn't expecting you back yet."

Kearwin grinned. "Can't keep away, Jack. How's it going?"

Jack Fiske pulled a face and sighed. "Nothing at all to report from the building where these guys are supposed to be laid up. I just hope you're right, and they're still there. But that's not the problem. We've been getting a lot of heat from somewhere high up about this airplane. My guess is Langley can't find it."

"Well, we had it fixed at Badanah at, ah, 18.30 yesterday, Saudi time, didn't we? All we have to do is pull the AWACS records since then, and see where it's gone. It'll take time, but we should be able to find it."

"That's just the problem, John. Someone out there has found out that it took off from Badanah at 19.00, headed for Tabuk." Fiske indicated it on the map. "It never showed up there. I tried AWACS records. It was before the alert, of course. There was no AWACS up last night – they stood down at 18.00."

Kearwin grimaced. "So what have you tried?"

"It's pretty hopeless, John, it really is. That plane could have travelled hundreds of miles, in any direction. Or it could simply have had engine failure, crashed or something. It could be anywhere. It's like looking for a speck of dust in a football stadium – worse, in fact."

Kearwin knew. When he had been doing his backtracking exercise, which had led all the way back to the container ship, he had at least known roughly where to look each time. Fiske was right. It would be pure luck if they found the Islander. "Any theories?"

"I've made just one assumption," said Fiske. "I've assumed that it has deliberately disappeared. After all, if it had crashed it would be out of the game and of little further interest. Working on the assumption that it's still operative, the last place we look is on its stated course, towards Tabuk. But that's about as far as I've got."

"I think you're right. So, where would it go?"

"My guess is, it doubled back and it's lying low somewhere out in the desert. It could even have crossed over into Iraq."

Kearwin thought about it. On balance, he agreed with Fiske. "Have you tried using the JSTARS?"

"I asked them to do one sweep about an hour ago." Fiske indicated the area, a tract of desert to the south of the border post which he had picked at random. "Then I lost my nerve. If we pull them off the watch on that building to do this, the vehicles could leave and we'd be none the wiser. Even if we assume the plane has gone a maximum of a hundred miles, it would take them two or three days of non-stop radar mapping to have any chance of finding it."

"I agree," said Kearwin. "We can't risk that. So that leaves us with . . ."

"The KH-11s and '12s." Fiske stifled a yawn. "Unless," he added, "the plane takes off again, in which case the AWACS will pick it up. I hope you don't mind, but I used your authority to order round-the-clock AWACS coverage from now on."

"Quite right," said Kearwin. "Well, I suppose we'd better try the Keyhole satellites, and see if we can spot the airplane from their photographic archives. Hell, that's how we first picked up the two vehicles, isn't it? We'll have to use archive material from, say, 18.00 to 23.00 Saudi time yesterday. There won't be any point in using anything more recent – the plane's engines will have cooled and it'll be too hard to spot." He made a decision. "OK, we might as well get a team of juniors on to it. It'll be the most boring job they've

293

ever had. We'll have to pull thousands of pictures, one by one, and run the aircraft template against each one. It could take days to sift through it all, and we don't even have complete coverage. Let's hope the plane interrupts us by moving. By the way," he asked, "do you know where Walter is?"

"Oh yeah, I meant to tell you," said Fiske. "He breezed in here about an hour ago. I've never seen him looking so smart. Wearing his best suit and tie. He said he'd been summoned to an emergency meeting of the NSC. It's scheduled for 11.00."

Good grief, thought Kearwin. The Walrus, at an NSC meeting. He was always beefing about the "cowhides" – and now it looked as if he'd become one himself!

50

At 17.55, as Palmer was ordering his second drink in the lobby of the Sheraton, Harris was standing at the reception counter arranging check-out formalities for himself and Sullivan, who was still upstairs in his room. Two police officers approached the desk and demanded to see the hotel's duty manager, who duly appeared from his office. Harris heard the senior of the two officers ask to see the hotel register; he would normally have paid little attention, but because of the suspicious circumstances of his failure to talk to Mr Patel in Mombasa that afternoon he was more than usually alert. He pricked up his ears. Harris understood enough Arabic to follow some of what the police were saying, but it was only when he heard the word "Darcon" that alarm bells began ringing in his head. Then he saw one of the policemen hand a copy of a photograph across the counter and ask the duty manager if he had seen the man. Casually, Harris moved closer to get a look at the picture.

His heart sank. The photograph, though not a good one, was plainly identifiable as Sullivan. Harris just had time to interpret the first three letters in Arabic script of Sullivan's name, putting it beyond doubt, when the duty manager shook his head regretfully and handed the picture back to the police officer.

Harris thought quickly. He thanked God that he had taken the precaution of having the other room registered in Denard's name and that both men were recorded as being employees of Pan-Arabian Petroleum, not Darcon. The manager had not recognised the photograph, which was another blessing. It was just as well, thought Harris, that he had insisted that the American shave off his moustache on arrival.

But the fact remained that they were blown. He finished settling his and Sullivan's hotel bills, collected his own and Denard's passports, and walked over to join Palmer. Talking rapidly in a low voice, he outlined his suspicions. "Chris, we're in trouble. The police are on to Sullivan – I've just seen them flashing his photo at the reception desk. Unfortunately, we have to assume they're also on to us. I got suspicious yesterday when I couldn't get hold of our agent in Mombasa who's supposed to be looking after the freezer container and restocking it for the return journey."

"Shit," said Palmer succinctly. "What do we do now?"

"Well, let's look on the bright side. In the first place, your journey wasn't wasted. The boss was right to insist on the precaution. It means we have to let Sullivan go, and I mean *now*. In a way, he's served his purpose – it was really only his ID papers that were needed, for Andy. Getting the plane out afterwards would have been a bonus, but it may not be essential. I guess it'll have to be ditched. So; the first thing I have to do is hand over Sullivan's papers and get him to the airport. He'll have to take his chances there. At least he doesn't know any of our names; the worst he can do if he's picked up is give descriptions of me and Andy – we're the only two he's met."

"OK," said Palmer, "but what about the cars? Maybe they've got the registration numbers."

"Exactly," said Harris. "That means your Land Cruiser sitting outside could be hot. We have to assume it is. What I'm going to do is this. I'll take Sullivan to the airport by taxi and hire another car there – a similar-coloured Land Cruiser, if I can get one. Then I'll put its plates on your car so that we can continue to use the same vehicle. I don't want to run up a huge mileage on a hire-car – it might attract attention. Anyway, we might have to abandon it and that would lead back to me – I'm going to have to hire it with my own credit card. It'll be better if we use your car with the other one's plates – we can take them off if we do have to abandon it."

"But if you're going to swap the number-plates round, all that does is make your hire-car the hot one. How does that help?"

"Ah," said Harris, "I've got an idea for that." He quickly outlined his plan; then he relieved Palmer of Sullivan's document case and went upstairs.

Passing the door of his room, Harris ducked into the service pantry and looked around. There was a plumber's tool-bag on the floor; he opened it, selected a hand-drill, a hacksaw and a screwdriver, and put them inside his briefcase. His eyes lit on the large worktop surface, which was covered with a thin sheet of off-white formica. Using a kitchen knife, he levered off a large piece of the formica; this he snapped into two pieces small enough to fit into his briefcase. Then he went back to his room to collect the Texan, who had finished packing and was ready to go. The two men descended to the lobby with their bags. Avoiding the front desk, Harris quickly guided Sullivan straight outside to find a taxi. Palmer remained behind; Sullivan was unaware of his presence.

On the way to the airport, Harris informed the puzzled Sullivan that the job had been cancelled but that he would be paid anyway, as agreed. He handed him a slip of paper, giving him details of a Belgian bank which, on receipt of instructions containing the code number written at the bottom of the slip, would telegraph the ninety thousand dollars anywhere in the world.

Harris decided he owed the genial Texan something of an explanation. "Listen, Ray," he whispered, to avoid being overheard by the taxi-driver, "it's possible that there may be trouble at the airport. Keep a low profile and don't draw attention to yourself. The fact is, you've been registered all along at the hotel under a false name. I'm trusting you now not to blow the whistle on me. But there may be trouble. Do you follow me?"

Ray Sullivan pulled a wry face. "I guess for ninety thousand bucks there was bound to be a hitch somewhere along the line. Don't you worry, Mitch, I'll act as dumb as I can. But I guess," he mused drily, "Mitch Hoskins ain't exactly the name your dear momma gave you, is it?"

Harris grinned and side-stepped the question. "If you do get picked up, the heat may be quite fierce for a while. But all you have to do is insist that you were at the hotel the whole time and don't know what all this is about. There are plenty of witnesses there who will attest to it and identify you. All I want is for you to give as vague as possible a description of me if you're asked."

"No problem, Mitch. Listen, it's been good knowing you. I'd love to know what this has all been about, but I guess I'd better not ask."

Harris smiled again. He had grown genuinely fond of the easygoing Texan. "It wouldn't be good for your health, Ray. But you may read about it some day. And by the way – I wouldn't go back to the States either, if I were you. If the cops are looking for you here, they're probably after you there too."

"Bad as that, huh? But don't worry. I wasn't planning on returning there anyhow. There's just the matter of some money I owe my sister, but I guess I'll wire it to her. I think" – Sullivan chewed his lip reflectively – "I'll head east. I've always fancied making a trip to Thailand," he added, with a roguish wink.

They arrived at the airport and Harris paid off the taxi. He said a final goodbye to Sullivan, who disappeared in the direction of the ticket counter. Harris went straight to the Avis car-hire desk and enquired what cars they had available; the clerk began reeling off a list. "Do you have a Toyota Land Cruiser?" asked Harris. "That would suit me perfectly. But I want a pale-coloured one. Dark colours don't reflect the heat so well." The clerk gave him an odd look but confirmed that they did indeed have a Land Cruiser available. Harris hired it on the spot, using his credit card.

Out in the Avis section of the car-park, he located the vehicle, which was cream in colour, and started it up. He drove the car the short distance to the public section of the car-park, found a space and reversed the Land Cruiser into it, almost up against the bumper of another car. He got out, and taking his briefcase round to the rear of the car he knelt down. Hidden from view by the other car, he opened the briefcase, took out the screwdriver and unscrewed the rear licence-plate.

Back inside the car, he used the hacksaw to cut one of the pieces of formica to size. Working carefully to avoid snapping the brittle material, he made two holes with the drill to correspond to the screw-holes on the licence-plate. Then he began to make a faithful copy of the plate on to the formica, using a waterproof black marker pen. When he had finished, he compared the two plates. Not bad, he thought; the copy wouldn't stand up to close inspection but it should do well enough for what he wanted. He thought briefly about the risk involved, and wondered whether it would not after all be safer to use the hired vehicle. No, he decided; he had been right. If they had to abandon it, he would be implicated by name through the rental agreement. There would also be the matter of the mileage on the hired car. A substitution was the only answer.

He got out and attached the copy plate where the real one had been, using the screws. He drove the car out of the parking slot and then back in, this time head first, so that the front was now hidden from view, and repeated the procedure for the front licence-plate.

Placing the two genuine plates and the car-hire documents inside his briefcase, he locked the vehicle and headed back to the airport terminal, where he hailed a taxi to take him back to the Sheraton.

Palmer had been unobtrusively hanging around the hotel car-park where he could observe his car. "No sign of any interest at all," he told Harris. Harris decided to get it over with. While Palmer kept an eye open, he worked on the car, replacing the hot plates with the ones from the hire-car. He was grateful that the section of the car-park where Palmer had parked the Land Cruiser was only poorly lit. The job took five minutes; both men breathed a sigh of relief when it was completed. Palmer's Land Cruiser now effectively bore the identity of the hired one; a close scrutiny of the documents would have revealed the anomaly of the stated vehicle colour – cream instead of beige – but the car was sufficiently dusty after Palmer's journey for the true colour to be difficult to discern. The two men went back into the hotel, where they had a quick snack before setting off on the long drive back to rejoin Denard.

They left the Sheraton at 19.25; Harris would have been relieved to know that Sullivan had by then passed through passport control without incident and was waiting in the departure lounge for Saudia flight SV 384 to Bangkok to be called for boarding. The flight was due to leave at 21.10.

Harris need not have worried. The Saudi police had through an administrative oversight failed to notify the immigration authorities that Sullivan was to be detained. It was an error that, when it came to light twelve hours later, was to cost the police lieutenant responsible his job.

It also ensured that Ray Sullivan got clean away.

51

Jonathan Mitchell, speaking from the Learjet to the British Embassy in Riyadh, gave instructions that the possibility of Darcon's direct involvement be communicated to "The Office". He stressed those two words, and the SIS staffer who had interviewed Hughes knew exactly what he meant. This man immediately faxed copies of the documents he had been given to SIS Headquarters in London; they were rapidly passed on to Commander Jones at New Scotland Yard.

Jones read through the faxes – by now faxes of copies of faxes – that Hughes had produced as evidence that he was only acting on instructions. Jones frowned when he saw the signature at the bottom. He knew of Dartington. The man was a prominent industrialist, highly respected; it was scarcely credible that a man such as he was implicated in this. But the evidence before him appeared to be quite clear. He buzzed his administrative assistant, and a few seconds later DS Mike Archer appeared in the doorway.

"Mike, I want you to get hold of DCI Hallam for me. Tell him I want him to leave his boys working on unravelling those bank transactions; I've got another job for him, which I want him to attend to personally."

Archer withdrew, leaving Jones still thinking about the implications of what he was about to set in motion. Yes, he thought; Paul Hallam was the right man for the job. He was used to investigating the rich and powerful, and had an almost infallible nose for a lie or half-truth. He was also extremely discreet. Well, he would certainly have to be on this one. The telephone rang. It was Hallam calling in; he would be there in fifteen minutes.

As Jones outlined what he had learned, Hallam sat silently, listening. His pale eyes, behind the heavy-framed glasses, gave no clue to his thoughts. Jones handed over the papers and concluded his briefing. "Be very careful, Paul. This must not leak out. Not to his staff, not to anyone. I don't want to be accused of starting a rumour about Dartington or his company."

"Absolutely understood, sir. I'll make up something to get past his people." He rose and left, glancing at his watch. It had just turned four o'clock in the afternoon.

Hallam arrived at Darcon's head office thirteen minutes later, and at 4.20 appeared at Dorothy Webster's door. He knocked and went in without waiting for an answer. Mrs Webster was startled and began to protest, but he cut her off by producing his warrant card. "DCI Paul Hallam, Metropolitan Police, madam. I wonder if I could see Sir Peter Dartington immediately, please?"

Mrs Webster was too taken aback to think straight. How on earth had this policeman managed to get up here unannounced? Without thinking, she went straight into her standard routine. "I'm afraid that will not be possible without an appointment, officer. May I ask what this is about?"

Hallam made a quick assessment of the middle-aged lady in front of him. She was on the defensive, but that was only natural. He had given her quite a surprise. "May I ask how long you have worked here, madam?"

Dorothy Webster blinked at the unexpected question, then drew herself up to her full height. "I have been Sir Peter's personal assistant," she said proudly, "for twenty-five years."

Good, thought Hallam. He had been right. There was one word that summed up this woman's approach to her job – loyalty. She would be discreet and fiercely protective. Anything he said to her would go no further. All he had to do now was feed her a story that she wouldn't dare repeat to anyone – especially not her boss.

"Forgive me, madam, but this is a very, ah, *personal* matter, involving a certain young lady. I am afraid that it is essential that I talk to Sir Peter at once." Hallam had deliberately adopted an uncharacteristic air of embarrassment. His normally steady gaze dropped, and when he raised his eyes again, he saw the expression of utter shock on Dorothy Webster's face. Her cheeks had turned crimson, and her mouth was pursed in a soundless "O". Hallam gave her an apologetic look, and made towards the door leading to Dartington's private office. "Do you mind if I go in now?"

Dorothy Webster recovered her composure. "There would be no point, officer. Sir Peter is away from the office today."

It was Hallam's turn to be caught unawares. He pressed on. "Could you please tell me where I will be able to reach him today?"

Dorothy Webster was not giving up without a fight. How dare this man come in here, she thought, and suggest these unspeakable things about her employer? "I am afraid that will not be possible, officer. Sir Peter left express instructions that I was not to reveal his whereabouts in any circumstances."

"I am afraid I must insist, madam." Hallam's pale gaze bore into Mrs Webster for a moment, then he lowered his voice and took on a confidential tone. "Off the record, you understand, we think that the allegation that has been made is a malicious one. We would like to be able to clear the matter up as quickly as possible. That way, we may be able to avoid any adverse publicity."

Dorothy Webster cracked. The possibility of a public scandal was unthinkable. Of course Sir Peter would be able to clear it up. There had obviously been some grotesque mistake. She sat down at her desk, and began to write out an address. She handed the piece of paper to Hallam without a word.

Oh damn, thought Hallam as he read the address. *The bloody Bahamas.*

52

"So, gentlemen, let us deal first of all with the known facts." Brent Scowcroft, National Security Advisor to President Bush, looked around the table and began to summarise. "In early December last year, a man with a South African accent purchases a light aircraft, a Britten-Norman Islander, in Ireland. He has it delivered by its owners to Southampton, England, where it sits on the ground for four months. Someone fitting the description of the South African is seen coming and going, working on the plane; five or possibly six other nondescript men are also seen there from time to time. Meanwhile, an Englishman, possibly disguised, has been setting up dummy corporations and renting industrial workshops in southern England, using funds from a Liechtenstein bank laundered through various British bank accounts. This Englishman is the only person any witness can remember seeing at the industrial premises. A sea container is delivered to the premises and modified; it is fitted with a new doorway, power-supply sockets and air-conditioning units, all concealed. This container is shipped out to Mombasa, Kenya, with a declared cargo of frozen vegetables. While this is happening, a Texan pilot, name of Sullivan, sells up his air charter business and flies to England, arriving there on 28th March. He flies out of England in the Islander aircraft on 7th April. On 8th April, the Englishman and the South African show up in Saudi Arabia at the offices of a British construction corporation, Darcon International, with authority to take over one of their old construction camps, at Badanah, in the north of the country. The authority is signed by the Chairman of that corporation, a Sir Peter Dartington. In accordance with Dartington's instructions, four long-wheel-base vehicles have been positioned at Badanah for these men's use. The Islander aircraft arrives in Jeddah, Saudi Arabia, on 11th April. The pilot flies it on to Al Wajh, where he stays for two days, then on 13th April he flies to Ar'ar. He stays at Ar'ar until 23rd April, at which stage he obtains permission to base the plane a few miles down the road at the construction camp. Eight men are seen at the construction camp; none of the descriptions is good. They work on the vehicles, painting two of them to look like military ambulances and stripping another for spares. Yesterday evening, 25th April, the three working vehicles, along with the aircraft and the eight men, all vanish; the aircraft has filed a flight plan for Tabuk and is observed setting off on the correct heading, but it never shows up at its destination. This morning, 26th April – which is to say late last night by our time – the container arrives in Mombasa and is found to be empty. None of the ship's crew has noticed anything untoward during the voyage.

"Those," declared Scowcroft, "are the known facts. They have all been verified by on-the-spot investigations carried out by CIA, FBI and British police and intelligence personnel. Now let us move on to supposition." He glanced at the faces round the table. "I have to say that what I have heard from the National Reconnaissance Office makes it ninety-nine-per-cent certain, as far as I am concerned, that their suppositions are correct. They run as follows.

"Two or more men are concealed inside the sea container for its voyage from England. On the night of 12th/13th April, during the ship's passage south through the Red Sea, they empty the container and depart from the vessel in a rubber dinghy with an outboard motor, possibly with contraband items on board, making for the Saudi Arabian coast. They land there in the early hours of the 13th, are collected by an accomplice driving a pick-up vehicle, and are driven to Al Wajh. They board the Islander and fly to Ar'ar, then travel from there up the road to Badanah. Last night, 25th April, the two ambulances drive north, cross-country, to the Iraqi border, where they cause a diversion and fire at an Iraqi border post. They enter Iraq and travel north-east on the Kirkuk road. Before dawn this morning, Iraqi time, they lay up in a large building east of Hadithah, where they still are. The third vehicle and the aircraft have meanwhile departed for destinations unknown; they have not yet been located.

"Now," said Scowcroft, "I said that this was supposition. I must still place it in that category as I am not sufficiently conversant with the technological capabilities of the NRO to know whether all this detailed information can reliably be determined from satellite photography and radar imaging alone. It would seem to me," he added sourly, "that if the NRO has the capability to shadow such a small and apparently insignificant group of people over distances of thousands of miles, and record their activities with such precision, then among other things we ought to be looking to this technology to solve some of our domestic law-enforcement problems.

"But that is beside the point. Before we go on to theorise about what these people might be up to, I am sure you would all like to hear from the Director of the NRO. I have asked him to bring with him to this meeting the senior supervisor of the NRO section initially responsible for bringing this affair to light. Mr Director, I would be grateful if Mr Sorensen would explain to us how this was done."

All heads turned to stare at the big man with the large drooping moustache. The Walrus looked uncomfortable and cleared his throat, about to speak. Then he seemed to have an afterthought, and leaned across sideways to whisper something to the man sitting next to him.

Martin Faga, Director of the NRO, smiled at Sorensen's whispered question and replied, loud enough for everyone in the room to hear. "Yes, Walter, you may take it that all these gentlemen have the necessary security clearances." A few uneasy looks were directed at the Walrus, and a frog-faced man with a sallow complexion and a grey suit scowled at him from the far end of the table. The Walrus recognised him as Douglas Longmire, Assistant Treasury Secretary.

Ten minutes later, the Walrus finished the detailed explanation and began to summarise. "So you see, gentlemen, the initial sighting was made purely by chance. I have to say that the tracking work, however, was of the highest quality and was largely the work of just one of my analysts. I think I can safely say that nothing involving such fine detail has been attempted before. In the normal course of events, a seemingly insignificant incident such as this would probably have been ignored, but it occurred in a relatively slack period and the Director considered that it merited further investigation." He tweaked his moustache and turned to the National Security Advisor. "Perhaps if you have any questions, sir . . . ?"

Brent Scowcroft shook his head and looked round the table. "Any of you gentlemen have a question for Mr Sorensen or the DNRO?"

The man on Scowcroft's left spoke up. "If I may, Mr Chairman . . . ?"

"Go ahead, John."

Under-Secretary of State John Kelly leaned forward in his chair, made a steeple of his hands and looked directly at Sorensen. "In view of what this may be leading to – and I believe we will be moving on to a discussion of that shortly – there could be serious implications here for US foreign policy. In that regard, we at State consider it essential that we get a handle on these people and put a stop to their activities. I believe that the President" – he glanced at Scowcroft, who nodded – "is at one with us in this. It would unfortunately appear that the men now inside Iraq are temporarily beyond our reach; while they are there, we simply can't get at them. So there remain just two avenues of investigation open to us. The first is obvious, but may lead to nothing: to interview Sir Peter Dartington and find out what he knows. It is possible, if he is involved in this, that he may have some way of recalling these men. The second you say is difficult: the locating of the airplane. Again, the pilot may be in contact with the men and might be persuaded to call them off. My question is this: what chance do you consider you have of finding the plane?"

The Walrus tweaked his moustache more vigorously than usual before answering. "Very little, I'm afraid, sir, unless it takes to the air again, in which case it will be spotted almost immediately by AWACS. The problem is, while it is on the ground we don't know where to look. So far, we have tracked these people by knowing roughly where to look each time. Even that has been difficult enough. Our best chance would be to use the E-8A JSTARS radar-mapping capability. But we dare not reallocate the JSTARS aircraft from the watch on the building. Of course, if we had more JSTARS at our disposal . . ." He left the statement hanging in the air, shaking his head mournfully.

"That is a good point, gentlemen." The comment came from a powerfully-built man with short, iron-grey hair, wearing the uniform of a US Air Force general. He cast an approving look in Sorensen's direction. "We have been pressing hard for additional JSTARS procurement. It has demonstrated its value beyond question, both during the 1991 Gulf War and again now."

"Thank you, General Burnside," said Scowcroft smoothly to the Vice-Chairman of the Joint Chiefs of Staff. "Your point is noted. Unfortunately, for the time being we must make do with what we have."

"If I may, sir?" the Walrus interjected. "When I said we would

306

have the plane located if it moved again . . . well, it's possible that by then it will be too late to do much about it. If this plane has gone into hiding, it may be that it's waiting until the men in the vehicles have completed their task and are heading for home. The plane may be their means of escape, and I would guess that it will sit tight until it's called for."

Across the table from him Robert Gates, Director of Central Intelligence, raised a forefinger and spoke. "The CIA would agree with that assessment."

"I think," said Scowcroft, nodding to the DCI, "that this brings us on to the possible reasons for the activities of these men. Unless," he added, "there are any more questions on technicalities?"

There weren't, and the Walrus got up to leave.

"No, please stay, Mr Sorensen," said Scowcroft, "we may have further queries for you."

The Walrus sat down again.

"Now," continued Scowcroft, "we have rather been skirting round the issue here, but I felt that it was important to be quite sure that there was no possibility of a mistake in our deductions. Independently, the NRO, the CIA and the State Department have all arrived at the same conclusion. By now, others among you may have done the same. There does not appear to be any other reasonable explanation for the presence of such a well-organised and resourceful team of men inside Iraq. In brief, we believe they are engaged in an attempt to assassinate Saddam Hussein."

There was a gasp from the frog-faced Longmire at the far end of the table, and a muttered "About goddam time someone did" from General Burnside. Under-Secretary of State Kelly looked daggers at Burnside. The General was smiling broadly at the Walrus, who concealed a grin behind his moustache.

"That is beside the point, General," said Scowcroft firmly. "The question is, how do we handle this? The President would like to hear our recommendations."

Charles Burnside was not to be put off. If he had been a Navy man, he would undoubtedly have been given the nickname "Broadside", but being an Air Force general he had instead become known affectionately as "Blockbuster". In the absence from the meeting of the quietly-spoken Defense Secretary, Dick Cheney, who would otherwise have spoken for the Defense Department, Burnside

307

weighed in forcefully. "I say we let 'em get on with it. We should've been allowed to finish the job last year, when we had the chance. It's about time someone settled that sonofabitch's hash. Good luck to these guys."

"If I may, Mr Chairman." Under-Secretary of State John Kelly cut in, his voice icy. "There are issues of foreign policy here that General Burnside perhaps fails to appreciate . . ."

"Policy, schmolicy," said Burnside. "Look where your goddam foreign policy has gotten us. No-place, is where. We get told to spend sixty billion dollars setting ourselves up to get rid of this bastard Saddam; then you weak-kneed sonsabitches at State pull the plug on the job at the last minute, and now that skinny faggot down the end there from Treasury starts chipping away at the defence budget."

"Mr Chairman!" Douglas Longmire was up on his feet, his high-pitched voice squeaking in protest. "General Burnside really must not be permitted to talk in this disrespectful –"

"Asshole," growled Burnside, grinning.

"Gentlemen! Gentlemen!" Scowcroft had also risen to his feet, holding up his hands in a placatory gesture. "Please!" The Assistant Treasury Secretary subsided back into his seat, an expression of outrage on his froggy face. Burnside winked at Sorensen, whose mouth was hanging open in disbelief at the exchange. Scowcroft waited until the undercurrent of murmurs around the table had ceased, then he addressed Kelly. "John, I think it would be a help if you explained the situation as the State Department sees it. I have to say" – Scowcroft shot a warning glance at Burnside – "that the President is entirely in agreement with the State Department's assessment. John?"

Kelly began to speak, controlling with an effort his irritation at Burnside's irreverent intervention. "The issue at stake, put simply, is the future of the Iraqi state. Iraq consists essentially of three separate states within a state. Without strong leadership at the top, there is little doubt that it would fragment – probably very fast. In the north, the Kurds would seek to establish an independent Kurdistan. In the south, the Shi'ite Muslims would also secede, possibly in an attempt to create a state based on the old Ottoman Empire province of Basra. That would leave the minority Sunni Muslims of central Iraq holding what remained. The point is that none of these three states could possibly survive as a separate entity. The vested interests of neighbouring powers would simply be too strong. I speak here principally of Turkey, Syria and perhaps above all Iran. All three would be sucked into the vacuum created by the collapse of the state of Iraq.

"Let us take these three countries in turn," continued Kelly. "Turkey has its own serious internal problems, with ten million ethnic Kurds living within its borders. The Government would be unlikely to countenance a new and almost certainly hostile and troublesome neighbouring state of Kurdistan, from where political and possibly military attacks might be mounted against Turkey.

"Syria's action would partially depend on that of Iran; the Syrians hate the regime of Saddam Hussein, and have long wished to absorb Iraq into a greater Syria. President Assad's regime is in many respects just as unpleasant as Saddam Hussein's. With one exception – Lebanon – he has stopped short of the sort of foreign intervention we have seen undertaken by Iraq, but there is no doubt that Syria would seize on the collapse of the Iraqi state as an excuse to intervene. The ruling parties of both Syria and Iraq describe themselves as Ba'athist; both are modelled on Nazism, but that doesn't stop them hating each other. One thing is certain: Assad would certainly not tolerate any Iranian intervention. Unfortunately, such intervention by Iran would, in our view, be inevitable."

Kelly paused for emphasis, then went on. "For years now, Iraq and Iran have balanced each other off in the power struggle in the Mid-East. You will recall how convenient – for want of a better word – the war between these two countries was. Quite simply, the fragmentation of Iraq would leave Iran the dominant economic and military power in the Gulf, and there would be nothing anyone could do to stop it. Iranian intervention would initially take a similar form to that of Turkey. Iran has problems of its own with the Kurds; it too has a large population of them living within its borders. Approximately five million of them, in fact. For reasons similar to Turkey's, Iran would strongly resist the creation of any independent Kurdish state. The second likely step for Iran, while the attention of the world was being distracted by the Kurdish question, would be the raising of arguments concerning the sovereignty of various seemingly unimportant islands in the Gulf; and the third step, while all this was going on, would be the all too familiar one of vigorously exporting

309

Islamic fundamentalism into the remaining central and southern regions of Iraq, and beyond.

"Some of you gentlemen may be thinking that I am painting an over-gloomy picture here, and that Iran is no longer as extreme in outlook as it was just a year or two ago. Iran would indeed *appear*, following the death of Ayatollah Khomeini and the accession of President Rafsanjani, to have shown signs of adopting a rather more reasonable stance in its dealings with the West. I stress the word 'appear'. I can assure you, gentlemen, that this appearance is only skin-deep. Furthermore, Rafsanjani's hold on power is at best tenuous. The hardliners still wield huge influence.

"Can any one of you here," asked Kelly, looking round the table and reserving an especially hard stare for General Burnside, "honestly say that you would be happy to see Iran become the unchallenged and dominant power in the Mid-East in general, and the Gulf in particular, with all that that would mean?"

There was silence in the room. Kelly ran his gaze slowly round the faces at the table; all eyes were upon him. "So. We must therefore accept that the continued existence of the Iraqi state is essential to a balance of power and thus stability – albeit an uneasy stability – in the region. Unfortunately, there is only one man who can guarantee, for the time being, to hold it together. Much as we may all dislike the man and despise the cruel treatment he metes out, even to his own people, Saddam Hussein is the undisputed strong man of the country. He has, after all, disposed of all his potential rivals. There is no one else. I can assure you, gentlemen," said Kelly forcefully, "that this is the case. I know the man, and have had personal dealings with him over a period of many years. If Saddam went, Iraq would almost certainly collapse.

"It therefore follows," he continued, "that this attempt on his life – if that's what it is – is fundamentally against the national interests of the United States and the West. What is at stake here is the peace of the region, and possibly of the whole world. That is why these men are so dangerous. That is why, if it can possibly be managed, they must be stopped. There is therefore only one question of any importance that we should be addressing. How can this be achieved?"

"We could warn Saddam." All heads swivelled round towards the new speaker. It was Douglas Longmire. He shrugged at the expressions of scorn on some of the faces. "Why not? All we have to do is tip the wink to that guy, ah, Alan something, the Iraqi Ambassador to the UN. He passes the warning on to Saddam. Simple."

"Mr Chairman?" Robert Gates, Director of the CIA, spoke up. "Unfortunately, it is *not* that simple. For one thing, it is unlikely that any credence would be given by Mr al-Anbari to such a warning, even if, as one would attempt to arrange, it was passed on by a neutral party. Unfortunately, there are no neutral parties on whom we could rely both to convince the Iraqis of the genuine nature of the warning and at the same time not to disclose its source.

"This leads on to another factor, which we should not lose sight of." The DCI paused briefly, tapping his forefinger on the table for emphasis. "The act of providing any form of support – which is what, after all, such a warning would constitute – to a stated enemy of the United States – which Saddam still is – would be regarded as an act of treason. If you think we had enough trouble with the Iran-Contra affair and its ramifications, just imagine the stink that would be caused, both domestically and internationally, if it got out that we had actually intervened to save Saddam's life."

Scowcroft, at the head of the table, cleared his throat and avoided Longmire's frog-eyed glare. "I think we must rule out any idea of a warning," he muttered hurriedly. "Does anyone else have a better solution?"

"All we can do, Mr Chairman, is to hope that the attempt will fail." The speaker this time was the Director of the Federal Bureau of Investigation. "These men have been lucky, so far. I am surprised, in view of the calibre of the personnel they have selected, that they have got as far as they have. We investigated the pilot. He is a nobody, a bum. The leader of this team, whoever he is, appears to have exercised poor judgement in his selection of colleagues. Furthermore, the prime mover behind the plot would appear to be a British industrialist – hardly a man well versed in the arts of military adventurism. One can reasonably hope, I think, that he and the men he has selected will have made other mistakes. Further enquiries should reveal more, possibly enough to put a stop to this. It could, after all, be nothing more than an amateur operation that just happens so far to have enjoyed an undue degree of success."

The anodyne words of the Director of the FBI failed to convince the Walrus. Glancing sideways at his boss, he could see that Faga, too, remained sceptical. Both had developed a feel for this team. The fact that their existence had even been discovered was a pure fluke. They had not made any mistakes so far, at least not avoidable ones.

"There is one way they could be stopped. One way that would guarantee it." All heads turned again towards the source of the gruff voice. It was General Burnside. He sat, his brow furrowed, deep in thought. He added, almost to himself, "Yes, it could be done."

"Please explain what you have in mind, General Burnside," said Scowcroft quietly.

"Right now," enunciated Burnside, "the USS *Missouri* is on station in the northern Gulf. If the NRO can give me the exact co-ordinates of the building where these guys are holed up, they can be flashed immediately to the *Missouri*. The necessary weapons-programming could be completed within about fifteen minutes. From then on, it would depend on the exact distance to the target; at a rough estimate from the map, it looks about five hundred miles. Time of flight would therefore be an hour, or thereabouts. I would say that within approximately seventy-five minutes from now . . ." – he looked at his watch –" . . . say at about 19.45 Iraqi time, I could guarantee that a couple of BGM-109C Tomahawk sea-launched cruise missiles could fly in through the window of that building and blow it and everyone inside to pieces."

For a full half-minute, there was dead silence in the room. The President's National Security Advisor looked at the faces round the table. He saw no dissent. Slowly, he lifted the receiver of the red telephone in front of him. He spoke briefly, then handed the receiver to Burnside. The Walrus watched, fascinated, as Burnside listened to the voice on the other end of the line.

"Yes, Mr President," said General Burnside finally. "I will give the launch order at once."

53

"Peter, there's someone from the Consulate to see you."

"Eh?" Sir Peter Dartington's eyebrows rose fractionally, and he pushed his dark glasses up on to his forehead. "What does he want?" He set down his glass of planter's punch on the table beside him and raised the back of the sun-lounger. He sat up and looked at his wife.

"He didn't say, dear. He's waiting in the study."

Dartington slipped his feet into a pair of flip-flops and pulled on his shirt, grumbling. "Dammit, how did anyone find out that I was here?"

"I expect your office informed them, dear. Do you want to ask him if he would like to stay to lunch?"

"No." Frowning at the interruption, Dartington disappeared inside the villa, still grumbling. He found his visitor in the study.

"Sir Peter Dartington?" The man rose to his feet as Dartington entered. He was wearing a pale-grey lightweight suit; he had a high forehead and wore a scholarly expression.

Dartington regarded him coolly. "Yes. What can I do for you?"

"My name's Smith – Detective Sergeant Smith. I am on attachment to the British Consulate in Nassau." Smith produced a warrant card; Dartington waved it away with a gesture of irritation. Smith continued. "I have been asked by my colleagues in London to investigate a security matter, and we believe you may be able to help us."

"What security matter? Couldn't this wait until I get back to London?" Dartington was wary.

"I'm afraid not, sir." The man opened his briefcase and produced a slim folder of papers. He selected a sheet from the top of the pile and handed it to Dartington. "I wonder if you could verify that this is your signature, please, sir?"

Dartington frowned again. "Just a minute, I'll need my glasses. Where the hell . . . oh, there they are." He retrieved his reading glasses from the study desk and put them on. Smith watched his face closely as he peered at the paper. "Yes, this is my signa . . ." Suddenly, Dartington's expression changed. "Just a minute, what the hell is this? This is a confidential doc . . ." The frown on his face deepened as he read through the copy of the fax Bourne had sent to Hughes. Suddenly, he raised his voice in a series of staccato sentences. "I never sent this! What the hell is all this about? This is a forgery! Where the hell did it come from?"

Smith continued to study the angry bafflement on Dartington's face, until eventually the protests petered out. Was there something else there in the businessman's expression? He remained silent, watching Dartington carefully.

Half-way through reading the copy of the fax, Dartington had suddenly realised all too well what it signified. He was thoroughly alarmed; his instinctive reaction, that of indignation, had provided a good camouflage for his fear. It had given him a few seconds to marshal his thoughts. He sat down and shot a glance at his visitor. "I think you had better explain what all this means, Detective Sergeant Smith."

Smith was not in fact a Detective Sergeant at all. He was an officer with the British SIS; he had been carefully briefed on the case and had spoken directly to DCI Paul Hallam about the approach he should take. He was an intelligent and observant man, but he was not a trained interviewer of people such as Dartington. Hallam, had he been there, might just have spotted the fleeting moment when Dartington had realised the trouble he was in; Smith had missed it. Nevertheless, he could see something in Dartington's face that fitted ill with the demeanour of a man who was supposed to be backed into a corner. It was an expression of confidence. Dartington, thought Smith, had something up his sleeve.

Smith was right. All of a sudden it had dawned on Dartington how clever Howard had been. He guessed what was coming next.

"Sir Peter, perhaps you would care to look at the top of the paper. You will see a series of numbers and letters."

"Yes, yes," said Dartington.

"They give the identification code and telephone number from which the fax was transmitted. Would you please compare them with the number and code at the top of this second fax?" Smith extracted another document from his folder and handed it over.

Dartington examined it. It was an earlier fax, this time one he had sent himself, also to Hughes. "Look here, where did you get these papers? I demand an explanation!"

"Please compare the numbers and codes, Sir Peter, if you would be so kind."

"They are the same. The date and time are different, but all the rest is the same."

"It is indeed. In fact, both messages were sent by the same machine. Each model has an individual system of recording and transmitting its codes. These faxes were sent by a Canon Fax-220. Do you deny having sent these messages?"

"Of course I do. What I mean is, no, I don't. I sent the earlier one – I remember it. But this other one – the later one – is a forgery."

"I repeat, Sir Peter, that these two faxes were sent by the same machine."

Dartington frowned. Time to look really puzzled, he thought. He made a show of comparing the two documents. For a minute, he sat, apparently racking his brains. Then he exclaimed, "Just a minute!" and sprang up, going over to the desk. He took out his diary and riffled through the pages as he returned to his chair. He looked at the dates on the faxes again, then up at Smith. "That explains it," he said, sitting back with a smile and regarding Smith with interest.

It was Smith's turned to look perplexed. This wasn't going at all as he had expected. "Please enlighten me, Sir Peter."

"On the night of 19th November last year, my house in Kent was burgled. Youngsters. Among the items stolen were some papers and my personal fax machine – this machine. The date of this forged fax message is 2nd December. The machine clearly fell into the wrong hands. The transmitting telephone number shown on here doesn't mean a thing – you have to enter it in manually. All this means is that the thief didn't change the settings. I think you have your answer." He emitted a small sigh of feigned exasperation. "Now," he continued, imparting a hard tone to his voice, "you will kindly tell me at once what all this is about. What has been happening, and what are you people doing about it?"

Smith was taken aback. He jotted down the date of the burglary on a piece of paper, and made a mental note to give London hell for not

315

having checked their facts. Then he looked up. "It would appear, Sir Peter, that we owe you an apology, as well as an explanation. Perhaps you will understand the gravity of the situation when I inform you that the people responsible for sending this message appear to belong to an organisation that has made use of the facilities requested in this message to enter Saudi Arabia and conduct what looks like, ah, shall we say, a terrorist operation."

Dartington sat bolt upright; his surprise was genuine. In his embarrassment, Smith had made a mistake which Hallam would have avoided: he had not told the whole truth. Had he told Dartington the full extent to which the operation had already been compromised, Dartington might have shown some alarm. If he had gone further and made out that the identities of the team members were known . . . but he did not, and Dartington was able to maintain his composure. "I see," he said slowly, his face a mask of concern. "Good Lord. That certainly explains things. Look, I'm sorry if I was short with you. I had no idea. I hope you catch these people. Is there anything I can do to help . . . ?"

"Thank you, Sir Peter. It is kind of you to be so understanding. But we cannot be too careful, as you will appreciate." Smith got to his feet. "My apologies again for bothering you with this unpleasantness."

"Not at all, Detective Sergeant." Dartington walked Smith to the door and bade him good day. He stood in the porch of the villa as Smith climbed into his car. *In a pig's eye he's a Detective Sergeant,* thought Dartington. *He's got security written all over him.*

Julian Smith drove slowly away from the villa, irritated with the way the interview had gone. He hadn't believed a word Dartington had said. Oh, he had been glib and convincing all right. But it was too bloody neat, that story about the stolen fax machine. He had no doubt that it would check out all right, but it was too neat. Never mind, he thought. He had had time to wire the villa, and the telephone line was already being monitored. The two bugs and the tapped phone line would turn up something.

*   *   *

The prow of the great warship sliced through the calm waters of the northern Gulf, leaving a boiling phosphorescent glow stretching out far behind her in the dark as her four-shaft geared turbines, generating two hundred and twelve thousand horsepower, drove her northwards at thirty knots.

On her bridge, nearly a hundred feet above the sea, her captain felt a surge of hope following the order that had been received ten minutes before. Perhaps this meant a temporary reprieve. There were only three weeks to go until his ship, one of the four greatest fighting ships ever to have been built and the last to remain in service, was due to sail home to be mothballed. The *New Jersey* had been the first to go; the *Iowa*, oldest of the four, had been next; and the *Wisconsin* had followed shortly afterwards. Only three weeks left, and then it would be the turn of the USS *Missouri*. Was this really to be her final voyage?

Perhaps not. It was unthinkable. The *Missouri* was nothing less than floating, living history. And a great and proud history it had been, for her and her three sister-ships. With the exception of the ill-fated Japanese *Yamato*-class battleships, they were the fastest and most heavily armoured warships ever built; nothing could withstand their tremendous power. The Captain reflected once again on their illustrious past. Commissioned in 1943/44, nearly half a century before, the foursome had fought with distinction in the Pacific against the Japanese; when Japan surrendered at the end of World War II, the actual surrender ceremony took place on the USS *Missouri*'s deck. In the late 1940s, three of the four great ships were placed on reserve; the day of the battleship was considered to be at an end. Only the *Missouri* was kept operational, largely because of the history attached to her. In 1950, her three sister-ships were reactivated for use in shore bombardment during the Korean War; the *Missouri* also served as Fleet Flagship to the Commander of Seventh Fleet. At the end of the Korean War in 1953, they were once again mothballed – all four of them, this time. That, the pundits all said, was definitely the end of them.

The pundits had been wrong. The Captain could remember with untarnished clarity the first time he had ever seen the ship he now commanded. He had had a strange feeling, even then, that his destiny was somehow to be linked with hers. He was a newly-promoted lieutenant (junior grade) aboard a destroyer when, in late 1967, he heard that the *Missouri* was to be brought out of mothballs for use in the Vietnam War. The news filled the young naval officer with a strange excitement, and six months later he heard that his ship was

317

to be attached to her battle group. The night before the rendezvous, he couldn't sleep; the next morning at dawn, he looked out over the sea – and there she was. The sight took his breath away. Awesome, majestic . . . he did not have adequate words to describe her. He saw the large identifying figure "63" on her bow, saw the three triple turrets of sixteen-inch guns, the secondary armament of ten double turrets of five-inch guns, drank in every detail of her.

The acquaintance then proved to be a brief one, and it was with sorrow that he learned, only two years later, that once again the *Missouri* was to be decommissioned. His promotion to full lieutenant, with two stripes on his arm, followed a year later, in 1970; five years after that, he became a lieutenant commander.

In 1981, a year after his promotion to commander and a posting to a staff job in the Navy Department, a rumour swept through the department that the new Secretary for Defense, Caspar Weinberger, was considering once again reactivating all four *Iowa*-class BBs. The news caused a sensation of excitement, and gradually details of the refit filtered down. The *New Jersey* was to be the first, followed by the *Iowa*, the *Missouri* and the *Wisconsin*. The sixteen-inch guns were to stay. Although they were no longer in production and technically obsolete, there were still thirty-four spare barrels and over twenty thousand shells and charges left in storage. The new weaponry could be fitted into a relatively small area, at the expense of eight of the twenty five-inch guns, whose role as an anti-aircraft system had been superseded. The whole refit, including renovated accommodation and utilities, modernisation of all electronic and communications systems, engine conversion, and reshaping of the afterdeck for helicopter accommodation, cost the Navy less than one new frigate. As a full captain and in line for a second sea-command appointment, he attended the *Missouri*'s commissioning ceremony in July 1987, when she left to join the Pacific Fleet; again, he felt strongly then that his destiny, somewhere along the line, lay with hers.

He had been right. The Captain recalled now with pride the day when, eighteen months ago, all those years after he had first seen the *Missouri*, he had been given command of her. It had been the finest moment of his life. He had commanded her during the Gulf War in 1991, when she and the *Wisconsin* had played major roles. Soon, it was all to come to an end. Or did this action signal yet another lease of life for the old lady?

He shook himself back to the present and spoke into the squawk-box. "Gun boss? Report progress."

Commander James Boyd, the *Missouri*'s weapons officer, replied. "Two more minutes to ready, sir."

"Report when all set." The Captain turned away and smiled to himself in the dark of the bridge. There had been a barely-suppressed feeling of excitement on board since he had ordered "General Quarters" ten minutes before. The Captain ran over it in his mind. Sixteen hundred men, all suddenly sent scrambling into action. Had that been the last time that command would ring out through the *Missouri*?

He thought about the order he had received from the Joint Chiefs. A strange one. Still, better than nothing. He hoped that it was important. Surely it had to be, if they were targeting *four* missiles at it . . . He contemplated the four flat boxes on the top deck, between the *Missouri*'s two funnels. Each box contained four tubes with their deadly cargo: sixteen tubes in all. One tube from each launcher would be fired tonight . . .

Boyd's voice came over. "SLCMs ready, sir."

"Radio? Do we have confirmation of the order to fire?"

"Affirmative, sir," replied the communications officer.

"Commence firing."

The ignition of the tandem rocket-boost motor in the first launch tube hurled the thin cylindrical missile out horizontally over the sea, leaving behind a trail of white vapour from its burnt propellant. The three-thousand-four-hundred-and-fifty-pound missile, twenty-one feet long and twenty inches in diameter, seemed to hang momentarily in the air, standing on its tail, and then began climbing slowly, gathering speed. Half a second after departure from the launch tube, a pair of short, stubby wings in the centre of the missile and four smaller tail-fins at the rear unfolded and locked into place. On the underside of the missile, near the rear, an air inlet swung out, allowing air into the Williams F107 sustainer engine, which started and ran up to speed. The missile appeared to shake itself into life; its tactical INS guidance system began to take over. The booster burned out and fell away. The Tomahawk BGM-109C levelled off at five hundred feet and streaked off towards the north-west horizon on its pre-programmed course.

Boyd's voice came over the squawk-box again. "Missiles fired

319

18.52. Time of flight fifty-five minutes. Simultaneous ETA on target due at 19.47 local time."

The firing of all four cruise missiles had been completed within thirty seconds. The Captain, a mixture of pride and sadness on his face, gazed out over the sea and watched them disappear into the night.

54

"How's that traffic now, Mike?" Ed Howard looked up as Ziegler joined him.

"Worse than New York in the rush hour during a state visit. Never seen so much shit on one goddam road. Must be an entire division movin' along there, all nose to tail. Mile upon mile of it." Ziegler sat down and poured himself a cup of coffee. "Yuk. This is cold." He set it down with disgust. "How are our visitors?"

"Scared. Johnny's still talking to them." Howard jerked a thumb in the direction of the little group huddled in the far corner of the warehouse.

The old man had gone beyond fear. He was now resigned to the certainty of death. He had heard about the hard-faced *Amerikaaniyeen*, and he knew he could expect no mercy. He felt a sadness for his two sons; he had willed them not to arrive, just for once not to come to take over from him. But they had come, his good, dutiful sons, and the old man knew now that they would all be killed. That was the way of these people – he had heard it. His grandsons would be left without fathers, without a grandfather, the women without their men . . . He mourned for them. They were poor, they had nothing. This work, guarding the building, had been a miracle; unlike others, they now had a little money, enough to live. Now it would all end. He felt no anger, just sadness. He could not hate them, these *Amerikaaniyeen*, especially not this one who spoke like a true Arab. Had he not given him and his sons food, and coffee to drink? How long was it since he had drunk real coffee? And had they not treated him well? Had this *Amerikaani* not been polite? Had he not treated him with the respect due to his age? It was impossible to hate him. This man was a warrior, doing what he had to do. Fate was inevitable; he, an old man, and his sons – all three would die.

"*Sha'ib*," said Johnny Bourne. "Old man. Soon we will be leaving here. Maybe in one hour . . ."

"*Sidi*, I am a *sha'ib*. I am unimportant," said the old man. "But my sons here, they . . ." – he indicated the two younger men who sat with their wrists fastened by handcuffs round a steel girder – ". . . they are young. They are good sons. They respect their father. They work hard. They have women and children. I am nothing now; I am an old man. I am not important. Kill me; my days are over. It is God's will. But if you have it in your heart to spare my sons, God will surely smile on you."

"We have no personal quarrel with you, old man." Bourne's voice was flat and cold.

"I know it, *sidi*. You have treated us well. But you are planning to kill us. It is expected. I ask only for the lives of my sons."

Danny MacDonald sat a little way off, watching and listening to the exchange. He thought he understood a few words – not many, but it didn't matter anyway. He could tell what the old man was saying. In the wake of his initial stark terror, he seemed to have become resigned to his fate, to have accepted it. When they had first taken him prisoner, in his dirty rags, thin and bony, with the straggly beard, white before his time, he had been a pitiful sight. And yet now . . . Danny saw that he had somehow acquired a great serenity, even in the face of death. With a feeling of revulsion, Danny knew that death was what awaited this old man and his sons when the team left. They would not be allowed to live, perhaps to spread a warning . . . Danny could see the hard look on Johnny Bourne's face. An implacable, frightening look. He could watch no more. He got up and went over to join Howard and Ziegler. "Ed? Can I ask you something?"

"Go ahead."

"Is it really necessary to kill these three guards, the old man and his sons?"

Ed Howard regarded Danny curiously. "What do you mean, Danny?" he asked carefully, his dark eyes expressionless.

"Look, Ed, I'm not stupid. I know what Johnny did to that soldier, back on the barge. I could tell. You're going to do the same here, aren't you? No witnesses, that's it, isn't it?"

"Sit down, Danny." Howard's penetrating gaze didn't leave MacDonald's face. He waited until MacDonald had sat down.

"You knew the rules of the game when you signed up. We can't afford the possibility of anyone giving us away. You know that. Johnny knows it, we all know it. Yes, Johnny killed that soldier. I didn't have to tell him to do it. He knew it had to be done. For the record, he didn't enjoy it, even though the soldier was a thoroughly unpleasant type and had tried to skewer Mike with a bayonet. So I don't have to tell Johnny what to do here, with these three. Howard paused. "But I'll tell you something else." He leaned forward, his dark eyes still fixed on MacDonald's, his face unsmiling. "We're *not* going to kill them."

"Wha . . . ? Then why is Johnny giving them such a hard time over there?"

Howard sighed. "We've all had some sleep today, haven't we, Danny?"

"Yes, but what has that got to do with —"

Howard interrupted. "All of us have had a few hours. Two of us on duty, four resting. We've all had some rest. All, that is," he said, pulling on his cigarette, "except Johnny. He came to me soon after the two sons arrived this morning to take over guard duty from the old man. He said he wanted to try something. It was his idea."

"What do you mean?"

"It was Johnny's idea, not mine, to let them live. He said if he had a chance to talk to them, to strike up a relationship of mutual respect, there would be less chance of their hating us and wanting to blow the whistle. A large part of that mutual respect has to be based on their being afraid of us, which is why Johnny has been giving them such a grilling. When he tells them their lives will be spared, they will feel gratitude. It's the same feeling a kidnap victim often has towards his or her kidnapper. The Hearst girl in America was a typical case in point. She felt such overwhelming gratitude towards her kidnapper when he spared her life, and at the same time so resentful of her family and the authorities for doing nothing to rescue her, that she even joined him on his subsequent criminal activities. It's a well-known psychological trick, Danny. All Johnny's been trying to do is to telescope the process into the space of twelve hours, rather than several days or weeks. That's why he hasn't had any sleep."

MacDonald said nothing. What Howard had told him had taken him completely by surprise. He had misjudged Bourne completely. His mind felt slightly numb.

Howard was still talking. ". . . And there's one other factor we're going to throw in, which should guarantee their silence," he said confidently.

"Johnny will tell them that if they talk, we'll come back and kill them?"

"That too, but he won't put it quite like that. It'll be more a matter of trust, of honour. But that wasn't what I had in mind," said Howard. "We're going to give them some money. Quite a lot of it," he added.

"You mean, buy their silence?"

"No. That would be completely counter-productive. It would probably have the opposite effect on a proud individual, however poor. The money will take the form of compensation for the harm we have done him, his sons and his people. No strings attached. He will understand that. It will be accepted. It will also" – Howard grinned – "make it even more unlikely that he or his sons will go to the Iraqi authorities. He'll know that they would grill him about everything he's seen, and probably not be too squeamish about how they do it. If he talked to them, sooner or later they would find the money. And that would be the end of him and *all* his relatives."

"Oh," said MacDonald.

"Satisfied now?" asked Howard. "Good. Right, on to other things. It's nearly seven; I want to be away from here fairly soon, but we have a problem with the road. That big convoy seems to be endless. I'm going to give it till eight. If it hasn't cleared by then, we'll have to take advantage of a gap, forget about the road and go cross-country the rest of the way."

"I don't like that," growled Ziegler.

"Why not?" asked Danny. "Won't we be safer off the main road?"

"More likely to be noticed," replied Howard. "Less easy to bluff our way, like last night. What would a couple of ambulances be doing going down side-tracks? People would think it was odd. No, I want to use the road as far as possible. But I don't want to leave it too late. Anyway," he continued, getting to his feet, "we'll reckon to leave at 20.00, latest. Danny, go and give Tony a call, will you? Mike's going to get some chow and a brew going. We'll eat in about fifteen minutes."

MacDonald nodded and went off to wake Ackford. Ziegler turned to Howard, speaking in a low voice. "Do you think he's goin' flaky on us?"

Howard put another cigarette between his lips, lighting it from the stub of the previous one. "I don't know, Mike. I don't think so. But that business with the soldier last night must have unsettled him. We may need to nurse him along a little. That's why I let him think we're sparing these three guys out of the goodness of Johnny's heart. I didn't tell him the real reason, that if they go missing there will definitely be a hunt on. One soldier disappearing won't have surprised anyone – they'll just assume he's a deserter. But three guards, suddenly going missing from here? Too much of a coincidence. Come on, I want to take another look at this convoy."

*   *   *

The four cruise missiles reached the coastline within ninety seconds of one another. Two were following a course to the east, while the other two were directed slightly to the west. The eastern pair headed straight for the mouth of the Shatt al Arab, the waterway marking the Iran-Iraq border. As they dropped from five hundred down to one hundred feet, their TERCOM terrain-contour-matching program kicked in, scanned the area below and made a slight correction to the inertial navigation system. Initially the missiles attracted no attention, but their presence was detected by Iranian soldiers on duty at Abadan and Khorramshahr as they passed the wrecked remains of the huge oil refineries and storage depots. Unsure exactly what was responsible for the noise that roared past them in the dark, the Iranians were brought to a temporary alert. They had, however, received strict orders not to fire unless directly attacked, so no action was taken. The missiles continued up the Shatt al Arab, flying into Iraqi territory and straight past the eastern edge of the Iraqi town of Basra. Here, Iraqi forces were brought on to the alert and tracer lit up the sky as men from the Republican Guard Hammurabi armoured division fired aimlessly into the sky. By the time the firing started, the missiles, following the waterway faithfully and flying at five hundred and fifty miles per hour, were long gone.

The other two missiles followed the waters of the Khawr abd-Allah, skirting Bubiyan Island to the north and entering the narrows of the *khawr* at the border with Kuwait. Twenty miles further on, they picked out the Shatt al Basra canal, which took them, like their counterparts, past Basra – this time to the west. Passing between the civil airport and the military Basra West airfield, they caused temporary confusion but little action was taken. Again, the only reaction was small-arms and some anti-aircraft fire into the air, long after the missiles had passed. They reached the end of the canal and came out over the open water of the Khawr al Hammar, turning almost due west towards the town of Nasiriyah.

The eastern pair of missiles reached the end of the Shatt al Arab, the confluence of the two great rivers. Taking the right-hand fork, they turned up the Nahr al Dijlah – the Tigris – towards Baghdad.

55

"Tony? Peter here. Would you mind telling me exactly what the bloody hell is going on out there?"

"Peter! Am I glad to hear from you!" Tony Hughes's relief at hearing Dartington's voice was unmistakable. "Where are you?"

"I'm on holiday. I'm calling from the Bahamas. I've just had the police here with a story about some people who have forged some Darcon documents, including my signature, to get the use of some of our facilities in Saudi. What the hell is all this, and who are these people? What have they been doing?"

Hughes outlined what he knew, mentioning the conversations he had had with "security men from the British and American Embassies". Dartington interrupted him with frequent questions. After giving as much information as he could, Hughes concluded, "And that's all I know. Everyone seems to be taking this very seriously, but that doesn't surprise me. I'm sorry about all this, but the paperwork all seemed genuine, and your personal signature on it had me convinced."

Dartington stayed silent for a while. *That Howard is a cheeky bugger*, he thought, not without admiration. He injected a note of concern into his voice. "Listen, Tony, I want you to co-operate in full with the Embassy, and I also want you to report all this to the Saudi police . . ."

"Already done, Peter."

"Good. I'm bloody angry about this," spluttered Dartington. "Not with you," he added hastily. "It isn't your fault. I've been shown a copy of the fax you got, and it looked like the real thing. But I've had my holiday interrupted, and I don't like the idea of these people making monkeys out of us and stealing our gear from under our noses. I want these buggers caught," he said with deliberate emphasis.

"You do everything you possibly can to help, OK? You were right when you said this was serious. Apparently they are terrorists or something."

"I thought it must be something like that. Those guys from the Embassies didn't say, but whatever these people are up to, it isn't going down at all well here."

"No, I don't imagine it is." Dartington's voice was grim. "Anyway, please do whatever you can to help catch them. Phone me here if you learn any more." Dartington gave Hughes his number and rang off.

"Something wrong, dear?" Lady Dartington had drifted in from outside.

"It would seem so. There's been a fraud or something, with some criminals posing as Darcon people out in Saudi. By God," he muttered vehemently, "I'll be damned if I'll have any bugger getting away with that sort of thing, making a fool out of me." He turned on his heel and stomped out of the room.

Lady Dartington could scarcely fail to recognise the signs of her husband's anger. She decided to remain silent. *Oh dear*, she thought. *Now he'll be in a filthy mood for the rest of the week.*

Had she been able to see Dartington's face as he left the room, she would have been somewhat baffled. He was grinning from ear to ear.

*　　*　　*

Several miles away, Julian Smith sighed and switched off the tape recorder. *Damn*, he thought. *I'd rather hoped he would give himself away. Perhaps he's on the level after all. Or maybe he's just rather smarter than he appears.*

*　　*　　*

"Johnny?" Ed Howard called over to Bourne, who still sat with the hunched figures of the three Arabs in the far corner of the warehouse. "Grub's up."

Bourne turned his head and gave Howard a slow nod. "Be with you in five, Ed. I'm just going to explain the situation to them now."

A few seconds later there was suddenly an excited babble of voices from the corner. MacDonald looked up from the pot of thick soup he was ladling out into a line of mess-tins. In the dim light on the far side of the warehouse, Johnny Bourne was unlocking the handcuffs on the two younger men. As soon as they were free, they stood up and shook him vigorously by the hand, voluble in their gratitude. *He's told them*, thought MacDonald. *At last.* The two young men were all smiles, talking nineteen to the dozen. After a minute they came running across, still beaming broadly, and insisted on shaking the hands of the remainder of the team.

MacDonald's gaze went back to the corner. In the guttering candlelight he could see the old man rising stiffly to his feet. He was talking slowly and solemnly to Bourne; the hands of the two men were clasped firmly together in a gesture of understanding. The candle flared in a snap draught, illuminating the figures in a lambent glow. But for the stark surroundings and Bourne's military clothing, thought MacDonald, it could almost have been a biblical scene, something out of one of those old pictures hanging in the lodge at Carvaig. MacDonald's eyes were drawn to the face of the old man. It was a timeless face. The lines had somehow smoothed, and the formerly stooped figure was now ramrod straight. Despite the skinny old man's unkempt appearance, it struck MacDonald that he had never before seen such dignity in a human being.

Howard ate quickly from his mess-tin, then looked at his watch. It was 19.25. "Keep a plateful for Bob, boys. I'm just going to join him and see how that convoy's going. Start packing up, ready to go."

*   *   *

The two cruise missiles on the westerly route had picked up the course of the Euphrates after passing Nasiriyah. Further upstream at Samawah, they left the river and headed out further west into the barren wastes of the rocky desert to the south of Najaf. The TERCOM guidance systems had had some minor problems with the unpredictable radar signatures of trees in the Euphrates valley, but correlation from their on-board GPS position-locating systems had confirmed that they were on track. The TERCOM also experienced trouble over flat, featureless terrain; again, the GPS provided constant and precise updates of position. Leaving Najaf twenty miles to their east, they headed unerringly for the brackish waters of the Buhayrat ar-Razzazah, a large lake some fifty miles south-west of Baghdad.

The six-hundred pound thrust of the Williams F107 turbofan engines slowed momentarily as the missiles dropped altitude to skim one hundred feet above the water; four minutes later, they climbed again as they reached the northern end of the forty-mile-long lake. The two missiles banked to the left to avoid the bombed nuclear complex and military base at Majarrah, then headed north-north-west towards the Muhammadi-Ramadi gap. Screaming low over the Baghdad-Amman highway, they crossed over the Euphrates and settled down on a northerly heading.

The other two missiles had followed the course of the Tigris until Amarah, where they had left the winding river and taken a track out to the east, between the Tigris and the Iranian border. It was a sparsely populated area and there were few to hear them passing in the night; those who did hear something assumed mistakenly that they were Iraqi Air Force planes returning from yet another bombing raid down in the southern marshes. The missiles skirted Baghdad, giving the city a wide berth and passing over the Tigris again at Tarmiyah, south-west of Baqubah. This was the area of most risk: their course took them over a heavily populated agricultural region with a high concentration of military bases and airfields. Again alerts were sounded, but the anti-aircraft fire was as ineffective as it had been earlier. Once they were over the Tigris, the cultivations thinned again. The missiles now headed almost due west, screaming over the ground at low level towards the southern end of the Buhayrat ath-Tharthar. They reached the south-eastern arm of the big lake at the same time as the western pair were crossing the Euphrates.

The four missiles were now seventy miles from their target and converging. The two western missiles slowed; they were ahead of schedule by twelve seconds. It was 19.41. All four were due to impact simultaneously at 19.49, exactly eight minutes away.

*   *   *

The small side-door swung open as Howard reappeared in the warehouse. "The convoy has definitely gone. Nearly ten minutes since the last vehicle passed. Let's go."

Howard and Ackford drove the Land Cruisers out towards the gatehouse, using the NVGs and the IR spotlamps in the dark. Usher, muttering about having had his supper interrupted, helped Bourne and the three Arabs to close the big doors; then they all walked over to the gate, where Usher got into the back of the second car and resumed gulping down the contents of his mess-tin. By the gate, Bourne started talking in a low, urgent voice to the three Arabs; when he had finished, he shook their hands once again. Disengaging himself with trouble from the protracted expressions of gratitude, he climbed in beside Howard, who had moved over to the front passenger seat. The old man's two sons, at Bourne's urging, began hurrying home along a track; the old man would remain on duty for the night, as if nothing had happened.

Howard turned to Bourne. "You sure you're OK to drive, Johnny?"

"I'm fine."

"OK, let's roll."

*　　　*　　　*

All four missiles, now just two minutes from impact, had switched on their DSMAC terminal guidance systems. Each missile's computer, studying the terrain ahead, compared it with digital pictures programmed into its library. The fuses on each warhead armed; the missiles had nearly reached the end of their journey. One by one, they suddenly recognised their target and locked on.

*　　　*　　　*

The old man watched the two vehicles leave, then locked the gate. It was a fine night, he thought. He thanked Allah for his deliverance. These *Amerikaaniyeen* were not at all what he had been led to believe. They were honourable men; they had treated him and his sons with respect. And he was now a rich man; the unimaginable wealth they had pressed upon him, with the properly humble apologies for the inconvenience and worry they had caused, made the future look bright indeed.

He would be careful about the money, as would his sons, spending it slowly and inconspicuously. Vulgar ostentation would be fatal; at the same time, it would not be wise to be caught hoarding such riches. Nor would it be safe for him to conceal it on his person. No, he thought, he would hide it, straight away. He knew the place for

331

it. There was a large rock behind the gatehouse, with a small crevice at its base, hidden by scrub and a flat stone. The rock was inside the security fence, so no one would find the money by accident. Yes, he thought, he would hide it now. He walked over to the rock, pushed the dried scrub aside and knelt down to move the flat stone.

The action saved the old man's life. There was a loud *whoosh* as something passed overhead in the dark; then night suddenly turned into day and the whole world seemed to disintegrate about him. Stunned and deafened by the two-hundred-and-sixty-four-pound explosion, he never even heard the almost simultaneous arrival of the other three missiles. A small piece of falling debris from the building caught him a glancing blow on the side of his head and he fell unconscious.

Five minutes later he was found by his two anxious sons, who had hurried back to see if he was still alive. On regaining consciousness, their astounded father opened his eyes to the devastation of the warehouse, now a smoking ruin, and the gatehouse, flattened by the explosions.

The old man would retell, countless times, the story of how he had survived the terrible air raid, but neither he nor his sons would ever reveal to anyone just why he happened to have been sheltering behind the large rock at the exact moment the bombs fell.

*   *   *

"Jesus! Did you see that?" Bourne stamped hard on the brake, bringing the car to a halt. There was a corresponding screech of tyres from the second Land Cruiser as it pulled up alongside. All six men turned to look at the scene.

A mile behind them, Howard could see through his binoculars that the warehouse had disintegrated. He cocked his head to one side, listening.

"What the hell was it?" Bourne asked, shocked surprise apparent in his voice.

"I heard three or four explosions, very rapid succession," said Ziegler from the other car.

"So did I," said Howard. "But let's get going. I think we'd better put in a bit of mileage between us and this place."

They drove off again. For a while there was silence in the lead

332

ambulance. Bourne was the first to speak. "Must have been an air strike, I guess."

"I think so too," said Howard. "Too big for tanks or artillery, and we didn't hear any secondary report. But I didn't hear an aircraft – did you?"

"I thought I heard something, but I can't be sure. We might have missed it beneath the noise of our engine, especially as the explosions rumbled on for a while afterwards. It had to be bombs. What do you think?"

"I don't know," Howard admitted, his brow knotted anxiously. "But it's bad news, whatever it was. It was no bloody coincidence, that's for sure."

"It must have been," said Bourne. "If they were after us, they wouldn't just have bombed that place. They'd have sent a helicopter force, and they'd have blocked this road into the bargain. Or maybe," he added, "they *have* blocked this road. Don't you think we ought to reconsider, and get off it?"

"No. It doesn't change anything. We'd still be more conspicuous off-road, and if they haven't got helicopters up now, they soon may have. If we go off-road too soon we'll be sitting ducks."

"What about that convoy up ahead?"

"The tail end will be at least five or ten miles on up the road by now," replied Howard. "They'll probably have heard the explosions, but I bet none of them will have stopped to investigate. They'll have orders simply to keep going. They won't be expected to use their initiative and come back to see what happened here. Besides," he added, "they'll probably think it was a routine practice raid or something. That warehouse was in an isolated area, after all. I doubt they'll even question it."

"I hope you're right."

"If I'm wrong, we've had it anyway," said Howard grimly. "But we could still turn this convoy to our advantage. We'll catch it up and tag along behind it until just short of Tharthar airstrip, as planned. If we come to a road block, we'll just go through it as part of the convoy. They're only using their tail-lights; if we do the same, the last vehicle in the convoy need never even know we're there."

Bourne nodded and increased speed. Fifteen minutes later, they caught up with the convoy. Bourne was relieved to see that the long line of lights in front was still moving. He settled down to the slow crawl, maintaining station four hundred yards behind the last vehicle. At this rate it would take another hour, he thought, before they reached the turn-off.

Beside him in the dark, Howard was thinking hard. Something about that air strike, he thought, smelled very wrong. Very wrong indeed.

56

The long convoy's progress had been reported and monitored by the JSTARS; initially, Kearwin had been worried that the two vehicles would slip away from the big building and get lost among the hundreds of other vehicles. Then he had reasoned it out, realising that an entire division of the Iraqi Army was just about the last thing the men in the two vehicles would want to encounter. They would wait until the convoy had passed.

Sorensen came in just after 12.30, straight from the NSC meeting, looking flustered. He was still wearing his best suit. He hurried over to Kearwin's desk. "John, are we sure those cars are still in there?"

"Sure as can be, Walter."

"Right. I want you to keep a real close eye on that building for the next twenty minutes. Real close. And I want a good shot of it from the first Keyhole pass after 13.00. That's 20.00 in Iraq. OK?"

"Sure thing." Kearwin began tapping in instructions, setting up a "bounce" by a KH-11 at 13.05. He glanced up at the Walrus, who was still standing beside him, a preoccupied expression on his face. Kearwin studied him curiously. "How did the meeting go, Walter?"

"Don't ask, John. Don't ask." The Walrus shook his head in distaste. "Goddam cowhides," he ejaculated vehemently, wandering off to his own desk.

Kearwin smiled to himself and turned his eyes back to the screen.

At 12.42, the JSTARS scan showed movement at the building. The Walrus jumped to his feet and came hurrying across to Kearwin's station again. "Are you sure?"

"Yep. See for yourself. Two vehicles. They've stopped by that hut there."

The Walrus was concentrating intently on the screen. "Maybe, just maybe," he breathed.

"No maybe about it, Walter. It's the two vehicles all right."

"That wasn't what I meant. Keep watching, now."

Five minutes later, they saw the vehicles move off. "Son of a bitch!" exclaimed the Walrus with a broad grin, as the trace showed the cars drawing clear of the warehouse. "They've made it. Just in goddam time, they've made it!"

"Walter?" asked Kearwin, now consumed with curiosity. "Would you mind telling me what is going on here?"

"Never mind, John-boy," said the Walrus. "You just stick to following those cars." He consulted his watch. "But right now, take another look at that building."

Twenty seconds later, the on-screen picture of the warehouse dissolved in confusion; it seemed to take a long time to clear. When it did, the building had disappeared.

"It . . . it blew up!" said Kearwin, his voice suddenly shaky. "I don't believe it! It just blew up! Holy shit!"

"Exactly," said the Walrus. "Now, if you'll get back to monitoring the cars' progress, I've got a phone call to make. I'm gonna enjoy this," he added. "One in the eye for the goddam cowhides, that was. Oh, boy!" He stomped off, chuckling.

Kearwin gaped at him, then slowly turned back to his keyboard. Numb with shock, he began tapping in instructions for the vehicles' progress to be followed.

*   *   *

Harris and Palmer chatted easily for the first ninety minutes out of Jeddah, Palmer gradually relaxing in the passenger seat after the tension of the close shave they had had back at the Sheraton. They exhausted the subject of how they could have been found out, and were no nearer a firm conclusion at the end of their discussion than they had been at the start. They agreed to drop it. Harris was eager to know how things had gone at Badanah, and Palmer filled in the details for him. Gradually, tiredness began to overtake the big man; he half stifled a yawn. "Mel, if you don't mind, I'm going to get some shut-eye for a couple of hours, hey? It was a bleddy long, boring drive and I only got two hours last night at stops on the way. You OK to carry on?"

"I'm fine. I've done nothing but sit on my backside for the last couple of weeks; I've had all the rest I need. You go ahead and sleep. Is there anything I should look out for along here?"

"Yes, one or two things." Palmer yawned again. "Watch out for camels. Stupid bleddy things, they are. I nearly hit one near a place called Taima. They wander across the road – they don't seem to have any idea of danger, and what makes it worse is that they're the same colour as the bleddy desert, so they're hard to spot. I saw one car at Qulibah with a dead camel in the driver's seat. He must have hit it some wallop, I'm telling you. The bleddy thing had disintegrated on impact and gone through the windscreen. It was hard to tell which bits were camel and which were the remains of the driver." He wrinkled his upper lip. "And did it stink . . ."

"You'd better climb over into the back seat, just in case," said Harris with a grin.

"Maybe I will, at that," said Palmer. "Oh, and watch out for these bleddy floppies driving their little white Mazda pick-ups. They wander across the road, too."

"I've already seen a few samples of that sort of driving," said Harris. "But what do you mean by 'floppies'?"

"What we used to call the terrorists in Rhodesia, before it became the people's paradise of Zimbabwe," replied Palmer, a sarcastic edge to his voice. "When you shoot them, they sort of go floppy. These guys would probably do much the same," he grunted blearily. "OK, I'm going to get some sleep. There's the BBC World Service on the radio on those three buttons there, and Radio Israel on the right-hand one. You'll have to hunt around from time to time to get the best frequency for the World Service; it comes and goes. Wake me in a couple of hours or so, or if you get tired."

*   *   *

At 21.05, just as Sullivan's flight was taking off for Bangkok and Palmer's snores were beginning to rattle the windows in the third Land Cruiser, Howard spotted the turning off to the right. They had just crossed the Wadi ath-Tharthar, the river leading down to the huge inland lake that the eastern pair of cruise missiles had crossed an hour and a half before. The track looked reasonable, and the GPS confirmed their position. As the two ambulances turned off the

337

main road, the tail-lights of the convoy carried on away from them, disappearing into the darkness.

"That's it," said Howard. "Now for the last leg. It should be fairly open to start with, but the nearer we get to the Tigris the more risk there'll be of being seen."

All loose items had been carefully stowed or lashed down to prevent rattling, and at twenty-five miles an hour the two vehicles, their engines growling quietly at low revs, made little noise. After a while, one of the rear springs in the lead car began to squeak; Bourne stopped and Ackford administered a generous squirt of oil from a can. From then on, they moved almost silently. No one more than a hundred yards away would have been likely to hear them passing, unless he had an ear to the ground. They were greeted by the occasional vocal chorus from dogs as they passed scattered signs of human habitation, but Bourne knew that such dogs needed little encouragement to start barking or howling. When not being roundly cursed, or pelted with stones by angry residents attempting to get some sleep, dogs were ignored and reviled as unclean animals.

By 23.00 Howard calculated that they were no more than ten miles from their destination; he ordered extreme caution, and the vehicles slowed to a crawl. The signs of civilisation were becoming more frequent now and at 23.20, as they breasted a rise, they saw off in the distance the light of a car or truck moving from left to right, heading south towards Baghdad.

"About three miles away, I'd say," whispered Bourne.

"Uhuh. That open rocky area should be just up ahead on the left. About another half-mile." Howard was now using the large-scale satellite-generated map, which showed the ground in detail. Holding a beta-light to it and following each bend in the track, he saw by the dim green glow that they were very near the point he had picked out as a suitable lay-up point. Three minutes later, he said, "Here."

Bourne slowly turned left off the track and picked his way carefully through the rocks and scrub, leading up an incline. The second Land Cruiser followed. After ten minutes, the silhouette of a building appeared on the skyline four hundred yards in front of them. Howard got out of the car and was joined by Ziegler. Without speaking, the two men moved off on foot, moving fast and soundlessly in the dark.

Twenty minutes later, they returned. Howard had made a decision.

"It's perfect, Johnny. No point in going on to the quarry; we can get the cars into that enclosure. It's just a wall surround, no roof on it. Completely deserted, and no sign that anyone's been there recently. Just the occasional bit of sheepshit, that's all. Let's get moving."

*   *   *

"They've definitely stopped, Walter." Kearwin was categoric. "They first stopped just down here . . ." – he indicated the spot on the large-scale map overlay – ". . . and then moved on again. Just a few hundred yards. They haven't moved for thirty minutes now, and the vehicles are behind some sort of a wall. I'm sure this is a planned halt. They'd been moving very slowly for the last hour. It's half-past midnight out there now."

The Walrus tweaked his moustache thoughtfully and nodded his head. "They're about a mile short of that main north-south highway. Maybe they've decided not to go any further tonight. Could be they'll go on to Baghdad tomorrow." He pondered the possibilities, then decided there was little point in speculating. "OK. What's this town here? Just the other side of that highway?"

The name wasn't shown on the overlay on the screen; Kearwin looked it up on the map. "It's called Tikrit. That mean anything to you?"

"Nope. I'd better go call on the Director. Maybe he'll come up with a slant on it. Meanwhile, you keep an eye on them."

*   *   *

"OK," announced Howard in a low voice, "we'll be off. Johnny, make sure you check that route down to the track before first light for wheelmarks, and brush them over. And get some sleep, you hear? You look just about all in."

"I'll sleep in the morning, Ed. See you in about thirty-six hours, OK? And give the bastard one from me."

"Will do." Howard grinned, his teeth palely visible in the dark.

Howard, MacDonald and Ziegler were assisted in lifting their heavy packs on to their backs. MacDonald nearly staggered under the huge weight; a hundred and twenty pounds if it was an ounce, he thought. With a brief wave behind them, the three men set off, their

339

bodies bent forward under the unwieldy burdens, plodding slowly down the incline towards the highway.

Bourne watched them go, then turned to Ackford and Usher. "OK, boys, let's get cracking. We've got a lot to do. Let's start by getting all that shit off the vehicles."

*　　　*　　　*

"Tikrit, you say?" The DNRO looked with interest at the Walrus.

"Yes, sir. Just five miles outside it. They're well off the road, up in some rocks. There's an old wall or something, and they're hidden behind it."

Martin Faga thought for a while, then he spoke slowly. "Walter, I think I know what they're going to do. I think you can relax now. Those vehicles won't be moving again until the day after tomorrow. Get some Keyhole shots for me, would you? I'd like complete coverage of the town, including the place where these vehicles are hidden up. There's another emergency NSC meeting in an hour's time, and they want a full update on the situation."

"Do you want copies of JSTARS imaging as well, sir?"

"No, I don't think so. They're too difficult for the layman to interpret. Keyhole pictures will do. Can you get a full set of prints ready for me in half an hour?"

"No problem, sir." The Walrus stood up to leave. He hesitated for a moment, and then blurted out the question he had been longing to get an answer to. "Sir, I hope you don't mind my asking, but do you think they'll recommend another SLCM strike?"

Faga studied the Walrus's face keenly for a moment. "Walter," he said gently, "you're not by any chance going soft on these people, are you?"

Sorensen was seized with embarrassment. He tweaked his moustache hard and cleared his throat before replying. "I'm sorry, sir, but it just didn't seem *right*, if you see what I mean. And that kid, ah, I mean young Kearwin there, when he saw what happened, he looked at me as if I was some kind of monster or something."

The DNRO's voice hardened. "It wasn't your decision, Walter. And if a similar decision is made again, it won't be for you or your staff to question it or make judgements about it. Remember that!" Faga gave the Walrus a cool stare, as if to make sure that the point had sunk in. Then he spoke more softly again. "But if you must know, I rather doubt that it will happen a second time. If I'm right, and these people have reached their destination, there is one very compelling reason why a further strike at this stage could be counter-productive. I won't say any more; maybe you'll figure it out for yourself when you think about it."

The Walrus mumbled an apology and turned to leave. Outside the door, his face broke into a grin. He didn't know it, but behind him, alone in his office, the DNRO was now also toying with a smile.

*　　*　　*

Elbow grease, assisted by liberal applications of white spirit from a five-gallon jerrican, cut through the oily mess that had covered the vehicles, and the layer of accumulated grime began to peel off. The matt-green top coat of paint, thinned with extra oil, had never hardened properly and proved easier to remove than Ackford and Usher had expected.

When both Land Cruisers were reasonably clean, the two men washed them down with detergent and water; finally they sluiced the suds away with clean water to which Ackford had added a small quantity of paraffin. "Old chauffeur's trick, that paraffin," he said. "Much better than these fancy new wax finishes. Cheaper, too. We'll soon have these babies looking brand-new again. You'll see, when you start polishing with the shammy leather."

Once they had finished, they emptied the vehicles and cleaned out the interiors. All the medical equipment, except for their emergency first-aid box, was stripped out and stacked in a heap in the corner of the walled enclosure. The stretchers had already gone, but the pile of junked oxygen-bottles and other gear would not be needed again. While Usher went off to relieve Bourne on guard, Ackford began to unpack a large box that had occupied the space under one of the stretchers. Inside the box were various spare parts, taken from the fourth car. He and Bourne set to work, replacing broken light-fittings and cracked windows, fitting hub-caps and carefully pushing dented panels back into shape. The red filters on the revolving roof-lights were replaced with blue ones; only the IR filters on the spotlights

341

were left. A pole was attached to a vertical clamp at the rear of each car; then Ackford produced a flat package containing two new sets of number-plates, a new set of stickers and two large flags.

"We'll leave the flags till just before we go, Tony," said Bourne. "They'll stick out a bit here, if anyone flies over. Let's get the stickers on, then put the cam nets up and get some of that thorn scrub over the top as well." He looked at his watch. It was 04.00. "We've done well. I wonder how the others are getting on?"

"Oh, they'll be fine, boss," said Ackford easily, chewing on a stick of gum. "Sod it," he added, spitting out the gum, "but the stink of that white spirit has given me a bugger of a thirst. Fancy a brew?"

"Come off it, Tony. You know we can't risk the light from a cooker. It'll have to wait till after dawn. "

"Nah," said Ackford with a chuckle. "Got a thermos here, haven't I? Ready made up."

"Well, well," said Bourne. Ackford poured out the tea, and they sat and rested for a while. "Poor old Bob," said Bourne, helping himself to another cupful. "First he has his supper interrupted, and now he's dipped out on the tea."

"Wrong place at the wrong time, boss," said Ackford. "Never mind, it won't do him any harm to wait. Wouldn't do to have a bloke drinking on guard duty, would it?"

57

Howard had been worried about crossing the highway, but in the event they negotiated it without incident. Waiting in the shadows beneath the roadside bank, they watched and listened for a long gap in the traffic. After a little while there was a period when no vehicle lights passed and nothing broke the silence; they climbed on to the road together and walked across quickly, disappearing into the cover of some palm trees on the far side.

Through the night-vision goggles the scene ahead was strikingly different to the emptiness of the rocky outcrop where they had left the cars. It was an area of cultivations, of orchards and fields and small, scattered groups of houses. There were clumps of palm trees; MacDonald, following behind Howard, noticed that these were thickest near the buildings. The night felt warmer than the previous one; MacDonald guessed that this was because they were at a lower altitude, having descended into the Tigris valley. The next day would probably be very hot, perhaps hotter even than the temperatures they had become used to at Badanah. No wonder the Iraqis encouraged the palms, he thought – not only for the date crop but also for their cool shade.

They saw only eight people on their hike towards the town. The first was an old man who suddenly appeared from a doorway of a hut and walked off a little way to relieve himself; a little further on they passed a group of six men seated round a dying fire about fifty yards off to the side of their route, talking in low voices. The last figure they encountered was a lone youth who came hurrying along a track towards them. They had plenty of time to move aside into the cover of a thicket. As the lad approached, MacDonald watched him through his night-vision goggles. There was something furtive but at the same time confident in his manner; MacDonald decided that he had probably been paying a clandestine visit to a girlfriend. The boy had some nerve, thought the stalker; he knew from conversations he had had with Bourne that premarital intercourse was a matter that the father of any young Iraqi girl took extremely seriously.

After an hour and a half, they had crossed a main railway line and a second large road and were approaching the edge of the town; Howard began to skirt round it to the south. Gradually, the ground began to rise in front of them. By 03.00 they had reached the top of a shallow incline which stretched obliquely away from Tikrit to the south. From the ridge, they could see the town spread out beneath them, and beyond it, the lights of the Sahra military airbase some ten miles off in the distance. To their right, behind the ridge and down a steep scarp, would lie the Tigris and, on the other side of the river, a second airfield, Tikrit East.

The nearest buildings of the town itself were just over half a mile away. Howard, stopping to check his GPS receiver and the map more frequently now, began to move closer, working his way along the ridge. The ridge itself was deserted of buildings and largely uncultivated. There were occasional rough grassy areas, but mostly it consisted of thin scrub. A large open area came into view. It was just inside the town boundary and surrounded on three sides by buildings; it looked to MacDonald like a very large town square – almost an arena, he thought. On the far side, nearest the town centre, was a monolithic structure lit up by spotlights. There was some kind of design on the front of it, facing into the arena, but MacDonald could not make out what it was – the lights were so bright they dazzled the night-vision goggles.

Howard had stopped again. MacDonald saw that he was taking a compass bearing on the arena; then he took a second on the bridge where the north-south highway crossed over the railway. A third bearing, on the distant Sahra airfield, confirmed his position. "OK," he breathed to MacDonald and Ziegler, "by my reckoning, this is just about it. Mac, get the range-finder set up and give me the exact distance to that spotlit wall."

Gratefully, the three men unburdened themselves of their heavy loads. MacDonald erected the short tripod and assembled the range-finder, plugging in the small battery that illuminated the read-out scale. He slowly moved the instrument round on its pivot until the wall came into view. Under normal outdoor night-time

344

conditions it would have been too dark to see anything clearly enough through the range-finder's lenses to get an accurate reading, but the brightly-lit wall leapt into focus. With a start, MacDonald saw that the design painted on it was a giant portrait; he instantly recognised the smiling, benevolent-looking features of Saddam Hussein. Lining the split-image picture up on one edge of the wall, he turned the drum until the line was unbroken, then he read the distance off the scale. "Twelve hundred and ninety," he whispered to Howard.

"Good," said Howard. "This will do as our main position. Mike, you and Danny find the best spot within twenty yards forward of here, and I'll go back about a hundred and fifty yards up the slope and pick our secondary."

Ziegler spent some time prowling around the area immediately in front of them, like a dog sniffing out its territory. Several times he sank to the ground and lay down, testing the line of view down the gentle slope to the arena below. Eventually he decided he was satisfied; he beckoned to MacDonald, who came over and lay down himself to check the visibility. He nodded his satisfaction. They went back to retrieve the packs and move them forward the few yards to the place they had selected. Then they unpacked a large groundsheet and a spade each and began to dig.

58

Brent Scowcroft drummed his fingers on the table, frowning. "So the British have come up with nothing on this guy Dartington?"

"Apparently not, Mr Chairman," said Robert Gates, Director of the CIA. "He has been interviewed by the British Secret Intelligence Service in the Bahamas, where he is on holiday. I have the full details if you need them, but suffice it to say that he has a perfectly adequate explanation for what looked like some incriminating documentation. Furthermore, he has been there since this episode started, or at least since the men first appeared in Saudi Arabia. During that time, the Bahamian phone company records show that he has neither made nor received any overseas phone calls. Until today, that is." Gates paused to take a sip of water from the glass in front of him. "This call was monitored by the British SIS; Dartington called his head office in Saudi Arabia. He sounded convincingly baffled by the turn of events, and not a little angry. His villa was wired by the SIS operative, and subsequent conversations there reveal that his wife and various guests have been on the receiving end of his bad temper. During one conversation, she confided to a female acquaintance that the incident had upset him badly, and that she had only just managed to prevent him from flying home immediately.

"I have heard the tapes of these conversations, and I have to say that Dartington sounds genuinely innocent of the affair. However, neither we at the CIA, nor the British, are entirely convinced. They will continue to monitor his every move."

"Hmm," said Scowcroft thoughtfully. "Well, please keep me informed. He turned to Martin Faga. "Has the National Reconnaissance Office got any news about where these people have got to?"

Faga laid out the large composite photograph of Tikrit on the table, and the others gathered round. A red blob marked the location of the vehicles. After quickly running through the chronology, Faga looked at his watch and concluded his summary. "As of now, the vehicles have been there for two and a half hours without moving. And it would be my assessment," he added, "that that is where they will stay, for possibly the next thirty-six hours."

Scowcroft's head jerked up from the photograph. "Why do you say that?"

"Because Tikrit is Saddam's home town. And the day after tomorrow, by which I mean the 28th, is his birthday. It could be that he will put in a public appearance there to boost his image. At any rate," he shrugged, "these men seem to have some idea that he will."

Gates chipped in again, glancing across at Faga and nodding. "I would support that view. There have been celebrations in previous years, and the Iraqi News Agency announced this evening that there would be celebrations again this year. They did not, however, specifically say that Saddam would attend any one particular event, nor have we heard anything to lead us to believe that he will be going to Tikrit. Saddam's movements are probably the mostly closely guarded secrets in Iraq. There is never any prior announcement of when or where he will appear. These people could be acting on a hunch, but I repeat what I said at our last meeting, that I do not believe they are. It would be extremely interesting to know where they obtained their information."

"Does it matter?" asked Scowcroft. "If we know they are there, and that this time they are going to stay there, we could launch another missile strike."

"It failed last time," squeaked the nasal voice of Douglas Longmire. "A complete waste of twelve million dolla–"

"The strike did not *fail*, you idiot," snarled General Burnside. "All four missiles impacted and exploded, on schedule and exactly as planned. The building was destroyed. There was always the chance that these people might leave before the missiles got there; that was a matter entirely beyond our control. Mr Chairman," – he turned to Scowcroft – "could I perhaps ask that the Treasury Department confine itself to commenting on matters within its own expertise? The fact that Mr *Quag*mire here," he enunciated sarcastically, "does not appear to have any discernible expertise at all, on any matter, might ensure that he keeps his goddam stupid mouth shut at all times."

347

Burnside turned his head to fix his stare on Longmire. The frog-faced Assistant Treasury Secretary's mouth had opened in protest, but he caught the full force of the General's steely gaze and sagged back in his chair, silenced.

Martin Faga and Robert Gates were stifling their mirth; Brent Scowcroft, a weary expression on his face, opened his mouth to intercede. "A–"

"If I may, Mr Chairman?" Faga interrupted before Scowcroft had the chance to speak. "I have considered the idea of repeating a missile strike. In short, I think we may already be too late. If we are right in our assessment, and Tikrit is the place where the attempt will be made, then there must be some doubt that these men are simply waiting by the vehicles until the day after tomorrow." Across the table, Faga saw General Burnside suddenly nod in understanding. "The assassins," he continued, "will probably be moving into position. They would not take the vehicles with them. We do not have the capability to track individual humans by satellite. A missile strike might destroy the vehicles, but it would not kill the assassins or stop the attempt. These are determined men. The only probable result of cutting off their escape route would be that they would subsequently be caught. Now; we already know that one of their number, the pilot, is an American citizen. Who is to say that there are not other Americans involved? And what would be the consequences if they were caught and paraded in front of the Iraqi television cameras?"

Scowcroft had quickly realised the appalling propaganda implications. Aghast, he stared at the DNRO, who had deliberately left his devastating question hanging. For a few moments, no one spoke.

Burnside broke the silence, his voice calm and low. "Mr Faga is of course right. The actual assassination team will have left the vehicles already. It's early morning in Iraq right now; they'll have moved into position, ready for tomorrow. They'll have left someone guarding the vehicles for when they return. Unless, of course," he added, "they have abandoned them altogether and intend to escape by other means."

"That makes sense to me," said Scowcroft gloomily. "So what do you gentlemen recommend that I tell the President?"

"I think," said Faga, "that the best thing the President can do right now is to hope like hell that this attempt fails for some reason, but that the assassins manage to escape afterwards."

"All the way back to Saudi Arabia," said Gates, "where we can get our hands on them."

59

They completed the first of the two hides when it was still dark. Only when Howard was fully persuaded that it was satisfactory did they move further back up the slope to the secondary position; Howard and MacDonald set to work while Ziegler went off to put out the anemometers.

He returned an hour later; he had found suitable places for two out of the three, at distances four hundred and fifty and eight hundred yards from the front hide. The first of the tiny instruments was on an upper branch of a tall, bare thorn tree, and the second, as close as he had dared to approach to the arena, at the top of an electricity pole. "Those damn thorns," Ziegler muttered, picking up a spade to begin helping the others. "I'm all scratched to hell. Sorry Danny, but there wasn't anywhere suitable to put the third anemometer. It wouldn't have been any use just leavin' it on the ground where someone might find it."

"No," agreed MacDonald, "and at ground-level it wouldn't have given a true idea of the wind speed anyway. They need to be elevated a few feet. We'll just have to make do with the two of them."

By the time they had finished digging the second hide and had covered it over and camouflaged it with scrub, the first glimmers of dawn were beginning to appear. Clearing away any visible trace of their presence, they made their way back down the slope to the first hide, nearer the arena.

MacDonald swore that he would not have been able to find the hide if they hadn't marked it with the tiny beta light they had left by the entrance hatch. The hole they had dug was now completely invisible. The spoil from the hole, shovelled on to the groundsheet, had been taken away a load at a time and scattered in thicker areas of thorn scrub where it would not be noticed; enough was left to cover the roof of the hide. They had tested the strength of the roof by walking on it; it had felt as solid as the surrounding ground. Then they had completed the camouflage with scrub and uprooted thorn bushes.

Ziegler remained outside as Howard and MacDonald crawled in; he scoured the area minutely, brushing over their footprints and removing any sign that anyone had ever been there. Finally, he pocketed the beta-light and crawled in himself, pulling the hatch cover into place behind him, reaching out of the slit with a piece of brushwood to scuff over the marks it had made in the thin, sandy soil.

MacDonald admitted to himself that he was tired. It had been hard work, true, but all his life he had been used to hard work. It was something more – tension. Lying back as the first chinks of light began to filter in through the observation slits, he had to pinch himself mentally to remind himself that it was all real, that he was as deep inside enemy territory as he could possibly be. Was the psychological strain of the build-up to this beginning to tell on him? He forced himself to analyse his thoughts. Yes, he was a little scared, he decided. Equally, he reminded himself, he would have been less than human if he had not been a bit frightened of what he had got himself into. The project seemed to have acquired a momentum of its own, an unstoppable inevitability that left him powerless. He wondered if the others felt the same.

He glanced at his two companions. Ziegler, in the well of the hide, behind and below MacDonald's feet, was already asleep. He lay still and soundless, scarcely moving. How could the man relax so completely at a time like this? MacDonald felt that he couldn't sleep now even if he tried, despite the waves of fatigue that washed over him. Beside him, Howard lay motionless on his front, gazing out of one of the observation slits down towards the arena. He had taken the first watch; every minute or so he would crane his body round so that he could look out of the slits at the rear and the sides, covering every possible angle of approach. His face looked unearthly, covered as it was by streaks of brown and black camouflage cream, his eyes glittering in the pale orange light of daybreak. A dark-green Arab *shemagh* covered his head and neck. MacDonald knew he himself must look equally strange.

"Try and get a bit of sleep, Danny," Howard whispered, no even

351

turning his head. "It'll get too hot later on. It's going to be like an oven in here when the sun gets up."

"I'll try." MacDonald lay back again, looking at the ceiling of the hide a few inches above his face. Neat, that idea of using the stretchers, he thought. The sturdy steel and aluminium poles of the stretchers and their dismantled trolleys had been an awkward load to carry in. Now they formed a strong lattice-work, supporting a tough plastic membrane; a one-foot depth of earth had been spread on top, forming the roof.

The stretchers had by no means been the most cumbersome of the things they had carried in. MacDonald had been surprised by the single heaviest item: ten gallons of water. One hundred pounds' weight – more than a quarter of the total. Both Howard and Ziegler had been insistent. "At rest, a man can normally get by on a pint or two a day," Howard had explained. "But drinking only that amount in the heat means you begin to dehydrate. You need eight pints a day to stay in good condition in the heat, depending on how active you're being. More, if it's very hot and you're on the move a lot. And we can't bank on just taking supplies for a day and a half. We may be away for two or three days, or even more, if we run into trouble or can't move."

The food – all to be eaten cold as no cooking would be possible – had taken up little space by comparison, and was a mere fraction of the weight of the water. Then there had been the three AK rifles and ammunition, a couple of grenades each – MacDonald hoped fervently they would not be needed – and all the rest of the equipment: the range-finder, the spotter scope, the anemometers, the little computer with its spare batteries, the 35mm camera with its motor drive and long lens . . . and of course the big rifle. MacDonald could feel the padded rifle-case next to him as he lay in the hide. In his breast pocket was the flat wallet containing ten rounds of ammunition. "You'll have a lighter load on the way back, Danny," Usher had quipped, helping MacDonald on with his pack; "you'll only be carrying nine rounds."

MacDonald smiled at the memory. What else was it Bob had told him? *Keep smiling.* That was it. Make a joke of everything, he had said. Don't take it too seriously – always find the funny side; it's the only way to survive. Bob had been right. Humour, however black, was the antidote to fear, even to disaster. MacDonald thought he understood that a little better now. Gradually, he began to relax; twenty minutes later, he was asleep.

*   *   *

"Oh, hello, sir; I wasn't expecting you back." Detective Inspector Juliet Shelley raised her head in surprise as Hughie Carter came into the room. He looked exhausted, rumpled and cross.

"There's not much more I can do there for the time being," said the Detective Superintendent with a yawn. "Twenty-four hours of bloody nothing, so far. Bloody wild-goose chase, if you ask me. Bugger all to go on. How are things here?"

"Oh, pretty quiet. No problems at all, really." She hesitated, choosing her words. "Sir," she went on, "you look tired. Why don't you go home and get some rest? I can handle things here."

"Can't," said Carter briefly. "I've got to stay on call here – immediate notice, in case something else turns up. But maybe I'll crash out on the couch next door for a while," he conceded. "Give me a shout if I'm wanted, would you?"

"I'll get you a cup of coffee, sir," said Juliet decisively, standing up. "Would you like anything else with it?"

"Oh, thanks. Maybe a biscuit or something."

Juliet left the room. *A biscuit indeed,* she thought crossly as she made her way down to the station canteen. *The man probably hasn't eaten properly for twenty-four hours.* Marching into the canteen, she placed an order.

Five minutes later, she was back upstairs in Carter's office with a tray. The Detective Superintendent was sitting on the couch, loosening his shoe-laces. He looked up in amazement as she pulled over a coffee-table and set the tray down in front of him. "Hell, Juliet, I . . ."

"Come on, sir, get it down you. You look as if you need it."

Carter cast his eyes down at the plate of bacon, fried egg, sausage and tomato, then up again at his subordinate, who was standing over him with a severe expression on her face. Suddenly, he realised that he was hungry. He began to eat, motioning to Juliet to sit down on a chair opposite him. In between mouthfuls, he grumbled gently about how he been run ragged for the previous twenty-four hours. "Not a single bloody clue, would you believe? Clean as a bloody whistle,

353

they left that place. Well, nearly clean. Complete bloody waste of time, it's been."

"What's the panic all about, sir?" Juliet asked curiously.

"Terrorist group, so we've been told," replied Carter indistinctly through sausage and egg. He snorted. "Hah. Terrorist group, my arse. What sort of terrorist sets up an op here, then takes off for the Middle East? Should be the other bloody way round, shouldn't it? Anyway, why should we mind if they go and blow up the Saudi royal palace, or whatever it is they're up to? Let the Arabs sort it out themselves, I say. Teach the buggers a lesson. Dose of their own medicine," he rattled on, waving his knife. He finished his mouthful, took a swig of coffee and returned his attention to his plate.

"Saudi Arabia?" asked Juliet, puzzled. She felt a twinge of alarm. Johnny was out there. She hoped he would be all right, that he wouldn't be caught up in some dreadful religious massacre. "Why there?"

"Search me, girl," said Carter, swallowing another gulp of coffee. "All we know is, two men turned up there on 8th April, posing as construction workers. One English, one South African. There were others, including an American pilot and some blokes who smuggled themselves over there in a sea container, would you believe. They'd been using premises down in Swindon . . ."

Juliet had stopped listening. Her mind raced. *That date – 8th April. An Englishman, and others. Johnny left on 7th April – he would have arrived on the morning of the 8th . . .*

Carter was still speaking. ". . . Anyway, I'm buggered if I know. It's all a bloody riddle. Your guess is as good as mine."

Juliet was thinking furiously. Her mind went back, searching for inconsistencies, for something wrong. But her sudden rush of suspicion was ridiculous, she told herself. OK, Johnny hadn't talked much about his work, but the idea that he might be involved in something criminal . . . And *terrorism*? Never in a thousand years! She forced her voice to remain calm. "You said they left their base here clean – no clues?"

"About as clean as you can get. No dabs, no hairs, no fibres – nothing. Just a couple of spots of paint on the floor."

"Paint?" Juliet tripped the word off her tongue as lightly as she could manage; her stomach was like lead.

"Yeah. Must have been them – the place hadn't had a tenant

354

before, see? They were the first. It'll probably match up with the container."

"How do you mean?" she asked, barely audibly.

"The sea container they used to smuggle some of their colleagues out to Saudi," Carter explained, chewing on a piece of bacon. "Apparently, they cut a false doorway in it and then cammed it up. Painted over the cracks – you know. Yellow paint – it'll probably match up when we get the samples back."

Juliet's head swam. Her knuckles went white as she gripped the arms of her chair, and her gaze fixed blankly on the thinning red hair on the top of Carter's head as he bent once more over his plate. With an effort she got to her feet, then stood for a moment, swaying. "Excuse me, sir," she said. Her own voice sounded strangled and strange to her; there was a loud roaring in her ears, and she thought she might be about to black out. "I must just go and finish something off next door." She turned, holding on to the back of the chair for support, and launched herself towards the door. It seemed miles away, at the end of a dark tunnel.

She gripped the door-handle and turned it; then she was through into the next room. She hardly registered Carter's voice calling after her, "Thanks for the breakfast, Juliet, huh? I owe you one."

Juliet lurched over to her desk and sank into her chair. She stared at the blank wall in front with sightless eyes, her mind dazed with shock. *Yellow paint*, she thought numbly. *That mark on the jeans Johnny left at the cleaners. The mark they couldn't get out. That was yellow paint.*

*   *   *

"Mr President, I have Prime Minister Major on the line now."

"Thank you." President George Bush thought for a moment, then picked up the receiver. "John? George here. How are you?"

"I'm very well, thank you, Mr President. How are you?"

"Fine," said the President, "fine. Ah, listen, John, we have a serious problem here with this Iraqi thing, these, ah, people out there trying to kill Saddam. Have your people filled you in on that?"

"They have. It could prove quite embarrassing."

Quite embarrassing, thought the President. *That's one way of putting it. A goddam disaster, is more like it.* "Yeah. As you say,

355

embarrassing. Look, my people here say there's nothing we can do to stop this. They're beyond our reach. We can hope for two things: one, that they don't succeed, and two, that your people manage to get something out of the guy, ah, the head of that corporation. Persuade him to call them off. Are you having any luck with that?"

"Sir Peter Dartington? He has been interviewed. He appears to be an innocent party. He is a respectable businessman."

Jesus, thought the President. *A respectable businessman indeed. As if that makes him clean.* "Sure he is, John. But have your people, ah, sweated him a little? Leaned on him? You know what I mean. We can't afford to horse around here."

Major was emphatic. "No, Mr President. We have not done that. It is not something we could do. It would cause a scandal."

"Hell, there's going to be more than just a scandal if this plot to kill Saddam succeeds!" retorted the exasperated President. Major's unrelentingly matter-of-fact formality was getting on his nerves.

"I can understand your frustration, Mr President. I share it. If I may come back to your other point – the question of the probability of their succeeding. First, I think we may assume that these people are highly professional. So far, they have left no evidence of who they are, apart from the pilot, whom you know about. Police opinion is that they must be extremely capable, and have planned this operation meticulously. The view here is that there must be some chance of their succeeding."

The British Prime Minister had given the President the opening he wanted. "Well, John," he said, "one thing that puzzles us here is how these guys seem to be so sure that Saddam will appear in Tikrit tomorrow. We do not know where they could have got this information from." The President inserted what he hoped was an insinuating pause before continuing. "No one here, either at the CIA or at the State Department or anywhere else, knows anything concrete about his movements. I've specifically asked them." He paused again, then added carefully, "Can any of your intelligence people confirm that he will be there?"

"As far as I am aware, no one here has any knowledge of Saddam's movements either."

The question hadn't worked, the President thought. He reluctantly decided that he would have to prod the Prime Minister a little further. "Well, John, the question is what do we do about it, damage-limitation-wise? It's going to look real bad if they're caught by the Iraqis. We have one US citizen who appears to be involved, and there is also at least one of, ah, your people." The President put a slight but unmistakable stress on the last two words.

This time it worked. The Prime Minister instantly responded, a note of testiness in his voice. "There may well be British subjects involved, Mr President, but I can assure you that they are not 'our people'. Whoever they are, they are not employees of Her Majesty's Government, if that was what you meant. I wouldn't want you to think that they might be."

"Of course I didn't mean to imply that, John," said the President, his voice placatory. "For my part, I give you a categoric assurance that the Government of the United States is not behind this attempt on Saddam."

At the other end of the line, John Major sat silent for a moment. So, he thought, *that is what this telephone call is about. The President* does *suspect that the British Government is involved, and he wants a confirmation or a denial.* He thought hard for a few seconds, then spoke. "And I give you a similar categoric assurance, Mr President. These men are not acting for the British Government in any capacity, either official or unofficial."

The President wavered for a moment. He had been given the solemn word of the British Prime Minister. "Well, John, one rather wonders who they are. Our discussions here played with the possibility that this might be a South African job, seeing as how there is a South African national involved. But we can't see the sense of it. Why would they risk setting the thing up in England when they could do it much more easily at home? Anyway, they have no particular interest in Saddam, so far as we know. The other possibility is the Israelis, but we have, ah, contacts in Israel, and we would have heard about it. And as with the South Africans, it's difficult to see why the Israelis would go through all these shenanigans in England when they could run it much more easily, and with less risk, from Israel. We just don't know who it could be. Do you have any ideas?"

He's trying to catch me out again, thought the Prime Minister. He kept his voice dead-pan. "I'm afraid not, Mr President. We don't know who it could be."

The President could do no more. He had registered the irritation in the Prime Minister's voice, and the somewhat guarded responses.

He decided it was time to loosen up the conversation a little. "Well, John, there doesn't seem to be much more we can do about it for the time being. Incidentally, we haven't spoken since your re-election on the 9th. My congratulations. You got my cable?"

"Indeed I did. It was kind of you. It was a very pleasing result, I must say."

That was more like it, thought the President. The Prime Minister sounded much more relaxed now. "We're all very envious of you here, John. You're home and dry for another five years, while here, I've got plenty of problems. I wish I had my own election behind me. Right now, I'm getting plenty of heat from the opposition here. I could sure use some pointers from you, sometime. You certainly pulled it off in style."

The Prime Minister was clearly pleased and flattered. "That is very kind of you, George. Things have gone well for us. We got the deal we wanted at Maastricht, and the European Community is moving in the right direction. Everything's looking very good for us. I'm sure things will come right for you, too. If it's any help, my own experience is that opposition candidates attract rather more attention than votes. Anyway, I wish you equal success for this autumn."

"Thanks, John. We'll talk again soon."

George Bush put down the telephone and ran through the salient points of the conversation in his mind. Major was a difficult guy to read, he decided. He seemed straightforward enough – sometimes straightforward to the point of banality – but it was difficult to know what he was really thinking. Had he been telling the truth?

The President of the United States sighed and concluded that he had.

*   *   *

MacDonald awoke to hear a slight *twang*. He started; he was about to sit up when he remembered the low roof. He turned his head to one side and saw Ziegler crouched by one of the side observation slits, a catapult in his hand. There was a bleat and the noise of something scampering away.

"Goddam goats," muttered the American.

It was airless and stifling in the hide. The only ventilation consisted of the horizontal observation slits. Howard was still awake, lying in the same position. MacDonald looked at his watch. He had slept for five hours; it was nearly midday. Ziegler handed him a plastic water-bottle. "Thanks, Mike," whispered the stalker, unscrewing the stopper and taking a mouthful of the tepid water. It tasted of plastic. "What's that about goats?"

"Damn things have been grazin' along the ridge here. Whole herd of them. Problem is, where there's a herd of goats, there could be a herdsman. I've been stingin' them in the ass with this slingshot. If there's someone watchin', he'll think there's a wasp's nest or somethin' here, and keep clear." He loaded another lead buckshot pellet into the catapult and drew the elastic back, taking aim. He fired, and there was another bleat. MacDonald saw a scrawny-looking white goat jump into the air. It ran off about thirty yards, then resumed grazing.

"Danny?" Howard whispered. "I think we can leave Mike to defend us from the marauding killer goats for a while." He grinned and pointed through the front observation slit. "There's some action down there."

MacDonald rolled over on to his stomach and looked out of the slit, down towards the arena. There were signs of activity; he reached for his binoculars and examined the scene.

All around the big square arena, men were engaged in erecting flagpoles and hanging bunting. Huge Iraqi national flags now decorated most of the buildings on all sides, including the far one, behind the wall with Saddam's picture. Several large lorries were parked in the centre, and groups of men were unloading smaller posts and carrying them off to various points on the square.

"What are all those small posts they're putting out?" asked MacDonald.

"Markers, I expect, so that tomorrow's audience is formed up in neat lines. But take a look at the far side, just in front of Saddam's picture. Here – have a look through the spotter scope."

MacDonald put his eye to the scope. The scene, magnified sixty times, leapt into view. Just in front of the picture wall, sections of a large wooden platform were being unloaded from lorries and put into position. A team of soldiers was bolting the sections together; gradually the platform took shape. An officer was standing in front of it, directing operations and making sure it was lined up centrally. As MacDonald looked on, white-painted sections of a second, smaller structure were carried on to the platform and positioned in its centre. MacDonald watched as the sections were assembled and men began to fit small stanchion posts to the corners, stringing a thick white rope loosely between them. Finally four soldiers appeared with a set of three solid-looking steps, placing them against the rear.

MacDonald handed the spotter scope back to Howard, who immediately took in the set-up. "Bingo," he said quietly. "A saluting rostrum. And in just about the right place, too. If the picture wall is twelve hundred and ninety yards, that rostrum should be about twelve-fifty. Perfect. Let's get an exact range on it now."

Manoeuvring the large cylindrical range-finder into place at the observation slit was a clumsy business, but after ten minutes MacDonald had it mounted securely on its low tripod and was sighting through the eyepieces in the centre of the cylinder. He lined the split image up on the white edge of the rostrum and turned the dial; gradually, the two halves of the image came together. When he was satisfied, he read off the distance on the scale. "One thousand, two hundred and forty-two yards."

They dismantled the range-finder again and stowed it away.

MacDonald reached for the little portable computer and switched it on. Practice at Badanah, with further guidance from Usher, had made him proficient with the ballistics program.

"OK, let's do a little practice run," said Howard. "Wind speed," – he read off the little electronic panel beside him – "one knot, right to left. Barometer, nine hundred and eighty-nine millibars. Humidity, eighty per cent. Air temperature, thirty-one degrees."

"Temperature in Fahrenheit, please," said MacDonald, tapping in the other information.

"Sorry. Eighty-six."

MacDonald finished and tapped in "SUM". A few seconds later, the information came up. He read off the scale for twelve hundred and forty yards. "If I left the settings unchanged from the zero I did at twelve hundred yards, the bullet would go twenty-nine inches low and ten inches to the left. So it needs ten clicks up on the elevation drum and three clicks to the right on windage."

"Good," said Howard. "Does that read-out tally with your notes?"

"My notes are only down to increments of twenty-five yards, not like the five yards the computer can do." MacDonald flipped through his book and found the page with the nearest corresponding weather conditions. "Yes, the other figures fit. It must be right."

"I think we're in business, Danny," said Howard with a fierce grin.

Behind them there was another soft *twang* from the catapult. "Goddam goats," growled Ziegler.

60

The black rage had descended on him again.

The worse the rage became, the more it distracted him; and the more it distracted him, the worse it became. It was a brutal spiral downwards into a Stygian fury. At its worst the rage overwhelmed him, nearly drove him insane, made him lash out at anything and anyone in sight.

Still just in control, the big man flickered his eyes venomously over the food set out on the long table in front of him, then towards the figure of the attendant who stood, stiff with fear, at the side of the room. Useless, worthless little creature, he thought. All of them, useless! Smoking, murderous anger erupted inside his brain; the rage overcame him. With a violent flail of his arm he swept the food, the plates, the glasses and the bottles away on to the floor. The echo of the breaking china and glass died away as cold, dark eyes settled menacingly on the figure by the wall. The fathomless stare was transfixing; the voice was flat, icy, deadly. "Get out."

There was a quavering, reedy reply. "Your Excellency, shall I clear up the . . ."

"GET OUT!" The big man crashed a heavy fist down on to the table. He rose to his feet, his face crimson, shaking with wrath. The terrified servant needed no further bidding. With an anguished whimper he scuttled out of the room, closing the heavy door behind him.

Alone now, the big man aimed a ferocious kick at his chair, knocking it flying. He began to prowl around the room, a caged beast trying to force the rage from his mind. Always, he knew, it was the same thought that started the rage; every time, thinking of the same person. The person who had betrayed him, who had lied to him. The one foreigner whose word he had trusted, and whom he held responsible for his humiliation.

362

Kelly. The traitor, the deceiver Kelly. The very name drove the big man into a dark fury. He bared his teeth and snarled the name again to the empty room. Kelly! He had been Kelly's friend, had done his bidding. He had been faithful to Kelly and the United States. And he had been betrayed. He had since vowed to himself many times that one day he would have Kelly at his deadly mercy, as many before had been. Then he would . . .

The big man's hand found the pistol at his side. He drew it from the holster. The clash of the action as he cocked the pistol resounded in the room. Kelly! He levelled the weapon suddenly and fired two shots at the heavy wooden door. The noise was shockingly loud. One of the bullets ricocheted off the grey reinforced-concrete wall and spun into an ornate silver coffee-pot on the far end of the table, holing it and knocking it over. The big man ignored it. A pool of coffee formed on the table and dripped on to the floor.

No one would come now, he thought. No one would dare. Not after the shots. The word would rapidly go round. Everywhere, people would be trembling with fear, cowering from his wrath like petrified rats, their bowels loosening at the thought that they might be the next to be sent for. *Terrified* . . .

Good, thought the big man. Let that rabble live in terror. It would keep them in line. Let Kelly be the one to be brought to him in due course. Not for him the merciful release of a bullet; for Kelly it would be an endless madness of pain, a long, slow death of screaming torment . . .

Firing the shots had made him feel slightly better. Absently, he ejected the round in the pistol's chamber and replaced it in the magazine, adding two more from the drawer under the table to replace the ones he had fired. His thoughts wandered. Tomorrow . . .

Tomorrow. It would be dark outside now, above in the streets. Tomorrow would be an important day. Action had been forced on him by circumstances, but he would turn it to his advantage, as he always did. Forced on him, he thought savagely. There had been only two alternatives: it had had to be either the Iranians or the Syrians. He hated them both. But he hated the Syrians more.

A non-aggression pact. He had been left with no practical alternative but to propose the initiative. The economy was in desperate trouble. There had to be an agreement with one of them, before they both combined to squeeze him dry. The Iranian lackey would sign tomorrow. The man would be impressed by the display of force, would be left in no doubt about what could be done. He wouldn't throw away months of preparation and negotiation. He would sign.

But neither the minion nor his masters in Tehran could be trusted. They could never be trusted! They would try to deceive, or trick, or . . . Yes. That too was possible. It was always possible that there was a plot. There were plots everywhere . . . Well, he had already taken precautions for tomorrow. That had been simple. If there was a plot, it would fail, as all the others had. Did they think he was so stupid? Well, they would find out that he wasn't. Tomorrow, they would find out. Tomorrow . . .

Deep in the labyrinth of bunkers beneath the streets of Baghdad, Saddam Hussein continued to pace, alone in the darkness.

*　　*　　*

Eventually, to everyone's relief, the temperature in the hide had begun to fall. The cooler night air sucked the heat from the ground, from the roof of the hide. It had become tolerable again. Howard was at last taking some rest; he lay asleep in the well of the hide. Ziegler had taken his place, next to MacDonald. Below, in the town, most of the movement had ceased. Lights still burned and small fires were to be seen on the outer fringes, in the scattered encampments of the soldiers who had been working on preparations in the arena. The nearest was six hundred yards away down the slope.

All day there had been comings and goings, constant activity. Streams of people had passed along the track beneath the electricity line, past the pole where the second anemometer was mounted. The three men in the hide had watched closely, but no one had paid any attention to the three tiny revolving cups of the instrument high above their heads. Ziegler had been relaxed about it. "People don't usually look up, Danny. They look straight ahead, or down. They won't see it. If they do, they'll think it's meant to be there." MacDonald had seen the sense of that. Red deer were much the same; they tended to look downhill, too. There was less likelihood of their seeing you if you were above them on the hill.

In many ways, it had been a day of constant alertness, of tension. Danny had sensed that the other two were feeling it too, although it hadn't prevented them from snatching occasional periods of sleep between periods of watch duty. Living in such close confinement, and in such primitive conditions, was certainly one way to get to know your companions, he mused. Those sealable plastic bags – thank God they had brought them. A series of them now lay in a deep hole next to Howard's feet. Without the bags, the smell would have been . . .

Oddly, it had also been a day of almost stupefying boredom. There was nothing to do except watch the scenery – the same scenery, hour after hour – or eat, drink or sleep. MacDonald was a patient man, but the monotony of the routine in the hide had become almost too much for him. He wondered how his companions, men who thrived on action, could bear it. It was the waiting . . .

"Ssss." The soft hiss from Ziegler alerted Danny at once. He turned to see the American peering intently out of the slit to the left of the hide, and moved over to follow his gaze. Ziegler reached down behind him. His fingers closed on Howard's ear-lobe and pulled it lightly. Howard came instantly awake, reaching for his silenced AK rifle. All three men looked out of the slit.

A patrol of a dozen Iraqi soldiers was making its way along the top of the ridge towards them. Through the night-vision goggles, MacDonald could just make out the figures, some four hundred yards away. As they approached, he heard the scuffing of their boots on the ground. The patrol stopped two hundred and fifty yards away; voices were faintly audible. After a while, the lead men in the patrol moved on again, now heading down the slope – straight for the hide. Eight of them. Four had been left behind.

Still they came on. Fifty yards, then forty. They were going to walk straight to the hide. They would find it. MacDonald held his breath, his hands gripped round his AK. Howard was crouched by the escape hatch, ready to spring. Twenty yards, ten . . .

The eight men walked right past the side observation slit. A stone kicked up by a boot rolled in through the slit, coming to rest against MacDonald's rucksack. Then the patrol was past. MacDonald watched them disappearing further down the slope towards the encampments below.

For thirty minutes they observed the four men left behind, silhouetted against the sky on the ridge-line. The low voices of the soldiers carried to the hide. There was the flare of a match and the glow of a cigarette. Three of the four soldiers had sat down; the fourth wandered about for a while nearby, picking up pieces of brush and scrub. Another match flared, and MacDonald could see a fire being lit. The fire caught. The light from the fire illuminated the faces of the four men, now sitting round in a circle.

An hour passed; three of the soldiers unrolled blankets and lay down. The fourth remained sitting until the embers of the fire began to dim; then he got to his feet and began to walk backwards and forwards, working the stiffness out of his body.

"Danny." Howard's whisper was only just audible. "You stay here. Mike and I are going to see to these guys."

"But they haven't seen us."

"No, but if they're still there in the morning they will, when you fire that rifle. And they certainly will when it's time for us to pull out."

"But won't they be missed? Or won't someone come to relieve them?"

"That's a chance we'll have to take. If the Iraqi Army was even half competent, I'd say that they would be missed; but you only have to look at them. They're a shambles. No, I doubt this lot will be missed for a while. They aren't in radio contact – they haven't got one. My guess is that their orders are to stay there until everything's over tomorrow. They probably don't even know their big boss is coming."

MacDonald nodded uncertainly, and the other two prepared to leave. Soundlessly, Ziegler pushed back the entrance hatch and climbed out, followed by Howard. MacDonald kept them in sight as they moved off, crawling stealthily up the slope. After only ten yards, even with the night-vision goggles, he had lost them in the scrub. A detached part of his mind approved; they would be good men to be out with on the hill . . .

For nearly half an hour, MacDonald anxiously watched the sentry on the ridge. Every few minutes he would return to stoke up the fire and sit by it for a while, then get to his feet again and resume walking backwards and forwards.

A shadow seemed to rise up behind the patrolling sentry, and MacDonald saw him fall silently to the ground. The three soldiers lying wrapped in their blankets did not stir. Then, less than a minute later, MacDonald thought he noticed a slight twitching motion. Then nothing. There had been no sound, hardly any movement. MacDonald had expected to hear the low cough of the silenced AK, but there had been nothing.

His heart pounded. What had happened? Suddenly he felt alone, as alone and exposed as he had felt in the rubber dinghy in the middle of the Red Sea. What if either Ed or Mike had been injured, or killed? Or if both of them had? How would he manage by himself? For long, uneasy minutes he waited. Fifteen. Twenty. Thirty. Forty! Something must have gone wrong! Why would it take them so long to return, when they didn't have to worry about being seen by the patrol? Why hadn't –

"Danny." MacDonald's head whirled round to the source of the voice. Ten yards away, he saw Ziegler rise from the scrub and approach. Howard followed. In a matter of moments they had brushed over the soil around the hide and were both back inside.

"What happened?" MacDonald spoke in a hoarse whisper.

"We took care of them," said Howard succinctly.

MacDonald's glance went to the large sheath knife on Howard's belt. "Why did it take so long?"

"We had to do a bit of clearin' up afterwards," explained Ziegler calmly. "Couldn't leave them and their gear just lyin' there, could we? Then we had to deal with the tracks, make sure there was no trace of anythin', all that sort of stuff."

"Where did you put the bodies?"

"Well," drawled Ziegler, "let's put it this way. I hope there isn't a change of plan and we have to use that other hide. It's kind of full right now, and the smell in there won't be too great once the sun gets on it in the mornin'."

"So it came in handy, after all," said MacDonald, forcing a grin. "I'm glad all that extra digging wasn't a complete waste of time and effort."

Ziegler gave MacDonald a strange look, then turned to Howard. "Ed? You know what?"

"What?"

"I'm thinkin' that just maybe we'll be able to make a soldier out of this Scotchman, after all," said Ziegler.

"Just what I was thinking myself, Mike," said Howard.

61

"JSTARS is showing heavy vehicular traffic approaching Tikrit, Walter."

"What does it look like?" The Walrus came over to join Kearwin in front of the big screen.

"There have been soft-skinned vehicles, mostly trucks, pouring into the town for the past hour. That's since . . . before 07.00 Iraqi time. No armour. My guess is, a lot of troops. Maybe they're going to be part of the big parade. Say," Kearwin side-tracked himself, "is that right, that today's Saddam's birthday?"

"That's what I'm told, John. What about these latest reports?"

"Up here, to the north. This airfield here. The Sahra/Tikrit North airbase. AWACS was reporting a lot of helicopter activity there an hour or so ago, but it all cleared off after about half an hour. Then, twenty minutes ago, a single helicopter flew in from the south. By itself. It's still sitting on the ground there. There was a large convoy of armour there too. Just after the helicopter landed the convoy moved off south, towards the town. See?"

The Walrus peered at the screen. It was extremely difficult to interpret the image, but Kearwin had had more practice at it, and as he explained it began to make more sense to the Walrus. He nodded.

"There's a second, smaller group of vehicles – light armour and cars – coming up the highway from the south, down here," said Kearwin. "It all seems to be converging on the town at once. Do you think something's about to happen?"

"I don't know, John, but it looks like it. Do we know what that armour is?"

"The heavy stuff, coming from the north, is MBTs. Main battle tanks. T-54/55s, T-62s – you know. Maybe even T-72s. The lighter stuff coming from the south, that's probably BTR-70s, BRDM-2s. Light armour – wheels, not tracks. That sort of stuff. Some jeeps and cars with it."

"OK. Starting now, I want every Keyhole satellite pass to bounce low-level over there. See where this stuff is headed and close in on it. I want prints of each pass. Got it?"

"Will do," said Kearwin. "You know, Walter, we'd learn a lot more if we had a TR-1 overflight as well."

"No chance, I'm afraid. I mentioned it. The Air Force said I must be crazy. They don't want the goddam thing shot down, and I can see their point. You remember those reports of SA-4 installations? One of them was reported to be right there at Samarra, just down the road from Tikrit. An SA-4 anti-aircraft missile could knock down a TR-1, easy. I think you'll have to forget that idea."

Kearwin began setting up the instructions for the Keyhole satellite low-level passes, keeping his eye on the main screen. Ten minutes later, he called the Walrus over again. "The armour all seems to be converging on this open area at the edge of the town, down here," he bubbled excitedly.

The Walrus said nothing. He was staring intently at the screen. Behind him, other analysts started to gather round. The radar picture on the screen became more and more confused as all the vehicles began to congregate in one place and come to a halt. All present had the feeling that something of great significance was about to happen. No one spoke.

"Hey!" exclaimed Kearwin suddenly, his high-pitched voice breaking the silence. "That helicopter's taken off again. It's headed down there too!"

*   *   *

The three men in the hide heard the roar of the tank engines and the grinding screech of their tracks long before they saw the tanks themselves. By now, down in the arena, thousands of people had gathered. Most were foot soldiers, marched in from the trucks arrayed in dozens of huge parking areas around the town. The soldiers now stood in massed ranks towards the front and sides of the arena, facing the platform and its white rostrum. Behind the soldiers in the centre of the arena, an area set aside for civilians began to fill up; the citizens of Tikrit had obediently responded to the blaring calls over loudspeakers bidding them to attend the ceremony that was about to take place.

A wide area around the platform beneath the picture wall had been left clear. The din of the approaching armoured column grew ever louder. Into the arena came a small convoy of wheeled BRDM scout cars, taking station over on the far right-hand side. Howard was puzzled to see a black limousine amongst the BRDMs; it was ushered into place in front of them and stopped. A small pennant was hanging from a miniature flagstaff on the bonnet of the limousine, but it was too small for Howard to make out what it was.

A small, fifty-strong contingent of purposeful-looking soldiers appeared to be controlling operations. Howard suddenly realised, looking through the spotter scope, that of all the soldiers present, they were the only ones carrying their own weapons. "Presidential body-guard," he breathed softly. "It's happening. Danny, get ready."

The roar and screech of the tanks were almost deafening now. MacDonald slipped the big rifle from its padded case and laid it out, its muzzle peeping through the front slit of the hide. From his breast pocket, he took out the wallet of ammunition and laid it down next to the rifle's barrel. He ran through the weather checks with Howard, entering the details swiftly into the computer.

At eight in the morning it was still relatively cool. "Nineteen Centigrade," whispered Howard. "Warming up. Set it for twenty, Danny. That's sixty-nine Fahrenheit. Better make it seventy."

"Wind?"

"Not a breath. Dead calm!"

MacDonald finished entering the settings. The computer gave the trajectory. He began adjusting the clicks on the telescopic sight's elevation drum. Howard was loading film into the long-lensed camera mounted on its squat tripod next to him.

The line of tanks thundered into the arena, fanning out to either side. The crowd of conscript soldiers shrank from them, huddling towards the civilians in the centre of the arena. The spectacle of the tanks' arrival was an awesome one, even to the three men in the hide twelve hundred yards away. They could only try to imagine what it must have been like for the soldiers and civilians crowded together in the arena. With the steel tank-tracks churning up the dry surface of the ground, a cloud of dust had soon risen, blotting out the view.

The roaring of the engines seemed to continue for many minutes; then little by little it began to abate. The screeching of tracks stopped, and engines slowed to idling speed; one by one they fell silent as they were switched off. Gradually the air cleared and the men in the hide took in the scene.

Tanks and armoured troop-carriers encircled the huge crowd. MacDonald could only guess at the number of men – ten thousand, he reckoned, possibly more. He was beginning to make an estimate of the number of tanks when his ears registered a clattering noise.

"Helicopter approaching!" Howard's voice was tight with tension.

The big helicopter came skimming in over the town. Over the arena it banked round abruptly and started to hover, descending slowly into the open space to the right of the platform. At a hundred feet above the ground the rotors began to raise the dust, and the scene became obscured once more. Just before the helicopter disappeared into its own dust cloud, Howard saw the massed foot soldiers and civilians clutch at their headgear, their clothing whipped by the downdraught from the rotor blades. Then the helicopter's engine slowed. The dust began to settle.

62

Slightly off to the right of the helicopter, Howard saw the door of the limousine open. A small man in black robes and a turban stepped out and walked towards the helicopter, escorted by an aide and a two-man detail of the Amn al Khass, the Iraqi Presidential bodyguard. "Looks like one of those Iranian ayatollahs," muttered Howard. "What's he doing here? I thought the Iranians and Saddam were mortal enemies." The Iranian approached the helicopter and stood outside the rotor circle as the blades slowed.

The noise of the helicopter engine winding down reached the three men in the hide. The rotor blades came to a stop and sagged gently downwards. The helicopter door opened and a burly figure in olive-green uniform and a black beret climbed out, followed by three other uniformed men. The guard-detail commander called his waiting men to attention and snapped off a salute. The burly man acknowledged him briefly, then walked past and approached the Iranian. There was a long handshake and a swift, passionless embrace between the two men. The Iranian fell in with the retinue, following a few paces behind the big man.

Howard kept his eye tight against the spotter scope, following the big man's progress. He had seen the face in photographs and newsreel clips countless times before; now he gazed at the man with a sense of unreality. It was actually happening. The bastard was here. "OK, it's him," he whispered fiercely to MacDonald. "Get ready. He's the one in front. Wait till he gets up on that rostrum on the platform. Ziggy, all clear?"

Ziegler was still covering the rear of the hide, his eyes shifting quickly from one observation slit to the other in a last-minute check against the approach of any intruder. "Yeah, clear," he answered tersely. "Go ahead."

MacDonald had already slid the barrel of the rifle forward and through the slit. He gradually eased himself into his firing position. He drew back the bolt of the rifle and gently fed the large brass case of the cartridge forwards with his thumb. It clinked softly as it slid into place in the chamber. He closed the bolt. His breathing was calm and slow. "I'll need absolute quiet and no movement at all, please," he said to Howard and Ziegler. "I have to concentrate."

The burly figure of the Iraqi President mounted the platform and walked towards the rostrum in its centre. The assembled crowd fell silent. Slowly he mounted the steps of the rostrum. The Iranian and his aide had taken up a position on the platform to the right of the rostrum, with the President's retinue on the left. Two senior Iraqi aides on the platform were talking quietly to each other. The figure of Saddam Hussein reached the top step of the rostrum and stood still. He raised his right arm to acknowledge the salute of the gathered troops below.

Behind the spotter scope, Howard's face suddenly creased with worry. "There's something wro—"

The crash of the rifle shook the hide as MacDonald fired. Howard's vision blurred as the spotter scope shook. MacDonald was reloading swiftly. "I said quiet, damn it!" he shouted angrily at Howard. "Watch for the strike!"

The big bullet took nearly two seconds to travel across the open ground towards its target. The motor drive on the camera, activated by Howard, began to whirr noisily. Both Howard and MacDonald were watching through their telescopes; suddenly they saw the burly figure on the rostrum lifted violently off his feet, as though by an unseen force. He was spun round and flung backwards, crumpling below the steps of the rostrum, dead.

The men on the platform stood frozen in shock. One of Saddam's aides drew his pistol and held it aloft, as if ready to fire. The aides made no move towards the body; they gazed wildly around them. In the crowd, the first cries and shrieks of alarm broke out.

Crash. The big rifle fired again. Howard and Ziegler were taken completely by surprise. They seemed to hear MacDonald yell "Allah!" at the top of his lungs.

"What the hell . . . "Howard turned furiously on MacDonald, whose eye was still glued to the rifle scope. "Stop it, for Christ's sake! What the fuck are you doing?"

MacDonald was still watching through his scope, his eyes ablaze. As he watched, the second bullet hit the aide with the pistol, low in the stomach. The man suddenly doubled up and fell to the floor, writhing. MacDonald's eyes were now triumphant.

"Mac, for fuck's sake!" bellowed Howard. "Stop now. Just stop! That wasn't Saddam, I'm telling you! It wasn't him!"

MacDonald turned to him. "What do you mean? He's dead! I hit him smack in the middle of the chest with the first shot. Look for yourself, man!"

Down below in the arena, pandemonium had broken out. People in the crowd were shouting and screaming, milling about in confusion and panic. The Presidential bodyguard, as confused and panicked as the rest, had begun firing their weapons at random into the crowd. The supersonic crack of MacDonald's first arriving bullet had disorientated them; by the time the rifle's report reached the arena, the chorus of alarm had already started and the distant thump of the rifle was drowned out. The men in Saddam's retinue had dived off the platform, leaving the bodies of their leader and his aide lying there. The big man in the black beret lay still; the aide wounded by MacDonald's second shot was moving weakly. The Iranian diplomat was grabbed by two men from the bodyguard and wrestled to the ground, his arms yanked up viciously behind his back, his face forced down into the dust. The bodyguard continued firing; men and women in the crowd fell dead and injured by the fire as civilians and conscripts scattered in terror.

BOOM! The ground shook as a tongue of grey-black smoke erupted from the barrel of a T-72 tank at the left-hand side of the arena. The 125 mm shell screeched over the heads of the terrified crowd and the unarmed conscript soldiers. The firing from the bodyguard slackened as they looked round in bewilderment.

BOOM! A second shell was fired by the T-72. Crowd and conscripts flattened themselves in the dust of the arena. The firing from the bodyguard ceased. The rumbling echo of the two shells reached the ears of the three men in the hide; then there was silence.

"OK, let's get the fuck out of here," said Ziegler, calmly. "I don't fancy stickin' around to watch the goddam celebrations."

"No!" snapped Howard, his eye still fixed to the spotter scope. "Wait. I'm telling you, that was not Saddam! It was a double!"

"What the hell do you mean?" asked MacDonald.

"He wasn't wearing a pistol," said Howard. "The bastard always has a pistol. He's never been known not to carry it. It's practically his trademark. That must have been a double. We have to wait."

"Aw, shit," said Ziegler.

All three of them now turned to watch the scene. At the side of the arena, heavy steel doors crashed open as a line of BMP-1 tracked personnel-carriers behind the T-72 disgorged their occupants. A hundred more armed men of the Amn al Khass Presidential bodyguard emerged; after assembling into a disciplined body they approached the saluting platform on the double. They cut a swathe through the crowd, trampling those already on the ground, until they reached the centre of the arena. The officer in charge shouted a harsh order. His men fanned out, their weapons trained on the men of the first guard detail around the platform. The officer bawled out a series of commands at them; the original bodyguard troops slowly put down their weapons and raised their hands.

The second detachment of the bodyguard advanced on the first. They snatched their weapons away and made them kneel down in the dust, cuffing them and shoving them roughly into a line. Protests were silenced with clubbing blows from rifle butts.

"I think they change the guard better at Buckingham Palace," commented Ziegler. "Those assholes don't have a clue what's happened."

The men of the original detachment of the Amn al Khass were now all on their knees; the new arrivals had taken charge. When the commander was satisfied that everything was as he wished, he barked out another order. Six men accompanied him as he marched briskly away to the side of the arena. He halted in front of the T-72 tank and stood stiffly to attention.

The turret hatch on the tank swung slowly up; the man inside began to lever himself out. His face, below a black beret, came into view; it was smouldering with fury and malice.

Saddam Hussein climbed heavily down from the tank and dusted off his uniform shirt with an elaborate gesture. For a few seconds he stood by the vehicle, staring malevolently around him, his eyes blinking. Inch by inch he unfastened his belt holster and drew his automatic pistol, cocking the action. There was absolute silence. Every man in the arena seemed to have heard the sound of the pistol being cocked; a few people raised their heads to look and then shrank back into the dust in fear. The bodyguard commander and his men wilted beneath the menacing glare of the tyrant. He waved them aside with his pistol and advanced steadily towards the platform in the arena. The bodyguard fell in at his side as he swaggered through the crowd of people still prostrate on the ground. Some scrabbled frantically to get out of his path; those too petrified to move were kicked and beaten aside by the guards.

Saddam took his time. He spun it out, well aware of the terrifying effect of his appearance. To Howard, MacDonald and Ziegler, it seemed that there was no one else in the arena. The man's presence was colossal and unmistakable. They knew, as did all those in the arena, that this time there was no doubt.

Saddam Hussein reached the platform and stopped. He glanced briefly at his dead look-alike, and then at the wounded aide, who was still alive and moaning in agony as blood continued to ooze from his stomach. He turned away from both and spat out an order to the guard commander.

Two soldiers unceremoniously lifted the Iranian diplomat from the ground and dragged him forward towards the Iraqi President. They flung him down at Saddam's feet. The Iranian struggled to raise himself; he was instantly clubbed back down by a rifle butt. His black turban came loose under the force of the blow and tumbled limply into the dirt. Saddam lifted his pistol and shot the Iranian in the back of the head. The corpse was dragged away.

The commander of the original guard detachment was next. He too was hauled before the President, writhing and babbling in terror and desperation. He looked briefly into Saddam's eyes and went slack. Again Saddam's pistol fired; the man collapsed dead.

One by one, the men from the first guard detachment were brought forward for execution. MacDonald realised that Saddam was not going to move. Each man was being dragged right to the spot where he stood, to be shot. Almost imperceptibly, MacDonald stiffened. Sensing that he was about to fire, Howard and Ziegler held themselves absolutely motionless and watched in fascination.

MacDonald gazed through the telescopic sight. The figure of Saddam was shimmering a little; the mirage effect in the gradually increasing heat was now more pronounced. Out of the corner of his eye MacDonald saw the shimmer of rising air at the bottom of the sight picture drift slightly off to the left. *A very slight wind*, he thought. Instinctively, he aimed off a foot to the right. He let out a slow breath. The cross-hairs of the telescopic sight aligned on the right-hand edge of Saddam Hussein's body and remained perfectly still. MacDonald squeezed the trigger.

The big rifle bucked in MacDonald's shoulder once more, and the bullet streaked towards its target, past the two anemometers, over the crowd of prostrate Iraqis, heading for the tyrant.

What made the shot go low was uncertain. A sudden downdraught of air somewhere along its route, an infinitesimal difference in the bullet weight or the powder load, a distortion of the sight picture due to the mirage, the minutest flinch by MacDonald, or the fact that the rifle barrel was now hot from the first two shots: MacDonald would never know.

Saddam Hussein was standing stock-still on the front edge of the platform with his legs slightly apart, his right arm outstretched downwards with the pistol ready to fire at the man sprawled at his feet. The rifle bullet smashed against the barrel of Saddam's pistol and ricocheted off the metal slide. The pistol flew out of his hand and the bullet, now partly spent, spun sideways on into the lower part of Saddam's pelvic bone. The bone shattered where the bullet hit it, and the bullet and small pieces of bone were driven back through his genitals, almost completely severing his penis and testicles.

Saddam let out a piercing howl and sat down heavily. The weight of his body on the cracked pelvis was instant agony, and he fell back on the platform, drawing his knees up and clutching his hands between his legs. Blood seeped through his fingers and torn uniform trousers on to the wooden platform. Those standing near him drew back in horror, and the man who had been on the point of being shot scrambled frantically away. The extent of the President's injury was suddenly visible to everyone in the arena as he lay squealing in pain.

For just one second, there was dead silence except for Saddam's noises of distress; then all hell broke loose. Once again, the noise erupted just in time to cover the rifle's report as it reached the crowd. The condemned men of the first Amn al Khass detachment, seeing their chance, broke free of their shocked captors and scrabbled for their weapons. The second detachment recovered in time to shoot down a number of them, but many managed to grab AKs and turn them on their rivals. A full-scale battle between the two factions of the bodyguard broke out around the platform. The guard commander was one of the first to be cut down, and with him died the last vestige of order. In less than a minute, more than sixty members of the bodyguard lay dead or wounded; many more of the crowd were hit in the wild crossfire. The bodyguard troops, firing off long unrestrained bursts from their Kalashnikovs, began to run out of ammunition and resorted in desperation to hand-to-hand fighting.

Among the conscript soldiers watching helplessly was a regiment of the Iraqi artillery. They were the remains of three entire artillery divisions from the 1991 Gulf War, practically wiped out by American B-52 bombing in the days preceding the land assault by the Allies. They had been helpless then, sitting in what they had thought were well-prepared defensive bunkers within Kuwait, waiting for orders to use their D-30 howitzers; the rolling thunder of the B-52s had rendered their pitiful defences useless. In one regiment alone, over ninety per cent of the men had been killed. The survivors, gaunt, deafened and thoroughly shell-shocked, were little better than zombies. Any spirit these men had once had was broken; they were listless and brutalised, and in most cases mentally unhinged. They had been reorganised into a single regiment; an injection of new officers from the Iraqi Republican Guard, drafted in after the war to reassert discipline and restore morale, had had little effect. The men's loathing and terror of warfare remained, and to a man they had focused their unspoken hatred on the one individual they saw as responsible for their own and their country's suffering. Saddam had indeed been wise not to allow such soldiers to be armed on occasions such as this.

Along with the thousands of Tikriti civilians, these men had scattered in panic when the firing from the Presidential bodyguard had begun raking through the crowd. Used to the perpetual, numbing barbarity of their existence, in no position to control their own lives, they would in most circumstances have submitted meekly to any further imposition of authority. They were fatalistic, mere ciphers, incapable of independent action.

Now in shock once again from the events of the previous few minutes, they would probably have acted in character and offered no resistance even if they themselves had been lined up, one by one, for execution. Except that this time, there was one extraordinary difference. They had seen it with their own eyes. Raising their heads, they could still see it. The sight of Saddam's élite bodyguard turning on itself was astonishing enough, but it was the other vision that now seared itself into their minds. It was the sight of the dictator himself, lying in agony on the platform, his manhood most visibly shot away, exposed for all to see. They gaped at him in utter disbelief. Then a young corporal started giggling.

Within seconds, impotent with laughter, others had joined in. The laughter became hysterical. Tears of frenzied hilarity and rage swept through the ranks of the conscripts. Somewhere within these men the last spark of spirit, which even they themselves had thought extinguished, was rekindled. Smoking anger, long and deeply buried, burst violently into life. Slowly, at first, and then in a sudden rush, they rose up and threw themselves with deadly purpose on the men of the Amn al Khass.

The surviving members of the bodyguard hardly saw them coming; within seconds they were overwhelmed. Buried beneath huge numbers of shrieking, snarling, maddened conscripts, they were clubbed and hacked to death. In two minutes, not one man from the bodyguard was left alive. The conscripts then turned their wrath on the armoured column, and stormed the lines of vehicles. They swarmed over them and engulfed the occupants.

The townspeople of Tikrit rose too. Brainwashed, bereaved, starved and impoverished by the policies of the ruler who had risen to brutal power from their own humble town, they too had seen the dictator lying helpless and humiliated on the platform. The Traitor of Tikrit! They converged on him, fury in their hearts.

Howard, MacDonald and Ziegler had been watching the spectacle unfold, unable to wrest their eyes from the tide of chaotic violence. Over half a mile away, they felt curiously detached from the events they had set in motion, yet the ferocity of the uprising down in the arena was almost tangible.

"What the hell are they doing now?" Howard muttered, more to himself than to the others.

A small group of civilians had commandeered an Army jeep, and were driving it into the centre of the arena. It was soon surrounded by a tumult of yelling people, waving and gesticulating excitedly. After a minute or so, the crowd parted to form a passage for the jeep, which started forward. There was a jerk, and then a howl from the seething mob. For a moment or two, the three men in the hide could see nothing. The roaring chant of the crowd reached their ears. "*Sahhl! Sahhl! Sahhl!*"

The jeep cleared the bulk of the crowd and began circling the arena. Behind it, tied by the feet and being towed by a rope along the ground, was the still-living body of Saddam Hussein.

"Christ!" breathed MacDonald. They watched open-mouthed as the screaming figure was dragged along at speed, flayed and lacerated by the stones on the hard ground, his blood mingling with the dust.

"Time to go," said Howard.

The three men hurriedly began packing essential equipment into the rucksacks. In the distance, the chants of the surging crowd continued. MacDonald forced himself to concentrate, stowing the big rifle carefully in its sleeve. He pocketed the empty cases of the three rounds he had fired, then turned to help Howard. Ziegler crawled out of the hide and kept watch to the rear.

Working as fast as possible, they took only a very short time to finish packing up the few items they would need: weapons, some water, the night-vision goggles, the film from the camera. The remaining equipment was left where it was. They moved off quickly, heading back towards the vehicles.

The arena was now almost completely obscured by dust; the three men did not look back. MacDonald's mind was churning with the images of what he had seen; he followed mutely as Howard and Ziegler picked their way through the palm orchards and fields.

Behind them, the death screams of Saddam Hussein seemed to rise high above the exultant roar of the crowd, and then fade.

PART THREE

THE SHADOW IS LIFTED

63

It was 01.35 in Washington when the first unusual Keyhole picture came through. A KH-12 had passed over Tikrit six minutes earlier, at 08.29 Iraqi time. Kearwin, who had been watching the JSTARS screen, had seen the arrival of the helicopter; nothing else had shown up except the movement of a small vehicle, probably a jeep, circling the open area where the mass of armour was concentrated.

The KH-12 image was unusual in that it indicated sources of abnormal heat in the arena, along with some smoke obscuration. After comparing the picture with that of a KH-11 pass of twenty minutes earlier, Kearwin did an analysis of the heat sources. "Walter, there are definitely six vehicles on fire there!" He spoke rapidly, his voice rising. "Now, look at this little jeep here. And you see all those other vehicles? They're all lined up perfectly. Here's the helicopter, and this looks like a staff car or something. The rest is all military – tanks, scout cars, APCs – the convoys JSTARS saw coming into town. And it's all lined up. All except the jeep. It's got to be the one we've been tracking going round and round this open area. Why would it be doing that? And if everything else is normal, why in hell would these six vehicles be on fire?"

Walter Sorensen was thinking hard. Something had happened; no question about it. But what? "OK, John, let's think this thing through. Twenty minutes ago, we have an orderly scene – vehicles lined up, everything looking just dandy. A helicopter arrives. Let's say Saddam's on board. He gets out to inspect the troops or whatever. Fifteen minutes later, things start to go haywire. Suddenly this damn jeep starts rushing around and six tanks are on fire. What's going on?"

Kearwin was emphatic. "They must have killed him, or tried to. What else could it be? There's something more," he added. "The readings from the open area are different from the earlier pass. It could be something to do with the smoke from the burning vehicles, but I don't think so. I was a bit puzzled about those readings, but I think what we saw earlier was a large body of people in that square. All lined up, like the vehicles. Foot soldiers, maybe – lots of them. Now the readings are different. I would guess there are still a lot of people there, but no longer in neat lines. The ceremony has fallen apart. It's chaos down there, is what I think."

"I agree. Let's assume you're right about the people. Maybe they've panicked. Six burning tanks, so would anybody. And that jeep running around. That makes three elements of chaos. So maybe there *has* been an attempt to get Saddam. That leaves just two questions, doesn't it?" The Walrus, still staring fixedly at the screen, spoke in a low voice, almost to himself. "One, how did a handful of Westerners manage to achieve that? And two, more importantly, is Saddam still alive?"

"He's dead, Walter," replied Kearwin without hesitation.

The Walrus looked at the younger man curiously. "What makes you say that?"

"The helicopter. It hasn't moved. Nor has anything else. Just that jeep, driving round in circles. If Saddam was alive, he would have got out pretty fast once that trouble started, wouldn't he? Nothing has got out. He's dead. They did it!" Kearwin's voice had risen to an excited shout. There was an outbreak of unrestrained cheering from the others in the room.

The Walrus held up his hands. "QUIET!" he bellowed. "God damn it, this is no matter for celebration! Hell, I know no one will be sorry to see the sonofabitch dead, but there are other issues at stake here . . ."

"Thank you, Walter." The Walrus spun round, and all eyes turned to the figure who, unnoticed, had entered the room. It was the DNRO. Kearwin jumped to his feet and stood stiffly to attention with the others. "Mr Sorensen is right," said Martin Faga calmly. "This is not necessarily a matter for celebration." He turned to Kearwin. "You have done a fine job, young man. So have all of you," he continued, looking round at the others. His voice hardened. "But you are to keep your personal feelings and opinions in this matter to yourselves. There are indeed other considerations at stake, as

384

Mr Sorensen has said. I don't want any repetition of this unruly behaviour. Is that understood?"

There were embarrassed mumbles of "Yes, sir," and "I'm sorry, sir," from the analysts. The Walrus, who had blushed a deep red, muttered, "It won't happen again, sir."

"Good," said the DNRO. "Now, you still have a job to do here. All of you. I still want those men to be shadowed. I'm relying on you not to lose them. You've done damn well so far, and I'm proud of you. I know I can rely on you to keep it up. Now, get to it! And no more of that stupid nonsense, please." Faga spun round abruptly and left the room; the analysts watched him go in silence.

Ten minutes later, as the subdued analysts were concentrating earnestly on their screens, Walter Sorensen was still trying to decide whether his section had just been given one hell of a roasting, or one hell of a big pat on the back.

64

The three men made little attempt to avoid being seen on the way back to the vehicles. In broad daylight, there would have been little point; and Howard had decided that speed was more important than concealment. Dressed in dishevelled and dirty Arab clothing, they carried the rucksacks slung over the shoulder, instead of wearing them conventionally. The AKMSs were concealed beneath their robes, their stocks folded. The only large item was the big AW rifle; MacDonald, without a rucksack, carried this slung across one shoulder with a bundle of sticks, to make it look as though he was simply carrying firewood.

In the event, they came across few people. Most of the local population, Howard assumed, had obeyed the summons to Tikrit to attend Saddam's birthday rally. Scattered groups of women and children gazed at them incuriously as they hurried past, but no one made any attempt to stop or question them. A party of women tending to a crop of water-melons in a field even waved at them as they passed.

As before, Howard's chief anxiety was the crossing of the main north-south highway; it was the only time when he stopped and made sure that there was no one to see them. There was no traffic and they crossed it unhindered and unobserved.

At 09.15 they were getting close to the vehicle hide. Howard took out his small VHF radio and spoke the single word "*Thalaatha*" – the Arabic word for "three" – into it. Bourne's reply of "*Arba'a*" – "four" – came back almost immediately. Five minutes later, they breasted the rise and approached the walled enclosure. As they drew near, Howard's simple thumbs-up told Bourne and the others all they needed to know; the three men were greeted with broad grins and pumping handshakes. Usher remained on guard while Bourne directed them to three large bowls full of clean water; stripping off their dirty clothes, they began washing off the accumulated filth of their thirty-hour stay in the Tikrit hide.

"Well, I think someone ought to put up a sign for this country sayin' 'UNDER NEW MANAGEMENT'," whispered Ziegler with a grin as he soaped himself down. "Mind you, I don't suppose anyone's figured out yet who's goin' to be takin' the job on. Nasty end, Saddam had. Just as well Mrs Saddam wasn't there to see it."

"What happened?" asked Bourne eagerly, laying out three sets of clean clothing.

"Well, our Scotchman gets the first guy clean through the ticker. Trouble is, it turns out he's not the real Saddam, see? Then Mac gets a bit overenthusiastic," confided Ziegler, frowning at the memory and darting a glance in MacDonald's direction. "He hauls off and plugs this other guy standin' nearby, just mindin' his own business. Anyhow," he continued, "all hell breaks loose, with the bodyguard people loosin' off their AKs into the crowd. Then a tank pops off a couple of shells of heavy-duty ordnance over their heads, to quieten them down a little. Then out jump some more bodyguard guys. They arrest the first lot. Assholes." Ziegler tossed his head disgustedly. "Anyway, guess who climbs out of the tank? Old Saddam himself. And I'm tellin' you, this time there's no doubt about it. He looks kind of pissed off, if you get my meanin'. So he takes over the show, and starts shootin' a few guys with his personal hand-gun. He starts with an Iranian mullah, which should be good for a diplomatic incident, and then carries on with his own people. That's when Mac lets him have it."

"Danny killed him with one shot?" Bourne's eyes were bright.

"Not exactly," grinned Ziegler. "But I'm tellin' you, he gave him the mother of all vasectomies."

"What?" asked Bourne, astounded.

"Yeah," said Ziegler. "Blew all his landin' gear off. Real nasty. Boy, was he squealin'. Anyway, at this point, the crowd decides to join in. Soldiers, civilians, the lot. They go crazy. They wipe out the bodyguard and stomp all over the tanks. Then they grab a jeep. They tie Saddam to the trailer-hitch and tow him around for a while, so everyone can admire Mac's handiwork. I guess they didn't really like him too much after all. That's when we decided to leave." Ziegler paused as he bent down to scrub the soles of his feet. "But I'll tell you somethin'," he went on, "jumpin' out of that tank when two of his guys had already been shot was a pretty goddam stupid thing for the man to do. I dare say he thought his bodyguard people had things under control by then, but he couldn't have been more wrong. Saddam was suckered, good and proper."

"Come on, you two," said Howard, towelling himself dry and pulling on a clean shirt, "stop gassing and let's go. Johnny, Ack, get the cam nets off those cars and put the flags up."

All six men were ready, dressed in ordinary civilian shirts and trousers, by 09.30. Bourne, Ackford and Usher had already shaved; MacDonald, Ziegler and Howard attacked their two-week-old stubble with electric razors and watched as the camouflage nets were pulled off the two Land Cruisers. With the dirt and the top coat of matt green now gone, the two cars were resplendent, looking almost brand-new.

They mounted up, started the engines and drove away, heading down the slope and then turning left towards the main highway past Tikrit. Now that all need for concealment had passed, they drove at speed. They reached the highway at 09.45 and turned north, towards Bayji.

Seven time zones away in Washington, John Kearwin breathed a sigh of relief as the JSTARS screen picked up the movement.

65

The road was eerily empty; they saw no traffic at all. Behind the wheel of the lead vehicle, Bourne was visibly tense. After a while, he asked Howard, "How long do you reckon before they put up some air cover?"

"Impossible to say," shrugged Howard. "With any luck, things are so confused right now that they're in a state of complete paralysis. We saw some Hind gunships flying around before the Presidential helicopter arrived, but they cleared off before Saddam got there. I expect they had orders to keep well clear until he had left. Maybe they won't be put up at all. Perhaps the road's empty for the same reason. Who knows? Anyway, from what we saw, those vehicles at Tikrit aren't likely to move. The conscripts took them out. They set fire to some of them, too. It couldn't have worked out better, from our point of view. It may be quite a while before any sort of order is restored."

"We've done nearly thirty miles from Tikrit already. Should be at Bayji soon . . . oh, *Christ*," said Bourne as they rounded a bend in the road, "look at that!"

Two hundred yards in front of them, the road was completely blocked with military vehicles and barriers. Armed soldiers leapt to their feet and levelled their rifles as the two Land Cruisers approached and slowed. There was no possibility of escape. "Red berets," muttered Howard. "Shit!"

"Republican Guard," said Bourne. "Bloody hundreds of them. Fuck it! OK, is it going to be you or me?"

"My turn," replied Howard, "but you'd better come along just in case. Danny, you stay in the car." The vehicles rolled to a stop in front of the barriers. Howard and Bourne slowly climbed out and faced the line of rifles and machine-guns pointed at their chests.

* * *

"They've had it, Walter," groaned Kearwin, despondently. "Jesus, they've had it this time. Look!"

The Walrus examined the screen. It was clear what had happened. The two cars had run slap into a major road-block. "Get a Keyhole picture of it, John," he said gently. "I want as much detail as you can get." He continued staring at the screen. Kearwin had identified the other traffic, and there was no doubt that it was military. Light armour and trucks – and plenty of it. Young Kearwin was right. They'd put their heads right into a noose, this time. "Damn fools!" grunted the Walrus vehemently.

* * *

Major Hassan Omair looked up, annoyed, as a lieutenant barged rudely into his command tent. "*Shu tureed?*" he snapped.

"*Ghurb,*" replied the officer insolently, jerking his thumb over towards the road. "*Ta'al.*"

"What do you mean, foreigners? What foreigners? And stand to attention, curse you! Remember who you are talking to!"

"*Inglizi.* English. They demand to see you – sir," drawled Lieutenant Saleh Masoud with a sneer.

The Major stood up, surprised. Squaring his red beret on his head, he followed his subordinate out into the sun. Two Westerners were leaning nonchalantly against the front car. One was drumming his fingers impatiently on the bonnet and the other was pointedly studying his wrist-watch. The Major grinned. "You fool," he said contemptuously. "Have you never seen such vehicles as these before?" The Lieutenant looked uncertain, and the Major continued acidly, "Have you checked their papers? No? A minor detail even such as that is beyond your limited capability? Well," – he waved his arm in disgust – "get back to your post, imbecile. I will do it myself. And smarten yourself up!"

Lieutenant Saleh Masoud scowled and moved off, muttering under his breath.

The Major walked over to the cars and addressed the older of the two men standing by the first vehicle. "*Sabaah al-khayr*," he said. "Good morning."

The tall man allowed his companion to answer on both their behalves. "*Sabaah an-noor*," came the second man's fluent rejoinder; he continued with a polite expression of hope that the Major was well, then finally introduced himself and his tall colleague.

"I congratulate you on your command of our language, Sayyid Bourne," said the Major in Arabic. "It will make our conversation much easier. May I examine your credentials and those of your colleagues?"

"Certainly, Major," replied Bourne, continuing in Arabic. "We have all the necessary documentation in the other vehicle. I think you will find everything in order. Perhaps if you would care . . .?" He gestured towards the second car; he and the Major walked over to it.

Ziegler wound down the window and flashed the Major a bright smile. "Hi," he said.

The Major looked momentarily nonplussed.

"The papers, Mike," prompted Bourne in English.

"Oh, sure," said Ziegler, fishing under the dashboard. He produced a folder of documents and handed them through the window.

The Major glanced through the papers in the folder, his face expressionless. Behind him, three soldiers had taken up station with their rifles, still suspicious of the foreigners. Ziegler's eyes flickered from one to the other. Underneath his seat, his hand closed on his AKMS.

"Where have you come from today, Sayyid Bourne?" asked the Major in a matter-of-fact tone.

"We have driven up from Baghdad, Major," answered Bourne.

"What's he sayin', Johnny?" asked Ziegler conversationally, his smile still fixed.

"Well, Mr Bourne," the Major said pleasantly, suddenly switching to flawless English, "it is unfortunate for you that not only can I speak your language, but also I can read it. Furthermore, I have had occasion to examine similar accreditation papers recently. There was a Mr Kay here in Iraq a matter of a few weeks ago, and I recall that he made quite a nuisance of himself. His papers, unfortunately, were in order. Sadly," he added, "your documentation is not, shall we say, quite of the calibre of his. These papers do not authorise your presence in this part of the country." He gave Bourne a look of unconcealed interest. "Well, Mr Bourne?"

While the Major was speaking, Ziegler had seen Howard slowly and casually inching closer, blocking the view of the three soldiers behind the Major. The Major's hand began to move to the pistol holster on his belt.

"Don't do it, Major," growled Ziegler, poking the silencer of his AKMS just above the window-sill of the car. "This here is a silenced AK. It's the real thing. Don't you even twitch a goddam muscle." He smiled brilliantly at the dumbfounded expression on the Major's face; the man had been taken completely by surprise.

Before the Major could react, Howard addressed him from behind, his voice light and affable. "OK, Major. As my colleague says, don't do anything rash. We are all armed, and we will not hesitate to shoot if we have to. Just keep looking at those papers and listen carefully to me. We'll take things one step at a time. Do you understand?"

"Yes," said Major Hassan Omair in a shocked whisper.

"Good. First of all, we'll try something very simple. When I tell you, I want you to turn round nice and slowly. Then I want you to dismiss those three soldiers right behind us here. Tell them to get back to their posts. And don't even think of warning them – Mr Bourne here speaks excellent Arabic, as you have heard. One word from him and Mr Ziegler will shoot you down. Are you ready, Major?"

"Yes."

"Good. Do it."

The Major turned round, his face a blank mask. "You three," he croaked at the soldiers in Arabic, "return to your posts."

The soldiers obeyed. Howard said, "That was fine, Major. Now; the next thing we're going to do is walk slowly over to the other car. Mr Ziegler will be covering you from here, and you can probably see Mr MacDonald there in the front car. He has a silenced AK on you too. Do you see him?"

"I see him," replied the Major. He could see MacDonald clearly; he wasn't to know that the stalker was unaware of what had happened. MacDonald's AKMS was in fact still stowed out of sight beneath his seat.

"Fine. Let's just walk over there now. When you get there, I want you to stand with your back to the front passenger door. Understood?" The Major nodded, and they walked the few yards across to the other car. Howard inclined his head to speak through the rear window. "Danny, keep your AK trained on the back of the Major's head. If Johnny says fire, shoot him instantly. Now, Major," he smiled, straightening up, the friendly note still in his voice, "we're going to try something a little more complicated. Let me explain exactly what you're going to do."

MacDonald had nearly had a fit when Howard had spoken; he carefully reached for his AK and held it out of sight below the window-sill, trained on the Iraqi officer's back. He listened as Howard gave instructions to the Major, stopping every now and then to check that he had understood.

The Major was still in a state of shock, and Howard's insistent monologue gave him little time to think. He nodded his acquiescence. Finally, mustering his thoughts, he said, "You cannot hope to get away with this."

Howard's mouth was still smiling, but his eyes were not. They bored into those of the Iraqi officer. "We have nothing to lose, Major. You know that. If it comes to it, we are prepared to die. I'm sure you will understand," he said sourly, "that from our point of view, death would be infinitely preferable to capture. But if we die, you will die first. There is no necessity for that to happen if you do exactly as I say. Do you understand?"

"I understand."

"Good. Give the orders."

"Are you sure you want that particular officer . . . ?"

"He is suspicious. I want him where I can see him. Call him over, now. And give him the orders."

The Major began to shake himself out of his numb stupefaction. Pointing at one of the soldiers manning the barrier, he ordered, "Go and fetch Lieutenant Saleh Masoud at once." The soldier trotted obediently off, and two minutes later returned with the sullen-looking Lieutenant.

As the Major explained what he wanted, Saleh Masoud's face darkened with indignation. Twice he tried to interrupt with objections. The Major, caught between the duress under which he was being obliged to act and the insolence of his subordinate, lost his temper with the Lieutenant and shouted at him to be silent. "Hold your tongue! Do as you are ordered! Go and prepare the vehicles! Now!"

The Lieutenant opened his mouth to protest one final time, but he saw the fury on the face of his commander and thought better of it. Turning on his heel, he strode off.

"Was that all OK, Johnny?" asked Howard.

"Everything just as you asked," replied Bourne.

"Fine," said Howard. "OK, Major. You've done well, so far. Here's how we're going to do it. You're going to travel in front here, with Mr Bourne driving. Mr MacDonald and I will be in the back of the car. Tell your lieutenant that ours will be the lead vehicle. He is to be in the BRDM armoured car, right behind us; our second car will be behind that, and then the two trucks bringing up the rear. Got it?"

"If you say so."

"I do say so," flashed back Howard, his eyes like steel. "When they're ready, get the vehicle commanders over here and tell them what we're going to do. And make it sound convincing. That way, we'll all live to tell the tale."

Ten minutes later, the small escort convoy had been drawn up. Ackford had reversed a few yards to allow a BRDM-2 armoured scout car to slot into place between the two Land Cruisers; two trucks, each with a complement of fifteen red-bereted Republican Guardsmen, were lined up behind. Lieutenant Saleh Masoud, a second officer and two sergeants came over to report to the Major, who began his briefing.

"These foreigners," he said, "have authority to proceed to the Jordanian border at Trebil and out of Iraq. I have decided" – he managed a faint swagger of self-importance – "that in accordance with standing orders, we will provide a standard escort convoy to accompany them to the border in order to make sure that they do not deviate from their route and compromise the national security of Iraq. I will travel in front, in their vehicle. The remainder of the escort will follow in its present order. Lieutenant Aziz Ali," he continued, turning to the second officer, "you will remain here, in charge of this position. You know the orders." The officer nodded eagerly. "We shall return tomorrow morning," concluded the Major; "now, get those barriers moved aside and we'll be on our way."

Lieutenant Aziz Ali, delighted with the unexpected responsibility he had been given, immediately began shouting orders to the soldiers on the barriers. Grinning unreservedly at the thought of the unlikable

Saleh Masoud having to spend the best part of two days cooped up inside a hot and uncomfortable BRDM, he gleefully took command. The barriers were pushed to one side, and the convoy moved off behind the lead Land Cruiser. As they passed through the barrier, the beaming Aziz Ali yelled a coarse comment at his colleague in the BRDM. The soldiers standing by the barrier laughed.

"I reckon," said Ziegler to Ackford as they followed the BRDM through, "you just heard the Arabic for 'Have a nice day'."

"It sounded more like 'Up yours' to me," countered Usher. "Jeez," he added, breathing a heavy sigh of relief, "I do believe we've pulled it off."

*   *   *

John Kearwin was studying a computer-enhanced KH-12 image of the road-block when the JSTARS screen showed vehicle movement. For a moment there was confusion; then the moving vehicles, drawing clear of the stationary ones, resolved into five distinct patterns. One light armoured, two large thin-skinned, and two smaller cars, he decided. The image was too hazy for Kearwin to be definite, but he thought on balance that the two smaller vehicles could not be the Land Cruisers. Why would one of them be in the lead? No, he thought, they couldn't be them.

He concentrated on the ten-minute-old print-out of the Keyhole picture. The two Land Cruisers were clearly visible in the road in front of the barrier. They had made no attempt to avoid it; at the same time they clearly hadn't crashed into it.

They must have been arrested, thought Kearwin. But how could they just have given up so easily, after all they had done so far? It didn't make sense. No . . . "Jerry? Keep tracking those five vehicles on the JSTARS, will you?"

Kearwin studied the Keyhole picture again. It would be 10.37 a.m. in Iraq now. It was the first time the two Land Cruisers had appeared in daylight. The previous day, there had been something obscuring them in the walled enclosure, and Kearwin hadn't realised what it was until he had compared the infra-red and the visible-spectrum pictures. Camouflage nets. They couldn't conceal the infra-red, of course. But after the first night, the morning after their arrival at Tikrit, there had nevertheless been something slightly different about them, even through the camouflage nets, even with cold engines.

He called over to Sorensen. "Walter, those ambulances were reported as having been painted matt green, right?"

"That's what the man said."

"Well, I know we can't tell colours from a Keyhole shot, but I'm assuming Iraqi light armour is matt green too, and I can at least tell that these two cars here can't be the same colour. They're giving off a different reflection signature."

"Maybe Iraqi armour is sand-coloured, not matt green. Maybe that would explain it. I don't know. Do we know the colour of Iraqi armour? I never thought of asking before."

"It doesn't matter," said Kearwin. "If it *is* sand-coloured, then our two ambulances are even paler still. Look at the picture!"

Sorensen studied the image and sighed. "It's not much of a difference, John."

"But it's there," persisted Kearwin. "I think they've done a respray job on them."

"What if they have? And in any case, how in hell do you go about respraying a couple of cars in the middle of the goddam desert? More to the point, why would they do it?"

Kearwin now had the bit between his teeth. "I'm sure these guys had something up their sleeves. Why else would they drive straight into that road-block in broad daylight? Surely they would do what they did before, and wait for dark before sneaking out? Hey!" he yelped, smacking his fist into the palm of the other hand, his eyes alight. "I'm sure of it! I think they've pulled off another stunt here!"

"John," said the Walrus calmly, "just think about it. What good would it do them, driving about in plain undisguised cars? Think about it. They'd be bound to be picked up, wouldn't they?"

Kearwin ignored the Walrus's reasoning. "Walter, the CIA man from Riyadh went to Badanah, didn't he? He was the one who reported the fact that they were matt green, wasn't he? Let me talk to him. Let me give him a call, right now!"

The Walrus gave Kearwin a resigned look. "OK, John. If you want. But I don't see how it's going to make any difference."

Kearwin grabbed the telephone and spoke rapidly to the NRO switchboard operator, demanding a flash priority call to the US

Embassy in Riyadh. While waiting for the connection, he shouted excitedly across to Freedman. "Jerry! Don't lose those five vehicles! It's them! I know it's them!"

Ten minutes later, Kearwin had spoken direct to Alvin Kennings in Riyadh. The CIA man initially failed to see the point of the call; he sounded somewhat impatient when Kearwin persisted in asking him about the workshop at the Badanah construction camp. Yes, he said, he had seen some cans of paint. No, the reason he knew the Land Cruisers were matt green was because the Pakistani cook had told him they were. OK, sure there were signs of paint in the workshop. Matt green, like he said. But come to think of it, the hulk of the fourth vehicle appeared to have been used for practice with the paint-gun . . . Yes, that was it . . .

Kearwin put down the receiver, his face puzzled. "White paint. Gloss white, Walter. What sort of a crazy outfit would use white paint in Iraq . . .?"

Walter Sorensen and John Kearwin stared at each other in sudden realisation. "I'll be damned," breathed the Walrus, his mouth broadening in a huge grin. "These guys sure have got *balls*! If that don't beat all! They're masquerading as a goddam United Nations inspection team!"

66

Major Hassan Omair sat silent and brooding in the front of the Land Cruiser. He had recovered from his initial shock. He realised, too late, that he should have made some attempt to avoid what had happened; but the tall Englishman, Howard, had given him no time to think. And the other man, Bourne, spoke perfect Arabic – any attempt to warn his soldiers would have resulted in his own death. Or would it? He pondered over the question. Yes, he decided, it would. These men were extremely determined. There was no doubt in his mind that they meant what they said. And the man Howard had been right. Capture for them would indeed be an unenviable experience. In the hands of the Mukhabarat, the Iraqi security service, they would suffer unimaginable agonies and lingering, hideous deaths. The Major grimaced in disgust. He had nothing but contempt for the methods of the Mukhabarat. Animals, he thought angrily; depraved animals, serving their despotic master.

The Major hated Saddam Hussein and his regime. He paid token lip-service to Saddam, as did his colleagues, mouthing the required protestations of undying loyalty which everyone knew were meaningless. Everyone hated Saddam, he knew – everyone except the stupid ones, the sycophants, the thugs, the career bullies, the ones not fit to be called human. Men like that insolent dog Saleh Masoud, who would certainly never have been promoted beyond the rank of lance-corporal but for his slavish devotion to the Ba'ath Party; who trumpeted aloud his ritualistic approval of Saddam's repressive rule and parroted Saddam's absurd claims of victory in the wake of each disastrous defeat.

But who were these spies, the Major wondered, and what were they doing? Where had they got these United Nations vehicles from? Perhaps they had stolen them in Baghdad. They seemed genuine.

398

The black "UN" letters on the doors and rear would have been simple enough to fabricate, but not the blue flags with the white globe-and-laurel motif. And the cars themselves . . . Yes, these men must have come from Baghdad, as Bourne had said.

Or had they? The road closure . . . It extended all the way south, down to Samarra. God only knew why. The Major's company had been ordered to the Bayji power station, to close the road to all traffic. Another company of his regiment had been sent to Samarra to set up a similar road-block there; the remainder of the Tawakalna division of the Republican Guard was still in Kirkuk, dealing with those miserable Kurds. With the road blocked both north and south, how had the spies managed to pass along it? They couldn't have come all the way from Baghdad – they would have been stopped at Samarra. That meant they must have joined the road somewhere north of Samarra – at, say, ad-Dawr, or . . . Great God! Tikrit!

The blood drained from the Major's face as he realised what that meant. If it was true, it explained the point of the road-blocks in the first place. He had been slow, he told himself, not to have thought of it. As usual, he had simply followed orders, without asking the reason for them. He had long ago given up trying to understand the sense of some of the things he and his men had been ordered to do. Now he thought hard. Today's celebrations . . . that must be it. Saddam himself must have been at Tikrit – his home town. It was the only explanation. So, had these spies . . .? Merciful God, they must have made an attempt on the President's life! He shot a keen glance sideways at the Englishman, Bourne. There was a smile on the man's face and his eyes were bright, the Major noticed; there was a look about him of confidence, of success. Could it really be true . . .?

Howard, in the back of the car, broke his train of thought. "What happened over there, Major?" He gestured to a large ruined building set back from the road, inside the half-flattened remains of a wire fence.

"What? Oh – I don't know. War damage, I would imagine. Why do you ask?"

"No particular reason. I just thought you might know." Howard was grinning. Bourne turned his head briefly and caught Howard's eye; he winked. Both men had seen the small group of people standing by the wrecked warehouse, and had recognised the slight figure of the old man gesticulating at the ruins for the benefit of the others. *So that old guy did survive*, thought Howard. *Good luck to him.*

The Major misinterpreted the glance between the two men. He frowned angrily. "I do not see why you should regard it as amusing that your Air Force has wrecked so many buildings in my country."

"Believe me, Major, we don't find it amusing." Howard was frowning himself now. Reminded of the incident, he was still trying to decide what the attack on the warehouse had meant. "I just thought you might happen to know something about that particular building."

"Well, I do *not* know," snapped the Major. "Why should I? We are rarely kept informed about such matters."

Good, thought Howard. The Major obviously felt a fierce resentment about the paucity of information he was given. That meant he probably wouldn't know anything about a missing guard on the pontoon ferry at Hadithah, either. In fact, he might not even know that the bridge there was down. It was the next danger point, a place where the cars and the escort would have to stop; where the Major might try something – if he knew about it.

As it happened, the Major did not know about the bridge at Hadithah. If he had, he might have been able to think of a possible course of action. He had decided that he was not going to let these spies get away with what they were doing. Spies. Assassins? Whatever they were, he admitted to himself, he had a sneaking admiration for them. They were clearly extremely capable, and highly professional. If they had disposed of Saddam, they had done Iraq a favour, in his view. Nevertheless, they must not be allowed to escape. Much as he hated Saddam, the Major was an honourable man, and a patriot. The history of his country – of the whole of the Middle East, for that matter – was little more than a long-running saga of interference and exploitation by Westerners. What these men were doing was just another example of that interference. It could not be tolerated. The Major had decided what he would do. At Trebil, he would have a chance to act, when they had to stop at the border with Jordan.

Half an hour later, the Major was taken by surprise when Bourne swung the Land Cruiser off the road and began to pick his way down towards the Euphrates. "What are you doing?" he asked.

"The bridge is blown, Major. Wrecked. We have to take a ferry."

Shortly afterwards, they arrived at the ramp, and the Major saw that what Bourne had said was true. "How did you know about the bridge?"

"Air photographs, Major."

"I see."

They reached the jetty at the bottom of the ramp. "Get out of the car slowly, Major, and stand next to the door," said Howard. "If the Lieutenant or any of your other soldiers gets out of their vehicle, order them to get back in."

Lieutenant Saleh Masoud had decided to take the opportunity to stretch his legs. No sooner had he climbed down from the BRDM than his commanding officer curtly ordered him back inside. Complaining vociferously, he complied. The Major stifled a grin. It would be baking inside that BRDM. It served the insubordinate Saleh Masoud right.

The pontoon ferry was at the far side of the river, and they waited fifteen minutes for it to arrive. Unlike on the night when they had used it before, it was now manned not just by a single soldier but by a daytime crew of five Army engineers, commanded by a sergeant. The Sergeant took one look at the red-bereted Major and was at once attentive, ushering the vehicles politely on board the large craft.

"Don't talk to him, Major," said Howard. "Just tell him to get on with it and take us across."

The Sergeant was slightly puzzled by the presence of the UN cars, but was nevertheless not about to ask any questions of the stony-faced Republican Guard Major who barked the instruction at him. He had had enough trouble two days before, when it had been discovered that one of his corporals had apparently deserted.

The crossing went without a hitch. On the far side, the previously deserted villages of Hadithah, Beni Dahir and Haqlaniyah were busy with people. The Major was startled when Howard switched on the siren, his headlights and the flashing roof-light — now with its blue filter in place of the red one; Ackford, in the second UN car, did the same. The lights and sirens had the desired effect. People hastened to clear out of the way, staring blankly as the unusual convoy swept past.

By 13.30, they were on the open road leading to Rutbah, retracing the route they had taken three nights before. Progress was slower owing to the lumbering presence of the two trucks at the rear, but Howard was well satisfied. The biggest potential problem, he thought, was the Major. The man had clearly regained his wits. He would need to be watched.

67

"Are you absolutely certain of this?" The DNRO studied Kearwin's face closely.

"As certain as I can be, sir. Can I show you what I've got so far?"

"Please do." Faga leaned over the table as Kearwin spread out the series of Keyhole satellite photographs he had printed out.

"Here they are at the road-block, sir. You can see from this one that the reflection signatures of the vehicles are different to that of the Iraqi armour. It's not much, as Mr Sorensen says, but we checked with the CIA agent who had been to the Badanah camp, and he confirmed that white paint had been used." Kearwin paused; Faga looked up encouragingly, so he went on. "We followed them from the road-block, using the JSTARS. At this stage we had no confirmation, but then at the river they had to stop, and we got a second Keyhole shot. Here it is. The template matches up. It's them, and they have an Army escort. We've kept tracking them since then."

"How do you know they haven't simply been arrested?"

"Two reasons, sir. First, if they had been, why would they be taking that road? I would have thought they'd be taken to Baghdad. This is the road to Jordan. Second, they're going back the same way they came. It's too much of a coincidence. It must be them."

"And you agree with this, Walter?" Faga turned to Sorensen for an answer.

"Yes, sir, I do. At first I wasn't convinced, but it makes sense."

Martin Faga nodded. "Well, I think you're right about them pretending to be a UN team. For one thing, I can't offhand think of any other way they could have convinced the Iraqi Army that they have any business even *being* in Iraq. They would certainly have been arrested, possibly shot out of hand. And there's another reason

403

why they must have altered their appearance from the ambulance disguise they were using before. They are breaking the oldest rule in the military book, and they wouldn't be doing that unless either they had no choice or they were now effectively a different outfit."

"How's that, sir?" asked Kearwin. "What rule?"

"You've never been in the military, Kearwin, so I suppose there's no reason why you should know," said the DNRO. "It's simple. If you're on a mission into enemy territory, whether it's a short or a long mission, whether offensive – as in this case – or purely reconnaissance, whether on the ground, at sea or in the air, the rule is always the same. You never, *ever* take the same route to exit as you took to enter. You always return by a different one. Otherwise you're just asking to be ambushed." Faga gestured towards the Keyhole picture and nodded again. "These people would know that, probably better than anyone. They wouldn't risk travelling the same route twice unless they were posing as something completely different. To my mind, it confirms it. The UN idea fits. It must be right."

"As you say, sir," said Kearwin, "I don't know anything much about the military. But I think I've got a feel for these people. They've been unorthodox right from the start. They've pulled some stunts that have surprised us all the way along the line. What you say about them breaking that rule just convinces me all the more."

Faga smiled. "Once again, Kearwin, I have to say that you have done one hell of a fine job with this. You too, Walter – and all the others involved. I'll be going to the NSC with this assessment. When they hear about the phoney UN cars, they'll probably have a fit. I don't think I have to tell you what a ruckus there would be if this ever got out. Which," he added, raising his eyebrows and keeping them there, "looks pretty unavoidable, as things stand. Anyway, thank you, both of you. And keep it up."

As he left the DNRO's office, John Kearwin was glowing with pleasure. Coming from Martin Faga, that had been high praise.

68

The tall, scrawny man sat hunched forward at the end of the long table. Ugly pockmarks pitted the face below his henna-tinted red hair. His eyes flickered around the faces of his colleagues, moving restlessly from one to another. He noticed that they were all glancing around too; all appeared unsure, uncertain, possibly even . . . yes, frightened. All except the waxen-faced, bespectacled former Foreign Minister sitting half-way down on the left; he appeared inscrutable and smiling, as always. Or was that a sheen of sweat on his brow? Would even he be just as scared as the rest of them? Of course he would, thought the red-haired man. They had all been stunned when he had broken the news to them just five minutes before. The stench of terror pervaded the room like a stinking fog. But there was no time now for idle speculation as to the state of mind of any of his colleagues. He must strike hard, fast, like a snake; he must give them no chance to think, leave no room for argument. It was his one hope. He must show no weakness now. If he failed . . .

He was already half-way there. He had taken the Chair – the Chair that none of the others had ever dared occupy. The significance of his taking the Chair had certainly not been lost on them. Startled, horrified, they had stared at him open-mouthed as they filed into the room and saw him sitting there, at the head of the long table. They were bound to have known immediately what it must mean.

It had a perfect symmetry, decided the red-haired man. As Vice-President, he was the automatic successor, the one who had been destined to occupy the Chair when the time came, as it now had. But if one of the others had heard the news first, it would not have been automatic at all; perhaps he, Izzat Ibrahim, would not be sitting in the Chair now. One of them would have grabbed it – probably that diseased hyena the Deputy President.

405

But Sa'adi Tumah Abbas, formerly Minister of Defence and recently demoted to Presidential Military Adviser, subservient to the last, had come to him for instructions when he had heard. Izzat had known that one day he would. Had he not flattered the man, cultivated him, praised his ability? Had he not led him to believe that the Vice-President's influence counted for something? And had the dolt not believed it all? Yes. And Sa'adi Tumah's loyalty had been assured with the craftiest touch of all – the rumour about the Vice-President's health. He, Izzat Ibrahim, Vice-President of Iraq, Deputy Chairman of the Revolutionary Command Council and Deputy Commander-in-Chief of the Iraqi Armed Forces, was unwell. He would soon need surgery. The day would come when he would have to step down, and then . . .

Oh, yes; that was the glittering prize that Sa'adi Tumah now saw, not far from his grasp. *Hah*, thought Izzat Ibrahim. He was not *that* unwell. The operation was booked; in a few weeks he would fly to Jordan, and return in full health. Sa'adi Tumah Abbas would soon learn. In fact he would learn one lesson right now. The others would do the work, wield the knife. Izzat Ibrahim addressed him direct. "Brother Sa'adi, we are all grief-stricken to hear your report. Do you have anything further to add?"

The Presidential Military Adviser looked around miserably. "Alas, no, brother Izzat Ibrahim," he said. "Details are still very sketchy . . ." He began to repeat some of the information he had already given. Perhaps, thought Izzat Ibrahim, he was under the misguided impression that it made him sound important. Well, he was about to find out just how unimportant he was. Izzat had seen at least two of the others round the table pretty well ready to explode. One, on his left, was Sa'adi Tumah's successor as Defence Minister, the *khinzîr* Hussein Kamil Hassan al-Majid. Izzat could see from his expression that he was furious at not having been informed earlier. The other, on his right, was the Deputy President, the hyena Taha Yasin Ramadan. He was the more dangerous of the two, thought Izzat, but by no means the only dangerous one. Which of them would explode first?

The hyena smacked the palm of his hand down on to the table, silencing Sa'adi Tumah Abbas with a poisonous glance. "You mean to say that this is all you can tell us? That our beloved brother the President has been assassinated and that there has been an insurrection? An *insurrection*? In *Tikrit*, of all places? What evidence is there of any of this? And what is being done about it?"

"And why was I not informed immediately?" The aggressive shout came from Hussein Kamil, Defence Minister and son-in-law of Saddam Hussein. Izzat studied Hussein Kamil's expression again and decided that he had misread it. The principal emotion visible on his pig-like face was alarm, thinly disguised as anger. It amounted to little more than an attempt to throw his weight about. He was badly rattled, clearly afraid.

Sa'adi Tumah Abbas attempted convincing answers to the questions. He failed dismally; he had none. Over the next couple of minutes further questions and criticisms were hurled at him by others seated at the long table. Izzat Ibrahim said nothing; sitting back in satisfaction, he allowed the man to become the focus of everyone else's rancour and dismay. Sa'adi Tumah Abbas was being skewered.

Eventually there was a lull; Izzat Ibrahim held up his hands. "Brothers, fellow members of the Revolutionary Command Council, it is with the greatest sadness that I feel we must conclude that the report, however incomplete it appears to be, must be true. We must for the time being suppress our terrible grief, and face the fact that our beloved brother and leader, Saddam Hussein, has been the victim of a treacherous and cowardly assassination plot. I can confirm to you that he travelled to Tikrit this morning," – Izzat paused, savouring the looks of hatred and envy on the faces of those who had not been privy to this information – "but he has not returned to Baghdad as scheduled. His helicopter has not appeared; indeed we have received word that it has been destroyed. As our brother Sa'adi Tumah Abbas has reported, attempts to contact the commander of the President's Amn al Khass bodyguard detachment in Tikrit have proved unsuccessful; however there were eyewitnesses to the events there early this morning. The commanding officer of the third regiment of the Medina division of the Republican Guard escaped with his life, along with elements of his command staff. It seems that they saw what happened and fled. Senior members of the Mukhabarat have conducted interrogations of these men. They did not . . . shall we say, waste any time in extracting information. The men all gave the same story before being executed, at my own behest, for cowardice. Tikrit is in turmoil; the Medina divisional commander has been instructed to proceed there at all speed, with Air Force helicopter support, to crush the revolt. On my instructions, the town has been sealed off. No information will emerge except via the divisional commander personally, and he will report direct to this council."

Izzat allowed himself another glance at the pig-like Defence Minister, Hussein Kamil. The man appeared speechless with fury on hearing that his authority over his own forces had apparently been usurped. Izzat bared his yellowing teeth at him in a parody of a smile. "I am sure, brother Hussein Kamil, that you will forgive me on this occasion for exercising my authority as Deputy Commander-in-Chief of the Armed Forces without prior reference to you. Swift action was required, and attempts to contact you at midday proved, ah . . . unsuccessful. It seems that you were temporarily absent from your ministry; I understand you had other important duties to attend to, at a certain address in . . . Khulafa Street." Izzat bared his teeth even wider; the hideous grin was now mocking. He knew where Hussein Kamil had been, and with whom. Yes, he knew which stinking trough the pig's snout had been exploring. Hussein Kamil had suddenly turned a deathly pale; his mouth opened, then snapped shut. Izzat saw him swallow nervously. Oh yes, thought Izzat, still grinning. This was one titbit that even that psychopath Kusai, Saddam Hussein's second son and head of the Mukhabarat, did not know about. No one had dared tell Kusai that his whore of a wife was having an affair with his own brother-in-law. But he, Izzat, had been told . . .

There was silence from the others; a few faces evinced a brief curiosity as to the possible significance of this snippet of information. Hussein Kamil eventually managed a response. "You were undoubtedly correct to take the action you did, brother Izzat Ibrahim," he spluttered.

"Thank you," purred Izzat Ibrahim. His yellow teeth flashed again, then he turned to the others. "So. The question to which we must now address ourselves is simple. What further action should be taken to avoid a major crisis and further domestic upheaval? The answer, or so at least it would seem to me, is equally simple. There must be a continuity of leadership. A leadership of the greatest strength will be required at this tragic and perilous time in the affairs of our great nation. There can be no doubt that all measures necessary to suppress any further dissent must be taken, wherever such dissent may occur. Harsh and drastic decisions may be called for. At this dreadful time, devastated as we all are, I find one shred of comfort: that you, my brothers around this table, are of the unquestioned calibre and heroic resolve to pledge your full support to the leadership that circumstances demand." There, thought Izzat Ibrahim. He had said it. There could be no possibility that anyone had failed to grasp the implication of his words. Even Sa'adi Tumah Abbas would have realised that this was a naked bid for the now-vacant Presidency. Izzat's eyes glittered as he hunched, vulture-like, over the head of the table and gazed around at the faces of his colleagues.

The first sign of dissent, when it came, was from a completely unexpected quarter. "I imagine that none of us, brother *Vice*-President," sneered the Minister of the Interior, "would dispute that strong leadership will be required. The question is simply one of identifying those areas of policy where strength – and experience – will need to be demonstrated."

Izzat was taken aback. He had anticipated a token protest from Taha Yasin Ramadan, but this was a surprise. Ali Hassan al-Majid was a cousin of Saddam's, and Izzat knew exactly what he meant by his remarks. Of all those present, this slavering, rabid dog had probably demonstrated the most ruthless and effective approach to the various assignments with which he had been entrusted. His record was horribly impressive. It was he who had ordered the gas attacks on the Kurds during 1987-88, and he whom Saddam had appointed Governor of Kuwait following the 1990 invasion. Along with his henchman, Ala'a Hussein Ali, he had presided over the rape and despoliation of Iraq's "nineteenth province". Since then, as Interior Minister, Ali Hassan al-Majid had been placed in charge of the operations to suppress dissent among the Kurds in the north and the Shi'ites in the southern marshes – and he had proved brutally successful. If anyone had adequate credentials for suppressing further internal disorder, it was he. So, thought Izzat, he was making his own bid for power, was he? It wouldn't work. The dog had too many enemies, had made too many fear him – they would gang up against him to ensure that he never rose to absolute power. Angered at the insolence and sarcastic emphasis with which Ali Hassan al-Majid had referred to him as "*Vice*-President", Izzat nevertheless bit back a retort and decided to let the others chop him down.

The hyena, Taha Yasin Ramadan, was not slow to begin the process. "Our brother the Interior Minister," he snarled, "is correct in one respect: experience in the exercise of power will undoubtedly be required. But experience merely of internal matters would hardly form an adequate basis for the formulation of a comprehensive Government policy. We are beset on all sides by enemies who will undoubtedly attempt to take advantage of the disaster that has today befallen Iraq. Strength, and a continued unshakable adherence to the principles pioneered by our glorious brother Saddam Hussein – Allah be with him in paradise – will of course be essential. They will be essential in our dealings with the predatory foreigners who even now have us in their sights. As Saddam himself reminded us all only three days ago, Iraq faces unprecedented assaults on her sovereignty. The leadership of Iraq would ignore the foreign dimension at its peril. Skill, and the utmost resolution in dealing harshly with all our enemies – external as well as internal – will be vital."

Izzat blinked in astonishment. The hyena had played into his hands. So keen had Taha been to strangle Ali Hassan al-Majid's bid for power that he had not made any bid on his own account. Not only that, but he had said nothing to jeopardise the position of Izzat himself. The strong players had spoken; surely, without any further discussion, it was now settled! His appointment would be confirmed!

"Our brother Taha has spoken well." Startled, Izzat jerked his head round to look at the new speaker. Half-way down the table, the bland face of the ex-Foreign Minister – now Deputy Prime Minister – was smiling broadly beneath his heavy spectacles. "One might almost think that with his eloquent advocacy of a leadership experienced in foreign affairs he was proposing my own candidacy for the Presidency." Tariq Aziz chuckled at his own joke; Izzat's eyes narrowed in suspicion. What was this wily old fox driving at? "Naturally, if such an honour were to be offered to me, I would decline." Tariq Aziz's expression became more serious. "Yes, my brothers, I would decline even this supreme honour. In truth, I believe that the office of President must, for the time being, remain unfilled."

Izzat Ibrahim was dumbfounded. There were murmurs of surprise and bewilderment from around the table; out of the corner of his eye Izzat noticed the hyena, Taha, sit back in his chair with an air of smug satisfaction. The two of them were in league! An ambush! Betrayal!

410

But what exactly were they up to? Colour suffused Izzat's sallow cheeks; mottled blotches of crimson highlighted the deep pockmarks as he fought to conceal the turmoil in his mind.

"Not only would any deliberation regarding a replacement for the President be premature at this stage," continued Tariq Aziz, "but I would go further. To make such an appointment now would be to court disaster. I hasten to say," he said with a disarming smile, "that by this I do not mean that there are no suitable candidates among those present in this room. Far from it. I am happy to acknowledge that many among you, my distinguished brothers, would be more than capable of carrying forward the burdens of that great office, until so recently held by our beloved brother Saddam Hussein. No; the reason we must not seek a new President is a more compelling one. It is also blindingly simple."

Izzat was now completely lost. What in the name of Allah was this grinning fox Tariq Aziz driving at?

"Any change, or even any *appearance* of change – however small – would be utterly catastrophic," declared Tariq Aziz emphatically. It would signal weakness, which would inevitably be exploited. No matter how strong a new President might be, no matter how capable, the authority of *the Presidency itself* would be seen to have suffered. If it became known that our brother Saddam had been assassinated, it would be a sign that *the Presidency*, not simply the President, was vulnerable – fatally vulnerable. If, alternatively, we were to issue an announcement that he had been replaced – something criminally unworthy of his glorious memory – it would be taken as a sign of internal dissent, and therefore instability, within this council. Either way, the leadership of Iraq would be dealt a blow from which it would be very unlikely to recover. There are enough enemies, both within Iraq and without, just waiting to seize on such news to their advantage, should it emerge. We must therefore carry on as before. No change must be apparent."

"This is absurd!" Izzat Ibrahim thundered, his carefully-maintained composure now in tatters. He jabbed a bony finger furiously towards Tariq Aziz. "How can we possibly carry on as before, now that Saddam himself is dead?"

The former Foreign Minister's smile did not even falter. He turned to Taha Yasin Ramadan. "Taha, my brother," he asked, "how many remain of the *tawâgît*?"

411

The hyena grinned, his lip curling as he glanced at Izzat Ibrahim; he noticed that the pockmarked face beneath the hennaed hair had turned very pale. "There are nine," he answered. "Of these nine, five" – he held up his right hand with the fingers outstretched – "bear only a superficial resemblance to our late brother and leader. Each of these has been used from time to time travelling in a motorcade to reward the people with an occasional glimpse of their beloved President. Two more" – he ticked off two fingers of his left hand – "are capable of more detailed duties, and have been featured in short clips of film taken of visits to military bases. No close-up pictures have been permitted, and the soldiers who have appeared in such film have on each occasion been members of the Amn al Khass in disguise. These clips have served a useful purpose – to demonstrate that the leadership is unafraid to venture among the people." The hyena paused, counting off two more fingers. "The remaining two are the best, the most convincing. They were selected to undergo special . . . *'ilm al-jirâha*, surgery. The first, the *tâgût* Bakr Abdullah –"

"Is dead." Izzat Ibrahim's voice was a hiss. "He was shot this morning, along with the President."

Shock distorted the hyena's face; it was his turn to go pale. "How do you know this?"

"The same way," snorted Izzat, rapping his bony knuckles on the table, "that I knew about the assassination. The interrogation of the witnesses, of course. You will kindly explain what this reference to the *tawâgît* is about. What possible use can they serve now? They should be eliminated."

"On the contrary," the hyena spat back at him, recovering his equilibrium. "They are now more vital to the security of Iraq than ever." He glared at Izzat Ibrahim. "The Deputy Prime Minister and I" – he turned to acknowledge Tariq Aziz, who smiled and nodded – "suspected this morning that something was badly amiss. A foreign diplomatic delegation failed to reappear from Tikrit, and we heard other rumours too . . . rumours that have unhappily proved only too accurate. We had an opportunity to discuss the matter briefly before this meeting."

So that's it, thought Izzat Ibrahim, fury and alarm rising in his gorge. *The two of them have been plotting!* He had a horrible feeling that he could guess what they had in mind.

"The news about the *tâgût* Bakr Abdullah is unfortunate," continued the hyena, "but no doubt he can be replaced in due course if necessary. The crucial thing is that the last one on the list, the *tâgût* Muhsen Hashim, remains at our disposal. He is the best of them all."

"So what exactly is it that you propose?" Izzat was now certain that he knew.

"It is simple. There will be no announcement of an assassination. There will be no announcement of a replacement as President. In fact there will be no announcement at all. Instead, a film will be made as soon as can be arranged. Two or three days should see its completion. This film will feature the *tâgût* Muhsen Hashim. It will be more comprehensive than anything he has featured in before. He is capable of it, I know; in accordance with direct instructions from our late brother Saddam Hussein, I supervised his training personally. Our late brother was concerned about the large number of public appearances expected of him, and wished increasingly to make use of the *tawâgît* to take his place whenever the occasion did not specifically require him to be there in person. Things will therefore continue precisely as before. Only a few people outside this room, other than the traitors responsible for this morning's outrage, will ever know the truth. The traitors, along with all witnesses and anyone else who might have heard rumours, will be eliminated. When this has been done, those who have conducted the investigations into the treason will in turn be eliminated. This *tâgût* will take the place of the President."

Izzat Ibrahim was staggered. The unthinkable had happened; his hopes of assuming power had been viciously – and, he had to admit, ingeniously – dashed. He thought fast. Perhaps not all was lost. The *tâgût* would not be as well protected as the President had been . . . "Are you suggesting that this *tâgût* should sit on this council? That he should become one of us?"

"Of course not," retorted the hyena contemptuously. "He will merely receive his instructions from us. He will do what he is told."

"Might I ask," hissed Izzat, "who it is that you have in mind to give him his instructions?"

"The matter is of no consequence," snapped the hyena. "The instructions themselves will of course be important, but the duty of relaying them from this council to the *tâgût* will be one of little

413

significance. The requirement will simply be to pass on to the *tâgût* orders detailing when and where he is to appear, and what he is to do – nothing more. However, as it appears to be something to which you inexplicably attach such importance, brother Izzat Ibrahim," he snickered, a note of triumph in his voice, "perhaps I might propose that you take on this task yourself?"

The deadly insult implicit in Taha Yasin Ramadan's words stunned the room into silence. For a moment, Izzat Ibrahim thought he had heard incorrectly; then, with mounting incredulity, he gradually took in that he had been duped into ascribing a weighty significance to what was merely a menial duty – and worse, it had then been suggested that he should take on that duty! Livid fury suffused his cadaverous, pockmarked face, and his claw-like hands gripped the edge of the table. He glared at the hyena with a bitter ferocity; finally he emitted a shriek of rage. "The idea is an utterly preposterous one! It is the product of a fevered imagination! It could never work! I suppose that part of this insane plan is that the *tâgût* should also carry the President's own *tabanja*, his pistol?"

"No!" barked the hyena, slamming his fist down on the table. "Not that! The existing rule must remain inviolate. This *tâgût* must understand that he is merely a servant of this council. He must on no account be given any indication that he is crucial to the security of Iraq, and he must not be allowed to get ideas above his station. Perhaps in a few months' time, if he shows himself to be utterly compliant, and if this council authorises it, he might be allowed to carry the *tabanja* on certain special occasions, if this is considered appropriate or necessary for the sake of appearances. But if I must answer your first point, *brother* Izzat Ibrahim, then I will briefly do so. This plan is infinitely less preposterous than any alternative on offer. Your reaction to it," he scoffed dismissively, "is no doubt purely a reflex one. I, on the other hand, have given the matter much careful consideration. This plan will work. It *must be made* to work. Our brother Tariq Aziz has already explained why it is our only option. If it fails, then we are all, every last one of us . . ." – the hyena, in full control now, slowly swept his malevolent gaze round the room – ". . . doomed."

Izzat Ibrahim, beaten, stared fixedly at the hyena Taha Yasin Ramadan. The small unblinking eyes in the pockmarked face radiated pure hatred.

414

69

Lieutenant Saleh Masoud was ready to explode with frustration. Despite the fact that the sun was now sinking fast, the BRDM armoured car was still baking hot inside; he had not had a chance to stop for a rest, for food, for anything. He imagined the guardsmen in the trucks behind would be about as fed up as he was. His driver certainly was, and had let him know about it at length. The driver's reedy voice had eventually got on the Lieutenant's nerves, and he had yelled angrily at the man to be quiet.

But the driver was of course right. Why should they, the Republican Guard, have to act as nursemaids to these hated foreigners? They should have locked them up, and left them to rot. Instead, they were escorting them, *helping* them – these people who were trying to strip Iraq of all its dignity! Yes, reasoned the Lieutenant, if his driver felt that way, so would all the others. If it came to another confrontation with that arrogant Major Hassan Omair, he would have the men behind him.

Curse the Major, he thought indignantly. It was typical of the man that he would ride in comfort in the foreigners' car while his men were being bumped about in these bone-shaking rattle-traps. Especially the BRDM. Whoever that idiot of a Russian was, the one who had designed the thing to have such non-existent suspension, with an engine that injected all its surplus heat into the interior instead of expelling it into the atmosphere, he, Saleh Masoud, would have liked to get his hands on the bastard. A curse on that Russian, and a curse on the Major, and, especially, ten thousand curses on these filthy foreigners. The Lieutenant made up his mind. Half an hour more was all he was going to give them. If they went on any longer than that without stopping for a rest, *he* was going to stop. Just like that. He would refuse to go any further. A plague on the Major

— he could say what he liked. He, Saleh Masoud, would have a thing or two to say himself. He began to rehearse some appropriate words in his mind.

The Lieutenant had by now become so used to the routine of following the car in front, and was so preoccupied with preparing the bitingly effective speech he would make to his commanding officer, that he didn't take any notice when Bourne turned off the main highway to Trebil and Jordan. The convoy had almost reached Rutbah; Bourne abruptly took a turning and retraced their tracks past the fallen road bridge and through the town. He headed south towards the Saudi border, the same way they had come. The Lieutenant, in the BRDM, assumed that it was a diversion because of the bridge, but he failed to pay much attention to the route they were taking. He was looking at his watch. Another twenty minutes, he thought. After that, he was damn well just going to stop.

70

Unlike his surly subordinate, Major Hassan Omair had realised straight away what had happened. He had had no warning. There had been no discussion between Howard and Bourne, no indication that the route to Trebil would not be followed. It was, after all, the logical one for the spies to take to get out of the country.

Now suddenly they were heading south – out into the middle of nowhere. Quickly, the Major thought about what he might do. His plan for having the spies arrested when they stopped at Trebil had now gone out of the window. He would have to think of something else. He immediately decided that he would give them no hint that he thought anything was amiss. Perhaps they would remain relaxed. If they thought he knew that they weren't going to Trebil, they would guess that he would be suspicious and might try something. No; the answer was to feign ignorance. Perhaps that fool Saleh Masoud, in the BRDM, would twig what had happened. If so, he would probably do something about it. Maybe even fire off his 14.5mm KPTV cannon at them. Good for him, if he did.

But what were the spies doing now? The man Howard had handed Bourne a flying helmet. There was something strange about the helmet – it had a device like a pair of binoculars fitted to it. Bourne was putting the helmet on, flipping the binoculars up clear of his vision. Of course – a light-amplification device! And the man was temporarily distracted . . .

Howard, in the back seat behind Bourne, had been watching the Major carefully. The Iraqi's face had betrayed nothing when they turned off the main road, but Howard had seen enough of the Major's ability to remain expressionless to suspect that he probably knew where they were now headed. As he reached for his NVG helmet in preparation for operating in the dark, it occurred to Howard that pretty soon the Major would know anyway. They had passed the turn-off to Rutbah South airfield, and the dirt track began only a mile or two further on. He passed MacDonald a second NVG helmet and handed another forward to Bourne.

Bourne was putting on his helmet when two things happened more or less at once. The first, unnoticed by him because he was concentrating on what he was doing, was that the BRDM behind braked to a halt; had he been looking in his driving mirror, he would have spotted it.

The second thing, occurring at about the same time, was that the Major, recognising what was perhaps the only chance he might have to cause a diversion, throw these foreigners off balance and alert his men in the vehicles behind, made a sudden grab for the steering-wheel. Bourne, temporarily preoccupied with his helmet, was wholly unprepared. Howard, however, was not. He hit the Major hard on the side of the neck with the edge of his hand; the Major slumped unconscious over Bourne's lap. Bourne, recovering quickly, pushed the inert Iraqi roughly back into his seat.

The incident was over in less than four seconds, but in that time the Land Cruiser had drawn about seventy yards clear of the rest of the convoy. Howard and Bourne registered the fact simultaneously; Bourne braked hard.

"Back up, Johnny. Slowly. Trouble. Danny, get ready to bale out fast when I say."

Ziegler, Ackford and Usher, sandwiched between the BRDM and the first of the trucks, instantly realised there was something wrong. "Not yet," said Ziegler tersely, "wait till we find out what this is about."

Lieutenant Saleh Masoud was already out of the BRDM. The lead car, he noticed, had not stopped immediately. It had continued on until the driver had seen in his mirror that the lights of the rest of the convoy were no longer following; presumably it would now reverse back to see what was up. Then he would give the Major a piece of his mind.

In the meantime, the Lieutenant decided, he would make sure these foreigners got a rough time of it. He walked back to the Land Cruiser. "Get out of the car," he snarled menacingly at Ziegler, jerking his thumb backwards in an unmistakable gesture.

Ziegler raised his AKMS and shot the Lieutenant in the throat.

He motioned abruptly with his elbow to Ackford and Usher. "Out now," he ordered. All three men dived out and rolled away, leaving the dead body of the Lieutenant lying by the car.

The Sergeant in the cab of the first of the two trucks was a veteran of the Iran-Iraq war. He had heard the soft cough of the silenced AK and the louder rattle of its recoil mechanism, and had seen the Lieutenant collapse dead. He reacted quickly. With a yell of "Out of the vehicle!" at his men in the back, he jumped out himself, loading his AK 47. He was about to fire when he heard a shout in English. There was a bright flash from somewhere near his feet, and he too fell dead.

The shout he had heard was "Grenade!" from Ackford. Almost simultaneously he, Usher and Ziegler had hurled hand-grenades at the two trucks behind. The first exploded between the front wheels of the lead truck, killing the Sergeant and setting the vehicle on fire. The second exploded near the rear of the truck, dispatching three soldiers who were in the process of dismounting, and wounding four more. The third grenade, aimed by Ziegler at the second truck, misfired.

Ackford and Usher were now raking the two trucks with AK fire. Many of the soldiers inside never managed to get out, but thirteen of the occupants of the second vehicle, which was undamaged by the grenades and a little further back along the road, jumped down to the ground and began returning fire. Ziegler took careful aim at the four headlights on the two trucks and shot them out, plunging the scene into darkness. Now only the lights of the BRDM provided any illumination, and they were pointing the wrong way.

The driver of the BRDM, despite his humble rank, had reacted with commendable speed and initiative when the first grenade had exploded. Wrenching himself up and back out of his seat, he grabbed the handle of the turret-mounted 14.5mm KPTV cannon and fired it without aiming. The cannon had been pointing directly ahead, down the road, and the first three of the burst of twenty rounds went straight into Howard's Land Cruiser as it reversed towards him. The car slewed off the road and turned over on its side, catching fire.

MacDonald had felt a violent thump on his right arm; the blow was strong enough to make him drop his AK. Immediately after that, the world seemed to turn upside-down, and he crashed down on his head. He was saved by the NVG helmet. He scrambled out of his door, which now opened towards the sky.

While MacDonald was climbing out of the door above, Howard dived over into the back of the car and kicked open the rear door. The RPG-7 anti-tank rocket-launcher was underneath the back seat; he grabbed it and rolled out on to the ground, lining up the weapon on the BRDM. There was a deafening bang from the RPG as the projectile fired; it detonated almost immediately on its target, punching through the thin armour plate. The front of the armoured car disintegrated, its lights went out and the interior began to burn. The BRDM driver was killed instantly.

Johnny Bourne had not been so lucky. Although the bullet that passed through MacDonald's arm had not hit Bourne, the next one had. It struck Bourne in the lower leg. The leg seemed to go immediately numb. The third of the three big bullets had hit a rear wheel and completely shattered it; it was this that caused the vehicle to swerve out of control and turn over on to the driver's side. As it did so, the body of the unconscious Major once again fell across Bourne, this time pinning him down. The vehicle was already starting to burn.

MacDonald felt utterly helpless. He couldn't fire his AK for fear of hitting Ziegler, Ackford and Usher, who were now engaged in an ear-splitting firefight with the remaining Iraqi guardsmen. The vicious cracks of the AK bullets overhead were completely disorientating; MacDonald had never experienced anything so confusing or terrifying. Flattening himself to the ground, he turned his head to see what Howard and Bourne were doing; he would take his cue from them. He saw Howard racing off to one flank.

It suddenly struck MacDonald that Bourne was nowhere to be seen. Behind him, the Land Cruiser was starting to burn; in a flash, he realised Bourne must still be inside. He ran to it and dived into the back. He found Bourne pinned down, and with a desperate wrench using his one good hand he pulled the Major's weight off his wounded leg.

"Thanks, Danny," shouted Bourne hoarsely above the din outside, as by their combined efforts they managed to get the unconscious Iraqi off him altogether. Struggling out from behind the wheel, Bourne dragged himself back out of the rear of the vehicle, following MacDonald. Outside, they flung themselves down and crawled away from the wrecked car, which was now burning fiercely.

"What shall we do, Johnny?" shouted Danny.

420

"Not much we can do at this stage," shouted Bourne, grimacing. "My leg's fucked, anyway. Best stay here and see what happens." Both men flipped their NVGs on and examined the scene before them.

Ackford had run out of grenades. He wormed his way back to his car on his stomach to get some more. As he yanked open the door and leaned in to grab a handful of them, there was a burst of bullet cracks very close by and he felt a heavy blow on his NVG helmet. *Shit,* he thought; then he changed his mind. *Good, I can still think. Must be OK.* Crawling away from the car, he pulled the pin on the first grenade and aimed it carefully at muzzle flashes of AK fire coming from near the second truck. "Grenade!" he shouted. Somewhere on his right, Usher was still firing.

Howard had seen that Usher and Ackford were on the right flank. He headed out to the left, where he knew Ziegler would be. Gradually, the crossfire laid down by the four men began to take its toll. The Iraqis, blind in the dark, confused, tired and caught completely off their guard, were no match for their adversaries. One by one, they were being picked off. Only eight out of thirty-five were now left alive.

One of the eight was the Sergeant from the second truck. A seasoned soldier, like his now dead opposite number from the truck in front, he had bided his time. He had taken cover; he waited to see if there was any pattern to the firing. He soon realised that these enemies were good. Very good, he thought. There would be an effective burst of well-aimed fire from one spot – he could see the muzzle flashes – but it would come only once from the same place. Then the firer would move. None of the enemy ever fired from the same place twice. Fire, then move, the Sergeant said to himself; that was what they were doing. Only a few feet each time, but enough to mean that he couldn't get a fix on their position and put down fire on it. He had seen one of them get up by the car and open the door to reach inside; he could have sworn he had hit him, but the man was back again, although the Sergeant was no longer quite sure where he was.

There was a sudden loud bang as the burning Land Cruiser exploded. The fire had reached the fuel tank. Major Hassan Omair died without ever regaining consciousness. The bright flash of the explosion instantly illuminated the scene – just enough for the Iraqi Sergeant to see movement from one of the enemy. He let off a long burst from his AK 47. The figure he had fired at jerked convulsively and then lay still. *Got him*, thought the Sergeant. Then came a series of shockingly forceful thumps to his own body. A wet salty taste came into his mouth; his head suddenly felt light and the noise around him began to dim. Before he could grasp what had happened, the Iraqi Sergeant drew his last breath, a look of surprise on his face.

The gunfire died away; the last Iraqi soldier was dead.

"Mike?" called Howard.

"Here. AOK."

"Johnny?"

"Here," called Bourne, his voice sounding strained. "Hit in lower right leg."

"How bad?"

"Bone's not broken."

"Good. Danny?"

"Here. Hit in left forearm."

"Tony?"

"Here. My helmet got hit, but I think the contents are still OK."

"Bob?"

There was a long silence. Ackford said, "I think he's over here, boss."

"OK. I think we're clear. Mike, take over. Find out if any of those vehicles are serviceable." Howard walked over to Tony, who was kneeling by Usher's body. Usher had taken three bullets in the head and chest. He had died instantly.

"Fucking shitty luck, boss," said Ackford. "We nearly made it."

71

Kearwin felt numb as he studied the Keyhole image on his screen. The vehicles had been stationary for ten minutes; this picture was from a satellite pass just three minutes earlier, and it was unequivocally clear now what had happened.

For some reason, there had been a showdown with the Iraqis. The "UN team" had obviously put up a reasonable fight; the armoured car, which was either a BTR or a BRDM, had been knocked out – Kearwin could tell from the heat signature. The thing was on fire. So was one of the large trucks. But . . . so was one of the UN cars. There was something else wrong with it, apart from the fire; it wasn't quite the same shape as before. But it had to be the UN car – the other four vehicles in the convoy were accounted for. Perhaps the car had turned over. He couldn't be sure.

They had come all that way, reflected Kearwin, only to fail. He felt a powerful wave of sympathy for them. He knew they would have been caught sooner or later – that was inevitable. Once they had got over the border into Saudi Arabia, there would have been no escape. But at least they would have lived, whereas now . . .

Kearwin wondered if they were all dead. It might be better for them than the alternative, capture. God only knew what frightful fate would await them if they had fallen into the hands of the Iraqi secret police – torture, public humiliation on television, more torture, the living hell of an Iraqi prison, perhaps even brutal execution . . . it didn't bear thinking about. No, he thought savagely, it would be better if they were all dead.

But maybe they weren't. Maybe they had beaten the Iraqis! He would soon know. It would depend on which vehicle moved, the other Land Cruiser or the second truck. Those were the only two apparently undamaged vehicles out of the five in the convoy. One of them would move. If it was the truck, or if another vehicle appeared, it meant that the Iraqis had won. If it was the Land Cruiser . . .

"John! JSTARS shows movement!" shouted Jerry Freedman.

"Land Cruiser or truck?" demanded Kearwin urgently.

"It's the truck."

"Oh." Kearwin's worst fears were confirmed. He sagged in his chair.

"It's moving down the track, heading south," said Freedman.

"South? Did you say *south*? Are you sure?"

"Yes. Definitely."

"Follow that truck!" screeched Kearwin. They had done it, he told himself. If it had been the Iraqis, they wouldn't have driven south towards the border. Thank God. Somehow, those guys had done it again.

*   *   *

"This effing truck's a pig of a thing to drive," shouted Ackford above the din of the engine.

"So would anything be, with a flat front tyre," answered Howard. He smiled weakly to mask his uneasiness. The second Land Cruiser had refused to start. On opening the bonnet, Ackford had soon seen why. It had taken several hits from Iraqi AK fire; the distributor and the battery were smashed, and there was acid and brake fluid splashed all round the engine compartment. They had emptied the stricken car of their equipment, and Ziegler had poured their last jerrican of fuel over the seats. Then he had tossed in a burning rag. A mile behind them now, the Land Cruiser was still on fire; Howard saw a flash in the truck's wing mirror as the car suddenly exploded. Thank heaven the second truck worked, he thought, despite the shot-out tyre.

Howard hadn't wanted to hang around at the scene of the fight a moment longer than absolutely necessary. It didn't matter that the truck's lights didn't work – they wouldn't have used them anyway. Ackford had discarded his smashed helmet and night-vision goggles, and was using Bourne's; he could see perfectly well.

"Just keep going as far as you can, Tony," said Howard. "I want to get as much distance between us and those wrecks as possible."

"I'm doing my best, boss. Sodding thing."

There was a tap on the cab and Howard turned round to see Ziegler poking his head through the canvas cover behind. "Andy's on his way, Ed. Airborne now. You got co-ordinates for us to give him?"

"Not yet, Mike. It'll take him a good thirty minutes to get here. We'll keep going for a few more miles and look for a suitable place for him to land."

"OK."

"How are Johnny and Danny?"

"Danny's OK. A big hole, but straight through the muscle. Not bleedin' too bad. I'm not so sure about Johnny, though. I've put a pressure dressing on it, but he's been losin' quite a bit of blood. We ought to stop someplace and have a proper look at it. He still can't feel his foot."

"The bones are definitely OK?"

"As far as I can tell, bumpin' around in the dark in the back here."

"You'll all just have to hang on for a while. We daren't stop yet."

"OK." Ziegler's head disappeared back behind the canvas flap.

Howard had an afterthought. He leaned his head out of the cab window again. "Mike?"

Ziegler's head reappeared. "Yeah?"

"Any dead Iraqis on board?"

"Yeah. Two who never made it out of the truck. I was about to start chuckin' them out of the back."

"Don't. We'll need them."

"Any particular reason?"

"I'm pretty sure we're blown in Saudi," said Howard. "We're probably going to have to ditch the plane on arrival and think of some other way."

"Shit," said Ziegler. "What makes you think that?"

"The air strike on that warehouse," said Howard. "I'm sure it wasn't Iraqi."

*   *   *

The Iraqi Air Force Colonel commanding the Rutbah South airbase looked up in surprise at the sudden loud knocking on his door. "Come in," he called.

The door flew open and an agitated Army captain appeared. "Sir, there has been a mutiny!"

425

"What? Explain yourself!"

The Captain explained. He had been driving back to Rutbah, he said, when he had seen something burning, about two miles away from the turning to the base. Then there had been an explosion, he said. He had gone to investigate. He had seen the vehicles and the soldiers' bodies. All dead, he said.

The colonel was perplexed and angry. "What was anyone doing down there?" he asked. "There's no convoy due down there this week."

"I don't know, sir," said the Captain. "But the Republican Guard never inform us of their movements in advance."

The Colonel knew. It was a sore point with him. How was he supposed to keep track of events in his sector, he wondered, unless he was told of such things? But . . . *Wait a minute!* "Captain, did you say Republican Guard?"

"Yes, sir. About twenty or thirty of them. All dead."

By God! thought the Colonel, jumping to his feet. He dashed out of the door, the Captain following. This was a major emergency! And if he did nothing about it . . . "Order a full alert at once, Captain!"

"Yes, sir!"

The Colonel hurried to his car and sped across the airfield to the control tower. All round the airbase, security lights were coming on as the sirens began to blare. A jeep raced up to the control tower; his operations staff jumped out and opened up. The Colonel followed them up the stairs at a run. He had decided what to do. "Get H3 airbase on the radio! I want to speak to Colonel Suba Ali! Urgently!"

"Yes, sir!" replied the operations officer with a salute. He made a speedy exit.

Yes, thought the Colonel. H3 airbase was the answer. There was nothing here at Rutbah South except transport planes. They had a squadron of Mi-24 Hind-A helicopter gunships at the H3 base, only forty miles away to the west. The situation called for nothing less.

*   *   *

"AWACS has got the Islander, John!" Peter Stannard called over to Kearwin. "It's airborne, crossing the border – northwards into Iraq!"

426

"Give me a plot on it. I want to know how long to target." Kearwin had been expecting this, but there was still something niggling at the back of his mind. He gave Stannard the co-ordinates of the truck, which had now stopped. No doubt a suitable landing site had been found. But how, he wondered, had the aircraft known exactly when to turn up? And how would it know exactly where to head for? The place could not have been pre-planned. The men in the truck would be acting in emergency conditions now. Kearwin was sure they would not otherwise have asked the Islander to penetrate into Iraqi airspace.

As Stannard interrogated the E-3 AWACS, Kearwin went over to talk to Sorensen. "Walter, is the ELINT section absolutely positive there have been no radio transmissions from that sector?"

"They say they've been monitoring it. Nothing."

"Nothing at all?"

"Only the usual stuff you'd expect, in Arabic. There are several airbases in the area. They can pinpoint each one."

"Can we check again? Perhaps there's been something from outside the bases. We know the exact route and present location of the truck – it's stopped, waiting for the plane."

The Walrus picked up the telephone and spoke to the Electronic Intelligence section's watch supervisor. He listened to the lengthy reply, thanked the ELINT man, then replaced the receiver. "Nothing, John, although there was some Arabic radio traffic a few minutes ago from somewhere south-west of Rutbah South airbase, and there's been some excited chit-chat between the ops centres of Rutbah South itself and H3 airbase."

"What did they say?"

"Rutbah's asked for air support. Possibly something to do with this. I guess the fight between the Iraqi soldiers and our guys was near enough for them to notice it."

"I didn't mean that. I meant the transmission from the truck. Let's get the tape and an English transcript of the conversation!"

The Walrus nodded, quickly picking up the phone again. "I see what you mean. You think they're talking in Arabic . . . Oh, Eddie," he said into the telephone, "it's Walter again. Yeah. Listen, Eddie, we think their radio traffic could be in Arabic. Could you get a translation of the transmission from the location I just gave you, south of Rutbah in the desert? Yeah. And a copy of the tape. And

427

have your language expert analyse the speech patterns, would you? Thanks again, Eddie." He put down the phone. "He says he'll get it to us as fast as he can."

*　　　*　　　*

Andy Denard was flying as low as he dared. On a course of 350 degrees magnetic, he had flashed across the Iraqi border, heading straight for the last reported position of the team. Harris, beside him in the co-pilot's seat, took down the co-ordinates again ten minutes later, and Denard altered course slightly to 342 degrees to compensate for the truck's new position.

It was obvious to Denard that the team must already be aware that something was wrong. There had been minimal chat between Harris and Bourne on the radio; Bourne had not said how the operation had gone, and Harris hadn't asked. They must already have realised that they were blown. Denard wondered how they knew. "How did they sound, Mel?" he asked tersely, his eyes not moving from the scene ahead.

"Hard to say, with Johnny talking Arabic and me trying to remember mine. I don't know. Tense, certainly. But so am I, the way you're flying this thing."

"Don't worry, man. We'll soon be there. Ten minutes more."

"I'll have aged ten years by then!"

"Close your eyes and think of tits, man."

"Right now, I couldn't," said Harris. "And don't you dare do that yourself!"

Denard laughed. Harris, glancing at the pilot's face, saw that just for once his eyes weren't laughing too. Shit, he thought grimly. If Andy thinks this is hairy, then it bloody well must be.

*　　　*　　　*

The Mi-24 Hind-A had almost arrived at the site of the reported incident. The Iraqi Air Force pilot was confused. What the hell was all this rumpus about the Republican Guard? What were they doing down here, getting themselves slaughtered? The pilot didn't like the sound of it. A serious mutiny was what it sounded like. Mutinies were nothing but trouble. The pilot liked the quiet life. H3 was a nice, peaceful place. Or at least, it had been, up to now. Not like down south at Nasiriyah or Basra. He had done a stint down there recently, at the Tallil airbase outside Nasiriyah. He, along with the others, had been given a job for which he had had no taste at all. Flying over those accursed marshes, day in, day out, mowing down civilians, was not his idea of fun. In fact, he had hated it, and had been thoroughly relieved when he had been posted to H3, two months ago. It wasn't that he had any affection for the men of the marshes – he had no time for them at all. It was just that what he had been ordered to do was not an honourable thing, especially when you were doing it to brave people.

Yes, they had been brave, those men of the marshes. Brave to the point of foolhardy stupidity. Hadn't they known that there was no point in resisting? After all, there was nothing they could do about it. And yet they had still resisted. Many of them had fired back at him as he swept in on yet another strafing run. Surely they knew that it was utterly futile to fire rifles or machine-guns at a Hind? The Hind was the most heavily armoured helicopter in the world. It was simply not possible to bring a Hind down with small-arms fire. He had felt completely secure as the bullets bounced off the armour plating; it had even been amusing. He recalled the look of terror on the face of a brand-new co-pilot sitting beside him on the man's first active mission. He, the pilot, had decided to have some fun. He had deliberately put the Hind into the hover, right in front of some resistance men, to make it an easy target. How the bullets had bounced off! The new co-pilot had screamed with fear, until eventually he remembered what he had been taught and realised that he was quite safe. The pilot smiled at the memory.

The navigator/gunner broke his train of thought. "Coming up to target now. One kilometre."

The pilot saw it straight away. Four burning vehicles, as reported. Two of them almost completely burnt out already. The pilot circled the scene. Bodies were strewn around; it had been a massacre. Where were the perpetrators? Which way had they gone? He spoke into his microphone. "Anything on the FLIR?"

The observer studied the forward-looking imaging radar display and answered, "Nothing except one aircraft approaching from the south. Twenty-two miles distant. But the infra-red imaging shows an unusual track pattern leading that way. A vehicle has left here recently. It looks as though it's got a damaged wheel."

"Aircraft? Coming from the south? Are you sure? What type?"

"I can't tell at this stage. The signal is intermittent. It's flying very low."

"We will investigate," said the pilot. "There are no airbases down there, and there are no scheduled movements in that sector. And that vehicle may contain the dissidents responsible for this massacre."

The Hind banked round and began to pick up speed, heading almost due south down the track.

*   *   *

MacDonald's arm was beginning to ache like hell. Beside him, Bourne lay on the ground, his leg raised as Ziegler finished binding up the wound. MacDonald could see his face was taut with pain; Bourne's wound was obviously nastier than his own. A Saudi hospital, followed by a long stretch in prison, MacDonald thought numbly; that was all either of them could look forward to now. They had so nearly made it.

"I think I can hear the plane, boss," called Ackford.

"Right," said Howard. "Lights now!"

*   *   *

"Three miles, Mel. Start looking for the lights."

"Can't see anything yet."

"I'll take her up a little."

"Thank God for that," said Harris.

Denard pulled back on the column and climbed to two hundred feet. Two minutes later, they saw the single line of torches on the ground. Denard banked round and came in to land; Harris felt a heavy jolt as the wheels hit the ground hard. They were down. He undid his harness and prepared to jump out. The Islander rolled to a halt, its engines still running.

*   *   *

"The aircraft has just landed," reported the forward observer in the

430

Hind. "It's a twin-engined light aircraft. The vehicle is stationary nearby."

"Distance?"

"Two kilometres."

The pilot spoke to the navigator/gunner. "Engage the vehicle. Fire one AT-3. Then prepare to engage the aircraft with the 12.7mm nose-gun. We're going to have some fun."

The navigator/gunner armed one of the four AT-3 Sagger anti-tank missiles on the starboard wing, and locked on to the target. He waited until he was one kilometre from the target and then fired. The missile streaked off into the night.

*   *   *

MacDonald never heard the missile coming. Forty yards behind him, the truck dissolved in a sheet of flame; the force of the explosion knocked him flat. As he sat up again, slightly stunned, something thundered overhead in the dark. He flipped on his night-vision goggles.

"Helicopter!" screamed Bourne, grabbing his AK and trying to raise himself to fire. "A Hind! Danny! Get the sniper rifle and put some armour-piercing rounds into it! That's the only thing that might stop it!"

"No good!" yelled MacDonald in reply. "It was destroyed in the fire in the Land Cruiser!"

Harris had just jumped down from the Islander when he saw the truck a hundred yards away from him disintegrate with a flash. The noise of the explosion reached him a third of a second later, but the drone of the Islander's engines masked the sound of the Hind flying overhead. By the light of the burning vehicle he saw Ackford and Ziegler firing their rifles at something airborne. He didn't wait. He ran to join them. "What is it?" he bawled.

"Fucking Hind, I think," shouted Ackford.

Harris suddenly saw it through his night-vision goggles. It was wheeling round and coming in again. It was going for the Islander. "Any weapon for me?" he shrieked.

"Back there, by Johnny and Mac," bellowed Ackford. "And bring some spare ammo!"

Harris sped off towards the others.

Denard hadn't waited. Ramming the twin throttles forward, he had begun taxiing the Islander. His goggles had given him a brief glimpse of the Hind, and he knew he was a sitting target. He also knew he would be no better off in the air. The twin three-hundred-horsepower Lycoming 10-540-K1B5 engines howled as Denard raced the plane along the strip, juggling the throttles and the rudder to throw it into a series of violent pirouetting movements. It was all he could do. He had to rely on the others to destroy the helicopter. He was powerless.

The pilot of the Hind had seen the aircraft's pathetic attempts to escape; he smiled. This was going to be more entertaining than he had thought. Bullets were now whacking into the side of the helicopter; just like old times, thought the pilot. He ignored them, and brought the Hind into a static hover, to get a standing shot at the aircraft with the 12.7mm nose-mounted gun. It would be more fun than using the 57mm rockets. Good target practice. Then he would finish off those idiots firing rifles at him. The 12.7mm nose-gun began to chatter beneath his feet.

Harris reached Howard, who was in the process of loading the RPG-7. "Let me take it," he yelled, "I'm good with an RPG! You load for me." Howard nodded and thrust the anti-tank weapon at him. Harris shouldered the RPG and brought it to bear on the Hind, which was hovering two hundred yards away. He fired.

The Hind's co-pilot saw a sudden flash of light over near the remains of the truck, and momentarily caught sight of something streaking past him in the dark. "Missile!" he screamed.

The pilot had not seen it; he was concentrating on the aircraft, which was proving a difficult target, spinning around in crazy circles, going backwards and forwards. "What missile?" he asked.

"It just missed us! I'm sure of it!"

The pilot frowned. That put a different complexion on things. He would have to deal with it – urgently. He pushed the control forward and applied throttle, to take the Hind forward out of the hover. As he did so, a second RPG-7 projectile impacted on the thick armoured-glass cockpit window beside him. The shaped explosive charge in the nose of the projectile was designed to penetrate six inches of solid armour plate; it detonated, punching a neat half-inch-diameter hole in the heavy glass. A stream of white-hot metal plasma was blasted through the window into the cockpit, where it exploded with a dazzling flash, killing all the crew instantly.

The Hind lurched, and its nose tipped abruptly downwards. It fell from the sky like a dead bird, smashed into the ground and burst into flames.

Harris and Howard remained kneeling where they were for a few seconds, staring in silence at the burning wreckage of the helicopter. Then Harris spoke. "That was bloody good quick reloading, boss," he muttered.

"More to the point, Mel, that was a bloody good shot," said Howard. They both watched as the Islander ceased its evasive spinning manoeuvres and began taxiing back towards them. Howard stood up slowly. "Come on. Let's get going. I think I've had about as much trouble tonight as I can take."

72

Kearwin had followed the events south of Rutbah as they unfolded. The Arabic translator in the ELINT section had provided the information that the helicopter requested was a Mi-24 Hind-A; Kearwin had watched his screen with horror as the Hind converged on the scene just after the Islander had landed. Then it had disappeared. It was impossible to work out what had happened, and he was going to have to wait another twenty-five minutes for the next scheduled Keyhole pass before he found out.

But whatever had happened, they had obviously managed to shoot the thing down. The Walrus had quickly filled him in on the Hind's capability, adding, "I think they really are finished this time, John." But they hadn't been. The aircraft had just taken off again! It was only about thirty-five miles to the border. What were they going to do when they crossed it?

There were two possibilities, thought Kearwin. Either they would fly straight on, hoping to clear Saudi airspace and maybe head for Jordan, or they would land and take to the road again. Kearwin considered each option in turn. He rejected the first almost straight away. The aircraft had gone missing and its pilot, Sullivan, would know perfectly well that he would have some explaining to do, even if he was unaware – as he must be – of the full extent of the search that had been mounted for him. No flight plan had been filed. No, they could not realistically hope to get away with flying straight out of Saudi Arabia.

So; they would have no real choice but to land. The question was, where? Kearwin decided that the Islander would have to return to where it had taken off. That would be where the third vehicle would be waiting. The problem was, AWACS hadn't spotted it immediately after take-off – it had been flying too low. Kearwin had the plot of the earliest sighting of it, and had retasked the JSTARS ground radar to that area. The JSTARS had picked up nothing. He had told the JSTARS to keep searching back along the course the Islander had taken, but so far still nothing had been seen. It didn't matter. When the plane landed, he would pick up the track of the third Land Cruiser from there. About twenty minutes' flying time, maybe.

Kearwin rewound the cassette the ELINT section had sent across and listened once again to the conversation in Arabic. He had been right. The first voice, which ELINT had pinpointed as coming from the area of the parked truck, sounded strained. Kearwin wasn't surprised. The language analyst had commented that the Arabic was fluent and perfect, but the accent wasn't a Saudi one. He couldn't put his finger on it, but he inclined to the view that despite the man's fluency he was probably not an Arab. That was certainly the case with the second speaker, in the aircraft: he had replied in a more stilted way, and the analyst had immediately recognised the voice as English. The man's poor mastery of the Arabic guttural consonants had given him away. Few English or Americans ever managed to get the hang of the gutturals, said the analyst. His opinion was that the speaker had probably learned his Arabic during military service in Bahrain, or possibly Oman.

Kearwin sighed. It wasn't really important. The real reason he had wanted the tape was to hear the voices of these people. He had just wanted to hear them speak. After all the time he had spent shadowing their movements, he had been intrigued at last to hear the voices of two of them.

He rewound the tape for the fourth time and played it again. *Who are you?* he wondered, as the voice of the first man crackled out of the speaker. *I will never meet you, but I would give anything just to know who you are . . .*

435

73

"Eight minutes, Ed. I'm going to start climbing now."

Howard looked across at Denard. The pilot's face was very pale and tense. There was a sheen of sweat on his forehead, and he had spoken through clenched teeth. Denard's flying seemed rather clumsier than he remembered, and he was not flying as low as he had when they had gone on their reconnaissance. Howard frowned momentarily, then swivelled round to shout the instruction to the others in the rear. The engines increased power as the Islander began to climb. He turned back to Denard. "Come on, Andy. Set the autopilot and come back to get fixed up with a 'chute."

"No point, Ed."

"Huh? What do you mean, no point?"

"I'm hit." Denard coughed.

Howard was stricken. Denard's face was now a mask of pain. "Oh God, Andy! Why didn't you say? Where? How bad?"

"Gut, somewhere. Losing blood. Can't feel my legs any more. Haven't you noticed? I've been flying without rudder control since we took off." Denard made a weak attempt at a smile, then screwed up his face again. "I've had it, Ed."

"I can fix you up, Andy! Don't give up now! We can do something!"

"No!" Denard's voice was a sudden shout. He coughed again; some blood ran down his chin. Almost whispering now, he forced the words out with great effort. "Autopilot's fucked. Tried it about ten miles back. That bleddy chopper got me and it, both. You and the others bale out. I'll give you the signal."

"Andy, *please* come! We can land instead! I'll get you to a hospital. I can't just leave you here!"

"No, Ed," whispered Denard. Howard strained forward to hear

436

him. "Never liked the idea of prison. Bleddy Arab food. No women either. I wouldn't make it, anyway. You go. Here's all my ID. Give my regards to Chris."

Numb with sadness, Howard stumbled into the rear of the plane and began preparing himself for the jump. First Bob, now Andy too. Had it all been worth it? The old, familiar doubts began to assail him. Going through the motions like an automaton, he finished strapping on the parachute. He had hoped they would not need to jump, but the fact that they were compromised now made it imperative. Harris's story of his and Palmer's near-miss at Jeddah had confirmed it to him. Usher's body had been stripped of all identification; Howard now had Denard's in his pocket.

He looked up; the others were ready. He could see from their faces that none of them had yet realised what had happened to Denard. Ziegler opened the large cargo door and the night air rushed in. The team began throwing all the weapons and other incriminating items out; they would smash unseen on to the desert below.

Howard watched Denard for the signal; when it came, he whacked MacDonald on the shoulder. The Scot, eyes tight shut, jumped out of the door. Counting a slow three, he pulled his rip-cord. Behind him, Howard and Ziegler were helping the injured Bourne out of the plane. Ziegler, Harris and Ackford quickly followed. Howard turned one last time to Denard; they looked at each other once more, then Howard was gone.

As he floated down to the ground under his parachute, the rumbling engine noise of the departing Islander gradually faded into the night.

74

Kearwin was puzzled. Forcing himself to look up from the Keyhole satellite image of the burning truck and helicopter, he turned his attention to the AWACS plot of the Islander's flight. The plane hadn't followed the same course. It wasn't going back to where it had taken off. Where was it going to land? He shrugged. It didn't matter. Wherever it landed, there would be the vehicle; JSTARS could follow that, until such time as the decision was made to intercept it. The Saudi Air Force, responsible for all air-traffic control in the Kingdom, would probably already have the plane on its radar. Kearwin wondered why the Islander was making no apparent effort to conceal itself this time. AWACS reports now gave its altitude as ten thousand feet; previously it had been skimming the ground and even the AWACS had had problems keeping track of it.

The track updated itself on Kearwin's screen. The Islander had now crossed over the TAP road. He had expected it to land earlier to rendezvous with a vehicle, but now it was heading straight out towards the Nafud desert — one of the biggest sand seas in the world. Where was it planning to go? The Saudi Air Force might be after it even now. They would send a fighter intercept, possibly helicopters . . . It was the first stupid mistake these guys had made.

Kearwin's instinct suddenly told him he had read it wrong. These people just didn't *make* mistakes. The plane must be a blind. They couldn't be in it. But nothing else had left the scene of the wrecked helicopter and truck — they *had* to have left Iraq in the plane! Yet it hadn't landed to let them out. That meant . . . "Jerry!" he shouted. "Get JSTARS to monitor vehicle movement at all places along the track of that airplane since it crossed the Iraqi border! I want to know about any off-road movement! Start off near the TAP road itself! They've jumped!"

438

Two minutes later, they had got it. It had been a very close thing. Kearwin at once saw how clever the team had been. The JSTARS had spotted it only just in time; its radar had picked up a vehicle leaving Al Mira, an abandoned airstrip only three miles off the TAP road. Five minutes more and it would have been just another car on the busy road. JSTARS was definite about it – the vehicle was close enough, being in Saudi Arabia, rather than way over the border in Iraq, for the identification to be certain. Kearwin could see for himself: the JSTARS picture fitted the template for a Land Cruiser. The third vehicle had surfaced at last.

*　　　*　　　*

The seven men in the Land Cruiser were subdued and silent. Howard's news about Denard had hit them hard. Harris and Ackford were squashed into the front passenger seat; beside them Palmer drove, grim-faced, as smoothly and steadily along the tarmac road as he could. Behind him, he knew, the others could do with as little vibration or sudden movement as possible, and Howard had ruled out a stop for the time being.

MacDonald sat in the luggage compartment in the rear with Ziegler, who was attending to the wound in the stalker's forearm. It was cramped for them, sitting amidst the team's baggage, but MacDonald felt quite comfortable; the injection the American had given him had already taken the edge off the pain, and he sensed himself becoming strangely detached and light-headed. He wondered absently what the injection had been.

"OK, Mac, you're goin' to feel this," said the American as he cut away the shell-dressing pad from the wound. "I'm goin' to have to clean this mess up. But it doesn't really look too bad, honest."

MacDonald looked down at it indifferently. The big bullet had gone straight through the muscle on the inside of his arm, leaving a large hole which was now matted with blood and clothing fibres that had been forced into the wound. His hand felt cold and numb. Ziegler broke open a sachet of antiseptic liquid into a bowl between his knees and started dabbing at the wound with a piece of clean lint. Gradually the dirt and clotted blood began to loosen and come away. MacDonald felt relaxed and strange. He couldn't understand why it didn't hurt. He could feel it, but somehow it didn't seem to matter. "What the hell was in that injection, Mike?" he asked dreamily.

"Morphine," grinned Ziegler. "Ten milligrams of morphine sulphate. You'll be flyin' for a while. Make the most of it, though. I'm not givin' you any more after this. You'll have to make do with pills when it wears off. Don't want to make a junkie of you." Ziegler inspected the clean wound and nodded in satisfaction. "OK, that'll do. Now I'll bandage it up. Hold still."

As Ziegler applied a clean dressing, MacDonald's mind wandered away. It was pain, this feeling, he realised calmly. Yes, it must be pain. It just didn't seem terribly important. An image of Glen Carvaig drifted into his mind, and he began floating away over the hills.

Bourne was lying across the rear seat, his damaged leg on Howard's lap. He had been nearly unconscious when they found him after the parachute drop, and Howard had lost no time in applying a tourniquet above the knee and putting in a plasma-expander drip. The plastic half-litre bottle of Hetastarch solution hung suspended from the coat-hook of the car, the tube leading down to a catheter in a vein in his forearm. His blood pressure had stabilised, but he was very pale. He had passed out soon after being hefted into the Land Cruiser, and Howard was now taking advantage of his semi-conscious state to attend to his leg. Working quickly, he cleaned it and packed the wound. It was nasty. Howard could not be certain, but it looked as if an artery in the back of the calf muscle might have been severed. If it had, Bourne would need surgery to repair it within the next twenty-four hours or so, or he would lose the leg. At least the bleeding had stopped. Howard wondered how much blood Bourne had lost. He guessed about two pints, possibly more; the guy was in severe shock. Howard pulled a long face. Somehow, Bourne was going to have to recover enough to be able to make it through the exit channel at the airport without appearing too ill to travel. He knew Bourne was tough, but things didn't look too promising.

*   *   *

Denard, near death, had adjusted the trim on the Islander after Howard had jumped out. The aircraft was flying almost straight and level now, needing no corrections. His sight fading, Denard had kept his eyes on the vertical-speed gauge that indicated the rate of

440

climb or descent, setting the plane to lose one hundred and fifty feet per minute. Immediately above the vertical-speed gauge, also within his field of vision, was the altimeter; at ten thousand feet, he was flying at seven thousand above ground-level. In theory, that would give about forty-five minutes before the plane came down, but the fuel loss would gradually lighten the load and thereby compensate to some extent. He tried to think, his mind fading fast. Was there anything else he should do? Maybe . . .

He died seventeen minutes after crossing the TAP road. The Islander kept on flying by itself, steadily losing height as he had predicted. Ten minutes later, it encountered a sudden downdraught of air which made the nose pitch slightly forward. The movement was enough to dislodge Denard's lifeless body with a jolt. He had undone his seat-harness shortly after he had been wounded, to ease the painful restriction; now, free of restraint, his corpse slumped against the control column, pushing it forward and sending the aircraft into a steep dive. Shortly after, it began to spin. It plummeted earthwards, taking just under a minute to fall. Unobserved except on the AWACS monitor, the Islander smashed into the ground in a remote desert region north-west of Sakakah and caught fire.

The US Air Force AWACS passed the information on the crash direct to the Saudi Arabian air-traffic-control authorities, and a joint Army and Air Force operation was mounted to investigate the incident. The first helicopters arrived on the scene three-quarters of an hour later, by which time the fire had largely burned itself out. Working by arc lights, the Saudi investigators extinguished the remains of the blaze and began sifting through the wreckage.

They found the remains of three bodies: those of Denard and the two Iraqi soldiers from the truck. It would not be until the following day that they discovered there was a fourth – Usher's. All four were burnt beyond recognition.

The Saudi police autopsies would be inconclusive, but the evidence of the bullet wounds and the aircraft's course would point overwhelmingly to the likelihood that the four men had been shot while attempting to flee from Iraq. The police would assume that the pilot, who had obviously died at the controls, was the one they had been seeking – Ray Sullivan.

441

75

MacDonald drifted in and out of a hazy sleep as the Land Cruiser sped through the night. He was oblivious of where they were, or even of how long they had been on the road. The constant hum of the car tyres on the smooth tarmac was soporific, and he was content to leave himself in the hands of the others.

Towards midnight, the effects of the morphine began to wear off and his arm started to throb; at first it was a relatively mild pain, but it got worse until at about two o'clock he found he could no longer sleep. His arm was aching badly. "Where are we, Mike?" he whispered to Ziegler, anxious not to wake Bourne.

Ziegler ignored the question. "How's the arm, Mac?" he asked.

"Sore," admitted MacDonald.

"I'm not surprised," said Ziegler, fishing in the medical box for a packet of tablets. "That was a 14.5mm bullet. That's half an inch diameter – makes a big hole. You've done well to last this long without needin' more pain-killers. Can you move your fingers?"

"Just, but it hurts."

"You'll be fine. Here," – Ziegler proffered two small pills and a larger capsule, together with a water-bottle – "take these."

MacDonald swallowed the pills with a gulp of water. "What are they?" he asked.

"The capsule is Magnapen, an antibiotic. The two pills are Pethidine, fifty milligrams. It's about two clicks down from morphine on the pain-relief scale, but it's fairly strong all the same. Should keep the pain at bay for a few more hours. By the time we get to Jeddah, I want to have you down another two or three clicks, to DF 118 or Co-proxamol. Wouldn't do to have you runnin' around the airport like a hop-head."

"Whatever you say, doctor," said MacDonald with a wry smile. "How long will they take to work?"

"Ten, maybe fifteen minutes."

"Where are we now?"

"I've no idea," answered Ziegler. "I'm just a piece of luggage in the back here, like you. Mel's doin' the navigatin'. Goddam borin' stretch of desert, is all I know."

"No problems so far?"

"No. All quiet. Well, reasonably quiet. One of those police patrol cars with a big green stripe came up behind us back at a place called Al Jawf, but they probably lost interest when they saw the licence number. Mel changed it back in Jeddah. Just as well Johnny's still lyin' down and you and I are out of sight on the floor back here — if the cops had seen seven people all in one car, they might have started wonderin' and stopped us for a closer look."

*　　　*　　　*

"They're coming up to Al Qulibah," Kearwin reported to Sorensen. "It'll be interesting to see which road they take from there."

"What are the options?" asked the Walrus.

"Either they go straight on, heading for Tabuk and then Duba, on the Red Sea coast, or they turn left towards Shuraif, Medinah and Jeddah. I'm not taking any bets on what they'll do. Trying to second-guess these guys is impossible."

"Well, let me know which route they take. Langley wants to know. They're closing in on them."

"OK," said Kearwin with a tinge of regret. "But something puzzles me, Walter. That's a very hot car they're using. The Saudi authorities have the licence number. I'm surprised they haven't been stopped."

"Cops have probably knocked off for the night," suggested Sorensen.

"I guess so," said Kearwin resignedly.

*　　　*　　　*

"Jonathan? Alvin Kennings here."

"Hello, Alvin," said Mitchell into the telephone. "What's the latest? Where have they got to?"

443

"I've just finished talking to Langley. They've taken the Tabuk road from Al Qulibah. There are only two ways they can go from Tabuk. One is to carry on to the coast, and the other is to turn left and head for Medinah. Either way, we've got them. I think it's time to go. If possible, we want to get to them before the cops do."

Mitchell frowned. "Change of plan, eh? Why?"

"Orders from on high. We're to stop and identify them at the earliest opportunity. Depending on who they are, we then get told how to handle it."

"D'you mind telling me why, Alvin?" Mitchell asked curiously.

"I'm surprised you haven't been told, Jonathan. Langley is convinced these people are agents of, ah, a foreign government. They want to know which one, although they're fairly sure. In fact, in the circumstances I'm *very* surprised you haven't been told."

"What – do you mean that because they're working for a friendly government, the CIA wants it hushed up?"

"Something like that," said Kennings. "The President's not convinced, but Langley is. If the DD(I) is right, Washington would be in danger of being implicated too, because of the close relationship."

Mitchell was exasperated; Kennings was talking in riddles. "Why? Which government do they think it is?"

"Yours, Jonathan," said Kennings slowly. "You Brits."

"Oh, Lord," groaned Mitchell. "Oh, Lord Almighty."

76

James Ansell, head of the CIA's Mid-East desk, sat in silence as the Deputy Director (Intelligence) read through the transcripts of the news reports that had just come in. The DD(I)'s cheek muscles were taut with concentration. "These are verbatim?" he asked.

"Pretty much, sir, yes."

"This Iranian news-agency report is very specific," said the DD(I). "And it fits with what we know about this assassination team and their movements. I mean, it says here that Saddam was shot. It doesn't just say killed, it says shot. It says he was shot yesterday at eight in the morning, Iraqi time. And one of their own people was killed too, a diplomat. Why would the Iranians specifically say he was shot, and give a time, unless it's true? He could have been blown up, or knifed, or poisoned, or any number of other things." The DD(I) paused, trying to piece it all together in his mind. "Apart from the fact that it fits exactly with the movements of the hit squad, can we confirm any of this?"

Ansell nodded. "It would appear to fit with a rumour that the recently-appointed Iranian Ambassador to Iraq has disappeared. He had an appointment at the Swedish Embassy in Baghdad last night, and he didn't show up. The Iranian Embassy at first seemed at a loss for an explanation. Then there was a burst of COMINT signals traffic from them to Tehran, which we're still trying to decipher. It looks as if it all adds up. I think we have to take it seriously."

"But then there's this other report," snorted the DD(I). "Look at this. The Iraqi Government denies it all. A ridiculous rumour, they say. There have been pictures broadcast of Saddam presiding over a meeting of the Revolutionary Command Council. The Iraqi cabinet, in other words. And there are reports of his birthday celebrations going on throughout Iraq. They deny the whole thing as complete nonsense."

"That's exactly the sort of thing one expects from the Iraqi News Agency," said Ansell. "I can't think of a single word of truth they've broadcast in the last ten years. Pure propaganda, all of their output. Look at it this way. If Saddam *has* been assassinated, they're hardly likely to tell anyone about it, at least not just yet. Not until his successor is announced, anyway. There would be massive civil unrest, possibly an uprising. The Iraqi hierarchy would want to suppress the knowledge for a while, until a new President had consolidated his power and taken full control."

"Hmm," grunted the DD(I). "Well, I must say I'm inclined to agree with you. The clincher is that it all fits exactly with the NRO reports on the movements of the hit squad."

"That's what convinced me, too," said Ansell. "But for that, I don't think I'd have attached quite so much credibility to it."

The DD(I) stared out of the window reflectively. "Why eight in the morning?" he mused. "Odd time to be shot, isn't it? What was Saddam doing holding a parade at breakfast time, for Chrissake?"

"The heat," said Ansell.

"What?"

"Tikrit is at low altitude, in the Tigris valley," explained Ansell. "It gets uncomfortably hot and humid after about ten in the morning, even at this time of year. If you have any physical work to do outside, either you get it done early, before the heat gets up, or you wait till late, just before dusk. I dare say Saddam didn't want TV pictures showing all his soldiers falling down, fainting from the heat."

"Oh, I see," said the DD(I) blankly. "Well, thanks for this, James. I'd better get it to the DCI. I guess he'll want to tell the President."

*　　*　　*

"Mr President, I have Prime Minister Major on the line."

"Thanks." The President picked up the telephone. "John? George here. I'm sorry if I woke you up."

"That's all right, Mr President," replied John Major sleepily. He had retired late, just half an hour before, only to be woken by the telephone. "What can I do for you?"

"John, you ought to know that the Iranian news agency has

reported that Saddam Hussein was shot yesterday morning. My people here are inclined to believe the report."

"Oh," said Major, suddenly awake. "How sure are they?"

"They can't be certain," answered the President, "but it all fits with our satellite monitoring operation of those people who busted into Iraq. We've been tracking them every step of the way, and the timings fit precisely. The question now is what are we going to do about it? On the diplomatic side, I think we have to prepare for the fragmentation of Iraq. On the practical side, I think we must decide what we do about the assassins. I would welcome your thoughts."

John Major mustered his thoughts and voiced them. "Diplomatically, things will clearly be awkward. If Saddam is dead, I suppose it rather depends on who takes over. If it's another strong man, fragmentation might be avoided."

"That's possible," drawled the President, "but we don't hold out too much hope. We don't think there is anyone else strong enough. It's interesting that Baghdad is denying the whole thing. If there had been a strong man ready to take over, he would probably already have made his move."

"Who do you think will take over?" asked Major.

"We think there are four main contenders, if one ignores Saddam's two sons, Udai and Kusai – they are just thugs. The first serious contender is Saddam's half-brother Barzan, who is based in Switzerland in his capacity as Permanent Representative of Iraq's Mission to the UN. Normally, he might be the one we'd expect to seize power, but he's out of the country, which can't help his chances. Do you have a view on him?"

"I would agree with your assessment," replied the Prime Minister. "Mounting a coup from outside a country is rarely successful."

"What do you mean?" retorted the President crossly. "It's worked in this case, hasn't it?"

"Oh, I see," said Major. "You think Barzan is behind this?"

"Of course I don't," spluttered Bush, exasperated. "What I meant was . . . Hell, we're getting nowhere with this. Let's get on with the list of candidates. The next contender is Tariq Aziz, the Foreign Minister at the time of the war and now Deputy Prime Minister. We don't think he has a sufficient power base or is quite ruthless enough to knock off his rivals. Third, there is Taha Yasin Ramadan, the Deputy President. He's smart – maybe smarter than the others –

but because of that, we see his position as precarious. Do you have any views on these two?"

"Well," said Major slowly, "I don't know much about Taha Yasin, but I would hesitate to rule out Tariq Aziz. He is a clever man too. I remember when I was Foreign Secretary —"

"Yeah, yeah," interrupted Bush. "I remember when I was DCI, too, but that's got nothing to do with this. Let's move on. The fourth contender is Izzat Ibrahim, Saddam's Vice-President. He is a hardliner, and he's ideally placed. We think he's the one who will make a grab for it. Do you agree?"

"Not entirely," answered Major. "Certainly he is a hardliner, but I would think he's rather too grey a character to be able to hold the job down for long. There are also reports that he is in poor health."

"We would broadly go along with that assessment, John," said the President. "And that is precisely my point. We don't think he will last. In the meantime, do you see Iraq holding together with him in charge?"

"It can't be ruled out," replied the Prime Minister, "even though he has been little more than a lackey of Saddam's. He has been absolutely faithful to Saddam, and he could probably be counted on to use similar means to try to hold on to power and keep the country together. If he lasts."

"OK," resumed the President, "let's say for the sake of argument that he doesn't last long. The problem then will be the upheaval that will result in the Mid-East if Iraq does break up. We'll end up with three rump states — the Kurds in the north, the Sunni Muslims in the centre, and the marsh Arabs in the south. We don't think any of these three states would last long either."

"Shi'ites," corrected Major. "We must remember always to refer to the marsh Arabs as Shi'ites. We can do so because of their religion. If we call them 'marsh Arabs' it makes them sound more innocuous. If people started thinking of them as harmless victims, public opinion might force us to do something about protecting them from Saddam. The term 'Shi'ite', on the other hand, has got itself a bad reputation — people think of Shi'ites as fanatics, and no one would want us to lift a finger to help them."

"OK, Shi'ites, if you like," grunted Bush, irritated at being lectured by the Prime Minister. "But that just reinforces my point. The Iranians are Shi'ites too, and they'll use that as an excuse to intervene. This is the main threat, as we see it – Iranian intervention. The implications of that are scary."

"Things in Iran aren't as bad as they were," countered Major. "They have recently held elections, and the moderates have done well, which is welcome news. Mr Rafsanjani has consolidated his power, and he is a moderate. We do not think that they will simply continue to act as before, spreading terrorism and revolution."

"We aren't so optimistic on that," said the President. "We are assuming that there will be little or no change in their attitude."

"Well, I don't think that is a wise assumption at all. I really don't think you can assume that, Mr President. I feel that the Iranian situation is a lot more promising now than it was under Khomeini."

"Then we'll just have to disagree on that," declared Bush. "Those goddam Ayatollahs and hardliners still have a lot of influence. I want to discuss with you a joint approach to Iran. In short, I think we must present a united front. I think we must offer Rafsanjani our support. We got nowhere confronting Khomeini, so maybe a more friendly approach would work better with his successor. If we stay on better terms with Iran, we might be able to persuade them that moderation pays."

"That sounds like a very sensible approach, Mr President," agreed Major. "Very sensible indeed. Perhaps my Foreign Secretary and your Secretary of State could put their heads together and come up with some recommendations."

"Fine," said Bush. "Now, we must also decide what to do about these assassins. The CIA should have caught up with them soon. The question is, what do we do with them?" *Major's answer to that might be revealing*, he thought.

"I suggest we let the Saudi police handle the matter," replied the Prime Minister simply.

The President was surprised. "What? Do you mean just hand them over to the Saudis?"

"Yes," answered Major. "These men have broken Saudi law. I don't think we should interfere."

"You do realise that we have tapes of radio conversations they had, and two of the voices had English accents?"

"I still don't think we should interfere," repeated Major firmly. "Apart from anything else, if they are tried out there, there will be less likelihood of the details of what they have done leaking out and causing a stir in the press. A Saudi court would be unlikely to tolerate a full account of their deeds in mitigation, in the way that a Western court would. Just imagine what a defence lawyer here would make of their story. No, I think it would definitely be better if they were arrested and tried out there. Perhaps if the sentences they receive under Saudi law are particularly harsh, we might appeal for them to be reduced; for example, if they are sentenced to death, we might ask if this could be commuted to life imprisonment. But there is no question of my asking for absolute clemency for people who have broken as many laws as these men would appear to have done. It would just annoy the Saudis."

"Well, I for one would like to know who was behind this job," said Bush with feeling. "It's going to mean a whole lot of extra work for everyone, and the situation out there is quite bad enough without people taking it on themselves to knock off heads of state, however nasty they are."

The Prime Minister considered his response. "It would certainly be interesting to know who was behind it," he began slowly, "of course it would." He cleared his throat briskly. "But what's done is done. I think we can do no more than let justice take its course."

"Well, I'll let you get back to bed now. It's been interesting talking to you."

"Good night then, Mr President," said the Prime Minister with relief, not entirely sure that their conversation had settled anything.

George Bush put down the telephone. He too was a little perplexed by the way the dialogue had gone. He mentally decided not to call John Major late at night again. The man obviously wasn't at his best when unexpectedly woken up. The President wondered about the last part of the conversation. Maybe the CIA was right about this, after all. If so, Major was a callous s.o.b., as well as a tricky one. OK, he thought; if the British Prime Minister was happy to let his own agents rot in a Saudi jail, so be it.

77

Howard had been sitting awake thinking; he hadn't slept at all. There were quite a few pieces to the puzzle that simply didn't fit. His suspicions about the air strike on the warehouse had hardened into certainty; there was no doubt that somehow they had been compromised. The difficulty lay in trying to fathom exactly how much was known. He turned to Ziegler. "Mike? How much do you know about the capabilities of aerial surveillance?"

"What – air photos, that kind of stuff?"

"Perhaps. Look, we've assumed that Saudi radar picked up the aircraft. We've been hoping they would think that was the end of it. What if something more sophisticated picked it up?"

"You mean AWACS? Yeah, it's possible. The Saudis have got AWACS."

"I wasn't thinking of the Saudis, Mike."

The implications of Howard's remark slowly sank in. "Shit!" said Ziegler. He sat up as straight as he could in the confined space of the Land Cruiser's luggage compartment. "You mean, our side?"

"Yes, I'm afraid I do. I can't see any other explanation for it. I think we've been shadowed since quite early on. And for some reason, they aren't acting friendly at all. The warehouse was evidence enough of that. The question is, if they're using AWACS, what can it do? Can it follow vehicles?"

"No, I don't think so," answered Ziegler thoughtfully. "Hell, Ed, I think you're right. I should've thought of it myself. It fits. That strike on the warehouse was too precise. It was laser-guided bombs, or cruise missiles. The Iraqis don't have either of those things."

"My conclusions exactly," said Howard. "But to get back to my question. Do our own Forces have the capability to track cars? Could they have been tracking us all along? Might they be tracking us right

451

now? My feeling is that they have – and they are. I don't see any other way they could have known we were in that warehouse."

"I don't know the latest technology. But there was some capability they used in the Gulf War to spot Iraqi tanks movin' about. It was a system similar to AWACS. Maybe if they could spot tanks . . ."

Howard had made up his mind. "OK. We'll play it safe, anyway. We'll assume they've got us on some sort of a monitor right now. Here's what we're going to do."

*   *   *

"They're just passing through Al Wajh, Walter," called out Kearwin. "They haven't stopped there. Where are the CIA boys now?"

"Never you mind about them," said the Walrus. "All you gotta do is keep your eyes glued to that Land Cruiser on the screen. It's after dawn there now, and there'll soon be other traffic on the road."

"That shouldn't be a problem. They're so close now. JSTARS is practically overhead. It couldn't miss that car, even in traffic."

Kearwin watched as the screen showed the Land Cruiser continuing south along the coast road at speed towards Yanbu and Jeddah. He wondered what they were going to do. Were they going to stop where they had landed the dinghy, and take to the sea again? If so, where were they going to go? There was no escape that way. Or were they going to carry straight on to Jeddah? Kearwin wished he knew. Somewhere down there a CIA intercept was waiting. Saudi police, too.

Twenty miles out of Al Wajh, the Land Cruiser stopped briefly; then it was off again. No more than ten seconds, thought Kearwin. Probably changing over drivers. An empty bit of road – no other traffic about. The new driver wasn't driving quite as fast. It was another fifty miles to the place where they had landed the dinghy, where the coast road was close to the sea. That would be the next point of interest – would they stop there? He leaned back and waited.

Forty-five minutes later, Kearwin sat up with a start. The Land Cruiser *had* stopped at the landing point. It had turned off the road, down towards the sea. They *were* going to take to the boat again! Yes – the car had definitely stopped by the shore. And there was no other vehicle approaching it.

452

Five minutes later, the information was flashed out to the American Embassy in Riyadh; from there it was relayed to Alvin Kennings, who was on the road just north of Yanbu. Kennings looked at the map and cursed. He was at least an hour away from where the Land Cruiser had stopped; they could be away in the boat before he got there. But it didn't really make any difference, he said to himself – in a way, perhaps, it was better. There was a US warship standing about twenty miles offshore, an FFG-7-class frigate. On board were two Sikorsky SH-60B Seahawk helicopters, ready to go. No dinghy was going to get past *them*. And that would avoid any possible trouble with the Saudi cops. Kennings put his foot down on the accelerator.

* * *

Unknown to Kennings, the rear door of the Land Cruiser had opened just before the vehicle had arrived at Al Wajh, a little more than an hour earlier. Ziegler, clad in several extra layers of clothing selected from the pieces of baggage in the rear, and wearing the last of the NVG helmets, had rolled out on to the road. The Land Cruiser did not stop; Ziegler hit the ground hard at forty miles per hour and then rolled for what seemed to him like a full minute, but was in fact a matter of just a few seconds. Picking himself up, he discarded the extra clothing, the outer layers of which were now torn, and the NVG helmet, which was almost shattered. Ziegler decided that apart from a headache and a few bruises he was unhurt. He waved at the departing Land Cruiser and set off at an easy jog along a side-road towards the north-west. Al Wajh airport was six kilometres away, he knew. The temperature at dawn was warm, but not too hot for him to run. He reckoned that it would take him no more than twenty-five minutes. There was no traffic about.

Twenty miles beyond Al Wajh, as Kearwin noticed on the JSTARS screen, the Land Cruiser stopped briefly. The drivers did indeed change, as Kearwin conjectured: Harris took over. What Kearwin could not have known was that everyone else got out of the car in the few seconds it was stationary. Howard and Ackford lifted Bourne out and laid him on the ground beside the road, while Palmer helped MacDonald to get all the luggage out of the rear. When the Land Cruiser was empty, Harris drove off. The stop had lasted for less than ten seconds.

453

They carried Bourne and the baggage well off the road to the side and took shelter out of sight behind a bush. Howard returned to the road and put out two small marker flags, the first two hundred yards back up the road from where they were concealed, and the second to mark their position itself. They sat down to wait.

Ziegler had arrived at the airport at 06.45, at about the same time the others had left the Land Cruiser. He went straight to the car-park and got into the hired Dodge Ram Charger he had used to collect Howard and MacDonald from the dinghy. He started it up and drove away, rejoining the main road through Al Wajh and following the route the Land Cruiser had taken just under half an hour before. At 07.18 he spotted the first of the two marker flags and slowed, stopping when he reached the second. Glancing up and down the road and seeing that it was clear, he tooted the car horn three times. Howard and the others emerged from cover and came across, carrying Bourne and the luggage. They climbed into the Dodge and drove off, still following the route south towards Jeddah.

Harris was a good thirty minutes in front of them. When he reached the spot on the coast road Howard had described to him, he drove the Land Cruiser off the road and down towards the shore, then stopped and got out. He removed the vehicle licence-plates with a screwdriver and set off at a fast jog down the road. He wanted to be well away by the time the Ram Charger caught up with him.

Half an hour later, Harris was nearly five miles clear of the abandoned Land Cruiser, on a stretch of the road that no one would have been likely to be monitoring. Harris heard the pick-up's car horn toot the signal; he looked round and prepared to jump on board. The pick-up slowed to a walking pace; Harris allowed it to pass, then sprinted forward and dived, panting, into the rear compartment. It was 07.51.

"He's in, Mike," said Howard.

Ziegler accelerated away. He glanced back at Howard. "Do you think we did it?" he asked.

"I hope so," said Howard. "Anyway, we'll find out when we get to Jeddah, won't we?"

Exactly thirty-five minutes afterwards, at 08.26, the Ram Charger passed a large Chevrolet saloon going in the opposite direction. Neither car took any notice of the other amongst the other traffic. At 08.52, the Chevrolet arrived at the reported location of the Land

Cruiser and stopped; Alvin Kennings and two burly Marines from the US Embassy climbed out.

"There's no one here," said one of the Marines unnecessarily.

Kennings ignored him. He was scanning the sea with his binoculars for any sign of a boat. How far could they have got? He radioed back to the Embassy, and just over thirty minutes later he saw a helicopter circling in the distance, way out to sea. "The Seahawks will pick them up," he muttered to himself. He continued watching.

He would have to wait another whole hour, until 10.32, before he received the message that neither the radar systems on the frigate nor its Seahawk helicopters had seen any sign of a boat. The frigate's captain was quite categoric about it: there was no boat there. Alvin Kennings immediately realised that the team must have changed vehicles and still be on the road, but neither he nor, several thousand miles away in Washington, John Kearwin would ever know exactly what had happened or how the team had managed to do it without stopping for more than ten seconds.

78

"It would therefore appear, gentlemen, that these men have temporarily slipped through the net cast by the CIA." The Director of MI6, Britain's Secret Intelligence Service, concluded his summary and looked up from his notes. There were a few raised eyebrows, but little other apparent reaction from the members of the Joint Intelligence Committee.

"Thank you, Sir Arthur," said the Intelligence Co-ordinator. "Gentlemen, before we discuss any further action that might be taken to identify the individuals concerned and deal with them, I think it would be useful to examine the possible repercussions of their actions in Iraq." The Intelligence Co-ordinator, himself a past Director of the SIS, paused for a moment and studied the faces around the table. "First of all, we should perhaps try to establish exactly what has transpired. The evidence, as you have heard from Sir Arthur, is compelling: in short, it is the view of the American intelligence community that yesterday morning President Saddam Hussein was assassinated by a sniper's bullet. The broadcast by the Iranian news service – not, perhaps, something to which great credibility would normally be attached – gave a specific time and place. These particulars happen to coincide exactly with observations made by American, ah, surveillance satellites. This alone, as I am sure you will all agree, is too much of a coincidence to ignore. There have, however, been other, contradictory, reports. Notable among these is of course the news emanating from Iraq itself. The official Iraqi news network has put out several broadcasts denying the Iranian report; Saddam Hussein himself has been shown on television presiding over a meeting of the Iraqi Revolutionary Command Council, and there have also been pictures of people celebrating his birthday yesterday at various towns and cities around Iraq."

The Intelligence Co-ordinator clasped his hands together in a decisive gesture, inhaled audibly and then went on. "We now firmly believe that these Iraqi reports have been deliberately falsified. This may not come as a surprise to any of you, given that agency's reputation for propagating falsehoods. We have, however, established that the pictures of the President are library ones. The BBC's archives already contain exactly the same clip of film; it was first shown on British television some six months ago. The implication must be that there was no film shot of Saddam Hussein yesterday, or if there was, it has been deliberately suppressed. I am further informed that one of the television sequences showing yesterday's celebrations, which the Iraqis claimed was of events in Tikrit, was in fact positively *not* of that town; the sequence was filmed in Al Mahmudiyah, a town just south of Baghdad. It has been conclusively identified as such by a journalist who has been there. I understand that this journalist is very reliable, and he is quite adamant on the matter. I think that these factors demonstrate, if any further demonstration is needed, that it would be quite safe for us to discount the Iraqi reports.

"There is a further report, which on the face of it would be less easy to discount. It appears" – the Intelligence Co-ordinator held up a newspaper – "in today's *Times*. The article reports at some length on the celebrations yesterday in Tikrit; it tells of tens of thousands of people swarming past a reviewing stand in the President's home town, shouting 'We all love Saddam'. The article also states that Saddam was not at Tikrit himself, because he was concerned about the possibility of assassination. Now; one might normally be inclined to take this report seriously, but for two factors. First, the journalist who filed it did so from Cairo. He wasn't even in Iraq, let alone in Tikrit. He was in Egypt. Second, he quite plainly acknowledges that the source of his information was the Iraqi newspaper *Al Jumhuriyah* which, as you will probably know, is the Iraqi Government's official mouthpiece.

"I think that you will therefore agree," continued the Intelligence Co-ordinator, "that the case is strong for believing the Iranian press reports. I would now like to move on to the Government's policy in this matter. I had a meeting early this morning with the Prime Minister and the Foreign Secretary . . ."

Max Goodale, Deputy Director of MI5, the Security Service, allowed his mind to detach itself from the proceedings as the

Intelligence Co-ordinator began to outline the new and more conciliatory approach the Government would be taking to the Iranians. Goodale was mulling things over. So it had been a sniper, had it? That was the first he'd heard of it. Interesting. He cast his mind back over the almost total lack of evidence the police had been able to obtain, and the dubious connection, still unproven, with Sir Peter Dartington. His thoughts wandered. He decided there were a few more things he needed to find out; he refocused his attention. The Intelligence Co-ordinator was winding up.

" . . . So, gentlemen, that is the proposed policy of Her Majesty's Government. Unless there are any comments, I would now like to discuss what action we might take against the assassins."

Goodale broke in. "Mr Chairman, I think it would be useful for us all to have an idea of the type of people we are dealing with in this matter. I am sure we all have our own opinions, but I think the view of the Director of Special Forces would be most useful."

The Intelligence Co-ordinator looked a little surprised, but he nodded his assent. "Yes, Mr Goodale, that might be useful." He turned to a man sitting at the far end of the table. "Brigadier? Perhaps you would enlighten us?"

The Director of Special Forces was a former commanding officer of the 22nd Special Air Service Regiment; now he co-ordinated all Special Forces activity, both SAS and SBS, from a headquarters in London. As usual, he was not wearing uniform. He spoke economically and to the point. "On the evidence of what they seem to have achieved, these are men of high calibre. It is certain that there are ex-Servicemen involved; most probably, they are ex-Special Forces. These particular men are unconventional but effective, and highly resourceful. They must also be very highly motivated and determined indeed. On a purely professional basis, I have to confess some admiration for their ability. But there is one thing that puzzles me about this affair."

"Yes, Brigadier?" prompted the Intelligence Co-ordinator. "What is that?"

"It is the question of where they got their information from. There are not many people in the world who could pull off a job like this; most of those who could do it are experienced soldiers, or ex-soldiers, from the SAS or SBS. But none of them," said the Brigadier with emphasis, "would have been able to do this job without information.

458

If we had been asked to do it ourselves, we could probably have done it, but I must stress that we would have got nowhere – in fact we wouldn't even have started – without accurate information. By that I mean precise information, well in advance, as to Saddam's whereabouts. The sort of information, in fact, that these men seem to have had. It would be most interesting to know where they got it from."

The Intelligence Co-ordinator had winced when the SAS Brigadier calmly talked of his men's capabilities; he was anxious now to bring the discussion back to the point. "Thank you, Brigadier. I am sure that the question of their source of information is one that will exercise us all until the matter is resolved. Perhaps we could now address the issue of what is to be done about these men, when they are found. Could I say first of all, although it perhaps goes without saying, that the Prime Minister is anxious that Her Majesty's Government be spared any undue embarrassment . . ."

Goodale was thinking hard again. Yes, he said to himself. That would certainly be the case. The Government must *of course* be spared any "embarrassment". He thought back to the words of the Brigadier. He considered the type of individual who would be capable of doing what these men had done. The Brigadier had confirmed it to him. Goodale had also come across such people, when he had been younger. In fact, he had once thought of volunteering for the SAS himself, but had instead found himself recruited into the rather more shadowy world of Army intelligence . . .

The Joint Intelligence Committee broke up half an hour later, and Goodale left the building to return to his office. As he sat back in his car, something was nagging at his mind, something he had forgotten. It had been only a small thing, something just to make him wonder if by chance . . .

"George," he said suddenly to his driver, "change of plan. Could you take me out towards Edgware, please?"

"Certainly, sir." The imperturbable driver swung the car round and headed northwards.

*   *

Three hours later, Goodale was back in his office, a gleam in his eye. He picked up the telephone and rang an old friend. They talked for a few minutes, and Goodale asked one question. He got the answer he expected. He made two further calls; one was answered by a machine which stated that the person he was trying to reach was away; at the other number there was no reply. Just as he had expected. Well, well, thought Goodale. He went down to the basement and picked out six files, returning with them to his office, where he sat down at his desk and read them one by one. When he had finished, he leaned back in his chair and let his eyes go out of focus.

There was a knock on the door and his secretary came in. She looked ill at ease. "Sir? Could you spare me a moment? It's something, er, personal, about a friend of mine."

"Certainly, Janey. Come in and sit down."

The young woman was relieved. Her boss was clearly in a good mood. She blurted out her story in a rush. "Sir, one of my oldest friends is in trouble. She has this boyfriend, you see, and I said I thought you might know what to do. I mean, she doesn't know who you are, but she knows I work in Security. It's all right – she's a police Detective Inspector. It's her boyfriend. Well, her fiancé, actually. She thinks he's mixed up in something and she doesn't know what to do. She'd like to talk to you."

Max Goodale smiled. "This fiancé of hers, Janey," he said, glancing at one of the files on the desk in front of him. "His name wouldn't by any chance be Bourne, would it?"

79

"The police checkpoint outside Jeddah is only about twenty miles away now, boss," Harris called out to Howard from the rear covered section.

"OK, Mel. What's the usual form there?"

"It shouldn't be a problem. If you smile at the guys and make an effort to speak a bit of the lingo, they normally just let you through."

"Do they check the paperwork?"

"Yes. Passports, vehicle documents – you know. No problem."

"Unfortunately, there *is* a problem. Two of the passports – mine and Danny's – don't have Saudi visas in them." Howard thought for a moment. "I tell you what," he said. "We'll hand them all the passports in a bunch, but we won't give them mine or Danny's – we'll give them Andy's and Bob's instead. There's a danger that they might match the faces, but I think it's a lesser risk than that they'll notice there are no visas."

"OK, boss."

Howard turned to Bourne, who was lying along the rear seat of the big double cab, his leg still up across Howard's lap. He shook his shoulder gently. "Johnny? Time to wake up. How are you feeling?"

Bourne opened his eyes. He was still pale. He had drifted in and out of a restless sleep, occasionally wakened by the pain from his leg. "Weak," he croaked. He cleared his voice and added, "I feel a bit light in the head. But the pain has eased. It's not so bad as it was."

"Good," said Howard. The pain-killers were obviously doing their job. He had had to give Bourne a second shot of morphine just after midnight, but since then he had been on the Pethidine tablets, washed down with a water-glucose mix to keep up his energy. The worst times for Bourne had been when the tourniquet had had to be released,

461

every half-hour for a couple of minutes, and the blood had flowed back into the leg. Howard had changed the dressing again an hour ago, and there had been no further bleeding. Bourne had now also had seven hundred and fifty millilitres of intravenous Hetastarch, and both his legs were bound up with pressure bandages to restrict the blood flow to the limbs. The treatment seemed to have worked, but Bourne was obviously in no condition for any activity at all; he ought to have been in a hospital bed, thought Howard. Well, it couldn't be helped. "Listen, Johnny. We're coming up to a police checkpoint. You're going to have to sit up and look reasonably normal when we pass through it. D'you think you can manage that?"

"Sure," said Bourne. He raised himself on one elbow. "Help me up, will you?"

"Not just yet, Johnny." Howard gestured to him to lie back. "I don't want you passing out before we get there. Wait until the last minute. OK, everyone," he announced, addressing the others, "time to smarten ourselves up. Get the electric shavers working on your faces, and clean shirts on. We want to look like respectable citizens."

"What a chance," grinned Ackford. "Us lot? Respectable? We look like we've just broken out of jail."

"And if we don't act convincing, jail will be right where we'll be going," called Harris from the rear. He rummaged in the bags for items of clean clothing and began passing them through into the cab.

There was a long queue at the road-block; Harris and Palmer both commented that the delay was worse than either had experienced before. Howard reassured them. "Look, they don't know about this pick-up. If they're looking for a vehicle, it's the Land Cruiser. And they don't know who we are or what we look like. The names they've got are false Darcon ones, not our real names. They don't even know how many of us there are. I think we'll be OK, as long as they don't try to match the faces to the passport pictures."

"What about Bob's picture?" asked Harris. "None of us is bald. They'll notice that."

"The picture in his passport is an old one," said Howard. "It's the same passport he had when we did time in the Turkish clink together. He still had some hair then. Not much, but some."

Howard eased Bourne up into a sitting position when they were

462

just two cars from the front of the line. He saw Bourne set his jaw in determination, but ten seconds after sitting him up he noticed the pale face grimace; the blood flow to his leg had brought the pain back with a vengeance. There was a sheen of sweat on Bourne's face, and Howard worried that he would pass out.

Ziegler gave the bored-looking Saudi policeman a radiant smile, and mustered his best Arabic. "*As-salaam aleikum*," he greeted him, "*Kayf haalak?*" He handed out the passports and the Ram Charger's hire documents, along with his driving licence.

The policeman seemed to take an age to check through the papers, and made a show of leaning down and looking into the vehicle to study each face. Somehow, Bourne managed to smile at him when it came to his turn, but he didn't try to speak. Then the policeman disappeared round the back of the vehicle to look into the rear, where Ackford and Harris were sitting with MacDonald. *Oh God*, thought Howard, *he's checking the faces thoroughly*.

Suddenly, the policeman was back. He handed the passports and documents back through the window to Ziegler and waved him on through. As the car started forward, Bourne gave a groan of pain; Howard gently lowered him down again, raising the injured limb. The relief for Bourne was almost immediate as the pressure came off his leg. "Ed," he muttered weakly, "I don't know how much more of that I can take. You'd better leave me behind. I'll never make it on to a plane."

Howard made up his mind. "I'm going to give you another shot of morphine, Johnny. All you have to do is remember not to talk too much. And don't go to sleep, either. We'll get you a wheelchair at the airport."

"What about the passports, boss?" called Harris. "How are you going to deal with that? Bamboozling a traffic cop is one thing, but trying to hoodwink an immigration officer is quite another. Neither you nor Mac looks anything like Andy or Bob."

"I'm going to change the photos. You, Mike and Tony drop the rest of us at the airport; then I want you to go shopping." Howard gave Harris a list of purchases.

Harris nodded in understanding. "Do you think it'll work, boss?"

"No. Not a chance," said Howard drily, grinning. "But at least I won't have to spend another couple of weeks in that bloody freezer container. Anyway, do you have a better idea?"

When they arrived at the airport, Howard and MacDonald hurried off to find an automatic passport-photograph booth, while Ziegler and Palmer went in search of a wheelchair. Harris drove the pick-up a short distance to a temporary parking space and waited in the cab with Bourne and Ackford. It was eleven in the morning and the sun was beating down; Harris left the engine running with the air-conditioner full on. Ten minutes later, he saw Palmer and Ziegler returning with a borrowed wheelchair.

"Luxury model, Johnny," beamed Ziegler. "It's got a leg-rest, so you'll be able to keep your foot up." They lifted Bourne into the wheelchair and Palmer trundled him off towards the terminal. Ziegler climbed into the front of the cab beside Harris and Ackford. "OK, guys; let's go shoppin'. Then I've got to check these wheels back in."

"Mine too," Harris reminded them. "But I'd better put some mileage on it first. We'll leave this and take my hire-car."

"No," said Ziegler. "They'll be stoppin' all Land Cruisers. We can't risk it. No, listen – Tony and I will do the shoppin', and you can drive your hire-car round the parkin' lot for a while."

Half an hour later, the team reassembled in the departure hall of the airport, Ziegler and Ackford returning last after a visit to the shopping centre. Howard had bought tickets for them all on the first available flights out; he and MacDonald would travel on a separate flight from the others. Harris had replaced the original licence-plates on the hired Land Cruiser and checked it in with eight miles on the clock; the check-in assistant had made no comment on the low mileage. The false formica plates had been snapped into little pieces and deposited in a waste-bin, along with all the medical kit except the Pethidine and Co-proxamol tablets for Bourne and MacDonald. Ziegler handed Howard a small bag containing the things he had bought and went off to check in the hired Ram Charger.

Howard had a brief word with each of the others; then he disappeared to the rest room and locked himself in a cubicle. He took out a scalpel blade and carefully slit around the edge of the photograph in Usher's passport, cutting through the thin transparent plastic film that sealed it to the page. He began to prise the photograph off with the blade. The glue was stubborn, and he managed only to get the edges away. It was enough; the replacement photograph would cover what was left. With a stationery embossing tool and a set of simple patterned dies, he began to copy the embossed Passport Office stamp on to a photograph of himself, taken in the booth. It was a slow process, doing one part of the pattern at a time, but after twenty minutes and on his second attempt – having ruined the first photograph – he was reasonably satisfied. It was crude, and it probably wouldn't fool a British immigration officer for one second, but it would have to do. Laying his photograph over the partially-removed one of Usher, he lined up the embossed lines and stuck it down lightly with glue. Then he took a thin sheet of transparent adhesive film, cut it roughly to size and laid it over the photograph and the passport page. Using the scalpel blade, he trimmed it to exactly the same size as the original, flush with the edges of the page. He left the cubicle and went to the hand-drier near the wash-basins. He held the page in the stream of hot air for two minutes, then placed the open passport on the flat surface next to the wash-basins and pressed down hard with his hands. The adhesive film, warmed and softened by the heat, moulded itself into the embossed pattern. Howard inspected the finished result. His own face stared out from Usher's passport; he just hoped the Saudi immigration officer would not notice the disparity in the stated height – he was nearly four inches taller than Usher. He began to repeat the process for Denard's passport, using MacDonald's photograph.

Howard emerged at 12.45; he found MacDonald sitting alone. "The others all get off OK, Danny?" he asked.

"Aye," answered MacDonald, a strange look on his face. He looked at Howard. "It seemed wrong, somehow, saying goodbye to them here. They're a hell of a good bunch," he added with sudden feeling. "I'll miss them."

"We had to split up at some stage, Danny," said Howard gently. "If we all arrived back home at once, we might attract attention. Especially with two injured."

"Why us two last? Was Johnny a guinea-pig, just to see if he would get away with it?"

"No," replied Howard. "Quite the opposite. He should be OK, with his so-called 'sprained ankle' bandaged up like that. Mel and Tony will look after him on the plane. He'll be comfortable enough in First Class, with his feet up. They'll deliver him home safe and sound – Mel's a trained medic too, you know. As for us two, we're the biggest risk, as we're the ones with false passports. So we go last, to give the others a chance to get clear."

"What about the passports at the other end? Will these fool British immigration?"

"They won't have to," said Howard. As soon as we're on the plane, I'm going to tear these two into tiny pieces and flush them down the khazi. When we get to Rome, we'll hang back and join a queue of people arriving from some other European country. Then we'll go through Italian immigration, entering on our own passports. Being EEC passports, they won't be stamped. I'll say goodbye to you in Rome – you'll have to get a ticket for the next flight back to the UK. There'll be nothing in your passport to show that you ever left Europe. Come on, let's go."

As they walked towards the immigration counter at the entrance to the departure lounge, MacDonald felt that every eye in the huge airport building was on him. He sneaked a glance at Howard.

"Keep it natural, Danny," murmured Howard casually.

In a half-daze, MacDonald handed over Denard's passport. He tried to appear nonchalant and carefree, but as the immigration officer flicked through the pages of the passport his heart was pounding.

Then there was a thump as the stamp came down on the page; the officer handed the passport back to him. "Thank you, Mr Denard," he rattled off in English. "I hope you have enjoyed your stay in Saudi Arabia."

"Aye," said MacDonald with a sudden smile. "I've had the time of my life."

PART FOUR

A BLINDING FLASH

80

The car turned off the Spean Bridge road into the cottage gateway and stopped; the Deputy Director of MI5 got out and walked up the path. He knocked twice and waited, glancing idly at a workbench standing under a lean-to shelter at the side of the cottage.

The door opened. Danny MacDonald stood framed in the doorway, one arm in a sling. His face registered surprise, and then pleasure. "Well, hello, sir! This is a pleasant surprise! Will you come in?"

"Thank you, Danny," said Max Goodale. He followed MacDonald through into the sitting-room. It was a warm, welcoming room; a pretty young woman with auburn hair was busy hanging a pair of cheerfully-coloured curtains on a rail. She got down from the stool as Goodale entered.

"Sir, I'd like you to meet my fiancée, Sheila." MacDonald introduced them; Sheila blushed and smiled.

"Delighted to meet you, my dear," said Goodale, also smiling. "And how did you come to know young Danny?"

"Oh, I live not far away," she replied. "In Carvaig village. My mother runs the inn there, and I help her."

"Oho," said Goodale with a twinkle. "You've left her to do all the work herself, have you?"

"Oh, no, not at all!" exclaimed Sheila defensively. "She's gone away on holiday — and about time too. It's the first one she's taken for years. She just suddenly decided to go. The inn's closed for three weeks."

"Oh, I'm so sorry, my dear," he apologised. "I really didn't mean to sound rude. Please forgive me. I hope she's gone somewhere nice?"

"Oh yes — Italy," answered Sheila, smiling again. "She's gone to

Rome. And it's a well-earned break. And now," – she put her hand up to her throat – "can I offer you a cup of tea?"

"That would be very kind," said Goodale. "And then I'm afraid I must have a private talk with Danny. I do hope you don't mind?"

Sheila looked puzzled, but a nod from Danny reassured her. She went into the kitchen to boil the kettle and the two men sat down. For a few minutes, while they waited, Goodale and MacDonald exchanged small-talk; then Sheila reappeared carrying a tray with tea and shortbread biscuits. Goodale thanked her for her kindness and she returned to the kitchen, leaving the men alone.

For a few seconds there was silence, then Goodale spoke. "Nasty wound, that, Danny," he said quietly. "Has a doctor seen it?"

MacDonald looked uncertain of himself. "Just a cut, sir, that's all it is." He forced a smile.

"From what I've heard, it's a bloody great big half-inch-diameter hole, not a cut," retorted Goodale, his eyes suddenly steely.

The blood drained from MacDonald's face. "Who . . . who on earth told you that, sir?"

"I saw a friend of yours yesterday," replied Goodale, his eyes never leaving MacDonald's face. "A fellow called Johnny Bourne. But he didn't give me your name. I already knew. And that nice suntan you have," he added caustically, "does rather confirm it."

MacDonald was shattered. His mouth opened and shut soundlessly; his voice, when it came, was a whisper. "How much do you know?"

"Most of it. I'm hoping you'll tell me the rest." Goodale's eyes drilled relentlessly into MacDonald's.

MacDonald spoke slowly, his voice low. "What will happen to me?"

"That rather depends on the answers you give me, Danny," said Goodale softly.

"But how did you find out? What gave us away?"

"A combination of things. Bad luck and sheer coincidence, mostly. But more of that in a minute. First, I'll tell you a story. Perhaps you'll correct me if I get any of the details wrong."

MacDonald nodded dumbly.

"I never knew how your brother Fergus died," began Goodale, looking keenly at the photograph above the chimneypiece, "but last

Wednesday I remembered something I had read in the newspapers and hadn't connected with you at the time. So I went to a library to look up some back numbers. Fergus was married to a Bahraini girl, wasn't he?" MacDonald did not contradict him, so he carried on. "He went to live out in Kuwait, to work for an oil company. He married and settled there. When the Iraqis invaded, he and his family were taken prisoner. He was tortured, and his wife and young daughter were beaten and repeatedly raped by Iraqi soldiers, right in front of him, then dragged away. Their mutilated bodies were found two days later. Your brother was held as part of Saddam Hussein's 'human shield' hostage programme, and eventually released with the others. He died about three months later, a broken man. Have I got it right?"

"Yes, sir," said MacDonald hoarsely, the pain of the memory showing in his voice. Then he blurted out, "It was only because of what happened to him that I agreed to do this thing!"

"I know, Danny." Goodale's tone was gentle. "Ed Howard knew about Fergus too, didn't he? That was how he recruited you?"

"Yes," answered MacDonald. "He said he knew of three reasons why he thought I would do the job, and I realised immediately what he meant. Fergus, his wife and his daughter." A look of incomprehension flickered across his face and he added, "How did you find out about Ed?"

"An acquaintance of mine called Henry Stoner remembered being asked about you by Howard. You've heard of Stoner. He wrote to you to try and get you to join his rifle-shooting team."

"Yes."

"The British Newspaper Library's records confirmed the connection. Howard had asked for the same cuttings, back in November last year. When I rang Howard's number, I got a pre-recorded message saying that he was away. I rang you here, too, and there was no reply. It all seemed to fit. Now, Danny," – Goodale again looked MacDonald straight in the eye – "I want you to answer my questions. First, what exactly happened that day in Tikrit?"

"Didn't Ed tell you?"

"I haven't spoken to him, only to Bourne. And I know Bourne wasn't there – he was guarding the vehicles. Now answer the question, please."

Danny MacDonald told him. The story took him nearly an hour

to relate; he described the events vividly and in unstinting detail. Goodale hardly interrupted. It all poured out of Danny with passion; his eyes lit as he told of the death of Saddam Hussein, then darkened as he recounted with sadness the deaths of two friends.

When he had finished, Goodale voiced his reaction at last. "Can you substantiate any of this? Apart from some rumours emanating from Iran, there has been nothing from Baghdad to indicate that any of it actually happened."

MacDonald seemed to be trying to make up his mind. Finally he nodded. He got up and went to a drawer, unlocked it and produced an envelope containing a sheaf of blown-up black and white photographs. He handed it to Goodale. "Ed had a camera on a small tripod. It had a long lens and a motor drive. He took these."

Goodale looked through the photographs, one by one, utterly engrossed. They were astounding. The first few clearly showed the shooting of Saddam's double, then of the aide; another sequence depicted the arrival of the real Saddam, followed by the murder of the Iranian diplomat; and lastly there was a graphic sequence showing the death of the tyrant himself. He looked up. "Howard sent you these?"

"They arrived in the post today."

For the first time, Goodale noticed the Italian postmark. *Good Lord*, he thought. *Is it possible that Ed Howard and Sheila's mother . . . ?* He decided not to speculate about it for the time being; he fixed his gaze once more on MacDonald. "Who was the other man you shot, Danny? The one standing on the platform behind Saddam's double?"

"His name was Ala'a Hussein Ali," said MacDonald slowly. "When the Iraqis invaded Kuwait, he was a colonel in their secret police, the Mukhabarat. Saddam made him nominal Prime Minister of Kuwait, the so-called nineteenth province of Iraq. He personally supervised the torture of my brother – Fergus told me, before he died. He showed me a photograph of him. I recognised him on the platform." MacDonald's voice had become tight and hard. "I deliberately aimed low, to make the bastard suffer, and by God, he did. Ed never asked me why I'd shot the man, but I think he knew. The other man with us in the hide thought I'd gone mad. He thought I'd yelled 'Allah', as if I was some sort

472

of religious maniac. It was the bastard's name, Ala'a, that I was shouting."

Goodale was silent for a while before speaking. "My next question, Danny. You have not mentioned any other names. You have only admitted to knowing Bourne and Howard. Give me the other names, please."

MacDonald's eyes clouded, and his face took on a look of iron determination. "I'm sorry, sir, but I am not prepared to betray my friends. You'll have to find out their names from someone else."

Goodale remained expressionless. Without knowing it, MacDonald had given him the answer he wanted. Even with his own future at stake, the Scot had refused to give his colleagues away. "I have one more question, Danny. I want you to think very hard before answering it." He paused and leaned forward, his eyes stern. "Do you know who was behind this operation? The man who recruited Howard?"

The reply was instant. "No. Ed never told me. He never told any of us. We often wondered. One or two of us used to talk about who it might have been. The general consensus was that the British Government was behind it."

Goodale appeared satisfied. "Right, Danny. I believe you. You've given me the answers I wanted." There was a look of puzzlement on MacDonald's face; Goodale continued. "I shall now tell you what is going to happen, and why. Before I do, I must ask you to give your solemn word that you will never again speak about what you have done, to *anyone*. You will cease all speculation about which person or organisation might have recruited Howard for this operation. Nor will you ever discuss any part of our conversation today. Is that understood?"

MacDonald nodded. "You have my word, sir," he said simply.

Goodale inclined his head in acknowledgement. "Good. Now; it would be possible to prosecute you, Howard, Bourne and the others. Between you, you have committed a large number of serious offences in this country. The list is a long one – there have been firearms offences, fraud, burglary, smuggling . . . but I don't think I need to elaborate. Suffice it to say that on conviction you would be liable to go to prison for many years. And I am talking only of offences you have committed in *this* country. Am I making myself clear?"

"Yes, sir," replied MacDonald miserably.

"However," Goodale went on, "any defence lawyer, even a

473

half-witted one, would use the background to the story, and the details of your deeds abroad, to the maximum potential. The full story would unquestionably emerge. Long gone are the days when such proceedings could be held in camera, with no leaks to the newspapers or arousal of public interest. And there would without any shadow of a doubt be the most almighty rumpus when the details became public knowledge. Quite apart from the possibly catastrophic diplomatic repercussions *vis-à-vis* a number of other countries – Saudi Arabia being the most obvious – it's quite clear to me that your prosecution would be pointless. Do you see what I'm driving at?"

"Not really, sir," mumbled MacDonald, now thoroughly perplexed. Was he not going to be prosecuted after all?

"It's quite simple, Danny. If the full story got out, which it would be bound to do, you and your colleagues would, in the eyes of public opinion, become national heroes overnight. Probably international heroes. I cannot see any jury in the land giving more than two minutes' thought to the matter. However compelling the evidence presented by the prosecution, they would ignore it and find you not guilty. There would immediately be scenes of pandemonium in the courtroom, with everyone cheering themselves hoarse and wanting to shake you by the hand. And there would hardly be a man or woman in the country – possibly even including the judge," interjected Goodale wryly, "– who would not feel exactly the same way. Do you see? You would get off scot-free, if you'll excuse the expression."

"Oh," said MacDonald blankly.

"So," Goodale pressed on, "I intend to spare the British taxpayer the expense of an unnecessary trial, the outcome of which would be not only a foregone conclusion but also a miscarriage of legal justice – which might encourage other hot-heads to think that they could get away with a similar exercise elsewhere. It is of course not really my job to decide whether or not you ought to be prosecuted, but in this matter I am comforted by three additional factors. The first is that the Government has let it be known that it wishes to be spared any embarrassment in this affair. The second is that yesterday I went to see the Director of Public Prosecutions. I took with me someone who has a personal interest in this, and we had an off-the-record discussion with the DPP, mentioning no names. The DPP was quite categoric on the subject. He confirmed to me and to the person accompanying me that a prosecution would not be in the public interest. The third factor is that only I and one other person – the one who came with me to see the DPP – know either your or your colleagues' identities, so there's no danger of the story leaking out, and police inquiries have been discontinued by order of the Home Secretary. So," concluded Goodale, "it seems that you and your colleagues escape the axe. This time. But don't ever, *ever*, even *think* of doing anything like this again."

MacDonald was dumbfounded. Goodale was going to let him off. He cleared his throat. "Thank you very much, sir," he managed to say, his voice shaking with gratitude and relief.

Goodale smiled and relaxed. "Johnny Bourne sends you his regards, by the way. His leg won't be quite what it was, but he will walk again. And I can assure you that when he does, he'll walk the straight and narrow. His first journey" – Goodale gave a little chuckle – "will be down a church aisle in two or three weeks' time, although it was a damned near thing. Have you met his fiancée? No," he went on without waiting for a reply, "I don't suppose you would have. She's a Detective Inspector with the Metropolitan Police. A quite remarkable girl. She came to see me, you know. It must have been the hardest choice of her life – whether to do her duty as a police officer or to cover up for her man. Too many people make the wrong choice, you know. She had found out what he was up to. But by the time she came to me, I already knew. It was her I took with me to see the DPP. When I saw Bourne later, he seemed very subdued. I imagine she gave him a pretty forceful ticking-off; at any rate, I think he'll behave himself in future."

"How did you find out about Johnny?" asked MacDonald.

"It was a simple matter of deduction, once I had Howard's name," replied Goodale. "Bourne was an obvious choice for Howard to make from among the people he worked with in his security company. I'd like to meet Howard himself one day, but he is proving, shall we say . . . elusive. So far, anyway," he added, thinking again of Sheila's mother. "I expect Ziegler is another, and possibly Harris, Usher . . . I don't know yet. The American pilot, Sullivan, is a bit of a riddle. And the South African . . . but I don't expect you to tell me, and I don't want you to. I am retiring next month – for good, this time," he said with a grin "– and it will give me something to do, thinking about it and trying to piece it all together. Fascinating. But never mind. Let's forget it, shall we?"

MacDonald felt as if an enormous weight had been lifted from his shoulders. "I don't know what to say, sir. I'm very grateful to you. I . . ."

"Nonsense, Danny, nonsense," beamed Goodale. "But I think I'd better hang on to these photographs, don't you?" Without waiting for an answer, he opened his briefcase and put the envelope inside, then snapped the locks shut. "It wouldn't do to have them fall into the wrong hands, would it?" He smiled again. "And if I were you," he continued, "I wouldn't leave those three empty cartridge cases up there on the chimneypiece. They look a bit too powerful for deer-stalking – they might attract comment. A bit of a risk, really, bringing those particular souvenirs back through Customs." Goodale shook his head reprovingly at the thought. "Now," he said, standing up, "I must be off. My congratulations on your engagement – your Sheila seems a delightful girl. And I much look forward to seeing you again at Glen Carvaig this October, for our annual outing on the hill. But," he added pointedly, "no more long-range shots, understood?"

Danny MacDonald grinned. "You have my word on that too, Colonel."

81

Sir Peter Dartington sat alone in his office in London, pondering the extraordinary events of the day. Tuesday 5th May 1992; he wouldn't forget it in a hurry.

First thing that morning, he had gone downstairs to the study in his house in the country. On top of the pile of post was a plain manila envelope addressed to him from Italy. He opened it and then sat down heavily when he saw the sequence of photographs. There could be no doubt about it – the photographs were time-stamped; they had obviously been shot with a motor-driven camera. The pictures clearly showed the shooting of Saddam Hussein. *Ye gods*, he breathed, *Ed Howard has done it. He's done it!* Hurriedly, he locked the photographs in his safe and left for London.

On his arrival at the office, the second extraordinary event of the day unfolded. Initially, he didn't understand the air of euphoria that greeted his entrance. Everyone was smiling, shaking his hand, congratulating him. Bewildered, he asked what all the fuss was about. Dorothy Webster broke the news to him. Darcon had been awarded three of the major contracts it had bid for. Not one, not two, but *three*! He felt triumphant, ecstatic. There was a brief twinge of guilt as he recalled how two of them had been obtained, but it lasted only a few seconds.

He thought about the two contracts he had been promised as payment for setting up the assassination. Yes, two of these three must have been awarded in that connection. One was obvious – the motorway-widening in the north of England – but Dartington could not think how the Government could have swung either of the others. But it didn't matter. He opened several bottles of champagne with his delighted staff to celebrate.

That was when the third thing happened. Dorothy Webster

announced a visitor, who was apparently very insistent on seeing Dartington in private. "It's a Mr Goodale, Sir Peter. He has shown me a card. He's from the police."

Dartington had soon found out exactly who Goodale was. He wasn't a policeman at all. The man had come straight to the point; Dartington had been badly rattled.

Now he sat in his chair, the champagne in the glass on his desk untouched. He had needed something stronger when Colonel Goodale had left; there was a tumbler of neat whisky at his elbow, now nearly empty. He reflected on what the MI5 man had said to him – Goodale, the sprightly little man with those intense blue eyes which missed nothing. Goodale had made him feel like a moth pinned to a board. Those eyes . . . Dartington could not remember when he had last felt so uncomfortable. Darcon would still get the three contracts, but MI5 . . .

He sat rapt in thought. What was it that Goodale had said about the contracts? For a moment, when Goodale had told him that he knew about the deal, Dartington had been too shaken to concentrate. Then, as he was leaving, Goodale had made some other remark. "Just give a bit of thought to those other two contracts, would you? Who do you imagine would have been able to swing those for you?" That was it. What could he possibly have meant by that?

It made no sense at all. None whatsoever, brooded Dartington, unless . . . No. That was ridiculous. If that were the case, then it meant . . . Dartington's mind quickly ran over the implications. The unease he felt turned to horror as he realised that it was a perfect explanation for the puzzle; it tallied with all the facts. And then there was Asher, revealed in death as a fraud and liar on a grand scale. A liar . . . Ye gods, NO! It wasn't possible! It couldn't be!

The truth of it, suddenly so obvious, hit Dartington in a blinding flash. He grasped the enormity of what he had done. He buried his face in his hands.

82

The Minister was on cloud nine. The meeting with the Prime Minister had gone even better than he had dared hope. In his car on the way home, he allowed his mind to drift back and savour again the words of praise that the Prime Minister had heaped upon him. He had been lavishly congratulated for the success of his plot to assassinate Saddam Hussein, and was now assured of promotion in the new Government.

Asher had had to be disposed of, of course. A pity, thought the Minister; the man had been useful over the years. A repulsive pig of a man, unprincipled, gluttonous and degenerate – but useful. Scandals had been looming; Asher had been involved in all sorts of financial chicanery, and in them up to his neck. If he had been exposed . . . No, he had had to be dealt with. The Minister had taken charge of it. The "accident at sea" had been his own idea, and it could not have worked out better; his men had made no mistakes, left no clues. The issue had been beautifully clouded by subsequent speculation. It had even got to the stage where the insurance companies were refusing to pay out because they considered it to have been suicide. The Prime Minister had expressed his pleasure about this too, and had not hesitated to sign the final approval for the two construction contracts to go to Darcon. Yes; the Minister had every reason to feel elated.

The Mercedes pulled into the drive of the Minister's luxurious house in the suburbs of the great city. His driver opened the door, and the heat hit the Minister with full force as he stepped out of the car's air-conditioned coolness. It was unusually hot, even for the time of year. A turbaned servant came down the steps of the house, bearing a tray with a glass and a jug of iced lemonade. The Minister took a refreshing sip of the drink; as he did so, the noonday call of the *muezzin* sounded in the distance. He smiled and set down the

479

glass; as Minister for Protocol in the Iranian Government, he knew that it would not do for him to miss the call to prayers. He decided to say a special prayer for the soul of his country's martyred Ambassador.

EPILOGUE

83

On Wednesday 6th May 1992, the Iraqi television service broadcast a short piece as the lead item in its early-evening news programme. It was not particularly newsworthy in itself; it was clearly nothing more than a propaganda piece, depicting the Iraqi President on a routine visit to a military base on the outskirts of Baghdad. The President was briefly shown inspecting a guard of honour; in the background, a large formation of armour could be seen, the soldiers standing to attention beside their vehicles. The President was not pictured talking to any of his soldiers, nor making a speech; he simply walked past the troops and weaponry on display, registering little apparent reaction. He was accompanied by Izzat Ibrahim, the cadaverous Vice-President of Iraq, and a number of Presidential aides in military uniform. One of the aides was carrying a newspaper which he held up to the camera as he walked past. It was a copy of *Al Qaddissiya*, the newspaper of the Iraqi Defence Ministry, and as it came close to the camera the date was clearly visible, showing it to be the previous day's edition, that of 5th May.

The American CNN, the British BBC and a handful of other broadcasting organisations around the world picked up the item and broadcast it, for the simple reason that it afforded the first confirmed new glimpse of Saddam Hussein that there had been for many weeks, and dispelled the now obviously false rumour of the previous few days. Iraq had been in the news frequently enough, but there had been no sign of the President himself. The man was, after all, news, even if he was being shown doing something of little general interest. The CNN report beefed the item up a little by adding a voice-over commentary, reporting on continuing unrest and repression in the Kurdish region of northern Iraq. Worldwide, the news clip was seen in one form or another by some forty million viewers. Most watched with vague attention, then switched off and dismissed it from their minds.

Some of the more observant viewers formed the distinct impression that the Iraqi President seemed rather more unsure of himself, perhaps less in control, than they remembered from previous footage. The customary swagger to his step was not there any more; his demeanour was altogether less animated, more wooden. He seemed in some intangible way to have diminished in stature and authority. Saddam Hussein appeared to be a shadow of his former self; he was no longer the larger-than-life figure they had been used to seeing on their television screens. There was nothing in particular they could put their finger on, but . . . it was almost as if, somehow, they weren't watching the same man.

Just a handful of viewers, however, were paying very close attention indeed. They noticed one other detail, ostensibly a minor one, which made them sit bolt upright in their chairs and reach for their telephones. There was something missing. The pistol holster on the President's belt was empty. The man was unarmed.

Appendix

BALLISTICS TABLE

Calibre:	.338 Lapua Magnum (8.6 × 70mm)	Location:	34 deg 35 min N, 43 deg 42 min E
Bullet weight & type:	250 grain FMJBT	Date:	28th April 1992
Ballistic coefficients:	.662(2953–2300 fps)	Time:	07.55 hrs local (B)
	.580 (2299–1700 fps)	Temperature:	70 deg F
	.522 (below 1700 fps)	Altitude:	320 ft
Muzzle velocity:	2953 ft/sec	Barometric pressure:	992 mb
Barrel length:	27 ins	Relative humidity:	83%
Scope height above bore:	2 ins		
Zero range:	1200 yds		

0–2000 YARDS: 100-YARD INCREMENTS

Range (yards)	Velocity (ft/sec)	Energy (ft/lb)	Drop (inch)	Time (sec)	Trajectory (MOA)	(inch)	5 mph Wind (MOA)	(inch)
0.0	2953.0	4840	0.00	0.0000	***	−2.00	0.0	0.0
100.0	2810.0	4383	2.06	0.1041	−33.9	35.49	0.2	0.2
200.0	2671.6	3961	8.52	0.2136	−32.7	68.58	0.4	0.9
300.0	2537.3	3573	19.85	0.3289	−30.8	96.79	0.7	2.1
400.0	2407.0	3216	36.58	0.4503	−28.6	119.61	0.9	3.9
500.0	2277.8	2880	59.27	0.5782	−26.1	136.47	1.2	6.2
600.0	2138.0	2537	88.66	0.7143	−23.3	146.62	1.5	9.2
700.0	2003.3	2227	125.74	0.8592	−20.3	149.09	1.8	13.0
800.0	1873.8	1949	171.57	1.0140	−17.0	142.81	2.1	17.7
900.0	1749.9	1700	227.51	1.1796	−13.4	126.42	2.5	23.3
1000.0	1625.0	1466	294.85	1.3576	−9.4	98.63	2.9	30.1
1100.0	1503.1	1254	375.58	1.5495	−5.0	57.45	3.3	38.0
1200.0	1391.2	1074	472.58	1.7570	0.0	0.00	3.8	47.3
1300.0	1290.6	925	588.53	1.9809	5.6	−76.41	4.3	58.1
1400.0	1203.2	804	726.74	2.2219	11.9	−175.07	4.8	70.4
1500.0	1130.4	709	890.27	2.4792	19.0	−299.05	5.4	84.1
1600.0	1071.4	637	1082.41	2.7523	27.0	−451.64	5.9	99.2
1700.0	1023.8	582	1304.40	3.0385	35.6	−634.08	6.5	115.4
1800.0	984.0	537	1558.45	3.3374	45.0	−848.58	7.0	132.8
1900.0	949.6	501	1846.42	3.6483	55.1	−1097.01	7.6	151.2
2000.0	919.1	469	2169.42	3.9699	65.9	−1380.46	8.1	170.6

1200–1300 YARDS: 5-YARD INCREMENTS

Range (yards)	Velocity (ft/sec)	Energy (ft/lb)	Drop (inch)	Time (sec)	Trajectory (MOA)	(inch)	5 mph Wind (MOA)	(inch)
1200.0	1391.2	1074	472.58	1.7570	0.0	0.00	3.8	47.3
1205.0	1385.8	1066	477.90	1.7678	0.3	−3.35	3.8	47.8
1210.0	1380.6	1058	483.26	1.7786	0.5	−6.73	3.8	48.3
1215.0	1375.3	1050	488.69	1.7895	0.8	−10.18	3.8	48.9
1220.0	1370.1	1042	494.16	1.8004	1.1	−13.67	3.9	49.4
1225.0	1364.9	1034	499.67	1.8114	1.3	−17.21	3.9	49.9
1230.0	1359.7	1026	505.23	1.8224	1.6	−20.79	3.9	50.4
1235.0	1354.6	1018	510.85	1.8335	1.9	−24.43	3.9	50.9
1240.0	1349.5	1011	516.51	1.8445	2.2	−28.11	4.0	51.5
1245.0	1344.4	1003	522.22	1.8557	2.4	−31.85	4.0	52.0
1250.0	1339.4	996	527.99	1.8668	2.7	−35.64	4.0	52.5
1255.0	1334.4	988	533.80	1.8781	3.0	−39.48	4.0	53.1
1260.0	1329.4	981	539.67	1.8893	3.3	−43.36	4.1	53.6
1265.0	1324.4	974	545.59	1.9006	3.6	−47.31	4.1	54.2
1270.0	1319.5	966	551.57	1.9120	3.9	−51.31	4.1	54.7
1275.0	1314.6	959	557.59	1.9233	4.1	−55.35	4.1	55.3
1280.0	1309.8	952	563.67	1.9348	4.4	−59.46	4.2	55.8
1285.0	1304.9	945	569.81	1.9462	4.7	−63.62	4.2	56.4
1290.0	1300.1	938	575.99	1.9577	5.0	−67.82	4.2	57.0
1295.0	1295.4	931	582.24	1.9693	5.3	−72.09	4.2	57.5
1300.0	1290.6	925	588.53	1.9809	5.6	−76.41	4.3	58.1

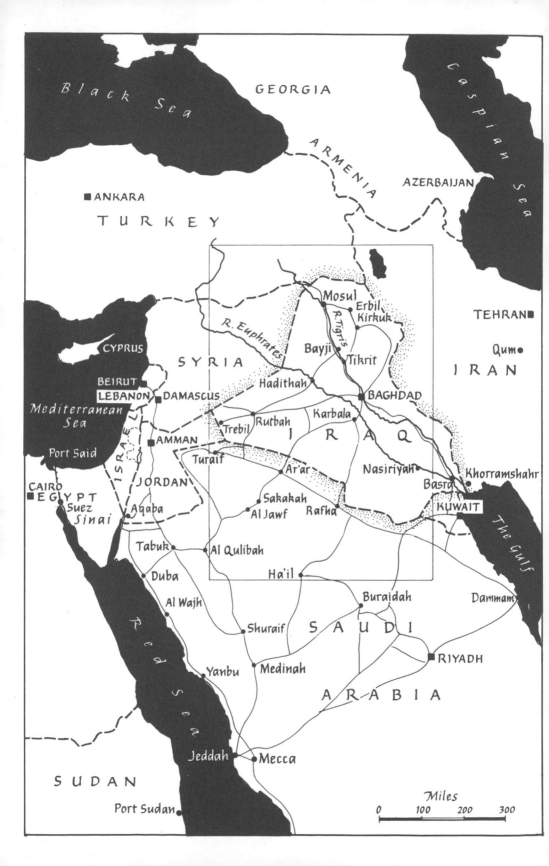

Miles
0   100   200   300